JERRY

To Carolyn Koontz
Please enjoy
Jerry Whitt

THE YEAR OF THE WOLF

A NOVEL OF CENTRAL TEXAS THE YEARS 1886-87

outskirts press

The Year of the Wolf
A novel of central Texas The years 1886-87

v2.0

This is a work of fiction. Names, characters, businesses, places, events, locales, and incidents are either the products of the author's imagination or used in a fictitious manner. Any resemblance to actual persons, living or dead, or actual events is purely coincidental.

Outskirts Press, Inc.
http://www.outskirtspress.com

ISBN: 978-1-9772-5419-1

PRINTED IN THE UNITED STATES OF AMERICA

A Word from the Author

In my second novel, *Jake's War,* I introduced a character named Levi Wolfe, a central Texas rancher. He and another rancher, Jake McIlroy, fought side-by-side to eliminate a well-established, well-organized, and very deadly criminal gang, a band of outlaws identified by several names. The Norwood Mob, the Mob, and the Buzzard's Water Hole Gang were three of the most commonly used.

The Mob operated with impunity in the fertile hills and valleys of the Texas Hill Country. The buffalo herds had been removed, as had the wild Indian tribes, leaving a perfect place for cattle. However, there was a great problem. There was no effective law enforcement. Certainly, sheriffs were elected and given authority to operate, but with few exceptions they were untrained, outgunned, and outmanned. And, in many cases, their loyalty lay with the Mob. In fact, that loyalty may have been the key to their very survival.

Facing little resistance, the Mob took hold and became as powerful as any criminal organization that existed anywhere at that time. Members of the mob engaged in the kinds of criminal activities one would expect. They rustled cattle. They intimidated legal landowners, claiming their land and giving them a day or two to vacate their property. They burned houses and crops. When other efforts failed, the Mob resorted to murder.

At first separately and then together, Jake McIlroy and Levi Wolfe evaluated their situation, already knowing what they would find. They could stand and fight, or they could quietly sell their land to Mob members and leave the area. They chose to stand and fight.

While Jake McIlroy's early life and his circuitous route to the ranchland around Norwood, Texas, are described in my first novel, *The List*, neither of my first two novels reveals much about Levi Wolfe.

The Year of the Wolf changes that. It begins with Levi—a young adult, twenty-five years of age—adrift in the thriving city of San Antonio. But to fully understand Levi, it might be good to understand just how he happened to be in that town—a place of great opportunity and excitement, a melting pot of humanity where anything could be found, a town where a life could be extinguished in an instant and few would notice or care.

For more information, read "Author's notes" at the end of the book.

Prologue

The plaza below was alive with people of all sizes, ages, and ethnicities—mingling and eating and drinking. The laughter drifted up to the balcony, where a young man named Levi Wolfe sat, drinking a beer as he watched the activity below. For a moment, he looked away as his eyes swept the historic Texas city, San Antonio. From his location Levi acknowledged for perhaps the hundredth time that the scene was beautiful. The fading light sent shadows across the buildings, somehow causing them to blend with the numerous trees and flowering shrubs that spread as far as he could see. Far to the west, the sun was approaching the thin dark clouds on the horizon, promising another beautiful sunset.

Levi returned his attention to the plaza, just as a pretty young woman in traditional Mexican dress approached a gringo who was sitting alone at a table. She smiled and whispered something in his ear. Returning her smile, he nodded his approval and invited her to join him at the table. Almost immediately a waiter brought two foaming glasses of beer and placed them on the table.

As if by magic, her hand reached out and touched him gently on his lower arm. Pretending not to notice, he casually inched his chair closer to hers. After a few moments and a few sips of beer, he placed a cautious hand on hers, as they continued to laugh and talk. Perhaps half an hour later, the man motioned to the waiter, paid his tab, and rose from his chair. His smiling female companion did the same. Holding hands, they strolled across the plaza and disappeared from sight.

"Ah," Levi said, smiling softly to himself, "Another business transaction consummated."

"Sure looked that way," came an unexpected reply. He turned quickly to gaze at the beautiful Mexican woman that now stood beside him. "May I sit with you?" she asked, speaking fluent English with a pleasing accent.

He smiled and nodded. "Selena! Of course you can sit with me," he replied. "You can always sit with me. You know that. A beer?"

"Wine," she replied.

He motioned to a waitress, but she was already on her way, carrying a generous glass of red wine. Turning back to the woman, he said, "You expected me to welcome you."

"Of course I did. You never fail me."

Pretending to watch the disappearing waitress, he glanced at the young woman beside him. The perfect teeth. The flawless skin. The quick smile through full lips. The brown, mischievous eyes. And the perfect body. Oh, yes! The body he knew so well.

"Are you hungry?" he asked. "I was about to order a meal."

"Yes, but let me order for both of us." Without waiting for a reply, she motioned for the waitress. Whispering softly in Spanish, she placed the order.

As they ate, he watched her, remembering the first time they'd met. He'd been in San Antonio for maybe six hours, trying desperately to locate a place of refuge, after spending his first twenty-one years on the family farm just outside Poteet. Somehow, his tired old horse walked up to her establishment, the Old Town Tavern, a very successful bar in the Mexican part of town. The horse then stopped, waiting for Levi to dismount and do whatever might come next. How he got there was a mystery. Selena, the owner of the bar, declared that it was providence, an act of God. He argued that it was nothing more than a happy accident.

He had walked in, expecting some sign of welcome. Instead, he was confronted by a huge Mexican bartender, threatening him with a double-barreled shotgun and accusing him of attempting to rob the place. It wasn't an entirely absurd accusation. In one hand he held his prized Henry rifle and on his right hip hung his deceased grandfather's Colt Navy revolver. After a few tense moments, he was rescued by Selena, the woman now sitting across the table from him. She directed the puzzled Levi to an empty table at the back of the bar and brought him a mug of beer and a hot meal.

At her urging, he had described the life of a dirt-poor farm boy—hopelessly fighting the elements, the endless labor, and his unforgiving father, as the family struggled to stay alive. He described events with self-deprecation and humor, which kept her thoroughly entertained. Then his story became more serious. He admitted that he'd gotten into some real trouble in Poteet. He had, in fact, killed a man. Although the killing was justified, Levi chose not to stay and trust the legal system. At the urging of his parents, he'd fled to San Antonio, seeking to lose himself in the mass of humanity.

Then it was her turn. She first assured him that she and her employees could easily hide him from any pursuers from Poteet. Then she told him how she'd grown up in the Mexican community in San Antonio, a poor girl who was *mostly Mexican but cursed by the presence of some Anglo blood* in her family tree. Seemed there was a Caucasian grandfather. As a result, she wasn't completely accepted by either the white residents of the city or the pure-blood Mexicans.

She was unusually pretty, developing into a woman by the age of fourteen. She had been told by a neighboring woman—perhaps with good intentions—that she had three possible career pathways ahead of her. She could join a Convent and become a Catholic Nun, she could marry one of the poor, unemployed young men in the neighborhood and expect regular beatings and constant pregnancy, or she could join one of the city's high-class brothels.

She stormed back at the woman, informing her that she would be none of those. Instead, she'd be a successful—and eventually rich—career woman, a business woman, right here in San Antonio. So she became a singer and dancer in the Old Town Tavern, quickly catching the eye of Jorge, the owner, and then marrying him. About five years later, her much-older husband died unexpectedly, leaving her the Tavern, as well as other properties. Against all expectations, she'd been successful, much more so than Jorge had ever been.

Seeing promise in young Levi, Selena offered him employment, with the understanding that he'd work hard, learn the operation of her businesses, and become something of a partner. Over the next few months, she taught him how to make sound business decisions, how to deal with unruly customers, and how to stop a poker game when a player was about to lose more than he could afford.

Sometimes his duties were less than desirable, but he approached each one with vigor and enthusiasm. He had worked for wages before, and he recognized Salina's plan. She was testing him, so he accepted each new assignment without complaint or question. Within a year, he was a significant part of Salina's staff.

To show her appreciation, she placed him in charge of what she called "Outside Operations," which included any of her business coming into or leaving San Antonio. A major component of Outside Operations was the hauling of goods by wagon to and from out-lying towns. Sometimes, Levi did the actual driving, but at other times he directed the work of other drivers. Again, Salina was delighted with his work.

Salina and Levi were young, single individuals who liked good food, good drink, and good times. They spent much time together, on and off the job. Soon they were spending nights together. They weren't in love, and both realized that there was no real future for them. They accepted their situation. She was almost ten years older than he, and her goals and his didn't quite mesh. And she really wasn't seeking a permanent relationship, but she certainly enjoyed the one they had. No, although he didn't fit into her long-range plans, he was young, handsome, and anxious to please.

"Well, Levi," she said, tearing him away from his memories. "I'm lonely. Would you comfort me tonight?"

He smiled at her request. "I can do that, Selena."

They lay in bed as the morning sun broke the eastern horizon, each deep in thought. He rolled toward her, placing his arms around her naked body. "I absolutely adore you, Selena," he said.

She flashed a knowing smile in his direction. "Yes," she said. "But you're feeling a bit of guilt, aren't you? I can tell."

He released his breath in a long sigh. "Some guilt, yes," he replied. "I've met someone." Nervously, he told her that things were changing in his life, and that he'd found the woman he wanted by his side for the rest of his life.

"It's Jovita. Correct?"

"How did you know?" he asked, quite surprised. "When did you learn?"

"I've known almost since you met her. Word gets around in this town," she said. "Especially in the Mexican community. At least twenty women made sure I knew. They meant well. Lots of people that I know don't want to believe what they hear. I mean, a poor white man courting a high-class Mexican girl, one from a prominent family? I don't mean to insult you, but you're not her people's first choice."

Levi smiled at the insult that wasn't intended as an insult. "I know that, and it may not last. She may take the advice of friends and family and church, but I have to try."

She took a deep breath and slowly exhaled. "Are you sure about this? You're stepping into a world that's different from anything you've ever experienced. You'll be expected to change, to accept her religion and customs and traditions. It won't be easy. Even if you do everything you're expected to do, some people still won't accept you. You're a good and honest white man, one that's been sleeping with a simple Mexican woman." She stopped to let him consider her words, and then she added, "And at this point in your life, you're little more than a common laborer."

"Yes, I'm sure," he said. "We've talked about it. She's explained her religion to me. I'm willing to adopt it. And she knows what I am."

She lay on her side, facing Levi. "I'm asking you again. Are you certain?"

"And again, I'm telling you that I am. I've thought this through, and my mind is made up."

"Then you surely know that our…our relationship is over. Jovita will not share you, and neither will I. This will be—it has to be—our last time together." She laughed softly. "I hate to lose you to another woman, but I've seen it coming. Actually, it's lasted much longer than I first expected."

Levi rolled away and swung his feet to the floor, sitting on the edge of the bed. "I don't know what to say," He whispered, reaching for his clothes.

"Then don't say anything. You've been a loyal worker, a very good friend, and a wonderful lover. As you must certainly know, I'm neither surprised nor angry. Fact is, I want to show my appreciation."

"Show your appreciation?"

"Correct. In the four years that we've been together, my businesses have prospered. You've been a big part of that growth, and I want to reward you."

"How?"

"You took over my freighting business, which was floundering, and you made it a great success. I want to sell it to you. Yes, you'll pay for it, but at the value it held when you took it over. You can pay for it over time, as it continues to grow."

Levi slowly nodded his head. "Selina, won't this be awkward?"

"Not for me. Our new relationship will be strictly professional. Business associates, that's all. I'll hire your wagons to transport my supplies. Others will do the same. You'll do well." She smiled wickedly. "Yes. I'll miss you, but I won't be alone for very long."

Laughing, he leaned across and kissed her. "I'll bet you won't," he said. "And you should know that I'll miss you, too."

Levi had made his decision. He knew which direction his life should take. In his mind, his destiny was decided. He would win the hand of Jovita, the approval of her mother, and the support of her church.

Chapter 1

The skinny white man in the clean, neatly tailored clothes stepped carefully from the porch of the house onto the muddy street. The only indication of his status was a shiny tin star pinned to his left breast pocket identifying him as a "Deputy Sheriff." Sam did, in fact, refer to himself as Sheriff Hammer's Chief Deputy. Perhaps the title was unofficial, but it was generally accepted. He dressed and acted the part, always letting his clothing and his aloofness serve as a deadly warning to the peasants, the human scum he now saw before him. He slowly picked his way through the mud and puddles of water to the point where a second deputy stood, carelessly keeping guard so that a growing crowd of onlookers did not get too close to the house.

"She's deader'n a herring," Sam said.

"Who is?" asked the second deputy, a young Mexican man named Ramon.

"The bitch inside. Beat clean to death. Messed up real bad."

"Who is she? What happened?"

"Don't Sheriff Hammer tell you nothin'?"

"He never does, Sam," Ramon said, shaking his head slowly. "He talks to you, not me."

"Well, I don't know much, neither. His Highness the Sheriff just tol' me for us to come out here with the ol' doc and find out what happened. Didn't say who or what or nothin'. Doc tol' me she's a Meskin girl named Jovita. Don't recollect her last name."

Ramon looked at his partner in shock. "Did you say 'Jovita'?"

Sam scratched his head and looked out into the night, not

especially interested in the girl's name. "Yeah. I think that's right."

"My God, surely not…not Jovita delos Santos. Why'd anybody kill her? She's too pretty to kill, but she's the only Jovita I know."

Finally showing some interest, Sam repeated, "delos Santos? Now that you mention it, that does sound like her name. You know this bitch?"

"She wasn't a bitch, Sam. Yeah, I knew her. Known her since we were kids. Every male in my part of town knew her, but not one of us ever touched her. I'd bet on it. I sure never got close. She was way outta my class."

"You shore must've thought she was something special, Ramon."

Ramon stared at a group of people standing in the edge of a growing circle, solemnly remembering the beautiful woman. "She was, Sam. She was. I know what you think of most women, especially Mexican women. You think they're all whores. Well, you're wrong about this one. She sure didn't deserve this."

"Don't nobody deserve what she got. Want to go take a look?"

"No. No, I don't think so. This ain't how I want to remember her."

"Well, anyhow, somebody shore done a job on her. She ain't gonna be sashayin' around San Antone no more."

The callous deputy sheriff was right. The young woman was dead. It didn't require the professional judgment of Dr. Afton Silverman to make that determination. One glance at the lifeless body by any of the solemn onlookers would have yielded the same conclusion, but the doctor had been called to perform his official function, and he was determined to do so.

As a cold spring rain fell steadily upon the restless group

of Mexican witnesses, the doctor examined the partially clothed body and prepared to officially record his findings. The two very different men who served as sheriff's deputies stood between the spectators and the crime scene, there to enforce Sheriff Dalton Hammer's version of San Antonio justice and to ensure that at least the appearance of legal procedure was observed.

If ever two men offered a study in contrasts, these two deputies did. One glance at Sam immediately revealed why he was held in contempt—as well as fear—by most residents of the Mexican community. His body was so long and wasted that it appeared unable to support the large bony head that sat atop stooped, razor-thin shoulders. Long, equally thin arms dangled loosely at his sides, scarcely moving when he walked. Large, gnarled hands hung open and cupped, as if waiting to strangle some unsuspecting victim. From all appearances, over half the length of his body was made up of legs, which rose out of expensive, well-polished boots and extended upward, seemingly forever, until finally ending somewhere near the waist, getting only slightly larger along the way. His buttocks were virtually nonexistent.

If the body was absurd, the face was frightening. Two small, reptilian eyes glared from beneath bushy masses of eyebrows that extended clear across the forehead like a windrow of dried wheat straw. Separating the eyes was an enormous beak-like nose that began at the brow, dwarfing other facial features as it descended and terminated almost even with the mouth. But the mouth was what most people remembered. The lips were narrow, appearing as a thin, hard line, turning downward at each corner in a half-smile and half-frown. From each corner trickled a rivulet of dark brown tobacco juice that stained parts of his weak, knobby chin and dripped onto the collar of his starched white shirt. Strands of reddish-blond hair protruded in all directions from beneath a clean gray felt hat, which protected the pockmarked, red and gray skin of his face. He appeared to be sinister and malevolent, and he was. He trusted no one, not even his fellow deputies.

Ramon was everything that Sam was not. Whereas most people remembered Sam, Ramon was easily forgotten or overlooked, the kind of man who preferred to blend into a crowd or linger silently in the background. He stood well under six feet in height and at first appeared to be chubby and poorly conditioned, an appearance that soon was dispelled by his actions toward anyone foolish enough to push him too far.

He moved like a cat, with grace and strength and precision. Unlike Sam's, Ramon's mouth was friendly and pleasant, possessing life and revealing at least the appearance of boyish humor. His nose was straight and fairly broad. His cheekbones were high and prominent, suggesting his Indian ancestry. His other facial features were not especially memorable, with the exception of his large black eyes, which constantly darted from side to side, as if seeking out danger and mischief. In most ways Ramon had the potential to be a top-notch police officer. He was sensitive, inquisitive, thorough, and intelligent—all attributes necessary for success in his profession. Unfortunately, he suffered a stigma common to that era. He was a Mexican. As such, he was given little training and little credit for whatever he accomplished on his own. With some resignation he accepted his fate. Although meager, his salary as a deputy sheriff was more than he could earn elsewhere, and he needed the job. For the most part, he kept his mouth shut and did as he was told. He learned that timidity was a way of survival, and he practiced it daily.

As the two deputies loitered near the crowd, and Dr. Silverman continued his observations, the previously quiet onlookers slowly began to murmur and speculate about the terrible event. Everyone in the small crowd knew Jovita delos Santos, and most were beginning to compare theories about the crime. For as long as anyone could remember, Jovita had lived with her mother, Maria, in a small house on the edge of the Mexican colony in San Antonio. Although modest by the standards of the white aristocracy of the city, the house actually was quite elegant, perhaps representing the vestiges of what was once a great family fortune. Approximately 150 years earlier, an ancestor, Dona Xavier Canto de la Garza, had inherited a huge tract of Texas land, which had been granted to her late husband by the king of Spain.

Dona Xavier's son, Don Jose, followed the example of his business-minded mother and became a prominent banker in the still developing settlement of San Antonio. In the early 1800s, King Charles IV of Spain commissioned Don Jose to mint gold and silver coins, one side of which bore the Lone Star, the eventual symbol of the Republic of Texas. The family was associated with numerous important movements and prominent people during the early history of Texas. Two family members fought as Confederate officers during the Civil War.

By the end of the Civil War, however, the de la Garza empire was in a state of collapse. Don Jose's bank was declared insolvent and was forced to close. Most of the family lands also were gone—some sold, others lost in unwise financial ventures. If it provided any consolation, the de la Garza family was not alone in its troubles. Many of the once powerful Spanish families of San Antonio were giving way to the onslaught of English, German, and other European newcomers in and around the city. Such certainly was the fate of the de la Garza family. A once vast fortune had disappeared.

Jovita's mother was one of dozens of descendants of the

family matriarch, Dona Xavier. Jovita's father, Rafael delos Santos, had once been employed as a bookkeeper in a clothing store owned and operated by the brother of Jovita's mother. It was rumored that he married Jovita's mother in the mistaken belief that the family was still wealthy. When he learned his mistake, he abandoned his pregnant wife, never even seeing his daughter Jovita.

Abruptly, one of the deputies remembered the instructions that he had been given by Sheriff Hammer. "Ramon," Sam said. "His Royal Majesty, the sheriff, said we have to check the place for clues. We'd better do it before that crabby old doctor leaves and we have to spend all our time runnin' them Meskin neighbors off."

"What the hell does he expect us to find? We know she's dead, and we know who did it," Ramon replied.

"It don't matter none. We still gotta do it. Let's go."

The two men went back into the house and spoke briefly with Dr. Silverman. Then they went about making a superficial examination of the crime scene. A close look about the house told much about how the family lived. Although the family was no longer rich, the two women lived reasonably well. The neat white stucco house had four moderately large rooms, each brightly decorated with tasteful pictures and tapestries on the walls. The oak floors were covered with elegant rugs, probably relics of a more prosperous past, and elaborately handcrafted curtains covered the windows. The furniture was simple and graceful, projecting a feeling of strength and culture.

After a few minutes, the silence was broken. "Sam, this doesn't make sense a'tall. The windows are unlocked. The doors, too. No sign of forced entry."

"You're right," Sam replied. "These folks ain't kept up with the times, I guess."

Indeed, a changing society had passed them by. Although there were locks on the doors and windows, the locks seldom were used. Until now there had seemed to be no need. All the residents knew their neighbors, and crime among these simple, honest people was rare. Now, the tranquility of the community had been shattered. The peace had been violated. Life in all parts of San Antonio was changing, as the city was evolving from a quiet Spanish settlement and outpost into a city of almost forty thousand residents. With this transition came progress, and with progress came lawlessness.

A cursory search and examination of the crime scene revealed nothing to change the minds of the two deputies. Even they could figure out what had happened. To further solidify the case, several witnesses were willing to testify that three white men had been harassing the beautiful young woman at Hernandez's Grocery, where she worked as a clerk. When Jovita had spurned their advances, they had gotten more determined and more vulgar in their comments. Finally, they had retreated, but not before threatening to return and enjoy a measure of revenge. One—a large, especially ugly man with dark, pig-like eyes and long, dirty hair—had chuckled and remarked that he was afraid of no one in town. Apparently, the three thugs had followed Jovita home, waited for just the right moment, forced their way into the house, and then raped and murdered her.

After their brief and pointless investigation, the two deputies sat on the floor of the living room of the house, each contemplating the horror and violence of the scene before them. Visibly shaken, Ramon finally spoke, "It still doesn't make sense, Sam."

"How so?" Sam already knew Ramon's meaning, but felt it best to let him express his disgust.

"This whole thing is damned senseless. Why'd anybody murder and rape a woman, when they can get anything they want almost free? It ain't like you gotta kill to get it."

"We both know it wasn't like somebody just...happened to stumble onto this defenseless woman," Sam replied. "Somebody wanted this particular woman."

Ramon considered Sam's statement. "Maybe," he said. "I know the bastard that did this, and he ain't particular."

"Really? And who'd that be?"

"Sam, you know good as me. It was George Tompkins and that scum that runs with 'im."

Sam chuckled softly. "You know that for a fact?"

"I can't prove it, but I know it."

Suddenly serious, Sam said, "Take some good advice. Don't tell our glorious boss that George done this unless you can prove it. In the first place, him and ol' George used to drink together. In the second place, George is downright mean. Hammer ain't gonna be anxious to take him in. Let's let his Royal Highness draw his own conclusions."

"Yeah. You're right," Ramon replied. "Still, it doesn't make sense. Killing a pretty little thing like her."

For a few moments, Ramon made another quick glance around the murder scene. Shaking his head slowly, he recognized the obvious. San Antonio was no longer safe for anybody. It had become a city of excesses, catering to the needs of the fun-seeking cowboy, the social outcast, or even the pathological criminal. The city had rows of elaborately decorated gambling establishments where huge sums of money were won and lost daily.

This was the town where a personal fortune, a home, a farm, or even a ranch might be gambled away in one careless act. Gunfights occurred with disturbing frequency in these establishments. In this district of sin and pleasure, two rival bar owners, John Bennett and Robert Marx, once killed each other over a simple disagreement. These men weren't bitter enemies. They once had been friends, but business and the heat of the moment had turned them violent.

Likewise, if a patron of an establishment wished to have female companionship, it was easily arranged. Women of questionable virtue frequented the gambling parlors by the hundreds. Houses of prostitution filled a red-light district that earned millions of dollars annually for its various madams, as well as for those city officials who supported and protected them. If a young adventurer had just experienced good luck at a gambling table, he could patronize one of San Antonio's finest brothels—one like the Arlington or the Three Fives—where the richest furnishings, the finest liquor, and the loveliest ladies were at his disposal. For the less fortunate visitor, one with limited means, numerous seedy, run-down houses provided entertainment of a much less opulent variety.

There was no lust, no sexual fantasies, and no deprivation of sexual fulfillment involved in the murder of Jovita. This had been an act of violence, wanton and horrible. A promising young life had been violated and viciously snuffed out for no reason. For what it was worth, Jovita did not die without a struggle. Strands of dirty blond hair were located near her body, and pieces of skin and flesh were embedded under her fingernails. Small pieces of furniture were overturned, miscellaneous items were strewn about, and most of the area was splattered with blood.

Concluding his duties, Dr. Silverman motioned for the deputy named Sam to come over to discuss his findings. Defiantly, the deputy rebuffed the doctor and motioned instead for the doctor to approach him. Totally oblivious to any appearance of relative importance, the doctor cooperatively worked his way to the deputy's side. Holding a page of handwritten notes in one hand while he adjusted a pair of gold-rimmed spectacles on the bridge of his nose with the other, Dr. Silverman remarked, "I think I need to talk to the sheriff on this case."

The arrogant young deputy cut him off before he could complete his remarks, and snapped. "That ain't gonna be necessary. I'll deliver that report. I'll explain what happened."

"You don't understand," the doctor protested, "This is serious. This woman wasn't a prostitute. She'd never even been with a man. Never would've been either. Not 'til she was good and married. Hell, she'd probably never even been in a saloon. She was respectable, comes from a good family. I've known her family for years. Another thing. Those people out there know who did this awful thing. Sheriff Hammer can't pretend this didn't happen. He's got to do something."

Sam looked at the old doctor with contempt. "Aw, she's just another Meskin. It's no big deal. We'll take care of it."

Still refusing to give up, Dr. Silverman continued, "No, Deputy, you still don't understand. It really is a big deal. Things are changing. The sheriff can't go on ignoring these people. He can't overlook this murder."

"Who's gonna complain?" Sam responded, wiping tobacco juice from his chin.

"What about that white kid she's been going around with? What's his name? Levi Wolfe, I think. He won't let this go."

"We'll take care of it," the deputy snapped again, a bit of anger and agitation creeping into his voice.

Shaking his head in disgust and disbelief, Dr. Silverman whirled around and walked quickly down the street to where his horse and buggy waited. The doctor bit his lip and tried to calm himself, wanting to lash out and knock some sense into the deputies. "Stupid sons of bitches," he hissed between clenched teeth. "Must have to pass a moron test to be a deputy these days."

Convinced that he had won his argument with the doctor, Sam turned self-importantly toward the curious crowd that had continued to mill around the scene and called out, "Okay, people! Vamoose! Go back home! Show's over." To Ramon, he said slightly more politely, "Come on. We've did about all we can do here. Let's go talk to His Highness, Mr. Hammer."

"Wait a minute, Sam," Ramon said, a troubled look on his face. "What that old doc said. It bothers me. What about this Levi fella? I've seen him around town. Kinda quiet, but I wouldn't want to rile him much. Young hot head. He may be a passel of trouble."

"You worry too damn much," Sam snarled. "Let our potbellied sheriff worry about it. He's the one what gets paid to worry. Not us." A cruel smile crossed his face, and he continued, "Come on, now, Ramon, wouldn't you like to see some young buck kick the hell out of old Dalton?"

"No, I wouldn't, Sam. People could die over this. I don't want a Mexican revolution here. I don't want that Levi person going after the sheriff, either."

"Okay, then you take the report to Hammer, and you tell 'im what you think he ought to know. I ain't gonna stick my neck out and get it cut off. I don't know nothin' about this thing, and that's what I'll tell the ol' bastard Hammer. You best think long and hard before you go spouting off a bunch of crap you don't know nothin' about."

An hour later the two deputies stood before Sheriff Hammer and told him about the murder. They explained the identity of the victim, the location of the crime, and other details. When they had finished, the sheriff asked the obvious question, "Any idea who might've done it?"

Ramon and Sam looked quickly at each other, and then turned their gaze toward the floor. Finally, Sam replied, "Didn't nobody see nothin'." He turned to go and then remembered, "Oh, yeah, here's ol' Doc Silverman's report." He handed the doctor's notes to the sheriff and left the room. Ramon followed him out.

Sheriff Hammer watched the two deputies cross the street and disappear in the direction of the nearest saloon. Shaking his head contemptuously, he said to himself, "Cowardly, lyin' horses' asses! They know who done this killing. I can tell by the way they act. They're afraid to tell me. Maybe they think they're keeping something from me, but they're not. I've already heard about it, and I know who done it."

Chapter 2

Levi Wolfe sat on a primitive wooden bench on a tree-covered hillside overlooking the San Antonio River. The day had been hot, but a cooling breeze had blown up from the river as evening approached. Birds called and sang in the trees and bushes, and a red-tailed hawk sat motionless in the tallest tree, closely watching the vulnerable song birds.

It was a familiar refuge for Levi. He and Jovita had come frequently, first just to talk and laugh about their daily routines, but later for more serious discussions about their future together. Today, he'd decided, would be a time of reflection, an opportunity to remember some of those times they had enjoyed so recently. For some reason, his mind kept wandering back to the day he'd first realized he might have a chance with her.

On previous visits he'd been studying her—unnoticed he thought—wondering why a woman so obviously out of his class would even be seen with him. She had beauty and she had grace. She had wit and intelligence. She had sophistication. Of course he was studying her. It was only later that she'd told him that she'd also been evaluating him, and she'd come to some conclusions.

Certainly, she'd recognized the obvious, which she enumerated matter-of-factly. He'd lived and worked in the city for almost four years, and he'd made admirable progress. But in some ways he was still the wide-eyed country boy from Poteet, Texas. His sunburned skin was at least as dark as hers, and his hands were still strong and rough from outdoor work. Like so many young men who had grown up in a farming environment, he had become a good, but not exceptional physical specimen, standing about two inches below six feet. He was muscular, but not exceptionally so, and he moved with effortless ease.

And he'd learned. Arriving in San Antonio, he had only a rudimentary education. He could read and write and do simple math, but all those were a struggle. He had laughed and told about his experiences in the one-room country school house near Poteet. He hadn't learned a lot, but his work in San Antonio had forced him to get better in those areas. True, he wasn't yet accomplished, but he'd get there.

Yes, of course, he was handsome, and she was well aware that other women occasionally cast admiring glances his way. Further, she acknowledged that it was an open secret that he'd once had a serious relationship with another young woman in the city, a woman named Selena.

His eyes and his mouth, she told him, were most telling. While kind and smiling most of the time, they occasionally reflected a sadness and occasional anger that she didn't quite understand. Outwardly, he projected self-confidence, but she believed it was acquired, not natural. Probably, she concluded, his time in San Antonio had shown that he had the intelligence and initiative to succeed in anything he chose to do.

Levi leaned back on the bench and laughed, as he recalled his reaction to being evaluated like a pig on the auction block. He was stunned. How did she do it so casually? He had been about to remark, when she interrupted him. Yes, she'd been sizing him up, as she'd admitted, but there was something missing, and she needed to know.

"Why?" she'd finally asked. "What on Earth compelled you to make such a change? You grew up on a farm or ranch or something. You worked hard for a good part of twenty-one years. Then you left." She stopped and studied him, as she searched for words. "You've told me that you're an only child, so you're probably needed there. But you left. Why?"

Levi smiled and replied. "You've never worked on a farm, have you?" She smiled in return and assured him that she hadn't. Of course, he already knew.

First he described the farm, telling her that it covered just a few more than four-hundred acres, and that it was about equally divided between farming and ranching. The farming part involved mostly vegetables and strawberries with some wheat and oats, mostly for grazing. The ranching involved the typical cow and calf operation common to central Texas.

He recalled telling her, "The work was so hard that I went to bed each night totally exhausted. Dirty work. Dangerous work. Burning hot in the summer. Freezing cold in winter. But, I'll admit it. Spring and fall were nice. Fall was my favorite. I like the crispness in the air and the relief from summer heat. Long, killing droughts were common, and they were devastating. Sometimes they wiped out entire crops.

"Livestock—cattle, sheep, and sometimes goats—just seemed to look for an excuse to die. There were diseases, but the worst were the screw worms. Flies would place eggs in a wound, and worm-like larvae would begin to eat the animal, sometimes killing it. And then there were chickens. They just seemed to be the dumbest animals on Earth. I've seen chickens sit in the rain and die, when there was shelter a few feet away."

"Was it just you and your dad? No hired help?"

"At peak seasons we hired farmhands and maybe a cowboy or two, but lots of the time it was just the two of us. I looked at the future, and I saw no end to it. It appeared that's how I'd spend the rest of my life."

"But if you'd stayed, wouldn't you have taken over one day? Inherit the farm? There don't seem to be any other potential heirs."

"If I'd stayed, it might've happened that way. But there are no guarantees in that life. A couple of really bad years in a row can wipe out a farm. Cause it to be lost to the bank or other creditors. And what if Dad dies before Mom, as he almost certainly will, and Mom remarries? Know where that leaves me? Besides, I'm not sure I even want the life of a farmer."

"Surely your dad misses you."

"I'm sure he does. He'll manage."

"You and your dad. You didn't have a good relationship, did you?"

"No. I got constant criticism. Nothing I did was right. I never heard a compliment from 'im. He saw me as a laborer. Not much more."

"Have you been back?"

"Only once. Didn't go well."

"Thank you, Levi Wolfe. I know enough. I know you've had a hard life, but you've come through it. You've done well in this city, and you have a bright future. You'll make it, and I'll be right there with you."

As the sun began to dip below the western horizon, Levi rose from the bench and walked to the edge of the river. He stood and watched the murky water roll past. He reconsidered what he'd told Jovita on the afternoon that seemed so long ago. He'd been accurate, but incomplete in his narration of his life in Poteet. He'd neglected to tell her that he'd shot and killed a man who was trying to steal a calf from the farm. He'd intended only to drive the man away, but he'd resisted, pulling a pistol and firing at Levi. Levi had returned fire, killing the man. Although it was self-defense, there were no witnesses, and the dead man was the son of a prominent neighbor, a friend of the local sheriff. Fearing arrest and prosecution, he had fled to San Antonio.

Levi stood, silently watching the sun disappear and darkness fall across the meadow. Then he turned and walked back toward the city.

Levi Wolfe was a troubled man. It had been almost three days since Jovita's funeral. Three whole days! Three days and still no arrest. So far as he knew, no charges had been filed. Officially, there weren't even any suspects, in spite of the fact that virtually everyone in the Mexican community knew who committed the atrocity. Levi knew the man. At least, he knew his identity. George Tompkins had appeared in San Antonio some five years earlier, accompanied by a small band of followers that were almost as feared as George was.

There were rumors about his history. Some ranchers swore that they had seen him several years earlier in cattle towns such as Abilene, memorable for their violence and lawlessness toward Texas trail-drivers. Others swore that he had once ridden with Quantrill's Raiders, and still others attempted to connect him to the James gang. Wherever he had come from, he had found a home in San Antonio. Hoping that George and his followers would simply move on, Sheriff Hammer had tolerated their presence until it was almost impossible to stop them. Now the day had arrived that the sheriff always knew would come. George had committed a crime that couldn't be ignored.

"That dirty, cowardly son of a bitch!" Levi said to himself. "He doesn't plan to arrest anybody. He's going to let those bastards go Scot free."

Levi was at a loss about what he could do. He had waited patiently, hoping that Sheriff Hammer's office soon would announce some significant development in the case. Perhaps, he assured himself, the sheriff was just being overly cautions, not wanting to arrest some innocent people. Or perhaps he was having difficulty in locating the perpetrators. Each day Levi had waited patiently, but to no avail. Each day, he feared, placed the murderers farther from San Antonio and farther from justice.

Levi walked quietly beneath the tall cypress trees along the San Antonio River. At times he strolled up the dusty road toward the Alamo, or back into the depths of the Mexican village that he knew so well. Perhaps he was reliving the pleasant times with Jovita, for these were the paths he often had taken with her. For three days he had been punishing himself for not being there when she needed him. Perhaps he could have saved her. If only he had married her six months ago, when he had become certain that she would accept his proposal. He knew at the time that he should ask her hand in marriage, but still he had waited—waited for a dozen reasons, all of them wrong.

Jovita and Levi were very different people, and there were many forces that logically might have kept them apart. She was a devout Catholic, while he embraced no formal religion, sometimes laughing to her that his God was found in the stars of the night and the solitude of the wooded hills that he loved so much. She was a Mexican, steeped in cultures and traditions that he admired and respected but still did not fully understand. There were numerous other reasons, each thoroughly discussed and ultimately resolved by the two.

He knew that those were not the reasons that had held him back, the reasons—perhaps excuses—that had kept them from becoming husband and wife. He knew that there was only one reason. That reason was much more selfish, more despicable to him now, but still he must face it. The fact was that he had been too immature, too irresponsible. He was having too much fun to tie himself down with a wife. He was enjoying the sights and the sounds of San Antonio. He loved his carefree bachelor life. He reveled in the nightlife of the gambling halls and the saloons.

In his selfish desire to enjoy the fleeting pleasures of a pagan city, he had pushed Jovita aside, expecting her to wait until he had satisfied his curiosity and filled himself with the vices of the town. With a great deal of pain, he remembered how he had first met her. It was strange really, and most unlikely. Usually, a simple, poor white cowboy would have little contact with a young Mexican woman who obviously came from a social class considerably above his.

She had been a cashier at Hernandez's small grocery store where he occasionally delivered produce. When he first saw her standing behind the counter, he could hardly believe his eyes. Why was a beautiful, sophisticated woman of high class working as a clerk in a grocery store? Later, he learned why. It was what she wanted to do. At first each one ignored the other, but the duties of their jobs required that they converse, at least on a business level.

As time passed, their business discussions became casual and friendly conversations. They made each other laugh, happy to be alive. Having grown up in the shelter of a protective family, Jovita knew little about men like Levi. This one was mysterious, charming, and—at least to her—handsome. She was drawn to him, and she made no attempt to resist the attraction.

In spite of their differences, they saw each other at every opportunity. He adjusted his schedule to allow more time with her, and she made sure she was available. Her mother, at first horrified that Jovita would become involved with a common gringo, gradually warmed to his charm and his obvious devotion to her daughter, and finally she gave her consent to an already flourishing courtship. Others in the Mexican village were equally reluctant to approve the relationship, but most doubters eventually were won over by the sight of the two young people walking together around San Antonio, obviously in love. Even

Father Pena, who had known Jovita since birth, saw hope in the relationship. Perhaps Jovita would bring this good, but worldly, youth to the Holy Catholic Church.

There was one group, however, that never viewed Levi as an acceptable suitor for Jovita. That group was the collection of young Mexican men in San Antonio. Each one knew Jovita and admired her beauty and sophistication. Each saw himself as the rightful recipient of her favors, the one most deserving of her attentions and her eventual hand in marriage. All were humiliated and embarrassed that she preferred a white man to them. However, the approval or disapproval of others meant little to the headstrong Jovita. She saw a promising future with Levi, and she believed she was making the right choice.

But what had appeared to be such a promising future for Jovita and Levi had ended in a few terrible minutes, and it appeared that nothing would be done to see that justice prevailed. The legal system was Levi's only hope. Jovita's family consisted only of her mother, at least as far as Levi knew. She didn't have the wealth or the political clout to force justice to be done. Levi's family, an impoverished farming family in Poteet, was equally incapable of bringing sufficient influence to bear.

Certainly, there was no real force in the Mexican community that would be heard. True, Father Pena would do what he could, but it would not be enough to impress Sheriff Dalton Hammer, and the priest knew it. Just yesterday, Levi had gone to the Father, requesting that he use the influence of the Church on the sheriff. To Levi's surprise, the priest at first was reluctant even to discuss the crime with him. After some persuasion, however, Father Pena did discuss it, and Levi realized that the priest wanted to help but was afraid to do anything.

"What do you hope to gain?" Father Pena had asked. "What good would it do? We can't bring Jovita back."

"Of course we can't!" Levi had replied, clearly agitated. "I know that. I'm not a fool. I...I just want to see justice done. Somebody needs to pay for this. You're an important man among your people. Maybe...just maybe the sheriff will listen to you."

"Among my people!" Now it was the priest's turn to be agitated. "Son, don't you know the sheriff doesn't care a bit about my people? The sheriff won't listen to me. My intervention would only bring more hardship to those you call 'my people.'"

"Then, you're saying you're not going to help?"

"I'll talk with the authorities, Levi. I'll do what I can." The priest smiled meekly. "Have you talked with her mother?"

Levi glanced at Father Pena, and then he looked away. "No. No, I haven't."

"Why not?" Father Pena asked, fully aware of Levi's reluctance.

"Look at me," Levi said, "I'm responsible for Jovita's death. I should've done more. Her mother knows that. I'm...I'm the last person she wants to see. I would only make things worse."

Father Pena nodded slowly. "I understand your hesitation," he said, "but she might surprise you. She has accepted you. She's very intelligent. She knows who's responsible for her daughter's death. Maybe you can comfort her. Go and talk with her. Express your sorrow. Be humble. Let her know you're grieving, just as she is."

Deep in thought, Levi watched a man in white peasants' clothing pull a cart down the cobblestone street. He turned again to Father Pena. "You're serious. She would receive me? She doesn't...blame me?"

"I've known her for many years. She's a gentle, loving woman. I believe she'd love to see you."

Levi stood in the dusty street and studied the white house. Turning his eyes away, he looked up and down the street. Several houses away, a flock of perhaps a dozen chickens clucked and fussed as they searched for grain that had been spilled by passing carts and wagons. In the other direction a small donkey silently argued with a man concerning the best route back home. Otherwise, the street was empty.

He directed his attention back to the house. Reluctantly, he took a step toward it, and then another and another. Walking haltingly, he considered turning back and abandoning his mission with each step. Finding himself facing a closed door, he raised his fist and knocked gently. He was committed. No turning back now. He had almost decided that no one was at home when he heard a bolt turn, and the door creaked open.

Not expecting Levi, Jovita's mother first stared at the young, disheveled white man standing in her doorway. Realizing it was Levi, she rushed to him and threw her arms around him, burying her face in his chest as she cried and wiped her eyes on his shirt. Unaccustomed to such expressions of affection, Levi was taken by surprise. His own eyes watered, and he tried to wipe them with his right forearm.

Finally pulling herself away, she said, "Please sit here at the table, and I'll get us some tea."

"Thank you," Levi said, haltingly.

Returning almost immediately, she placed two cups of steaming tea on the table. "I've been praying you'd come," she said softly.

"I'm sorry it has taken me so long," Levi said. "I...I was afraid ...." He wasn't sure how to continue.

"Afraid? Afraid you might not be welcome?"

Levi wiped his eyes again. "Yes, Ma'am. I guess I was."

She smiled slightly. "Why would you be unwelcome? To me

you're now part of my family. You're a son to me."

Levi had never felt so helpless...nor so guilty. "Because I feel responsible for Jovita's death." He was again fighting back tears. "I should've been there. I should've protected her. It was...it was my fault."

"Mr. Wolfe. Levi," she said, placing her hand on his. "I admit. When I first learned that my daughter was in love with you, when she first brought you here, I was not pleased. You were not the person I'd imagined for her. But she loved you, and you loved her. I saw the light in her eyes, and I saw the happiness in yours." Now tears were trickling down both her cheeks.

"Yes. Yes, I loved Jovita," Levi said, trying to hide his tears.

"You're not responsible for her death, Levi," she said, interrupting him. "We all know who is responsible, and we fear he won't be brought to justice. We have our own network in this community. We know what's going on. The sheriff pays no attention to us, but you already know that. I'm sure Father Pena told you. Others have too. The sheriff is a dangerous man. Be careful."

Levi was aware of the dangers in the path he was considering. "Someone has to stand up for justice. What kind of man would I be if I just let this pass?"

"I understand," she replied. "My religion teaches forgiveness, and I believe that's a good way to live. But sometimes things happen that challenge even the most sincere believer. For me this is one of those times. I'd like to see those animals who did this to my—no, our—Jovita brought to justice. I'd like to see them punished severely." She looked away for an instant. "May God forgive me," she added softly.

"I'm going to do everything I can," he replied, just as softly. "It may not be enough, but it'll be my best effort."

"Again, be careful," she said. "I don't want to bury you, a

son, along with my daughter."

He could tell that she was growing weary. "I'd best be going," he said. "I can't tell you how much I appreciate your willingness to talk with me."

"It was my pleasure," she replied. "Do what you have to do, and may God go with you." They rose, she hugged him again, and kissed him gently on the cheek. When he was gone, she prayed fervently for his safety.

Slowly, painfully, the truth became clear to Levi, as he left the house. Jovita's mother wanted justice, but she was powerless. All hope for justice rested solely on his shoulders. There was nobody else. His last hope for outside help had been Father Pena, a good man, but a meek and frightened one. Reluctantly, Levi admitted that Father Pena probably was correct. An attempt at vigorous intervention on the part of either the Father or the Catholic Church might well bring the wrath of the sheriff's office down upon the heads of both the Church and the Mexican citizens.

Levi had terrible feelings of inadequacy. He knew little about the law, about the intricacies of its enforcement, or about the depth of corruption in the local system. He didn't feel that he possessed the eloquence needed to argue successfully for justice, and he didn't have a power base from which to attack the corrupt system. He had no idea how, but he knew that if Jovita's death were to be avenged, he would have to do it.

Chapter 3

In the early morning light, Sheriff Dalton Hammer sat alone in his simple office, slowly reviewing his life—his successes and his failures—as men sometimes do in times of crisis. Slowly rising from an ancient swivel chair, he walked methodically down a narrow hallway between holding cells toward a small room at the far end of the building, quietly surveying his domain as he went.

The jailhouse seemed old even then. The main structure was a native limestone fortress with a tin roof overhead. Each cell had a heavily barred window, which opened to the outside of the building. The top of each cell was formed by two layers of heavy iron rods, arranged at right angles to each other, forming a checkerboard pattern. Heavy doors with metal bars opened into a long, common hallway, allowing access to each cell. There were fourteen cells, each measuring about six feet by eight feet. Each cell contained a narrow cot with a straw-filled mattress. Accommodations were primitive. The sheriff recalled with pride that in the twenty-three years he had been sheriff there had been only one successful jailbreak. A skinny kid from New Mexico once managed to grab a deputy's gun and make a clean getaway. Partly to save face and partly believing it might be true, the sheriff issued an official statement that the escapee was the infamous Billy the Kid. No one disputed the claim.

Reaching the end of the hall, Sheriff Hammer entered a small room and stopped before a crude washstand with a dirty mirror hanging above it. Looking into the mirror, he saw the reflection of a forty-six-year-old man with a deeply wrinkled, weather-beaten face that never had been handsome but once had possessed warmth that naturally drew others to him. Staring out beneath bushy eyebrows were hard, dark eyes that years ago had danced with humor and friendly mischief but now held little expression at all.

The muscles of his arms and upper body still were firm and strong, but he knew he was beginning to suffer some of the physical deterioration that comes with middle age. The beginning of a potbelly indicated that he both ate and drank excessively. Stretching to the full extent of his six-foot frame, he was not pleased that he had let his physical condition deteriorate, but he reassured himself, smiling faintly, that he still could hold his own in a street fight or a barroom brawl.

"Twenty-three years," he said to his reflection in the mirror. "Twenty-three years of bringin' peace and order to this godforsaken hellhole, and what's it got me? Nothin'! Not a goddamned thing, that's what. I've sweated in the summer, and I've froze in the winter. I've shivered in the miserable rain in between, and who gives a damn? Time was I at least could do my job without some crabby bunch of nosey bitches watchin' my every move. So what if I busted some greaser's head? The Meskins in this town behaved when I was around. Now, I gotta ask permission to piss. Then prove I done it right. Now this.

"Some damn Meskin slut gets herself raped and killed, and I have to deal with it. Course she wouldn't be just some worthless whore. No, she had to be respectable. Now, all the Meskins in town is raising hell. That ol' bastard of a Catholic priest is askin' questions, ever so polite. Most white folks don't really give a damn, but they're watching, too. Just waitin' for me to step in my own crap. Now, some damn cowboy that was shackin' with her is watchin' me. Lookin' for revenge, I hear."

Sheriff Hammer washed and lathered his face, took a

straight-edged razor from the shelf and prepared to shave. "To hell with that George Tompkins, anyway," he said, studying himself in the mirror. "I know he done it. Him and them snivelin' idiots that follows him around, lickin' his boots and tellin' him what a stud horse he is. Just the sort of sorry thing he'd do. Should've ran him outta town months ago, back when it would've been easy. Suppose I could bring him in now. I know where to find the worthless bastard. Probably he run to that bunch of no-account riffraff over in Bandera.

"Trouble is, he's got dangerous in the last few years. Pretty good with a gun, too. He may even have friends up there. Probably does. Well, not really friends. George ain't got no real friends, but maybe some people that'd help him. Anyway, why bring 'im back? Why risk my own life? No jury'll convict a white man for killin' a Meskin. Not even if they knew he done it. Besides, nobody seen nothin'."

He finished shaving, wiped away the remaining shaving soap, and combed his thinning, gray-flecked brown hair. Slowly, he returned to his office, which opened onto a muddy back street. He sat heavily into the swivel chair, leaned back, and placed his dirty, scuffed boots on the top of his desk. In the last few minutes he had made his final decision. He would not go after George Tompkins and his gang. It had been four—or maybe it was five—days since the murder. George well might be completely out of state by now, maybe even in Mexico. With luck, this thing would blow over.

Dalton was taking a calculated risk in choosing to ignore Jovita's murder, and he knew it. He had taken unpopular positions before and survived. It seemed to him that his entire life had been one long series of risks. He had appeared in San Antonio when he was only twenty-three years old. During the four years before that, he had served with distinction as a Texas

Ranger. Most of his service had been on the Texas border with Mexico, where he had dealt frequently with Mexicans on both sides of the Rio Grande and on both sides of the law. For the most part, he had treated all of them with fairness, dignity, and respect. His superiors spoke highly of him, and he appeared to be destined for a long career in the service of Texas.

Somehow, during that period he managed to meet the daughter of a south Texas rancher, and after an acceptable period of courtship they married. Dalton's future appeared even brighter than it had been before. His star was rising. It seemed that he could do no wrong. He was sure that he would conquer the world with his good wife at his side. However, there were things that he had not counted on. His new wife immediately objected to his life as a Texas Ranger, pointing out that it was dangerous and that it took him away from her too much of the time. His father-in-law was still a relatively young man, not ready to sit back and let Dalton run the ranch. Dalton was in a dilemma, as he now had a wife but no satisfactory means to support her.

He was very much in love with his wife and was willing to make all necessary sacrifices for her. Through contacts with others in law enforcement, he managed to find employment as a deputy sheriff in Bexar County. When the aging sheriff retired two years later, Dalton called in some favors and managed to take the old sheriff's place. As sheriff, he had found his calling. His experiences with the Texas Rangers served him well, as did his contacts with former Ranger colleagues and other law enforcement officers. He managed to apply the law fairly and firmly to all parties under his jurisdiction.

His practices drew the praises of the governor of Texas, who occasionally consulted him on law enforcement matters. It appeared that his career was back on track. Most importantly, his wife was happy in the developing city of San Antonio. As the wife of a successful—although minor—politician, she became visible in social and charitable organizations within the city, contributing countless hours to a local orphans' home. She found pleasure and contentment in the knowledge that she was helping her husband, while providing a useful service. When his wife was content, he was happy.

His happiness was short lived, however. His wife, never a physically strong woman, suffered a great deal of illness during their seventh year in the city. The winter had been unusually cold and wet, and she had considerable difficulty with various respiratory problems. Then spring came, and it appeared that now the approaching warm weather would bring improvements in her health. Unfortunately, during an early spring cold spell, she got soaked in a sudden rainstorm. She was ill again, very ill. Dr. Silverman did what he could, but his treatment was unsuccessful. She died of pneumonia.

Dalton became a different man. He was dark and brooding, frequently vicious. His wife's death left him alone with nothing to show for their time together. No children had been produced in the marriage. Twice his wife had become pregnant, but each time she miscarried. He blamed everyone, including himself, for his young wife's death. Most of all, he blamed the Mexicans. Of course, it made no sense, but he frequently singled them out for especially harsh treatment when they found themselves in his jail.

Once the example of honesty and fairness, Sheriff Hammer turned to graft and extortion to pay for his alcoholism, his gambling, and his women. At one time, virtually every saloon, gambling hall, and brothel paid the sheriff a sizeable fee for the right to do business. Ironically, at the time when he was making life miserable for many Mexicans, he was developing a preference for Mexican prostitutes and bar girls. Many such women were arrested by the sheriff or his deputies, only to find that the only way to win freedom was to provide sexual favors to the arresting officers. In the past few years, however, he had been forced to abandon or curtail many of his unlawful practices. An increasingly enlightened society constantly was clamoring for reform.

No fool, the sheriff recognized the winds of change. Instead of continuing his former practice of imposing his demands upon the unfortunate women under his control, the sheriff restricted his amorous activities to his Mexican mistress, a lovely young woman named Rosa Gutierrez. Rose, as Sheriff Hammer called her, had fallen victim to the sheriff just as other girls had. However, seeing an opportunity, she turned his harassment of her into an advantage.

Rose was never actually a prostitute. Even the life of a bargirl was distasteful to her, so when the sheriff made his usual proposition, she immediately accepted his offer. She had willingly served as his mistress ever since. Although they had been lovers for several years, they maintained separate residences. After all, openly consorting with a Mexican woman of questionable character might have been politically disastrous to the sheriff. At least, that was his claim. Whenever they wished to convey messages to one another, they sent simple, handwritten notes by courier. They used a Mexican boy about ten years old to carry their messages. Neither knowing nor caring the child's real name, the sheriff referred to the boy as Pedro.

Chapter 4

Levi stood on the edge of the muddy street, looking down toward the jail. Weary, bone tired, running on adrenaline and little more, he had slept little since the murder. But more, he was apprehensive, still unsure about how to approach the sheriff. Mostly, however, he was angry, angry with himself for acting too slowly and angry at a system that still had made no attempt to arrest Jovita's killer. Finally, unable to find another reason to procrastinate, he turned and walked toward the jail.

Sheriff Hammer shouldn't have been surprised when he looked up from his desk to see Levi standing before him. Certainly, in his years of law enforcement, he had experienced many more threatening and more surprising events. Hadn't he paid his dues? Had he not experienced terror? Surprise? Fear? Yes, his life of hardship and deprivation should have prepared him well for almost any event. However, he was startled by Levi's sudden appearance. The two men had never met formally, but the sheriff immediately recognized the younger man. They had exchanged casual greetings occasionally in some of San Antonio's business establishments.

The sheriff pushed himself stiffly out of the chair and extended his hand in an attempt to defuse a potentially ugly confrontation. "Howdy," he said, a wide smile covering his face. "I'm Sheriff Dalton Hammer."

"I know who you are," Levi replied, ignoring the offer of friendship. "I'm here on business, not pleasure."

The smile disappeared from the sheriff's face. "Well, seems

to me we can still be polite," he said. "What might your business be?"

"I think you know real well what my business is. I'm here about the murder of Jovita delos Santos. I want to know why you've been sitting on your ass while those bastards get away. A lot of other people would like to know the same thing."

Still trying to placate the young man but feeling his annoyance grow, the sheriff replied, "I'd like to accommodate you, son, but I don't know who them bastards are. I've got some suspects, but no real evidence."

"First off, I'm not your son. Next, you know damn well who killed her," Levi stormed at the sheriff. "George Thompson or Tompkins or something like that. That worthless, cowardly son of a bitch and those low-life friends of his." Then, very deliberately, Levi added, "He bragged that he was a friend of yours. Maybe that's why you haven't arrested him."

The accusation hit the sheriff in the face like a club. He struggled to control his anger. He knew that he might be considered a coward for not pursuing the men. He might be shirking his duties, but he wasn't protecting a friend. He knew George Tompkins and had even played a few hands of cards with him, but George was no friend of his. George was bad news, untrustworthy, and dangerous as indicated by his recent deeds. The sheriff had recognized all this many weeks ago and certainly realized he should have ordered George out of town, but at that time George had committed no known crime. If he ordered every potential troublemaker out of town, he'd have a fulltime job just delivering the messages.

Through the years of being in tough situations, the sheriff had learned to think on his feet, to plan quickly and skillfully to extricate himself from sticky situations. He was beginning to see the possibility of doing just that in this situation. Maybe he could scare this inexperienced, gullible boy so severely that he would be only too happy to go quietly on his way. It was worth a try.

In setting his plan into motion, the sheriff pointedly stated, "Now you know that I can't go giving information out to just anybody. Have to protect the rights of the victim and the accused. Now tell me, exactly what is yore interest in this case? Why do you want to know? What was the deceased to you?"

"If it's any of your business, she was my fiancée."

"Really?" Sheriff Hammer said, faking a sympathetic smile. "And you was plannin' to marry her?"

"That's right."

"Oh, you was?" the sheriff replied. "I guess you knew she was about three months pregnant?"

Now Levi had to redouble his efforts to control the rage and hate that were welling up inside him. "Like hell she was," he answered coldly.

"Was it yore baby?" the sheriff asked, ignoring Levi's denial and testing to see just how far he could push the young man.

Still struggling to control his anger, Levi again replied, "There wasn't any baby. What's it to you, anyway?"

"Could be a lot. Could be a whole lot."

"Like what?"

"Seems to me you sure are interested in havin' me believe ol' George Tompkins done this thing. Now, I know he ain't a model citizen. In fact, he's probably a lot of the things you called 'im, but he sure ain't a friend of mine. And I got no interest in protectin' the man, but I got no reason to arrest 'im. Yes, George can be kinda rough with a woman. I know that, but he ain't never killed one, at least not in this town. Men yes, but only in a fair fight. Look, you gotta understand, I got no real evidence against George. Just rumors. No reason to bring 'im in."

"Seems to me that Jovita's murder would be a reason."

"Boy, why're you so hell bent on havin' me arrest George? Do you have evidence—hard evidence that'll stand up in court—that he's guilty? Did somebody see somethin' that I don't know about? Maybe one of George's idiot friends has gone to some priest wantin' forgiveness? I don't think so. We're talkin' about a murder here. You gotta have evidence for a trial, and I ain't got any." Sheriff Hammer paused for just a moment, hoping his reasoning would influence Levi. Then he closed in for the kill. "It's occurred to me that maybe you have yore own reasons for wantin' me to arrest George. Personal reasons."

"Meaning what?"

So far the plan was working even better than the sheriff had planned. Now it was time for him to play his ace. He would send this greenhorn kid slinking back to his cage, like a dog with his tail between his legs. "Meanin' it seems to me there might be more than one suspect here. Seems to me that maybe you had good reason to kill that gal yoreself."

Levi was astounded. Could this moron really believe that he killed Jovita, the woman he loved and planned to marry? "You...you must think I'm crazy!" Levi blurted out.

"Crazy like a fox! I'm thinkin' you found yore gal in a family way, but you knew it wasn't yore kid. That'd make anybody mad, maybe mad enough to kill. Or maybe it really was yore kid, but you weren't ready—or man enough—to face the facts. Didn't want no family just yet. So you raped the girl, beat 'er up, and killed 'er. Just like that. Course you waited 'til ol' George was makin' eyes at 'er. That made *him* the perfect suspect. Everybody would blame him and feel real sorry for you. Real neat little plan."

"I'm telling you, she wasn't pregnant!" Levi shouted.

"Not what the doc said," the sheriff replied, knowing Levi

had no way to disprove the lie. "But let's just say she wasn't. Just pretend awhile. Maybe you found out she was takin' somebody else to bed. Or maybe she found an easy way to make a little extra money. There's a lot of possibilities in this crime."

Levi could stand it no longer. In his mind he had come to the sheriff's office to inquire about the progress of an official investigation. Now, he was being accused of his fiancée's murder, while the real killers were being allowed to escape. He was not perceptive enough to recognize that the sheriff's accusations were not serious, but merely a ruse to mislead him. In his cold, unreasoning anger, Levi did a foolish thing. He lunged at the sheriff, clearly intent upon beating the man to death.

Sheriff Hammer had not expected this reaction. What had seemed at first to be a brilliant plan had fallen apart. Levi's first punch was a wild hook, which struck the sheriff just below the left eye. The sheriff was quick on his feet, extremely agile for a man of his size and age. He saw the blow coming in time to deflect it enough to lessen its effect. He sent two quick, hard jabs to Levi's midsection. Levi grunted but came back strong, now using his youth and better physical condition to wear the aging sheriff down with short, hard punches and fast left-right combinations.

It wasn't an evenly matched fight. Twice the sheriff was knocked off his feet by his enraged opponent. Levi was viciously beating him, unleashing all the frustrations and fury that had built over the past several days. He might have beaten the sheriff to death, but Sam, the deputy sheriff, happened to report for duty just in time to save his life.

Levi was oblivious to everything happening around him. A dozen men could have entered, and he wouldn't have noticed. His sole mission at the moment was to destroy the sheriff. Realizing that very thing might happen, the deputy quickly stepped behind Levi and bought his large Colt revolver heavily down upon Levi's head. Levi crumpled to the floor, unconscious from the blow.

Sheriff Hammer held onto the edge of an open door in order to keep from falling to the floor. Sam attempted to assist his boss, but the sheriff brusquely shoved him aside, stumbled over to his swivel chair, and sat down. Looking at his deputy, Dalton pointed to Levi's unconscious body on the floor and said, "If he's still alive, put 'im in a cell. We're chargin' the bastard with murder, and by God I'll see 'im hang."

The news that Sheriff Hammer had arrested a suspect in Jovita's murder spread quickly through the Mexican community. At first the sheriff refused to reveal the name of the suspect. "Suspect or suspects," the sheriff was quick to say. There were security considerations, the sheriff explained. Many of the residents were ecstatic. Finally. Finally, the fat gringo sheriff had done something right. Finally, he was concentrating on something other than the body of Rose, his well-endowed Mexican mistress. Could it be, the Mexicans wondered, that times actually were changing? Did they dare hope for something approaching fairness from the despised sheriff? Would he actually place George Tompkins and his followers on public trial for the rape and murder of a Mexican woman? True, there were skeptics, but a feeling of cautious optimism pervaded the community.

Within three days of the arrest, word leaked—probably through one of the deputies—that the suspect was not George Tompkins at all. Instead, it was the young white man who had been seeing Jovita for over a year, Levi Wolfe. The residents were amazed when they learned of this obvious miscarriage of justice. It was unthinkable that he actually was the killer. Most of them knew him or knew of him. Certainly, they had not been pleased when the beloved Jovita began to spend time with him, a common gringo, but as time passed, they accepted him. Now he was treated almost as one of their own. Levi Wolfe, the killer of Jovita? Definitely not! As one member of the community stated, "For years Hammer has framed Mexicans for crimes against white people. Now he's framing a white man for the murder of one of us." Most people thought Levi soon would be released, that he simply was being taught a lesson for whipping the sheriff. At most he would be charged with nothing more than assault. It soon became clear, however, that such was not the plan. Three more days passed, and Levi still was locked in the cramped, dirty jail cell. The sheriff was forging ahead with his plans to prosecute Levi for murder.

When finally confronted about the matter by a curious newspaper reporter, Sheriff Hammer declared, "The man attacked me when I questioned him about the murder. He had no reason to try to kill me, but he give it his best shot. Don't it make sense that a man like that might kill the Meskin girl that was givin' herself to anybody that come along, makin' him look like a fool?" The sheriff clearly was on a mission of revenge, and he was determined to have that revenge.

Following the blow to his head, Levi had been largely unconscious for most of the day, finally regaining full consciousness late in the afternoon. He had lain for several hours on the crude bunk in the jail cell where he had been tossed, drifting in and out of consciousness. He was sitting on the edge of the bunk, nursing the worst headache of his life, when the sheriff paid him a visit. The sheriff was a sight. Both eyes were swollen almost shut. His face was bruised, and dark red welts were interspersed between the bruises. He hobbled in pain when he walked. Levi stiffened when the sheriff approached, not knowing what to expect. Clenching his fists, he felt pain shoot from both hands up his forearms. Then he remembered why the sheriff looked so bad. He waited to see what the sheriff had to say.

The sheriff stood in front of the heavy cell door, glaring at his helpless prisoner. "Today, I officially charged you with the rape and murder of Jovita...whatever her name was."

"Her name was Jovita delos Santos."

Sheriff Hammer nodded. "Right. I'm sayin' you killed her, and I'm chargin' you with it."

"You know damn well I didn't do it."

Just the shadow of a smile crept across the sheriff's face. "I don't know nothin' of the sort. Far as I know, you done it, sure enough. You had as much motive as anybody. Motive. Let's talk about motive. You understand motive, don't you, boy. Now, that's the reason you done something."

"I know what motive is."

"Good. I plan for you to learn a lot of legal words. Words like 'guilty' and 'execution' and 'hang by the neck 'til dead.' Them's some of my favorites. I plan for you to learn them real good." The sheriff grimaced with pain and hate as he spat the words to Levi. Clearly, he was serious about the charges.

"George Tompkins and two other hoodlums killed her. There were witnesses."

"Ah, witnesses. Now, that's another one of them legal words you need to learn about. A witness got to *see* somethin'. There weren't no witnesses. Nobody saw nothin'."

Despite his limited knowledge of law, Levi knew the sheriff was right. There were no actual witnesses. He continued anyway, "There were people who saw them messing with her."

The sheriff smiled again, this time the smile was almost genuine. "Where you been, boy? In this here town, men mess with women all the time. Most common thing in the world. Woman don't want it, she lets the man know, and he goes on to somebody else. It ain't like they's just one woman in San Antone. Besides, why's a shiftless bum like George think he could get away with messin' with a high class Meskin like her…if she really was all that high class?"

"He killed her, and you know it."

"All I know is that you had more reason than George did. We'll let a jury decide. Besides, I think the jury'll be interested in the fact that you come in here and jumped me, and tried to kill me. I'll take some pleasure seein' you pay for that."

"That's what this is about, isn't it? You're afraid of George Tompkins, and you want to get even with me, so you're going to try me for murder?"

"Boy, I ain't afraid of nobody. Not you. Not George. Not the devil hisself. But you're gonna pay for dishonorin' the office of the sheriff of this county. You'll see. If I have to, come trial day, I'll have witnesses that'll swear they seen you go in that house. That heard her scream and beg for mercy. That seen you run off after you done it." Sheriff Hammer's breath came in short, painful bursts as he described his plan to Levi. His swollen eyes gleamed with hate and revenge, and the corners of his wide, vicious mouth curled his thin lips up in a wicked smile.

"You'd do that? You'd buy witnesses? You'd lie and get other witnesses to lie just to convict me?"

"Goddamn right, I'd do that. Time was me and some of my deputies would've took you in that back room and beat a confession out of you. I'd love to do it this time, but I ain't. This'll be all legal and proper. Besides, you might die if we whipped you right good. I don't want nothin' to go wrong with this. I want to see you hang. Nobody whips me and lives to tell about it. Let's just say that I'm makin' sure that justice gits done."

The sheriff tried to whirl around and leave, but he turned too quickly and brought pain to his bruised body. He bit his lip hard to keep from crying out. He slammed the cell door, turned the key in the lock, and limped down the hall to his office.

Holding his throbbing head in his hands, Levi continued to sit on the edge of the bunk, listening to the sheriff limp down the hall. He knew he was in deep trouble. The sheriff was right. There were no witnesses to the crime. Even if Tompkins and his gang were arrested and tried, they likely would get off. If the sheriff got witnesses to lie to a jury by accusing Levi of being at the scene, then he indeed might be convicted and condemned to death. Finally, he was beginning to realize the seriousness of his predicament.

Chapter 5

With each passing day, Levi's fear for his life increased. At night he lay awake, pondering his fate. How could his life have changed so drastically in such a short time? How did this happen? Yes, he had acted foolishly, impulsively. He had attacked a public official, but should that be a death sentence? The men in the adjacent room—the sheriff and one of his deputies—fully intended to see him dead. They had made that quite clear, but why was his death so important? Why not some charge that would teach him a lesson—one that would make an indelible mark on him, while resonating throughout San Antonio's Mexican communities? Why not seek a long jail term? That would be easier to get.

The more Levi considered his situation, the more certain he was of one thing: He was being charged with murder, but that wasn't his real crime. Without fully realizing it, he had challenged an evil and corrupt system that had gone unchallenged for years. Yes, he was questioning the legitimacy of an institution that didn't want to be questioned. Not only that, he—a white man—was taking up the fight of the Mexican population. Perhaps none of this had been his intention, but it now was a huge part of his crime, and he would pay for it. If a trial took place, would he be convicted? After all, he thought, he was a white man, a definite asset at this time and place, and he had friends in San Antonio—not many but some. Then there was the jury, which would have to be convinced of Levi's guilt. Surely a jury—even an all white one—would hear the evidence and arrive at a just verdict.

Then his mind flashed back to reality. Actually, Sheriff Hammer stood a very good chance of getting a conviction. As the sheriff repeatedly stated, there were no legitimate witnesses, but for a person like Dalton Hammer, witnesses would be no problem.

A serious concern was that valuable time was being lost. Each passing minute made the apprehension of Jovita's real killers less likely. Levi examined his cell for the hundredth time, looking for some means of escape, but he found none. He had examined the windows, the roof, even the door. All seemed secure. The facility was old and primitive, but it appeared to be escape-proof. Even if he managed to get out of his cell, he probably couldn't get far. There always were two guards in the jail with him. Sometimes it was two deputies, but usually one of the men was the sheriff. Any of them, especially the sheriff, would shoot him at the slightest provocation.

Levi had tried to talk with his captors, hoping to establish some kind of rapport with them, maybe gain some sympathy that might be useful. It was immediately apparent that he had no chance with Sam. While Sam was illiterate and backward, he had a way of manipulating a situation to his advantage. Apparently, he had some personal goal that he hoped to achieve, and probably he planned to use Levi to achieve it.

Ramon was different. He was Mexican, and he knew why he had been selected as a deputy. Almost everyone understood. The sheriff had seen a need to develop some credibility with the increasingly restless Mexican community. In an effort to appease them, Hammer had hired a token, a Mexican deputy, to ensure that a buffer existed between him and the Mexicans. Although the plan had been only marginally successful, it had taken some heat off the sheriff, and it had provided a small amount of relief for the Mexican community. However, it had not been the stunning success the sheriff had wanted. He still had a restless group to deal with.

Ramon's loyalties were torn by the arrest of Levi. A young Mexican man, he had resented Levi's relationship with Jovita. On the other hand, he knew that Levi was innocent, and he was very much aware that Levi had the support of whatever leadership existed in the Mexican village, his village. At first Ramon was supportive and encouraging to Levi, assuring him that real justice would prevail in the case and even providing some physical comforts, such as blankets and shaving supplies. Unfortunately for Levi, that all came to an end as soon as the sheriff found out about it. Realizing that Ramon was the weak link in his chain of perverted justice, the sheriff carefully assigned the Mexican deputy to some duty other than guarding Levi.

Other guards were nothing more than nameless faces as far as Levi was concerned. Most had no opinion concerning Levi's guilt or innocence. They didn't know, and they didn't care. However, they held one thing in common. They had no intention of crossing Sheriff Hammer. To them this was just a job, a job that each one desperately needed, and they weren't going to jeopardize that job. They had seen the wrath of Sheriff Hammer, and they wanted no part of it. If the sheriff said that Levi was guilty, that was good enough for them.

By the evening of the tenth day of imprisonment, Levi had almost given up hope. Apparently, the sheriff and Sam, the deputy on duty, realized Levi's despondency, for their derision of him was especially intense on this evening. Sam brought Levi his evening meal but purposely spat in the food, fouling it in front of his boss. Knowing that the deputy was trying to gain the sheriff's favor, Levi lay face-up on his bunk, staring at the ceiling and ignoring the two laughing men. Levi's failure to respond brought a few more minutes of crude taunts. Then the two strolled casually back down the hall toward the sheriff's office. For the first time in several days the sheriff and his staff were relaxed, having successfully diverted attention away from George Tompkins and focused it upon Levi. Now, having an excuse for not pursuing George, Dalton could sit back and rest easy. The staff was relaxed because Sheriff Hammer was relaxed. A relaxed boss meant at least a short period of peace for them. Sam was feeling exceptionally good tonight. Perhaps his opportunity had come at last. For months he had wanted to be named Chief Deputy—officially, so that everyone would know—but the opportunity to plead his case had not come. Maybe this was the time. For sure, this was the best opportunity he would have. He would take his chances.

"Boss," Sam began. "I got to hand it to you. You played this real smart. Real smart. You got us a real, live murder suspect."

"Yeah, maybe," Sheriff Hammer began to reply, not sure what to expect next. He had known Sam for some time and knew better than to trust the man.

"Let's have a little celebration," Sam continued, reaching into the bottom drawer of a filing cabinet and withdrawing an almost-full whisky bottle and two dingy glasses. Sam filled both glasses. Handing one to the sheriff, he said, "Drink up. Let's talk." Sam seated himself in a chair across the desk from the sheriff. He leaned back and placed his well-polished boots on the corner of the sheriff's desktop.

The sheriff was puzzled. He was unaccustomed to such familiarity from his deputies. Certainly, he didn't encourage such behavior. He was boss, and he believed a great gulf should exist between himself and his subordinates. "Never treat them as friends. Treat them as servants," he once told a visiting dignitary from another city. However, on this occasion he decided to go along. He took a deep drink from the glass, settled back in his chair, and waited.

The two men sat in silence for a few seconds. Sam focused his eyes on the wall behind the sheriff, pretending to study some nonexistent object. He ran his bony fingers along the perfect crease in his pants. Silently, with well-concealed amusement and contempt, Sheriff Hammer studied this unsuspecting imitation of a deputy. Then the deputy began, "Sheriff, I been thinkin'. We can help each other out. We both got things the other can use, needs even. Now, you need me to make yore charges agin that kid stick. Hell, the whole world knows he ain't guilty, but if you want him to be, we'll make it happen. I'll swear anything you want, and I'll find half a dozen of the most believable liars in San Antone. They'll tell a jury any story I give 'em, and they'll make it sound real. Now, you probably wonder what I want in return."

Continuing to sit silently, the sheriff waited for Sam's proposition. "I don't want much, really. Just some recognition that I should've got a long time ago," Sam said. "A little reward for years of loyalty. I want to be named Chief Deputy, with a slight pay raise, of course. I want to be yore right-hand man. Help bring them Meskins back in line, with yore approval, of course. Hell, Sheriff, I been with you about five years now without no pay raise or nothin'. I been here longer than any other of the boys."

Hesitating for a moment to get his breath, Sam stole a glance at Sheriff Hammer, trying to determine whether his plea was having any effect on his superior officer. To Sam's disappointment, the sheriff stoically sat in his chair, sipping his whisky and deliberating upon each word the deputy had said. Now getting desperate for some response from the sheriff, Sam stammered, "I shore can be a lotta help to you in this here murder case, Boss."

For better or for worse, Sam had stated his case, laid it right on the line for the sheriff to see, and now he would wait for a verdict. The sheriff mentally was weighing all his options. Should he give in to this blatant blackmail? Hell no! Sam couldn't handle even the simple responsibilities required in his present position. He knew that Sam had been quietly promoting himself with the other deputies, leading them to believe that he soon would be their superior. Dalton also knew that some of the deputies might even expect Sam's request to be granted. But a real promotion was out of the question, of course. Maybe he should just fire Sam on the spot, perhaps accuse him of some offense, such as attempted blackmail, or maybe just declare him incompetent. No, that wouldn't work either. Sam knew too much. He was too much part of the plan. There had to be another way. Maybe it would be best to give up the whole scheme and free Levi. No, that wasn't an option. He had gone too far with the scheme. To bail out now likely would cause his own downfall. It might even result in his own conviction for tampering with evidence or something of the kind. The silence between the two men was becoming intolerable. Then, as if on cue, they were jolted back to reality by a gentle rapping on the heavy, locked front door. Recognizing his subordinate position, the deputy went to the door and peered out through the small, bar-covered glass window at the top.

It's yore messenger," Sam said, looking down at the smiling, up-turned face of a small Mexican boy standing just outside. The boy held up a folded piece of paper for Sam to see.

"Who?" the sheriff asked, uncertainly.

"Yore messenger. You know. Pedro. Rosa must be lonesome."

"Well, let ...." The sheriff was about to command Sam to let the boy enter, but his instincts warned him to be careful. "Look outside and see if anybody else is there."

Sam looked up and down the street and about the front of

the building, which was partly obscured by shadows. "No, Boss, I don't see nobody else out there," Sam said.

"Okay, let the little fart in," Dalton ordered.

Sam turned a key in the lock, and swung the heavy door inward just enough to admit the boy. Taking one look at the child, Sheriff Hammer knew he had been tricked. This wasn't Pedro, but another Mexican boy of similar size, stature, and dress. The sheriff froze only a moment in surprise and disbelief, but that moment was enough.

Two masked and armed men sprang from their hiding places on each side of the door and barged into the room. Training their revolvers on the sheriff and his deputy, the two men quickly disarmed the shaken lawmen. One of the intruders spoke in English with a heavy Mexican accent, "We want Levi Wolfe. Where is he?"

The sheriff started to protest but thought better of it. "Back there," he said, motioning toward Levi's cell.

The gunman again addressed the sheriff, "We're not here to kill you, but we will, if necessary. All we want is Levi. Do not do anything foolish." The man spoke precisely in a flat monotone, as though his words were well rehearsed.

Mustering all the courage he had, Sheriff Hammer replied, "Yore makin' a huge mistake. Wolfe's been charged with murder. You can't take him out of my legal custody. What do you want with him, anyway?"

Holding the gun against the sheriff's temple, the man lost his politeness and hissed at the sheriff, "This Colt says I can do what I please. If your life is worth a damn thing, which I doubt, you'd better see how fast you can get Levi Wolfe out of his cell. What do I want with him? Maybe I'm going to hang him!"

Levi heard the disturbance and the sharp, hostile exchange of conversation. Then he heard the men coming down the hall toward his cell. He had no idea what to expect. Was he being liberated, or was a lynch mob coming for him? The four men stopped in front of his cell.

"Open it!" one of the men ordered. The sheriff, now white with fear, motioned for Sam to comply. The two gunmen stood back, out of reach of the sheriff and his deputy, as the iron door swung inward.

"Out!" the man hissed at Levi, who had gotten off his cot and had moved to the front of his cell when the noise started. Levi complied. Without speaking, the man motioned for the two lawmen to enter the cell. Reluctantly, they did as ordered. The second gunman pulled the door closed and locked it.

Now leveling his gun at Levi, the first gunman, who appeared to be the spokesman, said, "Move it!" Levi walked toward the sheriff's office, still puzzled and unsure of his fate. One of the two men moved ahead of Levi, stuck his head out the door, and looked up and down the empty street. When he was sure that all was clear, he motioned with his pistol for Levi to follow him.

Once outside, Levi blinked and waited a few moments for his eyes to adjust to the darkness. His two captors had hurried around the corner of the building, making preparations for whatever was to come next. Almost immediately, one of the men stuck his head around the corner and motioned urgently toward Levi. Levi wanted to break and run, run for his life, run back into the jail if necessary, escape anyway he could. Even Sheriff Hammer's brand of justice would be better than what Levi expected from these two men.

If he'd ever had an opportunity to run, Levi had lost it now. He'd be shot down before going five feet. Having no other option, Levi moved toward the beckoning man. As soon as he was in the deeper shadows of the jailhouse, Levi noticed that the two gunmen had removed their masks. They were Mexican men about his age. He knew he had seen them before, but he didn't know their names. One of the men was holding a saddled horse—a very good horse from appearances—while the other man was hurriedly loading provisions into saddlebags. For the first time, Levi breathed more easily, finally sensing that he was in friendly hands. Almost overcome with emotion, Levi grasped the arm of the man who had done the talking inside the jail. Levi asked, "Why are you doing this?"

The young man looked steadily at Levi and then replied, "We did not like it when you entered our world and captured the heart of Jovita. Every one of us wanted her, and one of us might have had her. But you entered her life, and she loved you. I guess you loved her, too. At least, we know you didn't kill her. Besides, we wanted to teach that old bastard Hammer a lesson. We enjoyed taking you away from him, and we enjoyed seeing the fear and the hate in his eyes. We see the hate all the time, but not the fear. The fear was a real treat."

"Does this place you in danger? Will the sheriff take revenge?"

"Naw," the young man replied. "He doesn't know us. Sheriff Hammer can't tell one Mexican man from another. If he finds out, we can hide for a hundred years in the village. Or our friends can sneak us out of San Antonio, maybe all the way to Mexico. We'll be safe. Besides, he'll be too ashamed to do anything."

One of the men handed Levi a bundle and said, "You'll need these. We took them from your place." Levi opened the bundle and removed a heavy canvas pouch. Inside was an old Colt Navy percussion revolver that his father had given him when he left home. Along with the gun were about a hundred .36 caliber round balls, a flask of powder, and an old leather belt and holster for the revolver.

"You might want this, too," the man said, as he tossed a long object to Levi. Catching the object in his left hand, Levi felt solid metal smack into his palm. He ran his free hand across the tarnished brass receiver of a Henry rifle. The hand passed upward along the octagon barrel and then down the long tubular magazine beneath the barrel. Like the Colt revolver, the Henry rifle had belonged to Levi's family for many years. He had fired them both many times and had become proficient with each.

"Ammunition for the rifle is in the bag, along with one more important thing. You'll find all the money we could collect. Should be forty-seven dollars. Now, you'd better leave."

Levi mounted the horse, wanting to leave more than the two men could imagine. "One last question," he said. "Do you know where George Tompkins and the other two men went?"

Both of Levi's rescuers smiled and exchanged glances. "We knew you'd ask. Yes. We've followed their trail. All three are in Bandera. There's a big saloon just on the edge of town. It's called The Rose. They'll be there. We hear that George likes the whores there. And one more thing. We've heard there's another man runnin' with 'em. Don't know who he is. The story may not even be true, but be careful."

Levi sat silently in the saddle for almost a full minute, searching for just the right thing to say. Finally, he stammered, "I don't know how to say this. I can't ever repay you. I'll just say thanks."

All signs of humor left the faces of the two men. Then one of them said, "You don't need to repay us. Just kill the bastards. That'd be payment enough."

"I'll try," Levi said matter-of-factly. Then he reined the horse around and headed west in the direction of the outskirts of town. After he'd traveled a few yards, he looked back. Neither man was in sight. They had melted completely into the shadows. The jail and the entire street were dark, silent, and apparently empty.

For some time Levi traveled through the narrow, winding

streets of San Antonio. It took longer than he had expected to clear the downtown area, probably because he took extreme caution to avoid detection. On several occasions he made detours in order to bypass potentially dangerous areas. At other times he dismounted and led the horse past areas where human activity was in progress. Such caution might not have helped, but he felt that a dismounted man was more difficult to identify than one in the saddle.

Chapter 6

By midnight, with the lights of San Antonio a dim glow behind him, Levi reined his horse off the dirt road and into a small grove of live oak trees. There he hid himself and his horse as well as possible and settled down to watch his back trail, something he would do many times in the next few months. An hour's wait revealed nothing. Actually, he had not expected anything. In all likelihood Sheriff Hammer and Sam still were enjoying the inside of one of the sheriff's jail cells. Levi had no idea whether the sheriff would pursue him at all, but if he did, it likely would be after daybreak. Still, he felt better having watched.

Knowing that he should get far away from San Antonio as quickly as possible, Levi hurried his horse on down the dark, lonely path. As hours passed, he lost all sense of time and distance. He wasn't even sure that he was going in the right direction, but he was very much aware that he was growing more fatigued by the minute. The days and nights in the filthy cell with little sleep, no exercise, and barely edible food had taken their toll, and now he was paying the price. An occasional stumble told him that the horse also was beginning to tire. Levi needed to pass the time and maybe even to keep the animal more alert, and he had an idea. Looking about like a guilty, embarrassed child, he began to talk to the horse. At the first sound of Levi's voice, the horse broke stride in surprise. Both ears went back and then forward in attention. Knowing that talking would keep him awake and reasoning that it might actually be comforting to the horse also, Levi carried on a lively conversation with the puzzled horse for the better part of an hour. Finally, a gentle glow began to appear in the east, and Levi knew that daylight wasn't far away.

It was time to make some decisions. If he continued to travel after daybreak, someone might possibly recognize him on the road. Recognition was not very likely, but considerable commerce passed along this seemingly obscure road, and it was not impossible to meet some fellow traveler that would know him. If he moved off the road, he would lose time and possibly allow any pursuers to gain on him. On the other hand, he soon would have to deal with his overpowering weariness. He needed rest, but did he dare to go to sleep beside the road and surrender his caution for a few hours?

It didn't take Levi long to reach a decisions. He traveled perhaps a mile farther until he reached an area where the road crossed a shallow creek. Checking to make sure that he was unobserved, Levi reined his horse into the dry creek bed. Continuing on this path, he came to a small, dense grove of mixed live oak and juniper trees growing beside the creek. It was not a perfect shelter, but it would do. First, he made certain that he could see anyone approaching his location, but that he couldn't be seen. Then he checked to ensure that both his revolver and the Henry rifle were loaded and conveniently located. Finally, he unsaddled the horse, allowed him to graze for a while, and then tied him to a small nearby tree. Levi wished that he could turn the horse loose to graze in the open pasture nearby, but he couldn't risk the possibility that the horse might wander away.

Levi went back to the secluded place among the trees to sleep, but soon was distracted by the sight of the horse stretching to reach tufts of grass and leaves just out of his reach. "Damn!" Levi said. "Sure as I go to sleep, that horse will find a way to free himself. I can do better than that." Returning to the horse, Levi fashioned some hobbles from pieces of rope, and placed them on the horse's front feet. Next, he removed the lariat rope from the saddle and tied it around the horse's neck, using a knot that wouldn't tighten and choke the animal. He tied the other end of the rope to a small bush in the middle of a patch of grass. "Now, you old bag-o-bones, you eat while I sleep. And don't do something stupid. I'm the expert in the stupid department, if you'll remember." Levi looked apprehensively at the leaden sky, having been aware of the approaching rain since before daybreak. Rain or no rain, he couldn't fight his fatigue much longer. He removed an old rain slicker from among his supplies and threw it over the area among the trees that he had chosen for his bed. He slipped under the protective slicker and was immediately asleep.

At first, Levi thought he had been awakened by the patter of rain falling on the dry leaves near his head, but the sound was not quite right. It was different, not a steady drumbeat of rainfall, but the irregular cadence of human voices. That was it! Human voices. He noiselessly slipped from beneath the slicker and grasped the Henry rifle with his left hand. Ever so slowly, he rose up onto his elbows and gazed out toward the sound of the voices.

Levi's heart sank as he stared out into the small meadow where he had left the horse to graze. There in clear view no more than forty yards away stood the two deputies, Sam and Ramon. Sam was holding the rope that was tied to the horse's neck. Apparently, he was preparing to lead the animal away, but Ramon was arguing violently with him, gesturing in anger as he talked. Now fully awake, Levi could hear their conversation clearly.

"Don't do this!" Ramon shouted. "You don't even know it's the same horse."

"It's the same one, all right. It's gotta be. It just makes sense. This is the horse that was stol' last night. Why else would this animal be here? It's a good horse. It's him."

Ramon knew his companion was correct. "Well, what if it is. Leave him here, and let's get out of here!"

Sam brushed rain from his hat and shook his head. "Can't. Sheriff Hammer sent us to find that kid, and we've found 'im. Leastwise his horse."

"Why do you want to find him, anyway? What's he done to you? You know he's not guilty. Hammer's just too big a coward to go after the real killers," Ramon argued in frustration. Then, deciding to try a new angle, he continued, "Besides, what do you owe His Highness? Did he give you that promotion you asked for?"

Sam snorted. "You know damn well he didn't."

"Yeah. And what did he do when Levi got away?"

"He said it was my fault, and he slugged me." Sam sighed, gently feeling a large red lump on the side of his face.

"Bet there's something else you ain't thought of," Ramon said. "We have Wolfe's horse. We don't have him, but he can't be far away. I'll bet he's hiding and watching us right now. Probably got a rifle pointed at us, too. Don't know about you, but that don't make me feel too good. Specially after the way we've treated him."

In his haste to capture the horse, the slow-witted Sam had temporarily forgotten that his instructions had been to search for Levi. He stiffened, and his eyes darted from side to side, quickly surveying the countryside, as he considered Ramon's remark. In an instant, he identified several spots where Levi might be hiding.

"Naw. He's moved on by now," Sam replied, looking at his partner for reassurance but getting none.

Ramon chuckled nervously and said, "Without his horse? How would he leave without a horse?"

Sam scratched his bony head and looked at Ramon, doubt creeping into his voice. "Maybe he left it here just to throw us off his trail."

"Don't be such a fool, Sam," Ramon said with contempt. "Let's get outta here while we still can. You don't owe the sheriff anything."

"Maybe…maybe Hammer will be grateful when we bring Wolfe back in."

Ramon had heard enough. He whirled on his partner in anger and hissed, "You damned idiot. Are you all the way stupid, or just part? That man we're following is desperate. Can't you see? Can't you see that he'd kill us both just for one chance at George?"

The cold rain continued to fall, soaking ever deeper into the two deputies' clothing. Sam shivered and continued to search both sides of the creek with his eyes, desperately trying to locate Levi's hiding place. "I don't know, Ramon. I ain't sure about this. What'll we tell the sheriff?"

"Tell 'im anything. Tell 'im Wolfe must've gone somewhere else. Tell 'im we lost the trail. It don't matter what we tell the man. Long as he don't have to look for Wolfe, the sheriff don't care."

"I don't know, Ramon. His Royal Majesty can get purty riled. Just look at this bruise on my face."

"Okay, Sam. Let's do it this way. Up 'til now, I've always let you be in charge. Even when it was stupid, which was most of the time, I went along. Covered for you. Explained your mistakes. Apologized for you. Well, my friend, this is where all that ends. Now, I'm telling you. I'm not asking you. We're leaving here now, and maybe we can still get away."

In a rage, Sam lunged out, fists drawn back to strike. "You sorry Meskin," he began, but got no farther. Ramon's open right hand shot out, slapping Sam with such force that he fell back on the ground in a sitting position.

Ramon reached down and grabbed Sam by the front of his shirt and roughly lifted him back onto his feet. Then, as he brushed mud and leaves off his partner, he said, "Now, listen real careful, Sam. We're gonna tell the sheriff that we haven't seen a sign of Levi or his horse. We'll say that he must've gone some other direction. Got clean away."

Sam looked at Ramon with the eyes of a whipped dog, knowing that the other man had made him look and feel foolish. In one final act of defiance, Sam said, "And what if I don't go along with yore little scheme, Ramon? What if I tell Sheriff Hammer that you jumped me and held a gun on me while Wolfe escaped? What then?"

Ramon smiled coldly at his vanquished opponent, savoring his victory. After a lengthy pause, he replied, "Then I'll tell every Mexican in San Antonio that you helped rape and kill Jovita. I'll say that you enjoyed it, even laughed about it when it was happening. I'll tell them that you dared the entire Mexican population to lift even one finger in retaliation. And how do I know you participated? I'll say that you got drunk and told me the whole thing."

The color slowly drained from Sam's face. He tried to talk, but couldn't. Finally, he managed to stammer, "Who'd believe that?"

"They don't like you, Sam. Lots would believe it, but it'd just take one. Just one, Sam. Just one with a good, sharp knife. Ever see what one of those horrible weapons can do? Course you have. You're a deputy sheriff. You've seen it lots of times. A man that knows what he's doing can make you suffer for a real long time. Make you want to die. Make you beg to die. Remember that case we investigated about a year ago? Happened in one of them places over in my part of town. Seems one Mexican caught another one with his girl or wife or something. Remember what the victim looked like when we got there? Remember the parts of that man's body that got cut off? Better think on it, Sam."

Sam drew several quick, sharp breaths, then sat down abruptly in the same spot where he had fallen earlier from Ramon's blow. For a moment Ramon feared that he had overdone his threat, afraid that Sam would faint from fright. Slowly, Sam regained his composure and returned to his feet. Sam looked fleetingly at Ramon and said, "Okay, we'll do it yore way, but I'm just doin' this cause I believe Wolfe's innocent. It ain't 'cause I'm scared of you or yore Meskin friends."

"Of course you're not," Ramon replied. "After all, you're a deputy sheriff. Now, take that horse back over to that bush and tie the rope back like you found it. Maybe we can still get outta here alive."

Both men turned toward the road and began to walk the quarter mile back to the spot where they'd left their horses. Each man was terrified, knowing that a desperate and well-armed man was nearby, knowing that the man felt he had every right to shoot them down like wild animals. After taking only a few steps, Ramon stopped abruptly and looked at his companion. "I'm afraid of this, Sam," he said. "I feel like I'm already a dead man. I'm gonna take a chance. If it works, we're outta here safe. If not, we're both dead."

Before Sam could respond, Ramon shouted out, "Levi Wolfe! If you're out there, we want you to know! We're leaving now! Going back to San Antone! As far as we know, you've never been here! You got nothing to fear from us!"

From his hiding place only a few yards away, Levi replied in a quiet, level voice, "Go in peace, my friend."

No other words were spoken. Levi waited quietly while the two deputies hurried to their horses and headed for the road to San Antonio. He was cramped and sore from sleeping on the hard ground, but even so he felt better than he had felt in several days. Searching through his bundle of supplies, he found some hard biscuits and dried beef. He smiled, telling himself that his rescuers had thought of everything. He pulled the rain slicker about himself to ward off the increasing rain and the cold west wind.

Partly rested and partly fed, Levi saddled the horse and secured the bundle of supplies behind the saddle. Finding a quiet pool of water in a shallow creek, both Levi and his horse drank long and deeply. Levi still didn't like the idea of traveling in daylight this close to San Antonio, but he decided it was preferable to waiting for darkness. It seemed likely that Sam and Ramon represented Sheriff Hammer's major effort to recapture him. Surely, the sheriff wouldn't send more than two deputies to search any one place. Still, it would be best to be careful. Cautiously at first, Levi walked his horse along the edge of the creek back toward the main road. He immediately noticed that the tracks of the horses belonging to the two deputies had left a clear trail from the grassy meadow back to the road. Under different conditions, he would've been suspicious of such a conspicuous trail, perhaps wondering if he were being led into a trap. This time he had a different view. He knew Ramon had made sure there was clear evidence that he and Sam were keeping their word to pursue him no more.

The rainfall gradually increased as Levi rode on toward Bandera. After a while he was wet and cold, and generally miserable. Even so, he saw the adverse weather conditions as an advantage, for he was virtually the only person on the road. Once in the late afternoon, a freight wagon filled to capacity with a load of fresh cedar shingles approached him. He politely moved aside as the rig drove past. The neatly dressed driver tipped his hat to Levi and paid him no more attention. On another occasion Levi saw a group of four horsemen riding toward him from the direction of Bandera. Relatively sure that he hadn't been seen, he moved about two hundred yards into the junipers beside road and let the riders pass. Giving the riders plenty of time to move out of range, he returned to the road and continued his journey.

By nightfall the rain hadn't slackened. If anything it had increased in intensity. Although he hadn't traveled far, Levi decided to seek shelter and wait out the rain. In his experience these central Texas spring rains frequently developed into intense storms, then abruptly died away to nothing, completely spent. He didn't want to get caught out in the open if such a storm developed. After a period of watching the countryside along the road, Levi spotted an old shed located a good distance back from the road.

Checking closely, Levi found that it would serve his needs. It was completely open on the south side, but adequate walls existed on the other three sides. The roof was covered with leaky, rusty tin. This obviously was a crude shelter to protect livestock from winter storms. Levi barely had gotten his saddle and other provisions removed from the horse when the sky opened up and the storm descended with all the fury of an angry, vengeful god. Great claps of thunder roared, shaking the ground and Levi's simple shelter. Bright bursts of lightning lit up the dusky evening skies, occasionally sending long, crooked fingers of destruction to some unfortunate target on the ground. Vicious gusts of wind tried to rip the simple shed apart, as huge torrents of rain poured down upon the open countryside.

Levi was glad that some unknown builder had placed extra layers of dirt inside the structure to raise the level of the ground, so that water wouldn't collect there. Still weary, he had spread his damp bedding on the dry ground, being careful to avoid the numerous leaks in the roof above him. Stretching his aching arms and legs, Levi prepared for another period of rest. "Ah," he remarked. "It's not the comforts of home, but it's better than sleeping in the rain."

Curling up in his makeshift bed, Levi slept, but it wasn't a restful sleep. He dreamed of Jovita and the love they had felt for each other. He saw her face, her dark eyes, and her shiny black hair. He smelled her perfume and felt her soft, delicate body. He marveled at her beauty and her goodness. He walked with her through the peaceful, tree-lined streets of San Antonio, and he talked earnestly with her about their plans for a life together. In his dream he wondered how such a perfect woman could care for him, a very imperfect man.

Then he dreamed of Jovita being torn from him. He saw the terror in her eyes. He heard her cry out in agony, and he heard her plead for mercy, for her very life. He saw the vicious, cruel smile of George Tompkins as he crushed the life from her body. He saw the smiling, shadowy figures of George's accomplices as they stood by and encouraged George. He saw George in great detail. The wicked, rat-like eyes. The long, dirty hair. The foul whisky breath. The large, callused hands with dirty fingernails. It was an image that he had seen fleetingly before and one that would torment him for years to come. The worst part of his dream was that he could do nothing. He wanted to lash out and destroy George and the others, but he couldn't. He had to stand by and watch Jovita being violated and destroyed, unable to help, unable to save her.

Levi woke with a start, unsure of his surroundings. He felt

cold, but his body was sweating. His mouth was dry, and his muscles ached from the violent contractions that they had suffered during his terrible dream. His stomach was cramping, and he was sure that at any moment he would vomit. In an instant he remembered where he was. He got some relief from the fact that the rain had stopped, and the sky had cleared. Stars were out, and a gentle breeze blew out of the west. Levi guessed that the time was near midnight, perhaps a little later. He walked out of the old shed and stood facing the west, letting the cold west wind blow across his body. He stood in that position for a long time, looking into the heavens, trying to convince himself that none of this was happening, but knowing it was. Finally, as if seeking inspiration, he settled his gaze upon the heavenly constellations that he and Jovita had known so well, and said aloud, "Jovita, I'm sorry I wasn't there for you, when you really needed me. I know it doesn't help much now, but I promise this. I promise I'll hunt down the animals that did this to you, and I'll make them pay. Yes, by God, I'll make them pay." Then the tormented man turned away and returned to the shed, saddled his horse, which was resting peacefully in the far end of the shed, and prepared to continue toward Bandera.

Chapter 7

It was still dark when Levi caught first sight of a faint, flickering light in the distance. As he rode nearer, that light was joined by additional ones, blinking out the message that early risers were up and about, and that daybreak was coming soon. Levi reined his horse to a stop and surveyed the town. He had never been in Bandera before, but he knew something about the place. Nestled in the heart of some of the most beautiful country in the world, the town had become a haven for criminals and desperados. Bandera was a stopping-off place for those who had experienced trouble with the law and who were seeking to lose themselves in the solitude of west Texas and New Mexico. Generally, this lawless element came and went quietly, seeking not to attract the attention of law-abiding citizens.

Many questions flooded Levi's mind. Does anyone in town take note of who comes and goes? Does it matter whether a stranger enters town from the south instead of the north? And what does direction of travel say about a person's reasons for being in a place? Has anyone in town been warned of his plan to eliminate four of Bandera's murderous current residents? Does George Tompkins even know of his existence? Once in town, how should he proceed? He couldn't just walk up to George and shoot him, or could he? What about George's accomplices? Based on information from his rescuers, Levi assumed that there were now three, not just two. Surely they wouldn't just stand by and let him kill George. Should he seek the help of the local law enforcement officials?

To his dismay, Levi realized that he had no plan. Back in

San Antonio it all had seemed so simple. He would kill George, and the score would be settled. Now the time had come, and he didn't have any idea how to proceed. "Okay," Levi said to himself. "So I don't have a plan. Well, that's simple enough. I'll make one. First off, I don't think it matters what direction I come from. There must be riders going in and out of here all the time. Just to be sure, I'll circle around town and enter from the other end.

"I'll take my horse to the livery stable. Have a boy take care of 'im. Then I'll get a room in the hotel. There must be one. I'll clean up and find a meal. Go slow and easy, just like I'm some innocent traveler or trader. I'll spend a few days. Locate Tompkins and his scummy friends. Figure things out. I'll be all nice and polite. Then, when he least expects it, I'll drop it on 'im. Kill the son of a bitch—him and anybody else that gets in the way. Sure want to do away with as many of his friends as possible. Now, all that's easy to say, but that's when the *real* planning starts. That part's gonna be tough, and that's why I have to make those real, tough, detailed plans. I'll do that when the time comes. Killing a man's one thing. Killing four is something else."

Levi swelled with satisfaction and pride. His plan, the first part, worked like a charm. In the early dawn, well before good light, he quietly circled around the town and waited for the sun to show in the east. Just at daybreak he rode nonchalantly into town and headed straight to the livery stable, where he made arrangements to have his tired and hungry horse cared for. Just as Levi expected, a kid no more than thirteen years old was on duty. He watched the behavior and responses of the young man carefully as he transacted his business, determined to identify the slightest sign of suspicion on the part of the boy. There was none. The two exchanged small talk about the recent rainstorm.

Finally satisfied that the boy was harmless, Levi said, "I'll be in town for a few days. Need a place to stay. Got any suggestions?"

"Well, some cowboys just come in here and sleep at night. You could do that, if you want to."

"Appreciate the offer, but I'm thinking of something in the order of a hotel. I'd kinda like a little comfort for a change."

"In that case, you'd want to stay at Miz Quinn's Boarding House. Down the street on the right. Can't miss it," the boy said, pointing into the distance.

"Thanks a lot. Got any suggestions for meals?"

"Same place. Ol' Miz Quinn'll put more food in front of you than you can eat. Enough to fill a lumberjack."

"Sounds good, except I've never seen a lumberjack eat."

The kid looked at Levi carefully, at first thinking the older man was ridiculing him. With Levi's friendly smile providing reassurance, the kid smiled back and replied, "Me neither, but I hear they can put it away."

"Well, then that's the place for me," Levi replied cheerfully. He paid in advance for six days' care for his horse and then prepared to seek Mrs. Quinn's place. Careful to take no chances, Levi checked his Colt revolver and returned it to the leather holster on his right hip. He also made sure the Henry was fully loaded and ready for use. Then he picked up his roll of blankets and his canvas bag of supplies and headed down the muddy main street toward the boarding house.

The town was approximately what Levi had expected. It was so much like the other small towns that he once had visited regularly that he had to remind himself that he had never been in Bandera before. He walked past Leonard's General Store where the proprietor, a small, bearded man wearing too-large trousers held up with wide suspenders, was busily sweeping dust from his storefront into the street. The man hardly gave Levi a glance as he walked past. There were two offices across from the general store. From their appearances, Levi guessed that they must belong to lawyers, doctors, or other professional people. No signs were present in front to identify their occupants.

Moving on down the street, Levi identified the other small businesses so common to small Texas towns of the time. A small shop adjacent to the general store advertised saddles made to the specifications of the customer, in addition to leather repairs of all kinds. Another one—Johnson's Firearms Emporium—advertised the sale and repair of guns. On down the street, past two small buildings that appeared to be vacant, stood Bandera Metal Works, obviously a blacksmith shop. Just seeing it made Levi wince in pain, remembering the backbreaking trade practiced by the blacksmith that Levi had watched in his hometown as a child.

Also, there was a building with a sign announcing the existence of the *Bandera Sentinel*, the local weekly newspaper. At the end of the street, standing starkly alone, was a simple stone building with rusty iron bars on the windows and front door. A slight shiver passed down Levi's spine as he surveyed the local jail. Remembering the days he spent in Sheriff Hammer's jail, Levi whispered to himself, "I'm here to kill a man, and I know it's against the law, but they're not ever gonna put me in another one of those places. They'll kill me first." Turning away from the ugly structure, Levi continued on down the street past other offices and business establishments.

Mrs. Quinn's Boarding House was a large, rectangular frame structure of indistinguishable architectural style. The two-story building, which once had been painted white, had a porch extending completely around it. Above the porch a narrow balcony encircled the upstairs rooms. It could be entered in two ways.

A prominent, formal entrance from the main street opened into a large open sitting room. A small reception desk stood at one side of the room, and a wide stairway led to a series of rooms upstairs. A few rooms were present downstairs, along with a large dining room. The second means of access was a narrow wooden stairway leading from a side alley to the outside balcony. From the balcony a passageway led into the upstairs hallway. Standing momentarily in front of the structure, Levi carefully studied the building and its surroundings, attempting to fix in his mind every detail of its design and location in relationship to the rest of the town.

Mrs. Quinn's dining room was almost filled with early morning diners as Levi approached the counter and received the key to his room. As he expected, it was a small cubicle with only a bed, a small table, and a fully equipped washbasin. Depositing his gear, he locked his room and went back downstairs to the dining room. Levi felt good about his accomplishments so far. However, he had one major question. Would he be able to fade anonymously into the fabric of Bandera, or would the sheriff be waiting with a warrant for his arrest? Luck was going to help him find an answer to that question.

Against the wall, near the rear of the dining room sat a man wearing a shiny metal star on the left side of his shirt. Two other men hovered around, obviously feeling subservient to him. "The sheriff and two deputies," Levi said under his breath. "Now's as good a time as any to find out."

Levi walked over and noisily sat down at a vacant table near the sheriff. The sheriff looked up and studied Levi for a long moment, and then he rose and quickly covered the ten feet between them. Levi's heart rate quickened as he tried to anticipate the sheriff's next move. Before he could react, the sheriff extended his hand and said, "Howdy. Buford Rutherford. I'm the sheriff around here. Don't remember seeing you before. New in town?"

"Yeah, just passing through," Levi lied, accepting the hand. "I'll be here for a few days on business. Then I got to move on to Waco." Watching the sheriff carefully, Levi was reasonably sure that the man knew nothing of his true purpose in town. That's just like Hammer, Levi thought. He's too much a coward to inform his fellow law enforcement officials that a dangerous prisoner is on the loose. It was easier for him to pretend it didn't happen. He'd never alert the sheriff in a neighboring town.

"What'd you say your name is?" the sheriff queried.

"Matter of fact, don't believe I did. Name's Ellis. Thomas Ellis," Levi lied again, using the name he'd given the desk clerk at Mrs. Quinn's.

"Thomas Ellis…Ellis…Ellis. Nope, don't ring no bells to me," the sheriff replied, watching Levi for any suspicious behavior. All the time he was talking, the sheriff was mentally sorting through all his outstanding wanted posters, seeking to satisfy himself that Levi's face didn't appear on any of them. Largely, he disregarded the name, knowing that any wanted man would use an alias. "Tell me, Mr. Ellis, what line of business are you in?" the sheriff continued.

"Well, Sheriff Rutherford …."

"No," the sheriff interrupted. "Call me Buford. Sheriff Rutherford's too formal."

"Okay, Buford. Like I was about to say, I don't advertise my business too much. Success depends on a bit of secrecy, if you know what I mean. My boss sent me down here to look into the shingle market. Here's the thing. He's involved in building houses and such up in Waco. Been buying shingles out of Fort Worth, but he thinks he can buy 'em a lot cheaper here in Bandera, since they're made here. Sent me down to find out. Also told me to take a few extra days and rest. He thinks I've been working too hard. Real nice guy. Been kind of like a father to me. What do you think? Am I wasting my time?"

"No, Mr. Ellis, if you want a good deal, this is the place."

"Please, Buford. Please call me Tom."

The sheriff nodded slowly, focusing on the wall behind Levi. "Shore, Tom. I don't know what you're paying in Fort Worth, but you're right. Them shingles are made right here. Course you know that. Seems to me, if you buy enough, you can save money."

"I appreciate the information, Sheriff. I mean Buford."

"Sorry about all the questions, Tom, but I can't be too careful. Lots of riffraff comes through here. Town council's been on me lately to clean up the town. Well, I won't take no more of your time. Just keep that gun in its holster, and we won't have no problems."

"Don't worry and thanks again, Buford," Levi said, as they shook hands again. Levi had mixed feelings about his exchange with the sheriff. On the one hand he knew that the success of his mission depended upon deceit, and he had shown himself surprisingly capable in that department. He had never been a deceitful person, and he didn't feel comfortable as such. He returned to his chair, called the waitress over, and ordered his breakfast. Sitting quietly at the table, he was reasonably sure that no one in town knew his identity or his mission.

As he ate his breakfast, Levi again assessed his life and his mission in this small god-forsaken town. He was at a critical point in his life, and he was well aware of that fact. He faced many difficult choices, most of which held great peril for him. If he persisted in his decision to go after George, he would have to develop the most intricately detailed plan that he could imagine.

Any miscalculation probably would result in his death. If George or one of his henchmen didn't kill him, Sheriff Rutherford very well might. Even San Antonio's despised Sheriff Hammer might get another opportunity. There wouldn't be another rescue party if he were arrested and returned to San Antonio.

One choice—perhaps a very good one—would be to quit right now, just turn his back on the whole foolish plan to kill anybody and walk away. There was a certain amount of appeal to that plan. After all, he'd done enough, hadn't he? He'd attracted attention to Jovita's senseless murder and to a corrupt law enforcement agency that had refused to take appropriate action. He'd suffered the humility of being unjustly accused and charged with murder. True, he'd been forced to run for his life to avoid prosecution, but in doing so he'd struck a blow for honesty and justice for all citizens of San Antonio. At least in his mind, Levi had hastened the day when the city's Mexican population would receive treatment that more closely resembled fairness.

"Why not?" Levi asked aloud as he sat in his room reviewing his options. "Why not saddle that horse down in the stable and quietly disappear. I could go to Waco or Fort Worth or maybe way on up north into Colorado or even Montana. After a year or two I could go back to San Antone, if I wanted to. The law don't even really want me now. A couple of years would give them time to conveniently forget me completely. Besides, George isn't really going to get away. Person like him will get what's coming to him sooner or later."

As tempting as it was, Levi knew he wouldn't abandon the path he had chosen. Driven by grief and revenge, he would continue on his search for justice. But he was beginning to question his own motives. Maybe, just maybe, his real motivation was guilt, guilt for his own failures and inadequacies.

"What is it, really?" he asked himself as he had done dozens of times. "Am I just trying to stop the guilt-pains inside me? Is that what I'm here for, or am I really after justice?" As always he silently pondered the question, knowing he would arrive at the same answer. "It doesn't matter a lot," he finally said. "I've worked for this one chance. I've suffered, too. Now, by God, I'll have my revenge."

There in the solitude of a tiny hotel room in an obscure Texas town, Levi Wolfe made a final commitment. He had given himself an opportunity to walk away, and he had rejected it. So now he had to develop the plan he had been dreading—the real, detailed plan. The problem was that Levi had never been much of a planner. He had lived a careless and foolish existence, concentrating on the present and letting tomorrow take care of itself. He had never wanted to plan, had never thought he needed to plan, so he never had learned how to do it, but now he must. Therefore, like an inexperienced military strategist preparing for his first battle, Levi set about to devise a scheme to defeat four seasoned criminals in their own element.

Having no better approach, Levi began his task by addressing the factors that troubled him most. Where would he kill the men? There were many possibilities: in the street, in Mrs. Quinn's dining hall, or in The Rose, the bar that he had yet to visit. Everything depended upon the location that gave him the best opportunity to perform the deed and still escape. Even if he couldn't do both, he'd still take their lives and sacrifice his own. It was quite possible that he couldn't kill all four men, any one of whom was probably his equal, if not his superior, with a gun. Then there was the escape. After doing the deed, he'd have to choose a path and get out of town in a hurry. Probably, he'd need a hiding place, as well as a plan to deal with a posse that might follow.

To compound his problem, Levi had limited time to

accomplish his mission. Since Bandera lay fairly close to San Antonio, considerable travel took place between the two towns. Sooner or later, someone would accidentally—or perhaps intentionally—discover his identity. In all likelihood Sam wouldn't remain silent very long. Levi concluded that he would allow himself two weeks to accomplish his goals in Bandera. That was the maximum amount of time that he dared to stay in town. It would have to be enough. If he had failed in that time, he would quietly collect his gear and leave town, forever giving up his chance for revenge.

Levi decided that the first part of his plan should be to determine his route of escape from Bandera. Remembering a map on the wall of the livery stable, Levi returned to that location under the pretense of looking after his horse. The map was old, weathered, and crudely drawn, but all major towns and areas of the state seemed to be present. Levi studied it carefully.

One possible route would be to head almost due west toward El Paso. At points this route would pass fairly close to the Mexican border, possibly allowing the additional option to turn south and escape into Mexico. There were problems with this selection. Although it eventually would allow Levi to escape into New Mexico and Arizona, the distance between Bandera and El Paso was great. He was poorly equipped for such a long journey. It appeared that much of the distance was open, perhaps desert-like country, providing little cover for a man on horseback. Also, he had only one horse, and if that horse tired or became lame, he would be in real trouble. Certainly, it would be possible to buy a second horse, but he had little money, and he would have to conserve what he had. Also, a second horse might attract attention, a genuine concern. No, this route presented too many problems.

Another possible route would lead on a northwesterly

course in the general direction of San Angelo or Abilene. From one of those towns he might head due north, up through the Texas Panhandle. He could then escape into Indian Territory or on out into northern New Mexico. Like the route toward El Paso, this one was a long, tiring trip for both rider and horse. It offered more cover, but there was more population in that region, making detection more likely. An overriding problem with both these routes was that they would lead Levi through unfamiliar territory. From one point to the next he wouldn't know what to expect. Where could he find water? Which trails were impassible, and which were easy to negotiate? If he were pursued, where could he best stop and make a stand or stage an ambush? He had no idea.

This uncertainty led Levi to the third possibility, the route he knew all along he would choose. From Bandera he would head north, toward the small town of Mason, or perhaps Llano. Having once driven a wagon to deliver supplies to people in the area, he had spent considerable time there, and he knew some of the people. In an emergency he might be able to get some help. The country was open in some areas, but there were sufficient woods and hills to provide hiding places, either to avoid detection or to ambush a pursuer. From one of those towns, he could head farther north, passing through Brady or Lampasas. If unable to lose himself in the Hill Country, he could head east to the city of Waco. There was a German merchant named Hans Lowe there—a cousin of his mother—who would provide shelter. Levi stopped and reconsidered Hans. Could he count on the man? *Really* count on him? He had met the man only once, and that was years earlier. In fact, was Hans even still alive, and if so, how willing would he be to shelter Levi in the likely event that some party—either law enforcement or outlaw—was pursuing him?

Levi continued to study the weathered map, determined to remember its every detail. A smile crept across his face as he slowly took a step, then a second step, backward. He was pleased with his decision, imperfect though it was. Clearly, he had chosen the best of the three escape routes. He took one last look. Then he spun around to leave, coming face to face with Sheriff Buford Rutherford.

"Sheriff…I mean Buford!" Levi managed to say. For a moment Levi felt like a sheep-killing dog that had been caught in the act. Then he was angry with himself. He had done nothing wrong, yet he felt tremendously guilty, and he was certain his feelings were apparent to the sheriff.

"Sorry, Tom," the sheriff said. "Didn't mean to surprise you."

Trying desperately to appear calm, and failing completely, Levi said. "Not at all, Buford. Guess I was just too deep in thought. Wasn't a real surprise."

"Coulda fooled me. Looked like I'd just caught you with yore hand in somebody's pocket. You shore was lost in that old map." Sheriff Rutherford stepped closer to see what Levi had been studying. He then examined Levi more closely, more seriously.

"Yeah," Levi said, trying to sound casual. "Yeah. There's places on that map I've never been. Lots of 'em. El Paso. Amarillo. On out farther to Indian Territory. New Mexico. I want to see all of 'em someday. You kinda caught me in the middle of a daydream."

The sheriff shook his head and snorted. "Hell! Some dream. I've been to all of 'em. Believe me, they ain't worth the trip."

"Well, maybe not," Levi said, feeling a bit more confident.

"Guess I'd better move on," Sheriff Rutherford said, as he turned to leave. Suddenly, he stopped in his tracks and turned back toward Levi. "Oh, I almost forgot, Tom. I run into ol' man

Schmidt yesterday. He's the one that runs that shingle cuttin' operation just outside of town. Course you already knew that. I asked him if he'd been able to help you out, you needin' shingles and all. Funniest thing. He didn't seem to know what I was talking about. Appeared he's never even heard of you. Don't know. Seemed a little strange."

Levi's newfound confidence vanished and a wave of fear swept through his gut. "Schmidt's right," Levi admitted. "I haven't been out there. Wouldn't want my boss to know it, but I've been kinda taking advantage of 'im."

"Really? How so?"

Pretending deep remorse, Levi said, "Well, I've been using these past few days to look at property."

"Look at property?"

Levi knew it was time to be extra careful. One false statement likely would arouse even more suspicion in the sheriff. "Just little places, Buford. I love this part of the state. Trees. Good grass. Rivers. Beautiful country. I'd like to own a little piece of it. Not much. Maybe a few hundred acres." Levi let a pleading tone creep into his voice. "Hell, Buford, I can't afford a lotta land."

Having observed many wild schemes in his time, Sheriff Rutherford had just a flicker of doubt about Levi's story. "Land shore costs money," he observed.

"Oh, I've got some money," Levi said, sensing the sheriff's growing doubt, but determined to make the lie sound convincing.

"You got money? How much?"

"Few hundred," Levi said, now certain of the doubt on the face of the sheriff. "My folks are both dead. I'm their only child. They left everything to me. Wasn't a lot, but it's a start."

The sheriff stood, feet slightly apart, balanced as if he were about to spring upon Levi. His eyes were boring into Levi. Challenging. Intimidating. Questioning. Trying to sort truth from fiction. Levi had seen the behavior before. Its purpose is to unnerve, to rattle a weaker person. To force that person into a careless mistake. Although Levi recognized and understood it, it was having an effect. He felt dryness in his mouth, and beads of sweat developed around his collar and along his spine. Silently, Levi waited for the sheriff to make his next move. Without taking his eyes off Levi, Sheriff Rutherford removed a tobacco pouch from his shirt pocket with his left hand. Fumbling for a moment, he then found papers in the same pocket. Still silently staring at Levi, a strange half-smile on his face, he rolled a cigarette. From someplace he produced a match. Striking it with his fingernail, he lit the cigarette and blew a cloud of blue smoke in Levi's direction.

Finally, shaking his head slowly, the sheriff spoke. "I'm havin' a lotta trouble figurin' you out," he said.

"How so?" Levi said.

"Don't quite know," the sheriff replied. "Guess I've been sheriffin' too long. Sometimes I see trouble where it don't exist. Now, take you, for instance. You ain't been a minute's trouble. Not even a second's trouble. Somehow, though, I can't get this funny feelin' outta my head."

"You asking me to leave your town, Sheriff?" Levi asked the question forcefully, placing a hard edge on his words. He was careful to address the sheriff by his title instead of his name.

"No. No. Course not. You ain't done nothin' wrong. I'm just havin' trouble sortin' things out. That's all."

"Now, Sheriff, I don't mean to cause trouble for you."

"Well," Sheriff Rutherford said. "I've wasted enough of yore time, Tom. I'll be goin' on back to the office. Sorry about my silly questions." Without waiting for a response, the sheriff turned and strolled down the dusty street, never looking back.

Levi stood watching, waiting for Sheriff Rutherford to disappear. Questions rushed through Levi's mind, but he suppressed each one. No more time for contemplation. No more time for procrastination. Whatever time he'd had was gone. Maybe the sheriff knew something. Maybe he didn't. Maybe it was a bluff. Maybe it was curiosity. Probably it was nothing. Regardless, the time to act had come. Levi knew he had to move and move quickly.

Still shaken, Levi hurried back to his hotel room and began planning his escape from the town itself. He took little time, even though he knew his very life depended upon his performance of a task with which he was completely unfamiliar. On a piece of paper he made a crude drawing of the town, identifying each major building. On this map he designated different avenues leading to a specific point of departure, from which he would leave Bandera and head north. This task accomplished, he rode out into the countryside north of town, the area that he would be passing through on his escape. He made sure that there were no natural barriers—cliffs, flooded rivers, or deep ravines—to interfere with his plan, and he identified areas where either he or his enemies might hide in ambush. Rolling this information over and over in his mind, he soon knew it by heart. Finally, he identified an obscure cattle or wild game trail that went in the general direction that he wished to take. Taking every precaution, he followed the trail for several miles, checking every aspect, making sure that it would serve his needs. Now he knew how he would do it. He would leave Bandera along a well-used wagon road, and then at the first stream bed he would cross over to the trail and continue on it. This bit of deception might fool somebody attempting to follow him, or it might not. At least it was worth a try.

Levi was having difficulty in completing his plan. He had carefully studied George Tompkins and his three henchmen for nine days, attempting to establish a routine, a pattern, to their activities. He had reached only one conclusion: There was no dependable pattern. They had no set time for meals. They used different routes as they traveled around the area. They slept in various places, sometimes camping out, sometimes staying in the livery stable, and sometimes sleeping in some makeshift shelter. Once they even spent the night in Mrs. Quinn's place. As difficult as it was, Levi had watched, and he had learned. He had learned that George always rode a large gray gelding, while the other three rode a sorrel, a black, and a dun. He had learned to recognize their horses as easily as he recognized his own. He had learned about their clothing, as each man always wore the same trousers, shirt, and boots. He now knew something about their habits and the sounds of their voices. He knew well what kinds of weapons they carried and at what times they were most heavily armed.

Whether by old habit or by design, the four men were effectively camouflaging their activities. There was one activity that was entirely routine, but it gave Levi little comfort. They always arrived at The Rose at about the same time each evening, where they stayed—drinking, gambling, and whoring—until well after midnight. Levi observed that the men were less cautious at The Rose. Perhaps they felt protected with a crowd of people around. More likely, the liquor created a false sense of security.

Levi didn't like it, but he knew that if he had any chance of success, he had to strike while the group was in the saloon. He also was aware that nine days had passed since his arrival in Bandera. Sheriff Rutherford was growing suspicious of Levi's continued presence in town, and Tompkins and his gang were showing no signs of leaving. It couldn't have been clearer. Indeed, the time for planning was past. The time for action was at hand.

Chapter 8

Levi was watching quietly from a corner table in The Rose as George played out his evening's routine. Toward midnight, George was loudly berating a young cowboy who had just won a hand at poker. Apparently, George had been the big loser. After an angry and profane argument, George challenged the man to settle the dispute in a manner of his own choosing—guns or fists. Obviously drunk and dangerous, he intimidated the man into abandoning the table, along with his winnings. Scooping up the money, George shoved away from the table and stalked across the room, heading straight for Josephine, a young prostitute. After a brief conversation, the two headed up the stairs toward the room where the woman plied her trade.

At that moment Levi knew how he would do it. Let George get settled in with Josephine, and then quietly walk in—kick the door down if necessary—and shoot the bastard. If the girl got in the way, shoot her, too. Then, while people were creeping up the stairs to see what happened, he'd slip out the window and drop to the street. There was no better time than now.

After waiting about ten minutes, Levi nonchalantly stood up, stretched, and moved toward the foot of the stairs. Placing his hand on the smoothly polished banister, he casually looked about to see if anyone was watching him. Nobody seemed to be paying him any mind. He turned and started slowly up the stairs. He had reached the third step, when a harsh voice called out, "Where you think yore goin', Mister?"

Levi stopped and looked back. One of George's three followers was staring up at him. The other two were not immediately in sight. Acting as cool and innocent as possible, Levi replied, "I'm just walking around."

"George's up there. He don't need no help."

Seeing his chances slipping away, Levi felt anger sweep over him. Determined to finish his plan, he took a step back down the stairs and snarled at the man, "I don't give a damn whether George's up there or not. I'll go where I damn well please!"

The man—obviously one of George's followers—hadn't expected such a vicious response from this stranger, but he stood his ground and, taking a more cautions approach, he explained, "George just wants a little time with the whore. He'll kill me if I let anybody go up there. How about just come down and let 'im finish? We'll have a drink together. Ol' George won't be long."

Levi wasn't in a conciliatory mood. Letting rage overpower reason, Levi headed for the man, tearing at his gun as he went. Expecting Levi to be grateful for an opportunity to save face, the man was totally unprepared for aggressive behavior. Reflexively drawing his own pistol, the man fired wildly and harmlessly, as Levi was bringing his pistol up to fire. At the sound of Levi's pistol shot, the man's knees buckled, and blood began to appear in the middle of his chest. He crumpled to the floor, a look of complete surprise still on his face. He was dead.

Levi felt a wave of nausea mixed with terror pass over him. He had just killed a man before dozens of witnesses, and it wasn't even the man he was after. A knot of hard muscle formed in his gut, and he tasted bitterness in his mouth. He wanted to be sick, to purge his system of its load of emotion and guilt.

In an instant another surge of adrenaline caught Levi and swept away the physical weakness that was threatening him. Still fighting back his urge to vomit, he swept his pistol back and forth, covering the crowd of people, most of whom had taken refuge behind tables and benches. In a flash Levi saw a familiar face, another of George's companions. Not waiting to see whether the man was an immediate threat to him, Levi raised his cocked pistol almost to shoulder level, pointed it at the man, and pulled the trigger.

Levi's Navy Colt pistol was a marvel of ingenuity, an example of the percussion system of firearms ignition that revolutionized the weapons industry in the nineteenth century. It was small, light, and reasonably powerful, certainly adequate to take a human life. It allowed a proficient user to fire six accurate shots in a matter of mere seconds. However, it was far from perfect. It was prone to misfire. Already, the system had been rendered obsolete by the recently developed self-contained cartridge ammunition.

Levi's weapon made a hollow click as the hammer fell on a faulty ignition cap. In a split second everyone in the bar knew what had happened. Seeing his opportunity, the man smiled wickedly at Levi and slowly, deliberately lifted his revolver from its holster.

As Levi was reaching to thumb the hammer back to rotate the cylinder of his weapon, the bartender yelled at Levi, "Here, take this!" As he tossed a double-barreled shotgun to Levi. Without thinking, Levi extended his left hand, catching the shotgun by the wooden fore-end just in front of trigger guard. In the same instant he jammed the Navy pistol back into his holster. Throwing the shotgun to his shoulder, he pointed at the man and fired. The man's entire face disappeared in a mist of blood and tissue, as his own pistol discharged harmlessly into the floor.

Josephine had gone upstairs with George several times in the past few days. It was a trip she didn't enjoy, because George frequently became abusive and violent when he was drunk. In spite of the fact that he had consumed a large quantity of liquor,

George's violence didn't appear to be unusually bad tonight. They had just undressed and gotten into bed, when the sharp report of a pistol shot rang out in the saloon below. The deafening roar of a shotgun blast followed it almost immediately.

George jumped up, slipping into his trousers as he staggered to the door. He jerked the door open and stepped out onto the open, loft-like hallway just in time to see a man standing over the faceless body of one of his companions. The man was holding a shotgun. As George stood in momentary shock, looking down at the action that was taking place on the saloon floor, the man with the shotgun looked over his shoulder and saw George. Rage and hate filled the man's eyes, as he whirled the gun toward George. The shotgun roared, just as George dived wildly back into Josephine's room. A charge of buckshot tore into the wall exactly where George's head had been a fraction of a second earlier.

Levi stood looking at the silent saloon patrons, holding the empty, smoking shotgun in his left hand. His right hand rested on the butt of his revolver. The bartender, located less than ten feet away, motioned to Levi. "The gun!" he whispered.

"What?"

"The shotgun. Gimme the shotgun."

"Oh," Levi said, sliding the shotgun along the bar to the bartender.

Still whispering, the bartender said, "You'd better get the hell outta here while you still can. Nobody likes George and his pack of rats, but somebody's gonna notice that two dead men are laying out there on the floor. Besides, there's another live rat around here some place."

"Yeah," was all Levi could manage to say.

"Go on! Out the back door! Down the alley and outta here forever. Run, man, you ain't got no time to lose!"

Still in a daze over the magnitude of what he'd done, Levi obediently followed the bartender's instructions. The cool, outside air cleared his head, and he ran the few blocks to the stable. Quickly, he saddled his horse and rode out into the night. The streets were clear, but he could hear loud noises coming from The Rose. For a moment he debated. Did he have time to collect his belongings at the boarding house? Actually, he had little choice. He needed his bedroll and his gear, but most of all he need the Henry rifle. Like the Colt Navy on his hip, the big Henry was no longer the best weapon available. However, it was all he had, and it certainly beat nothing.

Tying his horse behind Mrs. Quinn's place, Levi casually mounted the stairs and went to his room. He returned within minutes with every possession he owned. No one had noticed his departure, not even the sleepy attendant at the desk. Quickly fastening his gear to his saddle, Levi led his saddle horse out of town, along one of his previously arranged escape routes.

The evening air was brisk, and the horse was well rested and full of spirit. Feeling Levi relax his hold on the reins, the horse broke into a long, ground-eating gallop, rapidly putting Bandera well behind him. Levi didn't know how long he let the horse run, but he suddenly was aware that the horse was breathing heavily. Reining the horse in, Levi began to search for the small wet-weather streambed that led to the game trail that he had chosen for escape. Just when he had decided that he had passed it, he located the trail, using a prominent landmark that he had noticed earlier.

Selecting the softest dirt that he could find on the road, Levi rode the horse well past the point where he intended to leave the road. He then doubled back upon his own path, this time riding in the hard-packed ruts of the road. He knew this ruse wouldn't fool an experienced tracker, but it might buy him some time.

The trail was difficult to travel. Tree branches lashed him, twice bringing blood to his face as he forced his way along the narrow path. More than once he found that he accidentally had guided the horse completely off the trail. It took him a while to find a solution, but he did. If he gave the horse his head, the horse would find the trail for him.

Levi pushed on through the night, stopping only for brief periods to rest and to check his horse. He really wasn't an expert horseman, but he realized the value of the animal. If the horse drew up lame, Levi was in serious trouble. He had no idea how far he had traveled, and he didn't know whether he was being followed but assumed that he was. He had killed two members of George Tompkins' gang, and he had attempted to kill George. George wouldn't let such an insult pass. He would seek his own revenge.

Levi smiled. It occurred to him that life takes some funny twists. For days he'd been stalking George, seeking revenge for a life that George had taken. Now, George probably was stalking him for much the same reason. "Well," Levi said. "We'll have us a meeting out here in these hills, and we'll see who rides away from it."

Another smile crossed Levi's face a few hours later, as he spotted a gentle glow on the horizon to his right. His judgment had been correct. The trail *did* lead north. He had gambled and he had won—so far, at least. Soon the sun was peeking above the horizon, lighting the eastern sky like a huge range fire. Levi stopped on a high ridge and watched the hills and valleys come alive with sunlight. "My God, that's beautiful!" he whispered, thankful to be alive to enjoy the sight. He said nothing more, just watched and rested.

Maybe it was fatigue. Maybe it was guilt or grief or maybe simply pain. Maybe Levi was suddenly overcome with the effects of events that had happened to him over the past several weeks. Whatever the reason, for the first time in his memory, Levi wept, gently and quietly at first and then in loud coughing sobs. He tried to resist, but he wasn't able. He clumsily dismounted, carelessly dropping his reins to the ground. Sitting down beside the trail, he held his head in his hands, his body shaking as wave after wave of sorrow racked his body.

Gradually, Levi's sadness was replaced with anger—anger at an inadequate and corrupt system of justice and its failure to conform to his set of standards, anger at Jovita for being dead, anger at her killers, anger at George for escaping, anger at himself for a dozen inadequacies and failures. For days the anger had been bottled up inside him, festering and slowly seeking the right time to explode. Now was that time. In a rage he charged to his feet, hurling stones and limbs into the trees and bushes beside the trail. He shrieked curses at Sheriff Hammer, at George Tompkins, at everyone who had stood in his way. Mostly, he cursed himself for his weakness, for his indecision, and for his failure to kill George Tompkins.

Exhausted, Levi stood, trying to regain his composure, cold and shaking, but dripping with sweat. Head bowed, he turned and approached the horse. Having observed Levi's strange behavior, the horse now stood carefully watching this madman, ears alertly forward and nostrils flared. As the man approached, the horse backed slowly away, staying just out of reach. This was a serious problem. He would be lost without the horse. Concentrating intensely, Levi spoke softly and soothingly to the frightened animal. Finally, the horse responded, letting Levi approach and pick up the loose reins.

For the next hour, Levi walked and led the horse. This

method of travel was slow, but it allowed Levi to regain his composure and the horse to get some rest. Although he couldn't understand how, his emotional outburst seemed to have served a healing and cleansing role. Levi now was more alert, his reasoning was clearer, and he felt more peaceful and more self-assured. After all, he had eliminated two of his archenemies. For sure, one of them had been present at Jovita's murder, and in his mind the other one was at least guilty by association. Although Levi hadn't killed George, he had satisfied himself of a lingering doubt. He had proven that he had the courage and the ability to do so.

The horse and rider traveled the faint trail all day, stopping only to drink from an occasional pond or stream and to let the horse graze for a few minutes. Before nightfall, Levi found a campsite, well off the trail and nestled back in the shelter of a small grove of post oak trees. He built a campfire, boiled water for coffee, and warmed a can of beans. During the days in Bandera when he was preparing for this journey, he had accumulated some basic food items to add to his supplies.

Levi loved the comforts of a campfire, but it was a luxury that he couldn't afford to enjoy on this occasion. He knew that a fire would make him far too visible to anyone who might be following, so he allowed the fire to burn down to a gentle glow, and then he prepared two beds. One bed consisted of some branches and leaves rolled up in a blanket and stretched out beside the embers of his campfire. From a distance this decoy looked for all the world like a sleeping man in a blanket. The other bed was prepared well back away from the campsite in a location from which he could observe the camp without being seen.

Giving in to complete exhaustion, Levi now took a chance that a more prudent man, a more experienced one, wouldn't have taken. He gambled that any followers wouldn't be able to catch him in this brief period of time, but he had gambled wrong. It was barely daylight when Levi awoke abruptly from a restless sleep, vaguely aware that something had disturbed the tranquility of the woods. Wild birds, usually singing and chattering at this hour, had fallen silent. Levi heard a twig snap, a very faint sound, back in the direction from which he had come.

Silently, he reached over and felt the security of the Henry, thankful that he had taken the time to retrieve it from his room in Bandera. He rose to a sitting position with the blanket still around him and the Henry resting across his knees. For minutes, which seemed more like hours, Levi waited silently, barely allowing himself to breathe. He strained his eyes, trying to find the thing that he knew must be out there. Could it be a deer? Maybe it was a mountain lion or a coyote. Then he saw it. A man, half-crouched and holding a rifle in his right hand, was silently creeping along the trail toward the camp. The man, whom Levi recognized immediately as one of the three that he had seen in Bandera with George, stopped for long moments to study the camp.

Finally deciding that everything was as it appeared, the man slowly raised his rifle to his shoulder and drew back the hammer. The rifle cracked, and leaves and twigs from the decoy scattered about the camp. The man was unable to believe what he had seen. For an instant, he stood motionless, letting the fact that he had been deceived sink into his brain. He began to back slowly away. Then he froze as he heard the hammer cock on Levi's rifle. The man had begun to turn toward the sound, when the Henry roared and sent a two hundred grain lead slug crashing into the base of the man's skull. The slug coursed upward, destroying the brainstem and killing the man instantly. The body lay on the ground, muscles occasionally twitching, making a slight rustling noise in the dry leaves. After a while the body was still, and the woods were silent again.

Levi made no sound. He didn't even eject the spent shell case, fearing it would make too much noise. There was still another man to kill, and then the score would be settled. He had to kill George, but where was he? Would George send this one man alone after Levi? Actually, he might, Levi reasoned. George was big and mean and vicious, but he wasn't brave. He might stay back in The Rose with Josephine and let this poor fool do his dirty work. Still, Levi wasn't convinced. He waited, every sense alert. An hour passed. A second hour passed. The sounds of nature had returned. Birds carelessly sang and flitted about. A pair of squirrels played chase in the canopy of one of the oak trees. A flock of crows called to one another in the distance.

"Just as I thought," Levi whispered to himself. "The coward's licking his wounds back in Bandera." Cautiously rising from his hiding place, Levi looked about the area. Nothing seemed to be out of order. Slowly, he walked over to the body and prodded it several times, making sure that no life remained. Using the barrel of his rifle, he rolled the body over onto its back. A gaping cavity existed just above the left eye where the bullet had exited. Levi ejected the spent cartridge case from the Henry, making a loud metallic sound.

As he turned to go back to his hiding place to recover his bedding and other gear, Levi looked back down the trail toward Bandera. For the briefest moment, he caught a glimpse of something that didn't seem just right. Maybe it was nothing, just a brief flash of light. Then he saw it again, and it was more than just a momentary flash. It was sunlight reflecting from polished steel. As George Tompkins raised his rifle to fire, Levi whirled and raced for the cover of the grove of oak trees.

Levi felt the searing pain of the bullet an instant before he heard the splitting crack of George's rifle. The bullet found its mark, but it wasn't what George had intended. George had aimed for the center of Levi's chest, but Levi's reflexive action had caused the bullet to strike high in the muscle between the neck and the point of the left shoulder. It was a painful and dangerous wound, but not an immediately fatal one.

Pain and anger raged within Levi. Once again he had let carelessness rule his actions. He lay hidden in the shadows of the oak grove, certain that George couldn't see him. Tearing some pieces of cloth from his shirt, he forced small wads into both the entrance and exit holes of the wound channel. The pain was intense, but he managed to complete the job. He found that he had only limited use of his left hand. With difficulty, he leveled the Henry on the spot where he had last seen his assailant, and he squeezed off a round. Then he fired a second time.

Almost immediately he regretted this action. Maybe, he thought, it would have been better to lie silently in the shadows of the oaks, and maybe George would have been tempted to come down to look for his body. If George had done so, Levi could have shot him from ambush. As Levi considered his next move, wondering just how deep his dilemma really was, the stillness was broken by a shout.

"Hey, down there! Does it hurt much? You know, you might bleed to death. Better come on out! You got what you wanted! Killed three of my friends, by God! That ought to make us even! No reason for either one of us to die! Come on up here, and I'll help you patch up that wound. Hell, we could go back to Bandera and discuss this over whiskey. I might even share Josephine with you. What do you say?"

Both men knew this approach wouldn't work. Levi wasn't sure just what George was trying to accomplish. Perhaps he thought Levi might answer and reveal his exact location. It was more likely that George was merely taunting a badly wounded foe. Levi remained silent, fighting pain and desperation.

"Hey, I finally figured out who you are!" George began again. "You're the guy from San Antone. The one that was shacking with that Meskin gal! Well, let me tell you. We done you a favor. She shore weren't much. Nearly any whore in San Antone was better! Hell, that's all she was anyhow, just a common whore!" Although Levi recognized George's tactic, he wanted more than anything to charge out and kill the man with his bare hands. He also knew that to make such an attempt would mean certain death. Instead, he continued to lie quietly in the shadows of the oak trees. The cedar-covered hillsides again were quiet. Nothing moved. Levi's wound was hurting more, throbbing with a dull pain deep inside his shoulder. Also, the dark brownish-red stain on his shirt told him that he was continuing to lose blood.

Another hour passed and Levi knew that George wasn't coming to an ambush. Finally, the stillness was broken again by George's voice. "Listen down there! I'm gonna give you a break! I ain't gonna kill you. Not today! Just let that bullet wound bleed! Who knows? Maybe you'll bleed to death. If you live, I'll know it. Remember this: Wherever you go, I'll be just around the corner! I could wait you out and kill you here, but I've decided not to! Wouldn't be no fun. I think I'll make you wait! Make you wonder! Make you worry! Make you wake up at night, afraid I'm out there, just outta sight! I'm leavin' now, but I'll be back! Count on it!"

There was silence again, and then Levi saw movement in a cluster of rocks some distance from where George had been earlier. Levi might have fired at him, but both men knew that the range was too great. In plain view, George led his big gray horse into a small clearing and mounted him. Next, he reined the horse around and rode back down the trail toward Bandera.

Could be a trick, Levi thought, but I have to chance it. The bastard probably means just what he says. He'll back off for a while and follow me. Then he'll spring his trap. Probably, he doesn't want me to die here. I've stolen a lot from him. Now, he wants revenge as much as I do. He wants to toy with me. Make me suffer. He really plans to kill me. Slow and painful, with me knowing every second what's happening. Killing me now would be too easy.

"Okay, George, I'll play your game," he whispered. "But first, I've got to get out of here and find some help."

Levi located his horse grazing a short distance from the camp. A few weeks ago, Levi had wished the horse were a bit more spirited, wilder. Instead, he had become as tame and docile as a big, friendly dog. Today, Levi was thankful for the horse's gentle nature. He caught the animal without difficulty; however, saddling him and getting all the equipment secured was more difficult. Levi accomplished most of this task with the use of only his right arm, as his left shoulder and arm had grown increasingly painful and stiff. With each exertion the bloody stain on his shirt grew larger.

At last ready to travel, Levi found that mounting his horse wasn't easy. He had never before realized how much he used his left arm. He choked back the pain and tears as he jerked himself into the saddle. Turning the horse toward the north, he headed up the narrow trail, having no idea where he was going, nor whether George Tompkins lay in wait around the next bend.

Chapter 9

Rachel Sandifer had risen from bed early this morning, as had been her recent custom. She especially enjoyed early morning in the springtime. The bluebonnets were in full bloom, as were dozens of other colorful wildflowers. The pecan trees along the San Saba River had not yet begun to leaf out, nor had the mesquite trees that were interspersed among the junipers and oaks on the rocky hillside away in the distance. Grasping a branch of a mesquite tree that stood less than twenty yards from her ranch house, Rachel closely examined it and found that the leaf buds were beginning to swell, but no leaves were yet visible.

Smiling faintly, she recalled the words she had heard her late husband say so many times, "There's one sure way to know that winter's over. The mesquite trees will wait until after the last frost to show their leaves. When there are leaves on the trees, there won't be any more real cold weather, at least no more freezing weather." Unlike most ranchers in central Texas, he had admired the tough, hardy mesquite trees that seemingly grew everywhere. "They're supposed to be here," he had said. "They belong, like the deer and the wild turkey. They're part of nature. Don't try to change that."

Along the river and even far up on the hillsides, especially down in draws and depressions where water could collect, many other trees and bushes already were in full foliage, and some had fragrant blooms that attracted wild honey bees and other flying insects. One small cluster of algerita bushes located a few feet away was covered with small yellow blossoms, a sure sign that honey bees would be present. Rachel reached over and pulled one of the tiny yellow flowers from one of the bushes, recalling an incident that had happened when she was new to the area. A local rancher had come to her tiny schoolhouse for reasons that long since had slipped from her memory. As he prepared to leave, the rancher had decided that a good way to make her feel a part of the community was to engage her in a brief discussion about her immediate surroundings. He pointed to a shrub with tough, spiny leaves and called it "algerita." In her youthful need to impress him, she informed him that the plant actually was named "agarita." Without further comment, he smiled at her, tipped his hat, quietly mounted his horse, and rode away.

Then she began to question herself, wondering if she might be mistaken. But she was reasonably sure that a recent newspaper article about local plants had called it agarita. It was a small thing, but she wanted to know. So she clipped a small piece of the plant and placed it in a box, and then she sent it to a professor of botany at the University of Texas. Along with the plant, she sent a letter, asking for identification and clarification of the name of the plant. Some time later she received a scholarly reply, informing her that technically the plant is a kind of native barberry. The genus name is *Mahonia,* and it has several common names, including agarita, agrito, and algerita. She also learned that it can be used to make jelly and wine, and that sometimes it's used to treat toothache, although the professor didn't explain just how.

A few weeks later she again saw the rancher, and she explained what she had learned. She concluded her remarks by saying, "I'm sorry. I guess I was just trying to impress you. Anyway, you were correct. Algerita is a perfectly good name. I wasn't as smart as I thought I was."

The rancher laughed good-naturedly. "It's okay," he said. "You're young and obviously smart, and you've learned a lot.

Just remember there's still a lot to learn, and the people around here have a lot of knowledge to share. Let 'em share it." She frequently recalled that incident and used it to remind herself that practical education can be as useful as the formal variety.

Returning to her morning ritual, she watched as hummingbirds buzzed about the flowers, especially the ones that were red or some shade of deep orange. Rachel was standing on a small hill, "surveying her kingdom," as Oscar Carson, her ranch foreman, laughingly referred to it. The kingdom was a modest ranch, about two thousand acres of grazing land, which bordered the crystal clear San Saba River. She had come to this community almost six years earlier for the purpose of teaching the children of the ranchers, farmers, and various merchants in the area. Almost immediately, she had met Sterling Sandifer, a young rancher who had inherited part of the ranch and purchased the remainder. After a courtship of about a year, they married and built a home on the ranch. Things had gone well for over two years. Production on the ranch was good, and they were showing a modest profit for their efforts. In addition, a bright, healthy son named Matthew was born during that second year.

Then Sterling began to receive letters advising him to sell his land to a certain group of landowners in the area. These letters were very polite and cordial, very business-like, at first. However, as time went on, they became increasingly threatening. Sterling refused to sell. This was his land, his and Rachel's. They had struggled and sweated to make the ranch successful, and now they were seeing some signs that it actually might survive.

One day on a visit to town, Sterling was confronted by a heavily armed ruffian who advised Sterling that he had ten days to get off the property. Livid with rage, Sterling beat the man severely, leaving him unconscious on the street. A few days later,

Rachel watched as Sterling's saddle horse carried him home after an afternoon of work down near the river. She noticed that Sterling held a strange, slumped position in the saddle as he approached, but she paid it little mind, thinking that he was just unusually tired. Still watching him through a kitchen window, she wondered why he hadn't dismounted. Why was he still sitting, slumped in the saddle? She immediately rushed to him, intending to help him down. It was then that she saw that he was bound and tied in an upright position in the saddle. He was dead, shot twice in the chest.

At the age of twenty-four, Rachel was a widow and the owner of the Double-S Ranch, with its lush pastures and herd of sleek cattle, but with little knowledge about running a ranch. Certainly, there were men who wanted to help her, a woman that appeared to be alone and helpless. Several had proposed marriage to the auburn-haired, green-eyed Irish beauty, but she politely sent each suitor on his way.

As Rachel saw it, she didn't need their help. Even when Sterling was alive and healthy, he couldn't manage the ranch alone, so he'd hired the most experienced cowboy he could find. Oscar, an aging survivor of the Indian Wars and an experienced cattleman, filled the bill. Since Sterling's death, Oscar had been Rachel's salvation, serving as a father, counselor, hired hand, and ranch foreman. He taught her everything he knew about ranching, such things as when to plant and harvest crops, how to judge the value of a horse or a steer, when to send cattle to market, and how to ride a horse better than most men could.

Determined to keep the ranch alive, Rachel threw herself into her work. Most evenings she went to bed so tired that she fell immediately asleep. One advantage of her demanding schedule was that she had little time to dwell on the death of Sterling. Also, the threats from the party that had tried to drive her and

Sterling from the ranch had stopped, at least for the present. Probably, she guessed, they were waiting for her to give up and move away voluntarily.

Rachel stood and surveyed and let her mind and her imagination drift in a hundred different directions. She enjoyed the warm sunshine on her face and the fragrance and beauty of the wildflowers. She looked up and down the sparkling river and thought how lucky she was to live at this time and in this place. Her mind wandered again, as she glanced down the long dirt road leading to the ranch house. Suddenly, she was shocked into rigid alertness by an object that she saw in the distance. There, walking slowly toward her was an obviously tired horse, carrying a rider slumped almost completely over the pommel of the saddle.

A chill surged through her body as she remembered Sterling's appearance on that unforgettable day a year ago. Was she seeing a ghost? Was her mind playing a trick on her? Was someone trying to remind her of what had happened to her husband? Bravely, she watched as the nearly spent horse came, head down, ever closer. In less than a minute she knew that the object she saw was real and that the rider was in genuine distress.

She hurried to meet them, careful not to spook the horse and cause him to throw the man. That wasn't a problem. The horse was too tired to shy away from her. Grabbing the bridle, she led the horse into the yard. Oscar, who had been cautiously watching the event unfold, came to Rachel's assistance. The rider briefly opened his eyes and loosened his death grip on the saddle horn. As Oscar and Rachel reached up to pull him from the saddle, the man gasped, "Shoulder. Shot. Hurts." As carefully as possible, they half-carried, half-dragged the filthy, bleeding man into the house and laid him on the bed.

Levi slowly opened his eyes and tried to focus on his surroundings. At first, all he could see were dim shadows, but slowly his vision and his senses began to clear. He was in a large room, lying in the most comfortable bed he had ever experienced. He was totally naked, resting on a clean white sheet and covered with another. Self consciously, he pulled the covering sheet about his body. As he moved, he felt stiffness and soreness in his left shoulder, but the fever and the searing pain he remembered were gone. Using his right hand, he felt the shoulder, locating a professionally applied bandage.

As Levi lay in bed trying to piece together his life over the past few days, a man and a woman entered the room and stood beside the bed. Levi attempted to sit up in the bed, but weakness and dizziness forced him to fall back abruptly. The woman reached out and placed a hand on his right shoulder. As she did so, she said, "You're not ready to sit up. You've lost a lot of blood. You nearly bled to death."

As Levi looked directly at the woman for the first time, his immediate thought was that she must be the most strikingly beautiful woman he had ever seen. Even in San Antonio, where beautiful women were encountered daily, this woman would have attracted notice. Her rich auburn hair, falling gently past her shoulders, glistened in the early morning sunlight. Her emerald green eyes were the most unusual and yet most stunning color he had ever seen. Suddenly embarrassed that he was staring at her, Levi blushed and turned away, momentarily avoiding eye contact.

"Where am I?" he asked weakly.

"I'm sorry. I should've told you sooner," the woman responded. "This is the Sandifer Ranch, sometimes called the Double-S. I'm Rachel Sandifer. You're a few miles outside of Norwood, a small town on the San Saba River." Rachel paused and motioned toward the man beside her. "This is Oscar Carson. He's the man who keeps the place afloat. He's my helper, my foreman, the only person in the world I really trust."

"How'd I get here?"

"Yer horse brought you," Oscar responded in a slightly exaggerated Texas twang. "You was pretty bad shot. Bleedin' real bad. You was a mess. It's a real puzzle to me. How'd you get on that horse, shot like you was? Then, how'd you stay on? Looked like you'd been on 'im for a long time. Anyhow, you can be real proud of that horse. He saved yer life. I took care of 'im. He's good as new."

"We had Doc Carpenter care for you," Rachel continued. "There weren't any broken bones. The bullet went completely through the muscle. Doc said it was a clean wound. No infection or anything, at least not now. But you lost so much blood. We just didn't know for a while."

"How long have I been here?"

Rachel looked at Oscar, uncertainty showing on her face. "More than a week. About nine or ten days, I suppose. You've been in and out of consciousness several times."

"What did I say?" Levi asked, guardedly.

"Quite a lot, actually," Rachel replied. "We'll tell you about it later. Right now you need some more rest."

"Yeah, I think I do," Levi replied. "I can't keep my eyes open."

Settling back on the bed, Levi immediately drifted into a restless sleep. Losing all track of time, he slipped into a dream. In most respects the dream was unreal, disjointed, senseless, but to Levi, in his state of fatigue and disorientation, the dream seemed very real. The memory of his terrible encounter with George Tompkins was haunting him again. In Levi's dream George repeatedly pointed a rifle at him, methodically terrorizing him by cocking and snapping the hammer. Each time the hammer dropped with a metallic click upon an empty chamber, and after each click George laughed hideously and cocked the rifle again, leaving Levi to guess when the hammer might fall on a live round. Obviously, George was enjoying the game, and Levi felt powerless to escape.

Maybe even more than fear of George Tompkins, Levi felt pain, a dull, throbbing pain in his left shoulder. Laboriously, he rolled to his right and immediately felt some relief. Still mostly asleep, Levi moved his hands across the smooth sheets, trying desperately to remember where he was. Slowly he opened his eyes, fully expecting to see George standing before him, a rifle in his hands and a look of sadistic pleasure on his face.

A faint glow of light filtered into the bedroom through the partially open door. Levi's eyes surveyed the room, finally aware that George had been nothing more than part of a very bad dream. Levi was alone in the room. His panic subsiding, Levi turned his attention to the shadowy furnishing of the room. An oak dresser with a tall mirror stood near the open door to the room. A lace cloth covered the top of the dresser, and pink tinted brushes and combs were neatly arranged on the cloth. An oak lamp table stood in a corner, holding a sparkling-clear glass lamp. Levi noticed that the lamp rested on a small lace tablecloth, matching the one on the dresser. A tall, dark-toned wardrobe took up almost half the wall across the room from the bed, and a wash stand stood beside the open window.

Continuing to study his surroundings, Levi concluded that he was in Rachel's room. The furniture was strong and functional, yet elegant and decidedly feminine. Any doubt was removed by the wallpaper, which bore repeating patterns of pastel pink and blue flowers that Levi recognized but could not immediately identify. His eyes drifted to the open window. On the distant skyline a faint golden glow told him that the sun was hovering just below the horizon. He studied the shades of red and orange and magenta that were captured by the wispy strands of clouds. A wave of uncertainty swept over him. For the first time in his memory he was completely disoriented. He had lost all sense of time and direction. Was he looking eastward toward a morning sun, or was it westward toward a setting sun? He had no idea, but he knew how to find out. Settling comfortably into the down mattress, Levi waited and watched. A thin sliver of gold appeared on the horizon, and the darkness began to melt from the landscape outside his window. He had his answer. He was witnessing a sunrise.

Magically, the colors in the bedroom came fully alive. Levi looked again and again, each time finding tiny objects and details that previously had escaped his notice. He was amazed. How could anyone bring such beauty and charm to a primitive ranch house stuck away in the wilds of central Texas? One last visual survey of the room brought his attention to the one object he hadn't yet seen. A picture in an ornate frame sat on a small table beside the bed. He reached over and turned the face of the picture toward him.

The image of a young man in a felt hat stared back at him. Levi grasped the picture and held it close, studying its every detail. The man was handsome and certainly quite young, but something about him was troubling. This was a man who had seen hard times. The face was smiling, yet lines of worry stretched across his brow. True, the lines were faint, but they were there. Additional lines, tiny thin lines, began at the corners of his eyes and radiated out, like the rays of the sun. Similar lines appeared at the corners of his mouth. An inscription spread across most of the lower right corner. It read, "With all my love, Sterling."

Levi heard a faint shuffling noise at the door. Looking up, he was staring into the huge, unblinking blue eyes of a child. The child, obviously a boy, had a head full of unruly hair, badly in need of attention. A white line of milk was on his upper lip, and traces of food were on his face. He wore light cotton pants and no shirt. Apparently, he had just recently gotten out of bed, and he had eaten at least part of his breakfast.

The two continued to stare at each other. Finally, Levi whispered, "Hello."

The child replied, "Hi. What's your name?"

"My name's Levi."

A broad smile spread across the child's face. "Levi?" he said. "I never heard that name before. It's a funny name."

Levi nodded solemnly. "Yeah, I've been told that before. What's your name?"

Deciding Levi probably was harmless, the child walked slowly into the room and stopped close to the bed. "Matthew," he said. "Matthew Sandifer."

"It's a good name," Levi said.

"It's lots better than Levi," the child replied.

Levi nodded, but hid his smile. "Yeah. Yeah, it probably is," he said.

Matthew silently studied Levi. Then, pointing to the picture that Levi still held in his hand, he said. "That's my dad."

Slightly embarrassed that Matthew had caught him holding such a personal object, Levi carefully, somewhat painfully, placed the picture back on the table. "Yes, I thought it might be," Levi said.

"He's gone, you know," Matthew said without elaboration.

"No. No, I didn't know," Levi said. "You see, Matthew, I don't know much about here. It's like I just got here. Do you understand?"

Ignoring Levi's question, Matthew said, "My mom said

you've been shot."

"She's right," Levi replied.

"That's not all. She thinks you might be a outlaw, too. Are you?"

Levi studied the child, silently admiring his directness and his obvious intelligence. "Matthew, do you know what an outlaw is?"

Matthew nodded. "I think so. It's a bad man."

"That's right, Matthew. It is, and I'm not an outlaw."

"There's lotsa outlaws around here," Matthew said. "Mom says we gotta be careful."

Levi leaned back in bed and chuckled. It hurt. "Your mom's right to be careful," Levi said, "but I'm not an outlaw."

Still not quite convinced, Matthew said, "Then how come you was shot?"

"An outlaw shot me," Levi said.

Nodding silently, while studying Levi with considerable skepticism, Matthew said, "Okay."

Rachel called from the kitchen, "Matthew, are you bothering our guest?"

Turning to Levi, Matthew whispered, "Are you our guest?" Levi nodded. Matthew walked back to the door. "We was just talking," he called to his mother.

"Well, come back in here," Rachel said. "He needs his rest," Matthew smiled at Levi and waved goodbye. He ran from the room toward the kitchen.

Levi listened to the hum of voices in the kitchen, but he could make no sense of what was being said. He could smell the aroma of food as it was being prepared, and he realized that for the first time in many days he was ravenously hungry. It was a good sign. Maybe he actually would live. He smiled at the thought. George Tompkins hadn't won yet. Levi looked down at his body and saw the bones of his ribcage. If he didn't get some food soon, George could turn his attention to someone else.

Levi didn't have to wait long. Rachel knocked twice on the door facing and entered the room, carrying a plate of food. She placed it on the table and said, "Eat what you can. I'll be back in a few minutes."

"I can eat all of it," Levi replied. "I might eat the plate, too."

Rachel smiled faintly at Levi's feeble attempt at a joke. "Decided to try to live, have you?" she said. "Well, if you eat this, it'll be the first solid food you've eaten since you've been here."

"I'll eat it," Levi said.

Rachel turned to leave, but stopped and looked back at Levi. "You shouldn't eat too much too soon," she said. "Your body has to adjust to food. You need to keep the food down." With that advice, Rachel left the room.

"Yes, I do need to keep it down," Levi whispered to himself, as he began to devour the food. "I need to keep it down and then I need to find my clothes and I need to get out of this bed. George really is out there somewhere, and these people don't need to pay for my mistakes. I've got to get well and take myself a long way from here."

Within minutes Rachel again appeared at the door. Silently, she took the plate and turned toward the door. Like before, she stopped. "I see that you met Matthew," she said. "He tells me your name is Levi."

"Yes. Levi Wolfe." Levi tried to laugh, but the pain stopped him short. "Matthew's quite a kid. He questioned me about my past. He thinks I'm an outlaw."

"Are you?"

Levi glanced quickly at Rachel, expecting a smile. There was none, so Levi looked away. "Guess that depends on who you ask," Levi said. "There's a sheriff in San Antone that would call me one. After all, he charged me with murder, and then I broke out of his jail, and then I killed three men, and another one almost killed me. Any one of 'em would probably call me an outlaw. Still, I'm not an outlaw."

"We have to be careful."

"Yeah. That's what Matthew told me."

"Matthew's right, Levi. This is beautiful, beautiful country. Clear rivers. Productive grasslands. Forests of pecan trees. Everything. So you wonder how it could be anything but peaceful. Well, let me tell you, it's sure not peaceful. It has become a bloody, violent place, and I don't see any end to the violence."

"Texas is a violent place, Rachel."

"Oh, our problem's a little bit bigger than that. It's special here, Levi. There's a war going on, and it scares me to death. And how do I know there's a war going on? How do I know this is a dangerous place?" Rachel stepped briskly toward the bed. For a moment Levi wondered if she intended to attack him. Instead, she reached down and lifted the picture from the table. "See this? This is a picture of Sterling Sandifer, one of the best men who ever lived. Kind. Generous. Considerate. He was my husband, and he was shot to death. Right here on his own property. Shot. Shot for no reason, and he's not the only one. There've been others. Mostly, good, innocent men. Just shot."

"There's no explanation?" Levi said.

Rachel stood silently studying the picture in her hand. For long moments she didn't speak. Finally, she returned the picture to its place on the dresser. "There seem to be some patterns, but it's still not clear. Some say the victims were told to sell their land and vacate it within a short time, maybe a day or so, but nobody's sure. Anybody who knows anything is probably too scared to speak up. Some say the judge and several city leaders are involved. I don't know, Levi. Maybe it's nothing. Maybe Sterling was killed by some cattle rustler that he caught in the act. Maybe, but I don't think so."

"What do you think, Rachel?" Levi asked.

Rachel was silent for moments, pondering the question. "I think we're in for a long struggle," she said. "I think there are evil men among us who want to steal our land, our homes, everything we have. I think they'll do anything to win, and I think they're not in a great hurry. In my case, not much has happened since Sterling's death. If somebody is after this ranch, maybe he's just waiting to see how long it'll be before the helpless widow starves out and goes somewhere else."

"And when I came in half dead, with blood all over me, you made an assumption."

"We didn't know what to think, Levi. When we first saw you, we suspected it was a trap of some sort. I believe Oscar considered just shooting you out of the saddle."

Levi winced and shuddered. "Glad he decided against that plan," Levi said.

"Actually, he didn't," Rachel said, flashing one of her few smiles. "The horse stopped, and you just sort of slid out of the saddle. Of course, Oscar wouldn't really have shot you. When we saw the wound, and we realized the blood was real, we thought you might be one of the land-grabbers, maybe one that had been shot by a land owner. Still, we couldn't just let you die."

Levi returned Rachel's smile. "So you and Oscar sent for the doctor and the sheriff, and you put me under heavy guard."

"We sent for the doctor, but not the sheriff. And, yes, we watched you pretty closely."

"Why not the sheriff?"

Rachel walked to the window and stared out. Finally, she returned and looked directly at Levi. "There are indications." She stopped and said no more.

"What kind of indications?"

"We wonder about his honesty. Sometimes he seems to give one person a lot more leniency than he gives others."

"Yeah. Sheriffs sometimes do that," Levi replied, silently recalling his experiences in San Antonio.

"Anyway, I don't trust him," Rachel said.

"And you really don't trust me either, do you?" Levi said with a smile.

Rachel returned the smile. "Why, Levi," she said. "I don't know you well enough to distrust you."

Levi knew he wasn't going to win his friendly argument with Rachel. He replied simply, "Oh."

Rachel turned and left the room, only to return almost immediately, carrying a stack of clothing. Placing the clothing beside Levi on the bed, she said, "You seem to be feeling better. I thought you might be ready for these."

As Levi examined the clothes, a puzzled look crossed his face. "These aren't my clothes," he said. "Where are my clothes?"

"Your pants were ripped and torn and filthy," Rachel said. "Your shirt was caked with dried blood and other things I'd rather not try to describe. Besides, it had a bullet hole in it. We burned them. We saved your boots and pistol belt and pistol and rifle. Somehow, you'd managed to tie the rifle to the saddle. That's about all. Oh, there was a little money in your pocket. I saved it for you."

"Where did these come from?" Levi asked, still studying the clothes.

"They belonged to Sterling. They should fit you. You're about the same size."

"But Rachel, these are your husband's clothes."

"They're just clothes, Levi. I've been saving 'em for somebody who can use 'em, not for any other reason. Around here we try not to waste anything. Can't afford to."

"Thanks," Levi said. "I can sure use 'em. I'll be leaving in a day or two."

Rachel studied Levi, finally smiling at his statement. "You've been awake for a couple of hours, and you're leaving in a day or two? This should be interesting to watch." Levi listened as Rachel walked toward the kitchen. She was chuckling as she went.

Almost immediately, Levi understood the humor—the absurdity—in his prediction. It took all the energy he could muster just to sit up and scoot to the edge of the bed. When he tried to stand, his head spun, and he felt himself losing consciousness. He lay back onto the bed until his head cleared. Then he tried again. By moving at a snail's pace and resting often, he managed to dress himself in the clothes. They were loose and baggy, but Levi guessed they'd fit well when he regained some weight.

Then Levi looked across the room at his boots, wondering how he'd even manage to get them on. Rachel stood in the doorway, smiling a superior smile. "Still planning to leave in a day or two?" she asked.

"Okay," Levi said. "Maybe it'll take four or five."

"Yes," Rachel said. "Four or five weeks, if you're lucky." Rachel followed Levi's eyes to the boots. "Need some help with those?"

"Much as I hate to admit it, I don't think I can do it by myself."

"Okay. I'll get you some help," Rachel said, disappearing into the kitchen. Within minutes she returned. Matthew, now clean and fully dressed, was beside her. "Here's your assistant," she said.

Matthew studied Levi, just as he had done before. "You still don't look very good," Matthew said, "and you need a bath."

Levi and Rachel exchanged amused glances. "Matthew kind of says what's on his mind," Rachel said, apologetically.

Matthew picked up the heavy boots and dragged them across the hardwood floor to Levi. Between the two of them, they managed to get the boots on Levi's feet. "Guess I'm ready now," Levi said. "Think I'll walk outside and wander around a bit."

"Just a minute," Rachel said. She disappeared again and soon returned with Oscar. "I asked Oscar to hang around the house for a while this morning," Rachel said. "I guessed you might need some help."

Oscar looked at Levi and turned away, shaking his head. Immediately, Levi knew Matthew's assessment of his condition had been correct. "You look like hell," Oscar growled.

"That's what I'm told," Levi replied. "Now, are we gonna talk about my good looks, or are we going outside?"

"Outside," Oscar said, moving to a position beside Levi. "Let's give it try." Wobbling like a newborn calf, Levi rose to his feet. His legs felt like lead, as he struggled across the floor. At the door he grasped the door facing and hung on. Rachel offered him a chair, but he declined. With Oscar beside him, Levi made it as far as the front porch, where he collapsed onto an old wooden bench. Holding his head between his knees, he breathed deeply for several seconds. Then he leaned back on the bench with his eyes closed. Finally, barely opening his eyes, he glanced at Rachel. "Okay, Rachel," he said. "It'll take a little longer than four or five days." Rachel smiled and nodded, but said nothing.

Chapter 10

Levi was young and healthy, but his recovery was not easy. By the end of the first week he was dressing himself, walking about the house, and exploring every inch of land within a hundred yards of the front porch. He pushed himself relentlessly, but his body needed time to recover. Usually, young Matthew followed his every step, chattering constantly and pointing out important things—things like how far a horned toad can spit blood and why a snake can crawl so fast without legs and where the biggest catfish live in the nearby river. Glad for the company and becoming fond of the boy, Levi listened attentively and always managed to ask just the right questions.

At first Rachel watched the two carefully. It wasn't that she feared that Levi might actually harm the boy. Clearly, he wasn't the outlaw she'd once feared. It was just that Matthew was all she had, and Levi surely didn't know how to supervise a child. Her maternal instincts drove her to be cautions. Soon, however, she realized that Matthew probably was safer with Levi than with either her or Oscar. After all, the threat from the men that killed her husband had not disappeared, and as Levi's health improved, he could better protect the boy. At that point she stopped worrying and enjoyed the unique relationship that was developing between the boy and the man.

Near the end of the second week, Levi and Matthew were venturing as far as the river, perhaps a quarter of a mile away. At first they sat on the riverbank and talked, casually throwing stones and clods of dirt into the clear water. Levi knew they needed something more, so as they prepared for their third trip to the river, he announced to Matthew that they needed a new adventure.

"I talked with your mom, and she told me that you're a great fisherman," Levi said. "So guess what Oscar found. The fishing poles you and your dad used to use." Levi produced two fishing poles. Previously, he'd asked Oscar if the objects still existed, and the foreman had scratched his head a few times and disappeared. A short time later he reappeared with the poles and a can of earthworms. Oscar didn't bother to explain where he found the poles, and Levi didn't ask. Within an hour Levi and Matthew returned from the river with more fish than all four people could eat in two meals.

Near the middle of Levi's second week out of bed—one of those rare occasions when he was alone—he walked to the corrals, a distance only slightly farther than the river. As Levi approached, his horse whinnied and trotted over to the fence to meet him. Reaching over the top pole, he stroked the horse behind the ears and along the neck, softly talking as he did so.

"That's a really fine horse, Levi."

Levi jumped and whirled toward the voice, fully believing that no one else was around. Startled by Levi's reaction, the horse sprang away from the fence and then ambled toward the middle of the corral. The voice had come from Oscar.

"I didn't know you were here," Levi said, trying his best to appear unconcerned.

"Good thing I wasn't that man that put the slug in yer shoulder," Oscar said.

"Well, I hope he's not around here," Levi replied.

"Prob'ly ain't," Oscar said, realizing that Levi didn't want to talk about George Tompkins. "That's a shore enough fine horse, Levi," Oscar continued, returning the discussion to the horse.

"Well," Levi said. "I'm sure no horse expert, but he does

seem to be special."

"Special?" Oscar said. "You really don't know, do you? That's a damn fine animal, Levi. Real fine." Oscar paused a moment to let Levi reflect on his words. "What's his name?"

"He doesn't really have a name," Levi said. "I just call 'im 'Horse,'"

"Horse!" Oscar spat the words out. "That horse's name is 'Horse'? Animal like that needs a real name."

"Well, Oscar," Levi said. "I haven't owned 'im long enough to choose a good name."

"Where'd you git 'im?" Oscar asked.

"He was a gift," Levi said, uncomfortable with Oscar's probing questions.

Oscar silently studied the horse for over a minute. "Stolen, ain't he?" Oscar said, matter-of-factly.

Levi, also studying the horse, waited almost as long to reply. "Probably." Levi waited another half minute. "Hell, Oscar, I don't know much about that horse. I was in jail in San Antonio, expecting every day to be my last. Then one night some Mexican men broke me out of jail, gave me this horse and my guns and some money, and told me to run. I did. Been running ever since."

"Why'd they do that?"

"Wasn't because they admired me. Mostly, they wanted to humiliate the crooked old sheriff. At least, that's my guess."

"Why?"

"Damn, Oscar, you sure ask lots of questions," Levi said.

"Sorry Levi. It's jist that I helped save yer life, took care of you, and nursed you back to health. Thought maybe I deserved some answers. Jist forget I asked."

Ashamed of his own behavior, Levi said, "No, Oscar. You're right. I'm the one that needs to apologize. I do owe you some answers. Let's find a comfortable spot and sit down. This'll take a while, and I still get tired pretty easy."

Sitting in the shade of a huge live oak tree, Levi told Oscar the entire story of Jovita's death, his own arrest and escape, his flight, and his encounters with George Tompkins and his gang. When Levi stopped talking, both he and Oscar sat for several minutes, reflecting upon the story.

Finally, Oscar said, "Damn, Levi. That's some story. Course I'd heard you tell some of it when you was sick, but that's the first time it's been put together fer me."

"It's all true," Levi said.

"I'm sure it is," Oscar said. "It's too wild to be made-up."

"Well, it's something you need to know," Levi said. "Someday Tompkins will show up here, asking all kinds of polite questions about me. I plan to be gone when it happens, but you still need to be ready. He's a dangerous man, meaner than the devil, a cold-blooded killer that wouldn't hesitate to kill everybody on this ranch. He'd do it without any regrets."

"Anything else?" Oscar asked.

"Yes," Levi said. "I'd appreciate it if you didn't tell Rachel."

"Don't she need to know?"

"I'd like to tell her."

"Okay," Oscar said, "but don't wait too long. She shore needs to know."

"I'll do it right away. After all, there's not lots of time. I'll be leaving pretty soon."

Oscar studied Levi. Satisfied that he was speaking truthfully, Oscar said. "Don't go rushin' off, Levi."

"What do you mean?" Levi said.

"Well, some people around here will shore miss you when you go. Matthew won't hardly let you git outta his sight, but he ain't by hisself. I've noticed Rachel smilin' a lot more in the last few weeks."

"Rachel?" Levi said, unable to contain his surprise. "Hell, she usually just pretends I'm not even there."

"Okay. Okay," Oscar replied. "I ain't sayin' she's goin' all gushy over a penniless drifter like you. Hell, she's smarter than that."

"Thanks for those kind words," Levi said, sarcastically.

Ignoring Levi's interruption, Oscar continued, "I'm just sayin' she's glad to have you around. It's true that she ain't got over Sterling. Not yet, but she will. Now, maybe you should be here when that happens."

"I can't stay around here. You know that. Tompkins probably knows where I am right now. He probably watched me ride in on that horse. If he doesn't know now, he'll know soon enough. I led him to this ranch. I have to lead 'im away."

Oscar silently considered Levi's statement. Slowly, he turned to Levi, smiled, and said, "Life's a real kick in the butt, ain't it, Levi?"

Levi shook his head. "You're just a regular philosopher, Oscar."

"I do my best," Oscar replied.

Nighttime is a special time in central Texas. Levi had known that since he was a child. Now, sitting alone on the porch of Rachel's ranch house, Levi again felt the peace he'd known so long ago. Dozens of different sounds floated up from the river. Each sound was different, yet each one complemented all the others. Air hissed through the outspread wings of an owl, as it swooped and searched for unsuspecting rodents, and a hawk's occasional screams were softened by the chirping of crickets and the hoarse croaking of frogs. Levi knew that if he listened closely, he might hear the yapping of a fox or even the distant bark of a coyote. Bobcats and mountain lions also prowled—always silently—along the moon-bathed riverbanks, seeking an easy meal, if such a thing existed in their world.

Down in the deepest canyons where dew hung heavy on the grass and light penetrated with difficulty, fireflies blinked and flashed like tiny electrical storms. If Levi was fortunate, a full moon would make its appearance, glowing like a huge silver coin and casting an eerie light across the landscape. Constellations blinked like beacons in the heavens, there to direct weary travelers toward their destinations.

Sometimes a gentle breeze blew up from the river, bringing with it the musty, yet not unpleasant, smell of mud and decaying wood and grass. Other times the breeze swept in from the fields, where it captured the sweet aroma of freshly cut hay or the ozone-charged smell of rain lying fresh on a pasture of oats. Perhaps, in the early spring it might carry the perfume of a field of wild bluebonnets or Indian blankets.

Levi sat on the bench, reflecting on the feel of the nighttime. For the moment he was at peace. He knew his peace wouldn't last long, but he would enjoy it while he could. Suddenly feeling great fatigue, he felt his eyelids grow heavy and then close completely. He didn't know how long he slept, but he suddenly was aware that Rachel was seated on the bench beside him.

"How long have you been here?" Levi asked, puzzled that he had not been aware of her presence.

"Oh, probably a minute or two," Rachel said. "I sneaked in while you were asleep."

The sound of a loud splash drifted up from the river, as a fish fought to escape the clutches of a hungry raccoon. For a moment the disturbance caused total silence. Then, as if on signal, the crescendo of usual sounds began again.

"Oscar says it's time for us to talk," Levi said.

"Oscar's usually right."

"Yeah, I've noticed that." Levi used a moment to collect his thoughts. "Rachel, what did I tell you when I was lying there in bed, trying my best to die?"

"Most of what you said didn't make much sense, Levi, but, yes, you did talk. It seems that your problems began in San Antonio. There was a girl named Jovita. You talked a lot about how she and all the other Mexicans were mistreated. You didn't give many details. Just bits and pieces, and you repeated lots of those over and over. So, there's a lot I don't know."

"What did I say about Jovita?"

"You talked about her quite a lot. Maybe the two of you were...well, I just don't know."

"I'm not even sure. I wanted Jovita, but I wanted my carefree life, too. I wanted both, I guess, but I didn't know which I wanted the most. I had decided it was Jovita, but there were lots of considerations."

"Such as?"

"Such as religion. Jovita was a devout Catholic. I wasn't much of anything, but I sure wasn't Catholic. And she had all that Mexican family stuff. She said it was her heritage. I wondered if I'd ever fit into her world. Or her into mine, for that matter. Jovita wasn't some cheap bar girl. There's lots of those in San Antonio, but she wasn't one of 'em. She sure wasn't a whore, either. San Antone has lots of those, too. Jovita was a high-class woman. She could trace her family back to Spanish nobility, or whatever they called it back then. I was just a simple gringo from Poteet. How could I ever measure up? Still, I wanted her and I loved her, and I'm sure she felt the same about me. Then she was killed."

"Murdered by this animal named George Tompkins, and you were accused? Exactly why?"

"He's a cold-blooded killer. He had a gang of outlaws in

San Antonio. The sheriff let him and his thugs run wild, doing anything they wanted to do. The sheriff and George used to be friends, but mostly the sheriff was just afraid of 'im. I guess it was easier to leave 'im alone. It's real clear that Tompkins and his thugs killed Jovita, probably because she resisted 'em."

"And the sheriff didn't want to face Tompkins and his band, so he accused you?" Rachel said.

Levi nodded and stared into the darkness. "Something like that," he said. "Course I played right into his hands. Being hot-headed and angry, I accused the sheriff of not doing his job. Hell, I even attacked 'im. Beat 'im up pretty good. Talk about stupid."

"You made it easy for him, didn't you?"

"Yeah. Yeah, I did."

Feeling the chill of the night, she moved closer to him. "Levi, you talked about escaping from jail and going after George Tompkins and about a gunfight in a saloon or something like that. Then you killed another man in the woods. That's where he shot you. Right?"

"That's pretty good, Rachel. Thought you said I didn't make much sense."

"You talked, off and on, for over a week. I could put together some of your story, but not all of it."

"You've put most of it together," Levi said.

"Here's the part I don't understand," Rachel said. "He shot you out there in the woods somewhere. You were bleeding, in pain, probably unable to defend yourself. Isn't that correct?"

"Yes."

"Why didn't he just finish it right there?" Rachel asked, still trying to piece the story together. "You'd killed all the members of his gang, if I understand everything. He must've been furious. Why not just shoot you there and let the buzzards have you?"

"He could have."

"But why didn't he?"

Levi looked toward the river, listening again to the night sounds. Rachel had asked a question he couldn't answer, one he had pondered many times. He had a theory, but no answer. "I don't know why, Rachel," he said. "All I can say with certainty is that George doesn't think like a normal person. He does things you wouldn't expect. He doesn't have a conscience. He'd kill you or Matthew and feel no guilt. Still, he's smart. He's careful about who and when and where he kills. Not that he minds doing it. He just wants to make sure all the cards are stacked in his favor before he makes a move."

Feeling Rachel tremble, he slipped his arm around her. He glanced at her in the faint light, seeing the beauty he'd seen so often, but now he saw something else. He saw a strong, successful woman who was facing overwhelming odds. He saw a mother determined to make a good life for her son and even for Oscar, whom she loved and protected as if he were her father. He saw a rancher trying to save the ranch her murdered husband had established and developed. Yes, she was a beautiful woman, but she was so much more. Levi felt his own body tremble as he sat beside her.

Maybe Levi was afraid of what was happening to him. Jovita had been dead for such a brief time. Surely she deserved a decent period of mourning, and she deserved to have her killer brought to justice. So far she had gotten neither. Levi thought he had no right to his feelings toward Rachel, yet they there, and he couldn't drive them away. Maybe it was just weakness on his part. Certainly, that had to be part of it. But was that all? After all, Jovita was dead. Nothing could change that.

"What happens now?" Rachel asked, interrupting Levi's thoughts.

"George doesn't want to just sneak in and kill everybody

here. If that was his plan, he'd have done it before now. He certainly could. He moves through the woods like an Indian. He wants me, Rachel, not the rest of you. On the other hand, if I stay too long, everybody here becomes my accomplice. That would make all of you fair game."

"How long is too long?"

"George knows all about my injury. He knows about how long it'll take to heal. That's how long."

She shook her head in sorrow. "How do you know all of this, Levi?"

"I've dreamed about him. I've studied 'im for the last several weeks. I haven't thought about much else. I just know."

"So what are you going to do?"

"I can't stay, Rachel. Much as I'd like to, I can't. That would get somebody killed, somebody besides me. Maybe you. Maybe Matthew. Maybe Oscar. Probably all of you. Probably, he'd kill all three of you first and save me for last. That's kind of what I've done to him. At least, that's how his twisted mind sees it."

Rachel shivered again. "You're determined to leave?" she asked.

"It's like I told Oscar. I don't have a choice. I led this madman here. I have to lead him away. He'll know when I leave. He'll follow me. It's the only choice."

"We want you to stay, Levi. I want you to stay. We could watch for this killer. We could contact the sheriff here."

Levi smiled at the plan, fully aware that Rachel still didn't comprehend the evil that George represented. "As I understand it, your sheriff is probably as crooked as the one in San Antone. Besides, even if he wanted to help, he probably couldn't. George could swoop in here, kill everybody, and be two hundred miles away before anybody even knew. The sheriff wouldn't know who did it or where he went."

Placing her hand gently on Levi's shoulder, Rachel asked, "How much longer do you plan to stay?"

"I should be able to travel in five more days. A week at most."

"Make it a week, Levi. We need time. You've become kind of a fixture around here. Mathew will be heartbroken when you go. I need time to prepare him."

"What will you tell 'im?"

"I'm not sure, but I have thought about it. I've known this day probably would come. Maybe I'll tell him that you're going on a trip, and that you'll come back. Would that be all right?"

"Would I be welcome, if I came back from this trip?"

Rachel looked away, choosing not to give a direct answer. "My husband was killed a short time ago, Levi, and it tore me apart. His death was so senseless. I blamed myself. I blamed him. I blamed everybody. I was so hurt and so furious. I thought about how unjust it was. Sterling died, and I lived. For a while I wanted to die, but that would've left Matthew with nobody to look after him. So I've struggled on, sometimes without direction or purpose. I kind of built a wall around myself. Guess I didn't want to get hurt again. Well, I see that wall cracking and crumbling just a little. That scares me."

Levi studied the moon that hung just above the horizon. "Leave the wall there, Rachel. It's not time for it to come down."

"So it's okay if I have a wall around me?"

"For now it's okay, Rachel Sandifer. I've got one, too."

"Thank you, Levi Wolfe," Rachel said. "You've become a fixture around here. You know how much Matthew will miss you." She stopped and smiled. "And Oscar is determined to make a real rancher out of you." She paused again, searching for words. "And you need to start riding Horse again. Oscar told me his name. Really, Levi. That horse needs a name. Anyway, Oscar and I will show you the ranch and the cattle and the crops.

Maybe it can make you really want to come back. Matthew will love it. He rides, mostly with me, but he does fine with horses. We'll ride all over the ranch. In six or seven days you'll be riding as well as ever."

Chapter 11

Oscar swung his arm in a long arc, following the general course of the river. "Jist look at that," Oscar said. "Ever see a purtier sight? See that grass? Look way back up where the river jist starts to bend, and follow that green band all the way 'til you can't see it no more. And look at them cattle. Fat. Sleek. Purtier than anything ye'll ever see anywhere else. This here's perfect cow country. Them cows drop a calf ever year, and them calves grow like weeds on that grass. Put good-blooded bulls with them cows, and ye jist can't fail."

Levi and Rachel exchanged glances and smiled but said nothing. They knew what was happening. For the past three days Oscar had been promoting the ranch specifically and central Texas generally with hardly a pause for breath. There was little subtlety in his manner, as he pointed out to Levi the unlimited potential of the area.

"What kind of bulls would you recommend?" Levi asked, trying to appear as interested as Oscar wanted.

"Some of the ranchers are startin' to use Herefords," Oscar said. "Course they cost a lotta money, an' there ain't much of that around. It's always been a dream of mine to cross them good Hereford bulls with ol' long-legged longhorn cows—or maybe with some part-longhorn cows. That cross outta git you some calves that're as tough as longhorns an' beefy like Herefords. Course that's way in the future, I guess. Seems like ever'thang's in the future."

"You've got a lot of dreams, Oscar," Levi said.

"It's a natural," Oscar said. "By the time young Matthew's

my age—hell, by the time he's yer age—this part of the world will be civilized. The outlaws'll be gone, leastwise most of 'em. The sky's the limit."

"If that's true," Levi said, "seems like there'll be a real rush of people to claim this land. There won't be near enough to go around."

"That's exactly right. Except that land rush happened thirty or forty years ago. Smart ranchers have knowed 'bout this country fer years. Ever hear of Shanghai Pierce?"

"No. Don't think so," Levi replied.

"Well, he come to Texas jist after the Civil War, I think it was. Built a cattle empire. Made a lotta money, bought a big spread down on the Texas coast, but he always said his heart was really in these here hills. He used to come up here all the time, buyin' cattle for his own ranch an' to trail north. Others did it, too. Some came an' left, an' some stayed on. There's one rancher that has a big operation over around Wallace Creek. He come here from Arkansas jist before the Civil War. Name's Riley Harkey. He fought Comanche an' Kiowa raiders an' outlaws of all kinds, an' he made a go of it.

"An' it's not jist the land, Levi. The livestock's better than anywhere else. Not sure why. It jist is. Feller named George Washington Miller come down here all the way from Missouri back in seventy-one or it could've been seventy-two. Miller an' his drovers took several weeks to git here, but they knowed it'd be worth the trouble. With Harkey's help Miller put together a herd of choice longhorns an' drove 'em north to market. Now, keep in mind he come all that way just to git this central Texas beef. Ol' G. W. used to say this is a cowman's paradise. Them wuz his exact words."

"He said that?" Levi asked. "He called it a cowman's paradise?"

"Shore did. He said it lotsa times."

"Ah, come on, Oscar," Levi said, certain the aging foreman was fabricating the story. "How do you know he said that?"

"Heard 'im say it. Heard it my very own self," Oscar said, looking at Levi and flashing a satisfied grin. "I worked fer G. W. while he was down here. Helped 'im an' Harkey put together that herd of longhorns. I was a bunch younger at the time, but I was good as any cowboy that ever rode a wild horse. I worked on a lot of the ranches around here, an' I learnt more than most cowboys ever git a look at." Oscar paused and glanced over at Levi. "Yeah, this ol' dog knows a lot about ranchin' that he could teach to a young pup like you." Oscar paused again, pretending to survey the river valley one more time. Then he said, as an afterthought, "An' don't thank them outlaw land-grabbers don't know this country's promise. They shore do. That's why a smart feller like you outta git in early."

Something lying on the ground a hundred yard away attracted Oscar's attention. Pointing at the object, he said, "Somethin' layin' over yonder. Could be a dead calf."

"Maybe you should check it out," Rachel said, looking in the direction of the object. "Take Matthew with you."

Oscar and Matthew rode away, leaving Levi and Rachel alone. Smiling across at Levi, she whispered, "Of course, you know he's trying to tempt you, you young pup."

Levi laughed aloud. "Really?" he said. "Fact is, I kind of like Oscar's wild ideas. Now, if George would just leave me alone, my choices would be a lot easier."

"I've thought about that some more, Levi," Rachel said.

"Rachel," Levi replied, "we've been over and over this."

"Yes, I know, but I've thought of another way."

Levi shook his head in disbelief. "Let's hear it."

"I didn't want Matthew to hear this conversation," she said.

"That's why they're studying that dead varmint. I already know it's a deer."

"Okay. So, talk to me."

"Well, I think we agree on one thing. The law can't help us. So maybe we should go outside the law."

"How?"

"George is a killer, so we hire another killer to go after him," Rachel said, as calmly as if she were discussing an upcoming picnic.

Levi turned and stared at her, realizing the full extent of her desperation. "Rachel?" he said.

"Think about it," she said. "If we can't get Tompkins legally, maybe there are other ways."

"Rachel! I know you don't mean that. It wouldn't work."

She turned and looked directly at Levi. "And why not? There are plenty of outlaws around here. Surely, one of them is for hire."

"Probably lots of 'em are. How much do you think you could trust one of 'em?"

"Well, we'd have to choose carefully."

"You can't trust 'em. That kind of person will turn on you every time. Maybe he'll take your money and just disappear. Worse, he might join up with Tompkins, and then they'd come after you together. And even if your hired killer played it straight and really went after George, George would win. Then he'd really come after you. Good idea, but it won't work."

She dropped her eyes and fell silent. After a moment she again looked, unblinking, at Levi. "I guess I knew that. I was just trying to find a way out."

"I understand," he said. "I know, and I thank you for it. There's just no easy way. This'll have to be between me and George."

Rachel's intention to respond was interrupted by Oscar. "That thang you wanted me and Matthew to check out wasn't nothin'," he said. "An ol' dried-up animal hide. Looked like it was a deer."

"Mom," Matthew said, "I'm tired of this. Can we go home, so Levi can take me fishin'?"

Rachel pointed toward the western horizon. "See that sun, Matthew? It'll be dark soon. You won't have time to go today."

Matthew shrugged and made a face. "Could we go tomorrow?" he asked, looking from Rachel to Levi.

Rachel glanced at Levi, seeking his approval. Levi nodded and said, "We can go, if you'll let your mom go with us."

Matthew frowned. "Moms don't go fishin'," he said.

"Of course they do," Levi replied, "You can show 'er how it's done."

"Well, okay," Matthew said. "I'll let 'er go, if I have to."

"You do," Levi said.

It wasn't a perfect morning for fishing, but it had to do. Levi didn't have many mornings left on the Sandifer Ranch, and everyone, with the possible exception of Matthew, knew it. Although no rain had fallen, heavy black clouds floated overhead and an occasional clap of thunder threatened the peace. Only Matthew had a fishing pole, and he didn't like the idea. In Matthew's mind Levi also should have one, but Levi chose to carry his old Henry rifle. Rachel fully understood Levi's thinking, but Matthew didn't. He offered Levi's pole to Rachel, but she smiled and declined, choosing instead to carry an oversized umbrella just in case of rain.

Matthew's attitude improved slightly after he caught two small catfish in rapid succession. With Matthew's busy mind finally occupied by fishing, Levi found a spot higher up on the riverbank. He motioned for Rachel to join him. She smiled and surveyed the location. It was perfect, allowing Levi a clear view in both directions up and down the river.

"Let's sit and watch the great fisherman catch his weight in catfish," Levi said. "Watching that kid kind of reminds me of my own childhood."

"Your childhood?" Rachel said. "You're sure you had one?"

Levi laid the heavy Henry across his lap. He looked up and down the river, searching every possible hiding spot. "Course I had a childhood," Levi said, somewhat puzzled. "Why would you think I didn't?"

"It's the only part of your life you haven't said anything about, so I just naturally thought maybe there wasn't one."

"My childhood is probably about the most boring subject you could think of."

"Could be," Rachel said. "I just noticed how you avoid it."

Levi was silent for a considerable period of time. "Childhood wasn't all that much fun for me. I don't talk about it much."

"In that case we'll talk about something else," Rachel said.

"Naw, there isn't much to it," he said. "It won't take long." His eyes again wandered up and down the river. He checked the mesquite pasture that led down to the river, and then he looked at the clouds. Finally, he turned back to Rachel. "My parents owned a place down in south Texas. Way out in the woods, some neighbors around, but they didn't live very close. Tiny little place. You could set it down on this ranch and never find it again. The place didn't have much water. Not much grass. Some skinny ol' cows. A few pigs and chickens. A garden. Not much else. Nearest town was Poteet, not too far from San Antone."

"Doesn't sound like the perfect place to be."

"Oh, we had some fun times, but not many. All Dad ever wanted to do was work. He was forever clearing land and planting crops behind those damned mules. If he wasn't doing that, he was working cattle, not that they really needed it. Why brand 'em? They were too worthless to steal. It went on and on, daylight 'til dark. Maybe even after dark. He never had much time for me, except when he needed me to help out. And I didn't mind helping out. It was the only time Dad paid much attention to me."

"Are your parents still alive?"

"Yeah, but they're getting old, and they can't go on forever. Don't know what'll happen to 'em."

"And I'll bet you left home as soon as you could," she said.

"It was time," he said. "Best for everybody, 'specially considering my dad."

"Tell me about your dad, Levi?"

"Seemed like he was always on me about something. I couldn't ever please 'im. Didn't make any difference how hard I tried. Course Mom tried to talk to me. She said his anger wasn't about me at all."

"Then what?"

"When I was born, my mother had a hard time. I don't know just how, but things didn't go just right. She didn't think she'd ever have any more kids."

"She told you that?" Rachel asked, surprised that Levi's mother would discuss the subject with her young son.

"She told me, but it was several years later, when I was really grown. Anyway, she did have another child. When I was ten years old, I had a little brother. Problem was, he was sick a lot. Oh, he usually did okay. It just seemed like he caught every little disease that came along. Dad was busy all the time, so I kinda took charge and taught my brother things. Things kids need to know."

"This story has an unhappy ending, doesn't it?" Rachel asked.

"My brother died," Levi said solemnly. "Not more than three weeks after his eighth birthday. One day he seemed fine. A day or two later he was real sick. Two days later he was dead."

"And your dad blamed himself?"

"He didn't say so, but he did. He was never the same after that. Actually, I wasn't either." Levi was silent for more than a minute.

Rachel could see that he was fighting back tears. She drew close to him and placed her head on his shoulder. "I'm sorry, Levi," she said. "I shouldn't have insisted on hearing about it."

"No. It's okay. I think about it a lot. Maybe I needed to talk about it. I really loved that little boy, and I miss him every day. I already knew about death, even as a little kid. Seemed like there was always some neighbor or some neighbor's kid dying. Just never thought it'd come so close to me."

"And you haven't been back home?" Rachel said. "Not since you left?"

"No," Levi said, after some hesitation. Then he was silent again. "That's not really true. I did go back once."

"And it didn't go well?"

"Not very," Levi replied, breathing a short laugh. "It was after I'd decided to marry Jovita. I wanted Mom and Dad to be the first to know. Things were okay 'til I told 'em she was Mexican. Then everything got real quiet and polite, like it does when people don't like what you've done but don't quite know how to tell you."

"So what did you do?"

"Politely said goodbye and went back to San Antone. Jovita was killed just a few days after that."

"And how did they react when she died?"

"They probably don't know."

"Don't you think they should?"

Levi surveyed the river again. "I haven't had a lot of time. Been kind of busy." He turned and smiled. "Don't you wish you hadn't asked about my childhood?"

"No. I'm glad I did," she said. "It helps me understand things about you, things I've wondered about."

"Like what?"

"Like the way you've taken to that boy down there," said, motioning toward Matthew.

"Yeah. Well, I'm not trying to replace my brother with Matthew." Levi paused and considered what he had said. "Memories of my brother make me realize just how important it is for young kids to get every opportunity life has to offer." He smiled over at her. "He needs more than what my brother had."

"More? Like what?"

"Matthew needs a chance, Rachel. We've both talked about how wild and dangerous this land is. He needs all the help he can get."

"And if you leave here, that improves his chances?"

"Strange as it sounds, it does."

"And just when are you leaving, Levi"

"Probably in the morning."

Levi and Rachel silently watched Matthew's mostly unsuccessful attempts to catch a fish. Just as he was about to give up, the cane fishing pole bent in a deep arc, and the water exploded in a spray of foam and mist. The struggle between boy and catfish went on for several seconds, with the outcome completely in doubt. Then the pole straightened abruptly, and the line sailed back over Matthew's head.

Matthew stood staring at the water. "Darn!" he said. "Lost 'im!" He turned toward Levi and Rachel. "He was huge, Mom! This big!" Matthew held his hands wide apart in the manner of all fishermen, regardless of age or experience.

Levi and Rachel rose and walked to the place where the excited boy stood. "That big, huh?" Levi said.

"Sure was!" Matthew said, still excited by his near miss. "Maybe bigger, and it was the only good bite I've had all morning."

Levi looked around. "I thought you caught a couple earlier."

Matthew looked sheepishly at Levi. "Threw 'em back," he admitted. "They were too little."

"That's probably best," Levi replied. "Maybe they'll grow up." Glancing at the clouds, he said, "We might want to just give up on the fishing, Matthew. This isn't the best weather for it."

"Maybe so," Matthew said. "Could we come back in the morning?"

Levi and Rachel exchanged glances. She turned and walked a short distance away. Levi knew she was crying.

Chapter 12

Matthew's fishing trip may have been a failure, but the day wasn't completely lost. In the early afternoon the sun broke through the clouds and warmed the steamy land. "Levi," Rachel said, "there's one place that you haven't' seen. I want to show it to you. Looks like today will be your last chance, at least for a while. So if you'd like to see it, we have time."

"Oh, I'd like it," Levi said, almost before Rachel could finish. "I really would. Now, where are you taking me?"

"It's my special place, down on the river. I'd rather not try to describe it. Seeing it for yourself is much better. There's a place where Matthew can play, and we can enjoy a warm, beautiful afternoon together. It's a pretty good distance. We'll need the horses."

"I'll have 'em ready in no time," Levi said.

The San Saba River began far west of the Sandifer Ranch, and it flowed for miles through dense hardwood and juniper forests and over beds of limestone and sandstone before emptying into the Colorado River. During the early spring, when heavy rainstorms fell along the course of the San Saba, the river might rage outside its banks, spilling its muddy contents onto the surrounding river bottoms. As summer set in, however, the river lost its fury and its load of dirt and silt, and its crystal clear water trickled like a mountain stream well within the confines of its banks.

That tranquility was its condition as Levi, Rachel, and Matthew stood high above and studied the river. Like a huge mosaic, an expansive field of almost perfectly flat rocks filled the bed of the river in front of them. As if it were undecided, the water of the river branched and branched again into dozens of small rivulets, each one seeking its own course through the limestone maze. At times when the river was carrying more water, an area extending perhaps half a mile downstream roared and thundered, like a whitewater rapids. At times like that the river could be treacherous, even deadly. Today, however, the water level was low, and each small branch passed with little more than a gentle hiss.

Matthew played in the shallow water of a natural pool between two large slabs of stone. Occasionally, he looked for reassurance from his mother and Levi, who watched from only a few yards away. "I can see why this is your special place," Levi said.

"Perfect, isn't it?" Rachel said. "On down at the end of these rocks the water gets quieter and deeper. Sterling and I used to come down here and swim on hot summer afternoons. It was wonderful, Levi. Look how the long branches of those cottonwood and pecan trees grow out over the water. They cast just enough shade to protect my skin. Sterling's skin was darker, and he didn't sunburn, but I do."

"How'd you meet Sterling?" Levi asked.

"I'd been in town maybe a year. I'd been hired to teach, and I was doing my best to do so. Problem was that lots of the children didn't much want to go to school."

"Yeah. I'm afraid I was one of those," Levi said.

"Oh, but that was just one problem," Rachel said. "There were so many things I wasn't allowed to do. It was like slavery had returned, but just for school teachers. No, just for women teachers. If a man was a teacher, he could do pretty much what he wanted, but I couldn't. I was a woman. A lady!"

"What was it you couldn't do?"

"Well, for one thing, I couldn't have a male friend."

"Really? Then how did you and Sterling get together?"

"I was in a store in town one day, and one of the cowboys—a really loud and obnoxious one—kept insulting me. I won't tell you what he said, but Sterling happened to be there, and he heard. Sterling made the man apologize. Then he showed the man the way to the door, so to speak."

"And it was love at first sight?"

"No, but love came along later."

"How, if you couldn't have a male friend?"

Rachel smiled her most defiant smile. "I had one in spite of the school board," she said. "Actually, I think they just looked the other way, probably because they all liked Sterling."

Levi smiled and shook his head. "You're a strong woman, Rachel Sandifer."

"I try to be, Levi Wolfe."

The late afternoon sun was filtering through the trees when Levi returned the horses to the corral. Oscar was waiting. The older man got straight to the point. "I hear yer leavin' in the mornin'," he said.

Levi looked at Oscar, his face showing surprise. "Rachel must've told you," he said.

"Yeah. I stopped by the house right after y'all got back from fishin'. She tol' me then."

"It's time, Oscar. Much as I want to stay, I have to go."

"You'll really come back? Yer not jist sayin' so?"

Levi shook his head. "I have a simple plan, Oscar. I'll lead George out there somewhere. I'll waylay 'im, and I'll kill 'im. No reason why I can't. I'm a better man than he is. When I'm finished, I'll come back. Could be a week or a month. Maybe a year, even. He wants to play games. I'll play."

"Ain't exactly a game, Levi."

"I think maybe it is to George."

"You thank so?"

"It's the only thing that makes sense. Think about it. How far do you suppose it is from Bandera to this ranch?"

Oscar silently pondered Levi's question. "My god, Levi, I ain't got no idea. Quite a piece, I'd guess. Maybe a hundred miles, as the crow flies. Some farther on the cattle trails."

"Pretty good trip for a man on a horse? A healthy man, that is."

"Yeah. Purty good trip."

"What about a man with a bullet hole in 'im—a man shot-up like I was? Could that man make it by himself?"

"Well, I dunno. It'd be hard." Oscar evaded the question, unsure how to respond.

Levi smiled at Oscar's evasiveness. "I've got my doubts, too, Oscar."

"How so, Levi?"

"I keep having this bad dream about how I keep falling off my horse, but somebody, somebody like George—big, stinking man with little pig eyes—keeps putting me back on. Cussing me. Telling me what a coward I am. Telling me I can't die this way. Yelling at me to get well, so he can chase me for sport. Laughing about how he'd toy with me and then finally shoot me down like a dog." Levi waited for Oscar to fully grasp what he was saying. "Would a man do that, Oscar? Did that really happen, or was I just dreaming?"

Both men stood gazing off into the distance, pondering the questions Levi had asked. Finally, Oscar declared, "There ain't no way to really know, Levi. But does it really make any difference? The main thang is that yer alive an' well. Whether Tompkins saved yer life or not, he's still gonna try to kill you. There's one thang I want to ask. Don't tell Rachel 'bout this dream. She's got enough to thank about without this."

"I won't tell 'er."

Levi squatted on the ground and picked up two small stones. Nervously, he toyed with them, first rubbing them together and then hurling them toward the distant river. Oscar closely watched him. "Yer nervous as a cat. What else is on yer mind?"

"There is something else that happened out there. It's pretty strange, and I'm not even sure I believe it."

Oscar leaned on the corral fence, his interests aroused. "Sounds important. Let's hear it."

Levi glanced at Oscar and then turned quickly away. "While I was out there, more dead than alive, my mind kept going back and forth, in and out of consciousness. Lots of the time I didn't know which was which."

"Sounds 'bout right, considerin' what I seen of you."

"I saw things, Oscar," Levi said, straining to make his point. "Strange things. Things besides George Tompkins. Things that couldn't possibly exist. There was a ghost…a shadowy ghost-like animal that followed me. Not real close. Kinda behind and off to the side. Sort of a floating thing. Maybe it was my imagination. Maybe a dream. But maybe it was really there."

"You seen this thang ever day you wuz out there?" Oscar asked, pushing his hat back and rubbing his forehead.

"I don't know. Seems like several times. Just following along and then disappearing then appearing again. No idea how many times this happened. Not even sure it really did."

"I ain't never seen no real ghost, Levi. Never believed they wuz real."

"Me neither, but something happened."

"Fer as you could tell, what kinda animal wuz it? A horse? A deer?"

Levi looked directly at Oscar, watching for a reaction. "That's the strangest part. I couldn't identify it at the time, but when I think about it, a wolf flashes into my mind."

Oscar laughed. "Levi, I've been all over this part of the state fer lotsa years. Haven't saw no wolf in…well, a long time. Ain't nobody else saw one neither. If they'd saw one, they'd of tol' ever body. Story goes that ranchers have kilt ever one of 'em, thinkin' they kill too many cattle."

"Well," Levi said. "I don't know what I saw. Probably nothing, but my mind thinks I saw a wolf."

"You had some strange company out there in them woods, Levi. A outlaw thet wanted to kill you, but actually helped you, and now a wolf thet might not even exist. Hard to believe it was all real."

"Yeah. I know," Levi said. "Hell, I should've died out there, but something or somebody kept me alive. I don't understand."

Shaking his head, Oscar replied, "Well, I shore kaint explain it."

"Oscar, we've been talking about what happened to me while I was wandering around in those hills and woods. There's a lot of strangeness about most of it, but there's nothing strange about George Tompkins. He's real. He's vicious. He's smart."

"Yeah. I shore believe thet."

"Well, when I leave, I'll leave at night, like I'm sneaking away. Tompkins might be watching. He might follow me right out of here, and you might never have the pleasure of meeting the man. But maybe he's not watching that close. Maybe he just checks now and then to see if I'm still here. Maybe he'll just notice one fine day that I'm not here anymore. When that happens, he'll come to the ranch and ask about me. He'll have some good story, maybe about how he's an ol' friend looking for me or maybe that he's a lawman and has a warrant for me. When he comes, listen to 'im. Pretend you're interested in his story. Tell 'im everything you know. Tell 'im I came here all shot-up and about to die. Tell 'im you thought I might be an outlaw, but you couldn't just let me die. Give him my real name and tell 'im when I left and what direction I took. Wish him good luck in his search for me."

"Thank he'll believe me?"

"I don't know, but if you tell 'im the truth, he won't have a reason not to. Main thing is that you don't do anything to make 'im angry. Here's another thing. Don't let him get under your skin. If he's in a playful mood, he might try. Just remember, he won't pick a fight unless he knows he has the drop on you, so don't fall into a trap, if he sets one. Give 'im the information he wants and get 'im on his way as fast as possible."

"I understand."

"I don't mean to suggest that you don't already know all of this, or that you don't understand how dangerous the man is. I just don't want to put Rachel and Matthew and you in any more danger than necessary. I want to be as certain as possible that he comes and leaves without incident."

"Really, Levi, I understand. I appreciate you goin' over all this again. My feelins ain't hurt."

It was a difficult time for Levi. He had to tell Oscar goodbye, and he didn't know how. Extending his hand to Rachel's foreman, Levi said, "I won't be seeing you for a while. I want you to know how much I appreciate what you've done for me. You've given me my life back, but you've given me lots more than that. Maybe someday I'll be able to really thank you for it. Until then, I'll just say goodbye."

Oscar shook Levi's hand. He tried to speak, but he couldn't. Finally, he managed to mutter, "Be careful, Levi." Levi turned abruptly and walked toward the ranch house, dreading the goodbye that would be much more difficult than the one he'd just endured.

Levi moved quickly now. His mind was made up. There was no turning back. It would be best to get the final goodbye out of the way as soon as possible. Rachel was waiting. He knew she would be.

"In the morning?" Rachel asked.

"Yes, Rachel. Before morning. I'll be gone well before sunup."

"And I won't see you again before you go?"

"No. I don't think you will."

"That's what I expected," Rachel said, struggling to maintain her composure. "There's something I want to give you." She disappeared into the bedroom and returned almost immediately, carrying a small box. "One of the times when you were talking out of your head, you talked about the gunfight in the saloon in Bandera. I never said anything about it to you. Guess I didn't think it was important."

"What did I say?"

"You talked about your pistol. You were pretty disappointed about how it failed you. There was something about it misfiring. You said it almost got you killed."

"Yeah. It's a good gun, but it has its faults."

"That's why I want you to have this," Rachel said, handing the box to Levi. "Open it."

Levi lifted the lid. In the box lay a shining blue steel Colt Single Action Army revolver. He picked the gun up and examined it carefully. It was chambered for the modern .44-40 caliber, a cartridge gun instead of percussion like his old Colt Navy. The barrel appeared to be about five inches long. The grips were polished smooth walnut. The gun appeared to be new.

Levi looked at Rachel and stammered, "I don't know what to say."

"It belonged to Sterling. He ordered it from the factory. He wasn't carrying it when he was killed. If he had been, maybe... anyway, it didn't save his life, but it might save yours. Take it. I want you to have it."

Levi examined the gun once more. He drew the hammer to half cock and opened the loading gate. Slowly, he rotated the cylinder, checking each chamber carefully. Then he pulled the cylinder pin and slid the cylinder out of the gun. He checked the barrel and the trigger and hammer mechanism. He had seen such a weapon before, but this was the first time he actually had handled one. It was all he had imagined it would be, a mechanical marvel.

Levi looked back at the beautiful, sensitive woman. Tears had formed in her eyes. "Are you sure?" he asked. "It belonged to your husband. It must mean a lot to you."

"Yes, it does. Sterling was very proud of it, but it needs an owner worthy of it. I know you're that owner. There's just one condition. You have to return it to me within one year."

Levi hesitated, remembering an agreement with Rachel. "I know I agreed to keep my distance, Rachel, but this is an exception," he said, putting his arms around her and pulling her close. He searched for just the right words, words that would comfort and reassure her. He had promised to return, but somewhere out there George Tompkins was waiting and watching for just the right moment. Did he, a rank amateur, have a chance against a professional killer like George? And he'd made promises to Rachel that he might not be able to keep. "I don't know what waits for me out there, but I have every intention of coming back." he said. "If I'm not back in a year, I won't be back. Wish me well and think about me. In the meantime, go on with your life. Look after Matthew. Trust Oscar. He won't let you down. And finally, expect me to come back."

It was midnight when Levi left the Sandifer Ranch. He guessed Rachel would be watching from the kitchen window, silently hoping he'd change his mind, but knowing he wouldn't. He wished he'd been more eloquent, more reassuring to her. He felt that words had failed him and that he had botched his chance to lessen her fears.

For just a moment Levi considered returning to Bandera and forcing George's hand, finding out once and for all which man would kill the other. Immediately, he knew the absurdity of the idea. In the first place, he almost certainly was no longer in Bandera. Also, Levi had lost the element of surprise. He had caught Tompkins unaware once. It wouldn't happen again. Additionally, he might still be wanted for murder. Almost certainly, Sheriff Hammer hadn't arrested anyone for Jovita's murder. And what about the three men he'd killed in and around Bandera?

No, Levi had to go on with his current plan to let George find him. He headed north for a few miles and then cut back east toward Waco. He traveled as light and as fast as possible, using well-traveled roads, but camping in secluded areas. Stopping often to watch his back trail, he saw no indication that he was being followed. He used every precaution he knew, and he saw no signs of Tompkins, but he was there. Levi knew it. He could sense and smell it, like a thirsty horse knows where there's water.

Levi arrived in Waco during the early evening, having timed his arrival about right. It had been dark for some time and there was little likelihood that the presence of another tired, dusty horseman would be noticed. He was tired, but mostly he was hungry, having eaten little on the trail to Waco. In his cautious state of mind, he'd been reluctant to build campfires, so he was unable to do any cooking. Rachel had packed some provisions that could be eaten without cooking, but those didn't take the place of a freshly cooked meal. More than almost anything else, he wanted to go to the nearest café and order the biggest steak in the house, but he resisted the urge. Instead, he went to the local wagon yard, where he fed and bedded his horse. Then he found a reasonably comfortable spot and prepared a bed for himself. He ate the last of a bag of cold biscuits and quickly drifted off to sleep.

Chapter 13

Levi was suddenly awake, somehow aware that something was wrong, very wrong. He was looking into the muzzle of a Colt revolver, a short-barreled .45 caliber Peacemaker, cocked and ready to fire. Without saying a word, Levi shook his head and rubbed his eyes, desperately fighting to remove the effects of sleep from his brain. His assailant was half-standing, half-kneeling about six feet away, just out of reach, yet close enough that a shot would be sure to find its mark.

For what seemed an eternity, Levi stared at the man, trying to make sense of the situation. Probably, he was still a wanted man in San Antonio, but this man didn't appear to be a lawman. Certainly, he wasn't a Texas Ranger. By the standards of the Rangers, Levi's offenses would make him a minor criminal, surely not important enough to attract their attention. It was possible that this was an outlaw, perhaps a friend of the men he had killed. If not that, maybe Sheriff Hammer had hired a bounty hunter to bring him to justice.

Whoever he was, he was not an amateur. The gun in his hand was perfectly still, like a rattler poised to strike. The cold gray eyes returned Levi's stare, hard and unblinking. Not even a glimmer of a smile showed on his face. Lines at the corners of his eyes, combined with a short stubble of gray beard, made the man look older than he probably was. However, one glance at the lean, muscular body told Levi that this man was perfectly capable and probably willing to complete the business at hand. Realizing the reputation of bounty hunters to kill instead of capture fugitives, Levi kept still and quiet.

Finally, the man spoke, "Who are you?"

"I thought you knew," Levi replied. "My name's Levi Wolfe."

"Levi? A bit unusual for this part of the world. Levi Wolfe. Huh. Where do you call home?"

Levi was determined not to reveal any more information to this stranger, this bounty hunter, than necessary. "I come from down south of here," Levi replied.

"Hell, man! Let's not play games. Half of Texas lies south of here. Specifically, where south of here?"

"Bandera most recently. San Antone before that." Levi saw no need to discuss his stay on the Sandifer Ranch. Rachel and Oscar needed all the protection they could get. "Which one are you taking me back to?"

"Why would I take you back to either one of them?" the man asked. Levi silently cursed himself. Already, he had said too much. "Now would be an excellent time for you to practice honesty," the man continued, the hard glint in his eyes warning Levi that this bounty hunter already knew the truth.

"I just figured that Sheriff Hammer sent you to bring me back."

"Hammer? You mean the fat bastard who impersonates a sheriff in San Antonio? Hell no. I don't work for that corrupt son of a bitch. There's still considerable pride left in this ancient body." The man frowned deeply, apparently disgusted with Levi's suggestion, and then he continued, "And why would San Antonio's glorious protector of the law be interested in a dignified young man like yourself?"

Levi sat staring at the man, puzzled by his strange way of speaking and certainly not wanting to reveal any more about his problems. Finally, the man grew impatient and said, "This Colt and I would certainly appreciate an answer."

"I was accused of killing a woman, which I didn't do. Before

I could go to trial, I escaped, with lots of help."

"You escaped from that fortress of a jail? Damn. I'm impressed. Now what's this about Bandera?"

It was apparent to Levi that he couldn't keep his past a secret from this man, so he replied, revealing as few specifics as possible, "After my escape, I went there. That's where the men were that killed the woman. I killed three of 'em. One's still out there, probably still looking for me." The man holding the gun stared at Levi for almost a minute, saying nothing, but carefully studying for any sign that he was lying. Levi asked, "If you don't work for Hammer, why are you after me?"

"Actually, I have no genuine interest in you," the man replied. "The fact is, I was just being careful. In my business one cannot be too careful."

"Hell of a way to be careful," Levi snorted. "I might've been killed."

"Only if you had reached for your weapon, and you are too intelligent to make a blunder of that magnitude." In one smooth, continuous motion the stranger stood fully erect, dropping the hammer on his revolver, and slipping the gun gracefully into its holster. He moved without thought or effort, conveying the message that he had complete confidence in himself and his ability to use his weapon. As Levi watched the arrogant gunman, anger and annoyance welled up inside him. In past weeks he had been falsely accused of the murder of a woman that he cared for deeply, and he had been jailed for the murder. He had been harried and pursued over half of Texas by both lawmen and outlaws, and he had been shot and apparently left to die a lingering death. In addition, he had been lonely, scared, cold, and hungry. Now, to top it all off, he was being accosted by a total stranger who apparently had no motive.

And who was this stranger who had so abruptly and rudely

intruded in his life and seemed to have no reason to be there? In spite of his denials, was he sent by someone in Levi's past to trick him into revealing damaging—perhaps fatal—information about himself? Actually, that seemed unlikely. So far this man didn't seem to be deceitful or treacherous. No, he appeared direct—shoot now and ask questions later.

Levi was well aware that his own pistol was lying in its holster on the ground about a foot from his right hand, where he had placed it last night for just such an emergency. For a fleeting moment his anger and pride urged Levi to turn the tables on this arrogant, self-assured intruder, make him pay for his brusque arrogance and for treating him with such total disrespect. There were ways to deal with such people. If necessary, this fool could join the three companions of George Tompkins.

The stranger casually rolled and lit a cigarette and was contemplating where to discard the smoldering match, to avoid igniting the loose hay scattered about. Carefully watching the man's every move, Levi recognized that if he ever were to get the drop on him, this moment of distraction was the time. His fingers inched slowly toward his Colt revolver, but the stranger wasn't fooled. In a flash he turned and slammed his foot on Levi's holstered gun.

"Maybe you don't have the intelligence that I expected," the man said in a cold monotone. "Maybe you have a death wish. One thing is certain. Your skills with Colonel Colt's invention are limited. That much is apparent to anyone. Fool mistakes like you were considering lead to an early grave."

The fear that Levi felt for this man multiplied, as a hard knot tightened in his stomach, and a cold sweat developed on the back of his neck. As much as Levi hated to admit it, the man was right. He had been a fool. He also suspected that he'd never been closer to death. As strong as it was, fear was only one of his feelings at the moment. Over the past few days he had given a good account of himself. He had proven his bravery, his worth, and his manhood. Now this man was taking those virtues away, humiliating and mocking him. Even worse, Levi was helping him, playing right into his hands.

Finally, the man relaxed, took his foot off Levi's gun and holster, and said, smiling faintly for the first time, "Okay, let's try this again. I'm not here to take your life, your horse, or your pride, nor do I wish to return you to San Antone or anywhere else. But friends of mine, good friends, have been killed by more harmless-appearing men than you. I can't take chances. Now, if you'll be kind enough to disregard my rudeness, I'll apologize and be on my way."

Having few options, Levi nodded and looked away, silently accepting the apology. The stranger started to leave, then hesitated and turned back toward Levi. "I have an idea," he said. "I owe you more than an apology. The very least I can do is offer to treat you to breakfast. There's a place down the street that's almost acceptable. How about it?" Still trying to regain his composure, Levi nodded again and got awkwardly to his feet.

The two men ate quietly in the crowded dining room of a small hotel. The meal was simple and poorly prepared. The fried steak was tough and over-cooked, the eggs were thin and runny, the potatoes were burned, but the coffee saved the meal. It was strong and hot. Levi couldn't remember the last time he had been so hungry. He ate like one of the starving pups that roamed the back streets of San Antonio. As Levi finished his plate of food, he looked at the stranger and asked, "You said you're buying?"

"Those were my words."

"Okay," Levi responded, signaling to the chubby young waitress. As the woman stopped at the table, Levi said, "I'll have another meal like the one I just ate."

The stranger looked at Levi in amazement and asked, "My God, boy! How long has it been since you had a meal?"

"Except for a few cold biscuits and such, two days."

Shaking his head and smiling at Levi, the stranger replied, "Eat as much as you can hold. It may be a while before I offer to purchase your meal again."

With Levi finally filled, the stranger started to rise from the table, but Levi motioned for him to remain. Hesitating for a moment, the man sat back down and looked quizzically at Levi. "Come now, Levi, can't we just forget this morning? Revenge isn't necessary in this instance. I apologized, didn't I?" the man asked.

"Yeah, but we're not even yet," Levi replied. "You owe me some more. You know who I am, and you know a little bit about why I'm here, but I don't know anything about you."

Relieved that Levi wanted only information, the man leaned back in his chair and eyed him, still a bit unsure of Levi's intentions. "Okay," he said. "I guess fair's fair. My unacceptable behavior this morning comes from another one of the peculiarities of my profession. I want to know everything but tell nothing. I'm a gambler, and my name's Shiloh Cole."

Before the man could continue, Levi abruptly sat forward in his chair and looked intently at him. "Damn! You are! I kept thinking that I'd seen you before, but I couldn't figure out where. Now I remember. I've seen you in San Antone. In the gambling houses there."

Levi remembered more than one occasion when he'd watched Shiloh and other notorious gamblers separate hapless ranchers, cowboys, and various other adventurers from their money. Sometimes he watched the games at Jack Harris's place. At other times it would be at the White Elephant or the Silver

King Bar. Levi often had marveled at the coolness of these gamblers, as huge fortunes changed hands in the boisterous, lawless establishments. Many participants lost their lives as well. It wasn't unusual for high-stakes games to be interrupted by gunfire. That was why so many successful gamblers like Shiloh Cole also were accomplished gunmen. If they couldn't handle a gun, they soon left the profession, one way or another.

"There's something else I'd like to know," Levi said.

"Yes? What?"

"You know why I'm here. What are you doing in this place?" Levi sneaked a glance at the gambler, wondering how he would respond.

Shiloh became silent, looking off into space, as if trying to decide whether or not to answer. Slowly, he took tobacco and paper from his pocket and rolled a cigarette. He lit it and deeply inhaled the smoke. Then he leaned back in his chair and exhaled, finally making eye contact with Levi. "I won considerable money in San Antone," he said. "Guess I got lucky. I won it honestly. Over eighty-thousand dollars."

Levi whistled softly and then asked, "Where is it?"

Shiloh turned and looked at Levi, a smile crossing his face. "I don't normally reveal that kind of information. It can be kind of dangerous," he said. "But some of it's in my money belt. Some's hidden away where I can recover it quickly." Again, Shiloh studied Levi and then decided to continue, "You see, there are people in San Antonio who would like to recover their money, even if it meant killing me. Some of them would even put out a contract on me. I had reason to believe that had been done, so I left town for a while. That's who I thought you were at first, a hired gun. Then I saw you in action and realized my mistake."

Levi blushed slightly at the good-natured insult and then said, "So I'm not much of a gunman, but I've managed so far."

"Yes. Well, you've been quite lucky. Just be glad you haven't come face to face with the man who's looking for you. What's his name again?"

"I haven't told you yet. His name's George Tompkins."

"Oh, yes, you're lucky indeed. I've heard of Tompkins. A vicious gunman from south Texas. Comes from down in the Del Rio area, I think. Ranchers once hired him and his bunch of vipers to settle disputes. Dangerous man. He certainly can use a gun." For a second time Shiloh rose from his chair to leave the dining room. Following the example, Levi also rose stiffly to his feet. "I have another idea," Shiloh continued casually. "It appears that we'll both be here in town for a few days. Why don't we join forces for a while, as long as we're both here anyway? It seems that we can at least stand one another's company. Besides, we're both being hunted, and two pairs of eyes are better than one. What do you think?"

"There's this tiny problem, Shiloh. I was planning to stay in the wagon yard for a real good reason. It's cheaper. You see, I can't afford a hotel."

"Then there's no problem," Shiloh said. "I already have a big room rented. Plenty of space. And I know what you're thinking. This is no gift, no charity. I'm a gambler, and gamblers don't believe in charity. You can earn your keep by helping me. Now, come on. Let's go. I need your help."

"Well, under the circumstances, I can't say no. Lead the way."

Levi realized that his temporary partnership with Shiloh was a challenge for both of them. They were very different individuals, coming from vastly different backgrounds and seemingly having different values. Although both recently had lived in San Antonio, their experiences in that city had been quite different.

Shiloh had lived the good life, enjoying the most expensive clothes, the finest foods, and the most beautiful women. In addition, he had developed a smoothness of manner and speech befitting his status as one of San Antonio's premier gamblers. In contrast, Levi knew his rural background had kept him from developing the social awareness that came so easy for Shiloh. So, while Shiloh had immersed himself completely in the excitement of San Antonio's fast-paced life, Levi had lived on the edge of that lifestyle, most frequently participating only as a spectator.

On the other hand, it may have been those differences that drew them together. Levi presented no real challenge to Shiloh, who was vastly superior in a card game, a gunfight, or a social setting. With no serious challenge, Shiloh was free to be himself, and Levi, having no desire to present a challenge, wanted only to learn from him.

It had been a week since Levi had arrived in Waco, and he and Shiloh had become almost inseparable. "It's been a few days since you made your dignified entry into town," Shiloh said. "We've spent most of our time together. Talked about a lot of things, but I don't know much about you." He gave Levi a casual glance. "For example, why were you even in San Antonio and what did you do there? I mean, somehow you survived for a few years." Shiloh paused again, long enough for Levi to respond, but he said nothing. "Since I've been chosen by God, fate, or some other mysterious force to be your protector and educator, I'd kinda like to know a bit more about you."

Levi rose from his chair and walked across the floor of Shiloh's room. He removed his dirty hat and held it in both hands, slowly revolving it. Stopping at a window, he stared into the distance, considering his response. "The woman that I was accused of killing was named Jovita. Yes, she was a Mexican, one that came from an aristocratic family that was way above my social standing. Anyway, she asked me those same questions not long ago," he responded. "First, she told me what she'd observed. That I'm industrious and determined and intelligent. All kinds of personal stuff." In an attempt to lighten the discussion, he decided to attempt humor. "Oh, and she mentioned my good looks and charm."

Shiloh nodded, considering Levi's comments. "Jovita must've had a strange taste in men," he replied, deadpan serious. Levi frowned at the reply, not recognizing Shiloh's attempt to treat humor with humor. Shiloh continued, "Tell me about your childhood, growing up in hell, so to speak."

With little emotion, Levi explained the hard work, the oppressive heat and the bitter cold, the devastating droughts, the crop failures, and the loss of livestock.

"That sounds like farming and ranching," Shiloh said.

"Yeah. I once overheard my father tell my mother that I just wasn't cut out for farming and ranching. Probably, he was right."

"And there weren't any other children to help with the work?"

Levi took a deep breath and then slowly exhaled. "There was a younger brother that was kinda sick a lot of the time. My father mostly ignored 'im, so I took over and taught 'im some things that my father should've taught 'im. Things like how to shoot a gun and ride a horse and skin a deer and such. One day my brother got really sick. My father paid little attention, telling us the boy would recover in a day or two."

"Did he?"

"No. He died. Doctor said his appendix probably got infected and burst. My father wasn't ever the same after that. He just got colder and more uncaring as time passed. He blamed himself."

"Maybe he blamed you."

"Me? That makes no sense."

"Doesn't have to. Sometimes people respond strangely to tragedy. Anyway, your dad never showed much interest, much concern, much love for you. Correct?"

"Pretty much."

For almost a minute, Shiloh sat, leaning back in a chair and staring at the dirt street outside. "That's something we have in common."

"Really? You were…were shunned by your father?" Levi asked.

"Well, we were never close. He wanted to see things in me that just weren't there. Guess I felt rejected."

"I know that feeling," Levi said.

Shiloh was quiet again. He rose and walked about the room. He stopped in front of Levi. "Yeah," he said. "I guess that would make you want to leave." He hesitated and thought again. "But you'd been on that farm for twenty years or so. Must've been something about it you liked." He stopped and ran his finger through his hair, carefully weighing Levi's account of his decision to leave. "Seems like…I don't know. Just doesn't seem to add up, but, hell, it's not important."

"Okay. You're right. There was something else," Levi confessed.

"Thought there was. Might help to talk about it, but that's your decision."

Unblinking, Levi turned to his friend and said, "I killed a man, so I had to leave. One morning I was checking on cattle, way down in a remote corner of the farm, and I found 'im skinning one of our calves. He'd killed it, and he was dressing it, preparing to steal it.

"One thing led to another. He pulled a pistol and fired at me, but missed. He was trying to get off a second shot when I shot him. One shot in the chest. He just sank to the ground, a look of surprise on his face."

"Sounds justified to me," Shiloh said.

"Yeah. Trouble was he was the son of a prominent man in town, a friend of the local sheriff. He'd been in lots of trouble, and the sheriff and a local judge always kinda overlooked his crimes. There were no witnesses. Just my word about what happened. They wouldn't have believed me. If I'd stayed, I'd have been tried and found guilty. I ran."

Shiloh nodded and asked, "After you got to San Antonio, how did you...well, how did you survive? A country boy with few marketable skills? Sounds like a plan for disaster."

Levi sat motionless, silently asking himself how much to reveal. Memories flashed through his mind. For four years he'd worked hand-in-hand with Selina, the owner of the Old Town Saloon, and for much of that time he'd shared her bed. And now, should he reveal that information to a man he'd known for such a short time? No reason not to, he reasoned. He'd violated no trust, no law and no confidence. Starting with the day of his arrival in San Antonio, Levi told his story. Then he sat, staring at the floor, waiting for Shiloh's response.

Nodding his understanding, Shiloh said, "You seemed a bit reluctant to tell that story."

"It's pretty personal, and I'm not proud of parts of it."

"I happen to know Selina," Shiloh said. "She's a lovely woman. A good woman. I have nothing but the highest regard for her. She used to hold high-stakes poker games in her saloon. They were fair, honest games. I participated, of course. Now, as I understand it, she wasn't *with* anyone at the time the two of you connected, and neither were you. So sure, you ended up together. Then, when things changed, you were faithful to Jovita. Now, get rid of the guilt, and move on."

Reassured by Shiloh, Levi described his imprisonment and escape from Sheriff Hammer's jail, the killing of the men in Bandera, and his flight to the Sandifer Ranch. At that point, however, Levi chose to omit significant details, revealing only that the Sandifer family had saved his life. He made no mention of Rachel.

He had feared that the gambler wouldn't take his story seriously, but that hadn't been the case. Shiloh had listened attentively, especially when Levi described the scene in which he killed the two men in The Rose in Bandera. Shiloh had stopped him repeatedly during the story to ask questions and to point out how Levi might have approached the job differently.

Finally, tired of Shiloh's constant badgering, Levi snapped, "You've already told me what you think about my ability with a Colt. If you're so damned good, maybe you could teach me a thing or two."

"I could, but I won't," Shiloh replied, then continued with a seriousness that Levi had seen infrequently. "Texas is changing. It doesn't need more gunfighters and gamblers. Our day is almost over. Believe it or not, I've been educated in some of the best schools my parents could find. I learned to read and write, and a lot more. I know what's happening back east and in the other developed regions of this nation. This country is becoming civilized. Indians are almost gone, as are the buffalo. Look at the changes that are happening as far west as California. I've watched it happen at other places. I've read about it, and I've even seen it myself a time or two. It'll happen here, too. Just be patient. You'll see."

"That's a long time off," Levi observed, unsure of his position but not wanting to acknowledge that Shiloh might be correct.

"Not so long, boy. It'll happen in your lifetime. When your children are our age, this state will bear little resemblance to its present condition."

Now it was Levi's turn to take on a very serious tone. "Let's say you're right, Shiloh. But I've seen you handle a six-gun. There are things you can do that I can't. You could teach me. I can read and write, too, but I don't know a lot about what's happening in other places. So, let's say you're right. If this country's gonna change like you say, then somebody's got to help it change. It won't change by itself. That means driving people like George Tompkins out, sometimes by being better than them with a gun. With your help, maybe I could be a part of that."

"I don't know, Levi. It doesn't seem quite right. I should be helping to civilize this state. Creating more gunmen certainly isn't the way to accomplish that end."

"You're not listening, Shiloh. I don't want to be a gunfighter. I just want a better chance to defend myself and other people, too."

Shiloh stared at Levi, silently considering his argument. "This is the only time I ever plan to lose an argument with you, Levi, but maybe you do have a point. Something tells me that you'll be more than just some worthless gunfighter. There's something about you—kinda spooky, really—something that says maybe you'll amount to something in Texas. You have potential, promise. Yeah, I'll show you a thing or two." Shiloh rubbed his hand across the gray stubble of beard on his chin, seriously questioning the wisdom of his decision. "It's against my better judgment, but I'll do it."

Smiling his appreciation, Levi said, "Thanks, Shiloh, you won't regret this. I won't let you down."

"I certainly hope not." was Shiloh's simple reply.

The two men found a secluded area on the Brazos River where large native pecan trees grew far out over the water and cast deep, cooling shadows on the riverbank. It was a quiet, peaceful place. The chirping of wild birds competed with the constant, raspy songs of cicadas to break the solitude. The sweet, wet smell of summer rose up from the river and floated across the hills and meadows. Back several yards from the river stood a steep dirt embankment, a perfect backstop for an improvised firing range.

"I believe this will be adequate," Shiloh told his student. "But let's look around a bit. Let's make sure your old buddy George Tompkins can't sneak up on us and assassinate us both while we're practicing. Now, that would be embarrassing, wouldn't it?"

"And let's not forget those friends of yours, either. We don't even know what they might look like," Levi replied.

"I would recognize 'em," Shiloh retorted solemnly.

At the beginning of their first lesson, Shiloh fidgeted about nervously, not quite sure how to begin. "Levi," he said. "I have never attempted to teach anybody before. I'm not sure how to do it. Maybe that's why I've tried to avoid it. Anyhow, let's start with what you could call my 'philosophy of survival.' It's nothing revolutionary, just some ideas that I've accumulated over the years. First, if at all possible, avoid a fight. Most of them don't even have to take place.

"Two damned fools, both too stupid to back off. Frequently, you can talk your way out of it. Always try that first. There isn't any sense in killing somebody over nothing. I've even seen men joke and laugh their way out of gunfights. You might try to persuade the other man that a gunfight isn't necessary. Anything's better than a fight, because if you fight, somebody's likely to die. No matter how many times you see it, death's still ugly. Especially if it's yours."

Having introduced Levi to his philosophy about gun fighting, Shiloh proceeded to coach Levi in the techniques of shooting and handling a gun. Levi was amazed at the ease and grace with which Shiloh handled the deadly Colt that he wore at his side. Sometimes it seemed that the gun was an extension of the man's arm. It was a tool of the gambler's trade, and Shiloh had no desire to be average. He had to be one of the best. The same was true of his teaching of Levi. At first uncertain, he soon found his way, and proceeded expertly. Both men took their roles seriously, and they worked well together. Just as Shiloh was a natural teacher, Levi was an enthusiastic student, hungrily absorbing each bit of instruction.

At points in each firing session, Shiloh offered more philosophy. "If you can't avoid a fight—and sometimes you can't—then make certain you have every advantage. It's not always the best shot or the fastest that wins. It might be the coolest, the one who doesn't lose his head and do something stupid. Bravery has much to do with it, too. A man who's fighting for a cause has advantages over one who's not. Being brave is easier for him. Of course, he still might die, but in anything like an even fight, he has my bet."

They sat in the cool evening shade of the trees, Shiloh quietly smoking a cigarette, while Levi tried to remember every detail that Shiloh had told him. Finally, Shiloh decided to conclude his dissertation, saying, "Here's one more thing. Too much is made of speed. People who write those books and stories about gunfights always talk about quick draw. Don't believe it."

Shiloh stuffed his still-smoldering cigarette into soft dirt, extinguishing it. Then tossing it into a small puddle, he turned back to Levi and continued, "Once, I witnessed a gunfight between two cowboys up in Kansas some place. Both were fast, but dreadful shots. They both emptied their guns and never touched each other. Both just turned and walked away, embarrassed I guess. A slower shooter with the ability to hit his target could've killed either, or both, of 'em. Now, Levi, I don't want to hurt your feelings, but you aren't especially fast. Not slow, just not exceptionally fast. But that's okay. You should concentrate on accuracy and skill."

Levi's lessons went on day after day, with Shiloh—accustomed to performing his craft, not teaching it—periodically recalling long forgotten points and adding them to his curriculum. He taught Levi to stand with his feet a comfortable distance apart, preferably about shoulder width. "When you draw your gun," he said, "bend your knees just a little, like you're just beginning to squat. Lean your upper body forward, toward the other man. This will give you balance so that you can move in any direction if necessary.

"Watch every move your adversary makes. Watch his hands. Watch his eyes. Sometimes he'll give himself away with his eyes, but a real professional won't. Instead, he'll use his eyes to mislead you. That's why you have to watch the hands, too. Oh, yes, something else, you cock your revolver while you're taking it from the holster and bring it up to fire. An amateur might wait until his gun is already lined up to cock it. Don't do that. It'll cost you precious seconds and probably get you killed.

"Watch out for an inexperienced gunfighter. A professional's dangerous, but I was always more afraid of some scared beginner, some kid. Many times a professional will look you over and decide you aren't worth the risk. He won't receive any pleasure from killing you, so why take a chance? Unless it's some case like your friend George. But there's no predicting what a beginner will do. As likely as not, after you think everything's over, he might pull his gun and shoot you, in the back usually. You just can't be careful enough. Most gunfighters die when they least expect it. Then again, everybody does."

It became routine for the two men to end each class by unloading their Colts and simulating a gunfight. These encounters allowed Levi an opportunity to put Shiloh's theories into practice. Levi quickly learned what it was like to stand face to face with a would-be killer. Occasionally, in the middle of these mock battles, Shiloh stopped and suggested improvements to Levi's technique. Mostly, however, he smiled and congratulated himself for doing a good job of teaching.

Shiloh often found himself puzzling over the position he was in. Here he was, one of the most successful gamblers in Texas, teaching an awkward, still-growing kid how to handle a gun. Why was he doing it? Why waste precious time that could be better spent in pursuit of a full house or a royal flush? Sometimes he had an eerie feeling that he was an unwilling pawn in some supernatural plan that he could neither understand nor change. He didn't buy into such things, but he wondered.

Twenty-nine days after his instruction had begun, Shiloh declared his efforts a success. Levi certainly wasn't the greatest or the fastest gunfighter in the West, but he was a far cry from what he'd been a few weeks earlier. If he kept his head, Levi could prevail over most adversaries, even most professional ones.

If Shiloh hadn't figured out why he was training Levi, Levi knew why. Aware that one day he would confront George Tompkins, he wanted to be ready. But there were other reasons, too. He remembered the stories that Rachel and Oscar had told about the growing cancer in central Texas—the crime wave created by the Buzzard's Water Hole Gang—and he knew that one day he would return to face that problem, which would require all the skills that Shiloh could give him.

Chapter 14

Ever a student of human behavior, Shiloh often had observed that active men suffer greatly when forced into inactivity. Certainly, that was a condition he was seeing in Levi, and he could feel it himself. The training of Levi had developed into an obsession for both men, providing an easy outlet for directed energies, as both men labored toward a common goal. But now that goal had been reached, and the two were restless.

Perhaps the inactivity was most difficult for Levi. For weeks he had used a succession of crises as distractions from his sorrow over Jovita's death. Then he complicated the situation by falling in love with Rachel and adding a burden of self-imposed guilt to his existing sorrow. Physically and emotionally exhausted upon his arrival in Waco, Levi had gained strength and self-confidence from Shiloh's successful instruction. But now that was over, and Levi felt himself falling back into depression. He desperately needed a new distraction, a cause, a mission.

Shiloh watched Levi's tormented emotional struggle with growing concern. He had no way of knowing that Levi was struggling to resolve his guilt concerning his love for both Jovita and Rachel, because Levi had chosen not to reveal it. Therefore, Shiloh mistakenly concluded that his young student simply was trying to rid himself of the painful memories of his beloved Jovita. To Shiloh, the facts were clear. Both men needed a change of location.

"Levi," Shiloh began cautiously, "I've been here too long. Men like me can't stay in one place. We keep moving on. Maybe we think a moving target is harder to hit. Also, harder to find.

Things will still be too hot for me down in San Antone, so that's out. Even Austin would be a mite warm. I thought I might wander up toward the Panhandle for a while. Maybe look up some old friends. Maybe even make some new ones. And I've gotten rather accustomed to having you around. How about coming along with me?"

Levi gave Shiloh a questioning look and then asked, "Why would things be hot for you in San Antonio? I know you won a bunch of money, but lots of people have done that."

Shiloh pretended to consider Levi's argument. "It's as I mentioned earlier," he said. "There are hired guns waiting to kill me and recover the money I won."

Levi persisted. "Naw. Been too long. Men like that'll go on to the next job before now. I don't think that's a problem."

Shiloh's plan wasn't working as well as he had hoped. Maybe he should try a new approach. "Well, what about George Tompkins?" he countered. "You've been here awhile. Surely, he's getting close to finding you by now."

"Might be, and I don't particularly want him to locate me here in Waco. There's too many places for him to ambush me here in town. Still, I don't know, Shiloh. It kind of seems to me that you're holding out on me. You're not telling me everything."

Shiloh took tobacco and paper from his shirt pocket and slowly rolled a cigarette. Holding it between his right thumb and index finger, he studied it carefully. With great deliberation he lit it and inhaled deeply. Turning toward Levi, he said, "You're getting pretty observant for a country boy. Yes, there was more to my leaving San Antone than I've told you.

"You see, I didn't know much about you at first. Didn't seem smart to tell the whole story. I'm sorry about that. Truth is, I killed two men in that card game I told you about. Oh, I won the money fair and square, but those two fools objected. Said I was cheating. Well, I wasn't, but they kept accusing me. I guess they couldn't afford to lose the money, so they decided to take it back. It turned out they were from prominent families. Killing them wasn't real smart. I left there in a hurry, and it seems about time for me to leave again. I suspect the same is true for you."

"I wondered about your story. Seemed a bit…well, made-up. So it looks like we've got more in common than you'd like to admit. Both of us are running from the law," Levi replied smugly.

Shiloh attempted to change the subject back to the Panhandle. "How about it, Levi? I know there's something back down south that's pulling on you. I've been watching you. I know you've been punishing yourself about the death of that woman in San Antone. I can't understand why, but you seem to want to go back down there. They'll hang you for certain, my friend, but that's your decision. It just seems that it can wait a few weeks, or months even. I'll bet you've never seen the Panhandle, the Llano Estacado they call it. Flattest place you've ever seen. Just like the top of a table. Then you come upon this deep, rocky gorge down the middle of it. Seems completely out of place. That's the Palo Duro Canyon. The last stand of the Comanche Indians. Man, it's a sight. Hard. Unforgiving. Beautiful in its own way. A person should see it at least once in his life.

"Besides, I know a rancher or two up there. Ol' Charlie Goodnight occasionally came to San Antone and gambled a bit. Mostly small stuff. Too smart to bet big. He knew he was no gambler, but he enjoyed the social activity that goes with it. We never were exactly buddies, but he'll remember me. He'd give us a job, if we wanted to try cow-punching." Shiloh frowned and rolled is eyes skyward. "Personally, I have no desire to mess with those contrary, stinking beasts.

"I'll tell you this, though. Charlie can tell you all you want to know about that part of Texas. In fact, he knows the entire state, and he knows the Comanche Indians. Knows some of them personally—Quanah Parker, for example. He once was a Texas Ranger. Charlie would love to tell you about his adventures. That is, if he's still there. Heard he was thinking about leaving the Palo Duro. I think he's getting his fill of his arrogant British partner. And I thought I might check out a few saloons up there and maybe stir up a card game or two."

Levi looked around himself, pretending to be considering Shiloh's proposal. "Well, it's not a trip I was planning, but I guess I don't have a better offer. Maybe I can spare a few weeks. George's gonna find me wherever I am, and I sure can't go back to San Antonio right now. Okay, I'll take a look at that strange country you talk about. And while I haven't had the privilege to know Mr. Goodnight personally, like some people have, I've heard about him." Levi smiled at Shiloh. Shiloh returned the smile and looked away, shaking his head. Levi continued, now more seriously, "Yeah, Shiloh, Goodnight's one man I'd like to talk to. If you want to go north, let's do it."

At last! Once again there was purpose in their lives, so they set about making arrangements for the journey. In no real hurry, the two men decided to wait for just the right moment to leave. Two days later, one of the late summer rainstorms blew in from the West. Under the cover of darkness, they left Waco, taking an obscure road northward and feeling safe in the knowledge that the steady downpour soon would erase their tracks.

For the next few days they traveled steadily northward, picking their way along old wagon roads and cattle trails. For the most part, they avoided ranch houses and small towns, making human contact only when it was necessary to secure supplies. Sometimes, when conditions allowed it, they traveled at night to further obscure their presence. Usually, they traveled slowly, often taking detours to avoid suspicious areas, or sometimes to view an area that Shiloh remembered from years past and wanted his companion also to experience. There was a distinct strangeness to their journey. On one hand, they were fugitives, sought by both those within and those outside the law. On the other, they were carefree explorers, retracing the routes of early-day pathfinders and experiencing the lust for adventure enjoyed by the likes of Jim Bowie and Sam Houston.

As they worked their way across Texas, Shiloh kept up a steady narrative of his version of the history of the territory they were passing through. He'd heard a thousand stories of Indian wars from visitors to the gaming tables of San Antonio. Many of the older ranchers, as well as army veterans, actually had lived through those wars, and most of them loved to tell about their experiences, both real and imagined.

During his earlier travels across the state, Shiloh had visited many of the old battlegrounds and had seen firsthand examples of the inhumanity displayed by both Indians and white men during the struggle for the Texas frontier. Shiloh clinched his jaw, and his face darkened as he explained to Levi how the United States government had pulled most Union troops out of Texas during the Civil War, leaving the settlers along the frontier to fend for themselves.

"True," he conceded quietly, as if debating with himself, "Texas *did* become a Confederate state, and the Confederacy did little to protect the settlers on the frontier. And it has been argued that the abandonment did lead to a new spirit of self-reliance on the part of the white settlers, but the bastards on both sides didn't seem to care." Shiloh then solemnly went on to observe that with the soldiers gone, the Comanche and their Kiowa allies realized their opportunity. As a result, these nomadic horsemen of the plains murdered, looted, and burned across the entire frontier. Many settlers were taken captive to be tortured, enslaved, or ransomed back to civilization, and thousands of Indians were murdered in revenge.

Determined as they were, the Indians were doomed to eventual failure, beaten by superior numbers and superior technology, not to mention the lying and double-dealing of the government. Perhaps the final death knell was sounded by the buffalo hunters who came with their deadly single shot, large-caliber Sharps rifles, killing buffalo at long range, usually taking nothing but the hides.

"I once got into a friendly card game with an old buffalo hunter in one of the gambling houses down in San Antone," Shiloh said. "He swore to me that he once came upon an open pasture where some hide hunters had worked two or three days before. Now, I didn't see the sight myself, but he claimed he came over a small hill and looked down on hundreds of dead, bloated buffalo. Nothing missing but their hides."

Shiloh stopped his narration, a scowl crossing his face as he pictured the scene in his mind. Then he continued, "Imagine the waste in that. And the smell was so bad that he couldn't stand it. Scared his horse nearly out of its wits. He said big, ugly, red-headed buzzards were everywhere. The sky was almost dark with the creatures. They were camped on top of every carcass. You could hear the wind hiss through their wings as they sailed just overhead. Some were so full of rotten meat they could barely fly. Enough to make a grown man sick." Shiloh shook his head in disgust, and then he continued. "Seeing sights like this, the plains tribes finally buried some of the long-standing distrust of one another and organized a resistance against this latest scourge, the buffalo hunter, but they were too late. At this point, they couldn't turn back the tide of invading whites."

Shiloh sat in his saddle and looked across the prairie at some imaginary buffalo herd. Reaching into his breast pocket, he pulled out tobacco and paper and rolled a cigarette. He lit it and carefully disposed of the smoking match. Levi watched the blue cloud of smoke rise quickly above Shiloh's head and then disappear into the atmosphere. "The buffalo slaughter," Shiloh said. "Now that's an event every Texan—no, every American—ought to know about. Especially you, Levi."

"Why especially me?"

"It's a gambler's business to evaluate people," Shiloh replied. "Can't help it. I just do it. I see something in you. I call it 'potential.' You don't have much formal education, so you need to learn every way you can. Now, we can't return to the time of the buffalo, but we can learn *about* it and learn *from* it."

"And I'd bet you're gonna tell me about it," Levi said.

"I'll try. Trouble is, I don't know that I fully understand it myself."

"What? Now how could that be?" Levi replied, his voice rising in mock disbelief. "You're telling me there's something about this country you don't understand?"

Shiloh hid a smile and ignored Levi's insult, pleased that his young companion felt comfortable enough to ridicule him. Few men would dare. "It was a conspiracy, really," Shiloh finally remarked. "You see, there were two herds. One to the south and one to the north. An imaginary line divided the two. An Indian agent told me once that some railroad divided the two, but I'm not sure. He was more than a little bit drunk at the time. The way I understand it, two or three years after the Civil War ended, the Sioux tribe signed a treaty that gave them and their friends exclusive hunting rights to all the buffalo north of the Platte River. Now, I suppose you're familiar with the Platte."

"I know where the Platte is," Levi lied. "I'm not stupid."

"Oh, no. Course you aren't," Shiloh said apologetically. "I didn't mean that."

"Well, it sounded like it."

Shiloh smiled and said, "Anyway, the treaty gave those Indians exclusive hunting rights in the north. My storyteller said that the words of the treaty said it would last 'as long as grass grows and water runs.'"

Suddenly interested, Levi turned his head quickly toward Shiloh, his mouth hanging open in surprise. "It said that? The treaty said that?"

"Well, I haven't read it, but I doubt it. My storyteller may have had it confused with some other treaty."

"I'll be damned," Levi said, shaking his head slowly. He was silent for a minute. Then he continued, "And what about the southern herd?"

"Oh, there were treaties there, too, but nobody paid any attention to 'em. The white hunters descended on the southern herd like a bunch of coyotes after a crippled goat. In less than ten years that army of cold-blooded assassins wiped out the entire southern herd. Probably weren't a hundred buffalo left in the entire state of Texas. A few years before there had been millions."

"What then?"

"Different things. Some of the hunters stayed on and homesteaded. Some worked for the big ranchers that were moving in. Some of 'em went home, wherever that was."

"And the others?"

"I suppose some of 'em packed their Sharps and Remington buffalo guns and went north, hoping to find a few more buffalo."

"What about that treaty with the Sioux?"

"Now why would *that* treaty be anymore important than any other one? Surely you don't believe those sons of bitches gave a damn about some agreement with a bunch of filthy Indians. And this is what I meant about a conspiracy, Levi. The army and the government were supposed to protect the buffalo for the Indians—all of 'em, north as well as south—but they didn't. Didn't even try. Know what I think? I think some high-ranking generals and government people got together and decided to let the hunters kill all the buffalo. Then the Indians would have no choice. They'd have to leave the plains and accept life on the reservations. Otherwise, they'd starve. Of course, the soldiers weren't the only ones that wanted the Indians and the buffalo off the range. Ranchers and farmers did, too, but mostly I blame the army and the government. Bastards."

Levi rode on in silence for several minutes. Finally, he looked over at Shiloh and said, "I suppose there's a lesson for me in all of that."

"Well, do you see one?"

After a minute's consideration, Levi replied, "Awful lot of destruction for not much gain. I mean all those buffalo gone for nothing."

"Some would say it opened up the West for white settlers."

"Yeah. There's that."

They'd been riding silently for perhaps an hour, when Levi broke the silence. "So you think I have potential?"

The question caught Shiloh by surprise. "Well, yes. You're smart, and you learn fast. You do have potential."

"Potential to do what?"

"There's a place for you out there. I don't know what it is, but it's there. My job, I believe, is to keep you alive and to educate you. I'd like to think I'm not just wasting my time. Now, your job is to learn as much as you can. Learn what happened here. Mistakes that were made. Learn how to keep from repeating 'em. Also, learn about ranching and about farming. About government and how it works and how it doesn't work and how it *should* work. We can do better. You can be part of that, a big part of it. Just stay alive. And learn."

"Okay, but the Indians are gone now."

"Not entirely. This state—hell, this nation—will be dealing with them for decades to come. Probably for centuries. To do that, we need to understand 'em. Understand as much as we can, I mean. It'll be up to you and others like you to decide what their place will be. That's why I continue to enthrall you with my fascinating stories."

Levi smiled at Shiloh's last remark. "You *do* tell a good story," he said.

As the men continued their northward trek, Levi was amazed at the constant change in the geography of the land. Although he had seen some of Texas, most of his travels had been confined to the southern half of the state. The transition from tree-covered, rolling hills to flat, treeless prairie was complete and unexpected. Levi hadn't been completely confined to his father's small ranch. In his efforts to scratch out a living, his father traveled on short trips in the areas around San Antonio, buying and selling horses and cattle, and sometimes Levi got to tag along.

A few years later, having left home to seek his fortune, he learned that his fortune was as hard to find in San Antonio as it had been in Poteet. Although it wasn't the perfect career, he took a job doing odd jobs at the Old Town Tavern in the Mexican part of the city. After proving his honesty and his worth, he was given the job of transporting freight between the city and the numerous small settlements in the area. It was a job of considerable responsibility, and it allowed him to be outside in the Texas air, suffering the stifling heat of summer and the frequent cold, wet storms of winter. With this occupation he had the opportunity to venture even farther from the city, sometimes hauling merchandise north and west into the post oak savanna country of Lampasas, San Saba, and Brady.

His early education involved more than weather and terrain. As a freighter, Levi developed judgment and caution that would serve him well in later years. Bandits and small, roving bands of desperados were scattered throughout the backcountry. Mostly, these were little more than scavengers who preyed on the livestock of area landowners. However, sometimes they sought out bigger stakes and attempted to rob a bank, a train, or a freight wagon. For this reason, he learned to recognize potential trouble spots on his routes, frequently taking detours around problem areas. If more than one route to a destination was available, he would take alternate routes, carefully avoiding any pattern to his actions.

Levi's early travels had prepared him well for his present journey. He knew what it was like to suffer through rough Texas weather. He also was prepared for changes in the climate, geography, and vegetation, as he rode out of Waco northward into the Cross Timbers. However, he was mildly surprised when he and Shiloh rode past Jacksboro into the flat, open grasslands of north Texas. It was late summer, nearly autumn, and the evening air sometimes was brisk and cool.

Late one evening after a long day on the trail, Levi was preparing camp in the shelter of a small grove of stunted hackberry trees when Shiloh came riding up at a gallop. "Come with me!" he shouted. "There's something I want you to see!"

The two men rode about half a mile to one of the few small hills in the vicinity. They ascended the east slope of the hill and were at its crest within seconds. Dropping off before them and extending almost as far to the west as the eye could see lay an open, flat, virtually treeless plain—a sea of grass. The plain was populated with hundreds, perhaps thousands, of cattle of every description.

The sun was sinking and darkness was upon them as Shiloh and Levi viewed the vast herd of cattle. A soft breeze blew in their faces, carrying with it the musty, pungent odor of the animals. Far off in the distance, well out of sight, a lone coyote yapped several times and then was answered from several different locations miles to the north. The only other sound was the soft lowing of the cattle on the prairie before them.

In the gathering darkness each animal lost its identity and appeared only as a large, dark, living object. After a silence of several minutes, Shiloh asked his companion, "As a child did you have a vivid imagination?"

"Vivid imagination?" Levi asked, trying to anticipate Shiloh's thoughts.

"Yes. Were you a dreamer? Did you pretend to be someone you were not? Maybe an explorer or somebody you never met, but learned about in school. Somebody you admired. I know I did. My dreams were really strange. I dreamed about being a pirate and traveling around the world and seeing strange places and people."

"Yeah. Me too. I used to dream I was a trapper in Canada or Alaska or some place. I don't think I knew just where it was. A place I've never been. I imagined the high, snowcapped mountains. The streams. The pine trees. The Indians. I remember dreaming about Indian girls. Of course, they were all beautiful."

"That's what I mean. Visualization. I want you to visualize, to imagine now. Think you can still do it?"

"I suppose I can do that. But why?"

"Well, before you, you can see both the past and the future of this state. Use that imagination we talked about, and those animals down there become buffalo, the life blood that sustained the Comanche and Kiowa and other mounted Indians for centuries. Now keep imagining and look again and see them as cattle, and you see the animal that will earn and lose fortunes long after you and I are dead."

Levi did as his mentor suggested, and indeed he could imagine a large herd of buffalo, extending beyond the far horizon. Casting himself even more into a trance, he could visualize a band of nearly naked Indians on wildly decorated paint horses, closing in from the west, intent on securing meat for the winter. He saw the Indian braves racing along beside the stampeding herd, dropping buffalo after buffalo. He heard their loud cries of success and disappointed exclamations of disgust when a shot was missed and a buffalo escaped. He felt the warm exhilaration of pride expressed by a successful brave and the dismal feeling of failure suffered by one who hadn't been so fortunate. After the dust had cleared, the women and children appeared out of nowhere, expertly taking the hides and carving huge pieces of meat to be sliced and dried in the sun.

"Well," Shiloh said. "Did it work?"

"Yeah. I think I did a good job of picturing what a buffalo hunt would look like."

Shiloh smiled with satisfaction. "I can't tell you how many times I've ridden across a piece of open range and imagined what it must have looked like when buffalo were everywhere," he said.

Snapping back to the present, Levi asked, "Whose are they? The buffalo. No, I mean the cattle."

"Don't know for certain. Gotta belong to Dan Waggoner's outfit. Nobody else has that many cattle in one bunch. Not around here, anyway. Dan came out here several years back and made peace with the Comanche. Somehow their truce has held and he's still alive."

There was almost total darkness as they rode their horses

slowly back to camp, each man lost in his own personal thoughts about the primitive culture that so recently had dominated this wild country, but that now had disappeared forever. Long after he had eaten supper and curled up in his blankets for the night, Levi pondered his strange experience. After a long period of restless meditation, he drifted off to sleep, but it wasn't as restful as he'd hoped. Instead of sleeping quietly under his warm blanket, he tossed about, sleeping for short periods, and then waking cold and tired. After repeating this pattern for a good part of the night and early morning, he rose from his bed and sat with the blanket over his back and shoulders.

A three-quarter moon hung in the western sky, bathing the night in an eerie half-light. Levi listened to the sounds of the night, still trying to find the rest that he wanted. Somewhere in the distance he heard the soft hooting of an owl. Smiling to himself, he whispered, "Those things must be in every corner of this state."

Back toward the small hill he and Shiloh had climbed, Levi heard the lowing of Dan Waggoner's cattle. It was gentle and peaceful, nothing disturbing about that. As he sat, still as a statue, a half-grown bobcat crept through the shadows, periodically stopping and sniffing, a predator careful to avoid a larger predator, such as a hungry mountain lion.

Levi heard Horse whinny, but it wasn't a typical whinny. It was harsher and deeper—more a snort, an expression not exactly of fear but maybe of interest, signaling that things weren't as perfect as they might seem. Almost immediately, Shiloh's horse nervously stamped his front feet. Horse did the same. Levi sensed that he was witnessing a smoldering, uneasy peace, one that seemed able to explode into violence, but what was it?

"This deserves some looking into," Levi said, again speaking softly. "Not impossible that somebody might be messing around out there." Rising slowly, blanket still around his shoulders, he buckled his Colt around his waist and grabbed his Henry rifle. Silently, he crept in the direction of the horses.

As Levi approached, both horses turned their heads toward him, acknowledging his presence. Then both turned back toward the hill, staring in the distance with ears forward and every sense alert. "Okay," Levi said, hoping the sound of his voice would reassure the horses, "I'm as curious as you are. I'll take a look."

Crouching low, Levi moved from bush to bush, working his way toward the crest of the hill that overlooked the cattle. Reaching the top, he found a cluster of wild plum bushes, and he settled behind them, searching the distant landscape. For about fifteen minutes, he watched the cattle below, mostly bedded down and apparently sleeping. He was certain that no humans were about.

He waited for another half hour. A pair of coyotes appeared in an open spot on the far side of the cattle herd, sitting on their haunches and watching the animals. After a time, the coyotes suddenly jumped up, turned abruptly, and trotted away, leaving the cattle undisturbed.

Levi smiled to himself. "If those beasts had really been the buffalo I imagined yesterday, I'd say those coyotes were waiting to come down and clean up whatever the Indians left." He thought for a moment. "Anyway, they left in a hurry."

Rising to return to camp, Levi turned to his left and stopped in mid-stride, unable to believe what he was seeing. Not more than sixty feet away, sitting on its haunches like its coyote relatives, a large gray dog was watching him. The animal stared through yellow eyes, panting with its tongue hanging out and saliva dripping from its mouth. The slight breeze ruffled its silver-gray coat, making it look even larger than it was.

That's not a dog, Levi thought. Not a domestic dog. Neither was it a coyote. It could be only one thing. It was a gray wolf. A lobo. But how could that be? Ranchers had made war on them years earlier, declaring them unwelcome in a modern world. As a result, wolves were shot on sight, trapped, and poisoned to a point approaching extinction, at least in Texas. But could a solitary individual have survived? Apparently so.

As Levi watched, the wolf rose and took another long look at him. Then it turned and trotted along the crest of the hill, weaving in and out through the brush and scrubby trees. At a high point on a ridge, it stopped and looked back in Levi's direction. For just a moment the wolf stood still in the fading moonlight. "That's a beautiful animal," Levi said, this time not bothering to whisper. In an instant the wolf was gone.

Levi walked noiselessly back into camp and crawled into his blankets. In a few moments he was asleep, peacefully dreaming about the mysterious wolf.

Chapter 15

Levi opened his eyes, stretched and rose up on his elbows. The sun already was peeking over the eastern horizon. A small fire was burning, and a soot-covered coffee pot sat on a rock in the edge of the fire. Arising slowly, he walked over to the campfire and poured himself a cup of strong black coffee. He sat back, sipping his coffee and enjoying its pleasant aroma, as he watched Shiloh ride slowly up to the camp.

"I thought maybe you were going to sleep all day," the gambler remarked.

"Sounds like a good idea. Where've you been?"

"Back up on that ridge we climbed last night, watching our back trail. Just watching for your friend. Or mine."

"See anything?"

"Nope. Didn't expect to."

"Why did you go then?"

"Well, I could've been wrong. I didn't live this long being careless. It's something you might consider."

Levi knew his companion was right. He had become far too careless in recent days, assuming that his increased distance from central Texas provided adequate security. He was well aware of the error in this thinking. Of one thing he was convinced: His trail would cross George's again, and he had to be ready. Silently, he vowed not to make the same mistake again. He and Shiloh had scarcely traveled three hours when they saw four small hills in an almost straight line running roughly northwest by southeast. In a geological sense, the hills were insignificant, each one rising less than a hundred feet above the floor of the prairie. The significance was that they were seemingly out of place, being virtually the only natural objects disrupting the even flow of the land.

Reining in his horse and looking toward the hills, Shiloh asked, "You've heard of the Medicine Mounds?" Levi looked quizzically toward the source of the question. Without waiting for a reply, Shiloh continued, "Well, now you've seen them."

"What are they?" Levi asked, obviously unimpressed.

"Now they're just hills, but once they were a place of importance and mystery for the Comanche Indians. For one thing, there are plants up there that the Indians use for medicine. There's more. Those hills held great mystical powers—kind of spiritual medicine. A young brave would climb up there on one of those hills and stay two, three, four days without food or water, trying to have a vision. A vision was necessary for him to become a man, a warrior. After a period of suffering, he'd start seeing things, imagining things. Maybe some of those plants growing in the area helped. I'd guess that more than one of 'em invented a good vision to avoid looking like a fool to his friends.

"Anyway, he'd come down and tell the tribe about his vision. If it was believable, he'd be accepted as a warrior. I don't know what happened if he wasn't believed. I guess he'd be required to do the same thing all over again."

"What was the purpose of this vision stuff? This medicine?" Levi asked.

"Have you ever heard of a 'rite of passage'?"

"I've never heard of most of the things you talk about."

"Well, as I said before, it was his ticket into the tribe as a full-fledged member. He could hunt. He could steal from his enemies. He could kill. But it was more than that. It was a religious experience. In his vision, a brave might see an eagle. After that the eagle took on extra importance to him. It was his inspiration.

At least in his mind it protected him, looked after him. In a sense he worshipped it."

"And you believe all that?"

"I don't know. I certainly don't ridicule it, though. There's a lot we don't know. Maybe Indians have a different god, or maybe God has a different bargain with the Comanche. The same could be said of the Apache, the Cheyenne, and all the others."

"Maybe so."

"It's important to learn about these people. For the most part, they're gone now, but their heritage lives on. I would like to see it live on for centuries to come. Ever since they walked out of the mountains onto these plains and traded for their first horses—probably out in New Mexico—they've been a force to reckon with. They were majestic, and they were terrible. In some ways they were like children, but they could be cruel, murderously cruel. They had a well-developed culture, a way of life that was both simple and complex. Not more than thirty years ago, they ruled half of Texas. They had been the undisputed rulers of this land for maybe a hundred years before that. Who knows how long, for sure? I certainly don't. A few years from now, your children and your grandchildren will read about how these people lived and died out here. You can tell 'em about it. You can make sure they learn it right, being fair to both sides."

Shiloh's stories about the plight of the Comanche and other nomadic Indians of the plains were troubling to Levi. The gambler had expressed a point of view that was unfamiliar to Levi. In early years, he'd been filled with much different stories, stories of atrocities committed by cruel savages, horrible beings that more closely resembled animals than humans. In contrast, Shiloh described them as a civilization of intelligent, sometimes noble humans who loved their children and cared for their families. In his view they wanted nothing more than to be left alone to live their lives as they had lived them since the introduction of the horse into their culture.

But Shiloh's stories about Indians and the atrocities they'd suffered were not the only events troubling him. His memories frequently returned to the gray wolf that had visited him a few days earlier. He wasn't even sure the animal was real. He'd been tired and sleepy at the time, so maybe he'd imagined everything. He'd considered that possibility several times, and each time he'd reached the same conclusion. The wolf was real. So why was the wolf there? In his mind, Levi was certain the animal had approached him intentionally. It didn't just wander upon a man with a gun. There had to be more to its actions. Finally, he reached a conclusion. Probably, it had never seen a white man before, and it was simply curious. Once the animal recognized Levi as a man, it wisely left. Nothing more.

Smiling at the simplicity of the conclusion, Levi whispered to himself, "One thing's sure. I'll never see it again."

Deep in thought as he tried to unravel the mysteries of past events, Levi was paying little attention to his direction of travel, aware only that his horse was following the lead set by Shiloh. Startled by his own lack of concentration, Levi looked all around but found only confusion. He stopped his horse and again carefully surveyed his surroundings, but still the confusion persisted.

Clearly, they had abandoned the wagon road that they had been traveling all day. Levi didn't know exactly when they did it. The main trail lay somewhat north of due west. With the early afternoon sun glaring ruthlessly at him, Levi could easily distinguish directions. He wasn't mistaken. Instead of continuing toward the west, Shiloh had chosen an alternate route, one that almost paralleled the main trail for some distance, but gradually branched off to the north.

"The bastard's doing it on purpose," Levi muttered under his breath. "Wonder what he's up to?" Levi had noticed early the previous evening that Shiloh was paying especially close attention to prominent landmarks along the trail. Today, by midmorning the gambler was so absorbed in the geography of the country that he noticed little else. Several times Levi had considered confronting his friend about his preoccupation with the countryside, but each time he decided against it.

"Guess he'll tell me when he's ready," Levi muttered again. This time Shiloh heard Levi speak, but couldn't understand any of his words.

"Sorry, did you have something to say?" Shiloh asked.

"Just talking to myself," Levi remarked. "Kind of wondering where you're going and what you're doing. Figured you'd eventually get around to telling me."

Shiloh gave a barely visible start and then grinned an embarrassed grin, somewhat surprised that Levi had noticed. Bringing his horse to a complete halt, the gambler withdrew the familiar "makings" and carefully rolled a cigarette. Placing one end of the cigarette between his lips, he cupped his hands around the other, and lit it. Levi watched the end of the cigarette begin to glow and the smoke slowly rise, understanding that he was watching the gambler play out his most effective diversionary tactic. Finally, Shiloh said, "Well, to be quite frank, I was trying to rediscover some long-forgotten landmarks. I guess I was practicing a bit of deception. I was trying to search without it being apparent. I hoped you wouldn't notice."

"Hell, I'm not blind or stupid. I've been outta the house a few times. The main trail's over yonder half a mile or more," Levi replied, gesturing wildly.

Shiloh nodded. "Yes. I'm aware. Here, let me explain. A few years ago I met a family of homesteaders out here. Lived with 'em a few weeks, maybe months. Helped plow. Milked a cow every morning. Did all those civilized chores. They were honest people, poor as dirt, trying to scratch an existence from an unforgiving prairie. Let's see. There was a man and his wife and three little kids, all in a row and about a year apart. Probably more than three now, at the rate they were going. Kaufman was their family name. He was Ernest, and she was Libby, for Elizabeth I suppose. And there were their rowdy boys."

Shiloh said nothing for a while, apparently lost in memories of time spent with this family. Restless to hear more and wanting to break an uncomfortable silence, Levi asked, "How did you come to know these folks?"

Drawing tobacco smoke deeply into his lungs, Shiloh slowly exhaled. "Oh, kind of an accident, I suppose. Like so many things that occur in life." There was another pause, this one shorter. "Actually, I was in a bit of legal difficulty at the time. I'd been in Fort Worth, as I recall. Playing poker and living the good life. A fellow there, an awful poker player, objected to the way I dealt the cards. Ordinarily, this sort of thing isn't much of a problem, but this time it was a close friend of the sheriff who complained. A lady friend found out that I was about to be arrested, and she warned me."

"And so you left?" Levi finished.

Shiloh smiled and nodded as he recalled the incident. "I had little choice. If I'd been arrested, my fine would've been whatever money I had on me. I happened to be carrying almost eighteen-thousand-dollars. It was easier to leave. Also cheaper."

"Yeah. I see your point. How did you wind up here?"

"I left Fort Worth at night and headed west. Seems like I do that a lot. I wandered around out here for a few days, mostly lost. I just happened onto the Kaufman's place. Divine providence, I've always said. I probably wasn't being pursued, but

I thought I was."

Levi wasn't quite ready to buy the story. "Gamblers don't exactly blend into the scenery out here, Shiloh. I've seen how most gamblers dress, you'll remember."

"Give me some credit, my friend. When I travel out into the wilderness—so to speak—I don't travel as a gambler. Like you said, we don't blend into the scenery. Under those conditions I take on the character of the common cowboy. Look at what I'm wearing now. Too many people expect gamblers to be carrying money, whether they are or not. Anyway, I just wandered onto the Kaufman's farm, and they welcomed me without question. From my behavior they probably thought I was an escaped criminal or something, but they never asked. Later, I told 'em, of course."

"So you just hid out here until the problem blew over?" Levi asked.

Again nodding his agreement, Shiloh said, "Yes, that's essentially correct, but actually there was more to it than that. I grew to admire Ernest. He worked hard. He was honest, and he genuinely loved his family, especially Libby. He adored her, and it was easy to see why. She had nothing out here, but she never complained. Just a tiny dugout house. Hot in the summer and cold in the winter. Plain clothes. Simple food and never really enough of it. Certainly not enough water to stay clean like a woman wants. In all this, the only thing she wanted was to please Ernest and the boys. That was her purpose in life."

The two horsemen rode on down a faint road toward a line of trees that apparently marked the margin of a stream. Along each side of the road grew thickets of wild plums, much too dense and tangled for a man to walk through. Somewhere within the thicket a mocking bird was lifting a crystal-clear voice in song. As if in concert, other birds, many of which Levi couldn't identify, joined in and contributed their own voices to the efforts of the mocking bird. The result was a discordant combination of sounds that somehow gave the impression of harmony.

"Actually, I had to leave," Shiloh said. "I watched this close family desperately trying to beat the odds. Happy. Contented. I had to leave." He looked at Levi, hoping to make the younger man understand. "I grew jealous. I envied Ernest. I wished I had his life, his family, and, yes, his wife. Yet I wished him no harm. I just wanted what he had, but I realized it was something I could never have. Not me, the footloose gambler. So I left. I planned never to return, but it appears that I have."

Indeed, Shiloh was about to return. As the two men rode along, casually talking about Shiloh's earlier visit to the Kaufman's farm, they rounded a bend in the road, and Shiloh came face to face with the past. Dominating a small clearing, surrounded by large post oak trees, stood a log cabin, standing out from its stark surroundings, simple yet somehow beautiful.

Eyes wide and mouth half open, Shiloh reined his horse to a stop. He stared in disbelief. This was not the way he remembered it. Where was the crude dugout? It was one of the few times Levi ever saw his friend taken completely by surprise. As the two men stood staring at the scene, a woman stepped out of the house and stood on the porch, waiting for the men to approach. She held an old Winchester rifle loosely in her left hand.

As Shiloh and Levi walked their horses closer to the house, the woman brought the Winchester up across her chest and placed her right hand around the grip, finger on the trigger. She cocked the hammer. "That's far enough!" she called out. "State your business!"

Shiloh looked over at Levi, surprise still showing on his face. "Libby!" he shouted. "It's Shiloh! You remember me?"

"Shiloh! My God, Shiloh! Is it really you?" she cried. Laying the rifle aside, she jumped from the front porch and raced toward the two men. Reaching Shiloh, who had dismounted and was standing beside his horse, she leaped at him, throwing her arms around his neck and holding him tightly. She clung to him, sobbing and laughing simultaneously. After a while she turned loose and slid down his body to stand on the ground. "My, how I needed to see a friend," she sighed.

"Looks like more than a friend to me," Levi murmured to himself.

"This is a rather elaborate dwelling," Shiloh observed. "What happened to the dugout?"

"Ernest thought it wasn't enough," she said. "I thought it was all right, but not him. He built this house a year or two ago. Cut the logs himself. Did everything."

Turning his eyes to the boys who now stood on the porch near the open doorway, Shiloh said, "Looks like those guys are doing well. Growing like weeds. Who's the youngster?"

"That's Seth, our youngest. Born after you left. Seth is everybody's favorite, I guess. His older brothers look after him like you wouldn't believe. Ernest said he was the smartest kid he'd ever seen."

"Where is Ernest?" Shiloh asked casually.

The smile faded from Libby's face. She dropped her head, then jerked rod-straight and pointed toward a small knoll about fifty yards north of the house. A small white cross marked a fairly new grave. "Up there," she whispered.

"What? How?" Shiloh managed to choke out, refusing to believe what he'd heard.

"Really don't know," she replied matter-of-factly. "A couple of cowboys brought him in one morning. He was dead. They said his horse drug him to death. Said his foot was still caught in the stirrup when they found 'im. I looked at his body. I don't know, Shiloh. It might've happened that way. The body was a mass of bruises and cuts. Looked to me like he was beaten to death."

Shiloh silently watched a hawk as it circled high overhead. After several moments, he said, "I remember you well, Libby. You wouldn't suggest this unless you had reason. Who would want him dead?"

"I honestly don't know. There are all kinds of desperate people in this country. Maybe he owed money that I didn't know about. Maybe he just stumbled onto some crime in progress, a robbery or something. Maybe somebody didn't want to leave a witness. Probably, I'll never know."

Shiloh looked deeply into her eyes, as if he were searching her soul for an answer to some unasked question. Libby returned his gaze with the same unblinking determination. Finally, Shiloh smiled gently at her and put his arm around her shoulder. "Be careful," he advised. "Whoever killed Ernest might return for you and the boys."

"Oh, I'm careful," she replied. "Careful as possible out here. That's why I had the rifle when you rode in. Believe me, I know how to use it."

Levi watched carefully during supper that evening. Libby had invited the two weary travelers to a filling meal. It was plain, mostly pinto beans and cornbread, but it was wonderful after the sparse and tasteless meals on the trail. The older Kaufman boys were delighted to see Shiloh again. Obviously, he was a hero to them. Seth still had his doubts about both strangers. But it was Libby who was truly glad to see the gambler. Her eyes sparkled and her face glowed when Shiloh talked of the places he had been and the things he had seen. When the meal was finished and the conversation over for the time being, Libby begged the men to sleep in the house for the night, but Shiloh insisted on a camp along the stream.

During the next few days Shiloh and Libby spent virtually all their time together. Levi watched from a distance as the man and woman strolled along the stream or across the fields, sometimes deep in serious conversation and at other times laughing and joking like children. Frequently, they walked hand-in-hand, and sometimes Shiloh slipped his arm around her slender waist and pulled her close. At still other times they were accompanied by young Seth, who was slowly warming up to Shiloh.

Late at night at the end of a week Shiloh came late to camp. "Are you ready to move on, my friend?" he asked.

Levi turned and stared at his companion in surprise. "I suppose so. Are you really going to leave?"

With no elaboration, Shiloh gave a simple reply. "Yes. If it's agreeable to you, we'll leave in the morning."

"Sure. That's fine," Levi replied. Hesitating for a moment, he continued, "Does she know you're leaving?"

Shiloh nodded slowly. "I informed her a while ago. We'll say goodbye in the morning."

"Suits me," Levi replied.

The men sat around the campfire in cross-legged Indian fashion until long after the fire had died to a gentle, copper glow. Shiloh rolled and smoked several cigarettes, the first that Levi had noticed since their arrival. Clearly, something was wrong, but Levi didn't dare to ask what it was. He woke several times during the night to observe his friend quietly smoking in the darkness or walking slowly along the stream in the moonlight, head down and shoulders hunched, deep in thought.

At the first light of dawn Shiloh was up, making sure he woke Levi, as he noisily began to break camp. Purposely leaving enough chores to detain Levi, Shiloh mounted his horse and rode alone toward Libby's house. She was sitting quietly on the porch as he arrived. Without speaking, he dismounted and sat down beside her. Two steaming cups of coffee sat on a rickety table in front of her. Obviously, she was expecting him. A thin sliver of sun hung low over the eastern horizon, bathing the farm in shadows and radiant colors. For minutes neither spoke.

Then, taking a sip of coffee and solemnly looking over at him, she said, "Shiloh, I owe you an apology. I lied to you."

"I know," he replied, his expression equally solemn.

"You know?" she asked.

"Yes. You killed Ernest, didn't you?"

She took a long breath, holding her hand near her throat, taken completely by surprise at his question. "How did you know?"

"I'm a gambler, Libby. A very good one. I've learned to read people. I usually know when they have a good hand, and when they're bluffing. I know when they're lying."

"After you left, he changed. Maybe he was jealous of you and your casual way of life. Maybe he noticed the glances we exchanged. He started drinking real bad. Anything he could get his hands on, just as long as it had alcohol in it. Oh, he was drinking some when you were here, but not bad. It had just recently started. He couldn't handle it. After a few drinks, he'd become a different person. It made him vicious, cruel. He'd do anything for a drink."

Her voice began to crack as she fought back the tears. Shiloh watched her carefully, concluding that she was telling the truth. With difficulty, she continued, "He beat me when he was drunk, Shiloh. That wasn't too bad. I could take it. Bumps. Bruises. A black eye or two. Ernest wasn't a big man, so he couldn't hurt me seriously. One night he decided to beat up one of the boys, just for fun. I told 'im if he did, I'd kill 'im. That got his attention, and he stopped. But later he started doing strange things.

Ugly, perverted things. Once he tried to trade me for liquor. Me! His wife! He would prostitute his own wife for a bottle of cheap whiskey. He couldn't do it because I wouldn't put up with it, but he sure tried.

"Then he started on the boys, again. It was Seth mostly. I fought 'im toe-to-toe. One night he came at me. The boys were asleep. He had a knife. At least, I thought he did. When he got close, I hit 'im with a poker. I hit 'im again and again. I beat 'im to death, Shiloh. I killed 'im, but it was him or me. I never did find the knife. I looked everywhere. I guess there wasn't one."

Again there was a lengthy silence. Then Shiloh continued her story for her. "Then you saddled his horse in the darkness, and you dragged Ernest's body outside to the horse. You wedged his left foot inside the left stirrup. Since he wasn't large, it wasn't difficult to do. Next, you led the horse around and around the farm, dragging the body along behind. Finally, you left the horse and dead man in a location where they'd be found. How did I do?"

"Pretty good, Shiloh. Pretty good. Now, where do we go from here? Do you go to the sheriff?"

Shiloh chuckled. "To the sheriff? That's the most ludicrous idea I've ever heard. Why would I do that?"

"Well, you know about a murder that was committed."

"I beg to disagree. I know nothing of the sort. All I know is what you said. Means nothing. Besides, didn't the sheriff investigate back when it happened?"

"Yes. Of course. He looked at the body, declared it an accident, and told me to bury him. He may have thought he was protecting some big rancher who killed Ernest for this land. I don't know. It probably wasn't official or legal. We're a little bit informal out here, Shiloh."

"Libby, why would I try to get you sent to prison or to a

hanging for defending yourself against a madman? What would happen to your boys? An orphans' home? I hope not. What would happen to you? To your farm? No, I think justice has been served, no matter how unconventional. Besides, this really is none of my business."

Unconvinced, Libby shook her head. "You can just walk away from it?"

"Certainly, I can. If you're smart, you'll walk away from it, too. Set it aside and start over. Move away, if you have to. Just leave well enough alone."

"He was so good at first, before the madness and the alcohol started. When he wasn't drinking, he was so kind, so full of apology. He'd do anything to make up for the abuse. That's why he built the house. I'll remember the good part."

"It's strange, Libby. I don't misjudge people very often. As I told you, that's how I make a living, but I misjudged Ernest. I didn't see his dark side."

"You couldn't have, Shiloh. You didn't misjudge him. Around people he admired, he avoided liquor. Oh, he might take a drink now and then, but no binges. When you were here, he was fine, just like when we first married. But when you left the madness really started."

Looking toward the stream, Shiloh saw that Levi had finished breaking camp and was riding uncertainly toward the house. "It's time for my departure, Libby. Would you tell the boys 'goodbye' for me?"

"Do you have to leave, Shiloh? I know you care for me, and the boys are crazy about you. We both could start over here on the farm. Or someplace else."

"It's tempting, Libby, but you'd regret it. Every man is different. That one coming up the trail needs a wife. I don't. In time I'd make you miserable. You don't need any more misery. I'm headed up toward Amarillo. I'll be going back to San Antone for the winter. I'll stop by and check on you."

"I wish you would, Shiloh. Maybe by then you'll change your mind."

Shiloh motioned toward Levi and shouted, "Come on up, boy. Amarillo awaits us." As Levi trotted his horse up to the porch, Shiloh pulled a sealed envelope from his pocket and handed it to Libby. "It's a little something I want you to have, Libby. Just a few dollars that I can spare. Gamblers don't have much use for money. It doesn't stay around long." Before she could protest, Shiloh kissed her gently and then mounted his horse and rode toward the West. Still puzzled, Levi followed.

As Libby stood watching Shiloh and Levi ride away, Seth came sleepily out of the house and stood beside her. Looking up at his mother, he asked, "Where's he going, Mom?"

"He's leaving."

The boy looked quickly at his mother and then back at the disappearing rider. "But I don't want him to go, Mother." Without waiting for his mother's response, he continued, "Will he come back?"

"I don't know, Seth," she replied, brushing her eyes. They stood watching long after the two men had disappeared from sight. Then they turned and went back into the house.

Chapter 16

Levi warmed his hands over the small, smoking campfire. He had spent the better part of an hour searching for enough solid wood for a fire to prepare meals for both the evening and the following morning. Finally, he had found a small supply along a shallow creek some distance from camp. Some of the wood—he wasn't sure, but thought it was hackberry—burned well, making little smoke. The remainder, however, burned reluctantly, giving off large amounts of smoke but not much flame.

Just as Levi finally succeeded in producing an almost adequate blaze, Shiloh suddenly appeared like a ghost in the edge of the light of the fire. Seeing him unexpectedly, Levi gave a sudden start and reflexively placed his right hand on the butt of the Colt that Rachel had given him. "Don't shoot," Shiloh said in jest, "I come in peace." Then, looking disapprovingly at Levi's campfire, he continued. "On the other hand, with all the smoke signals you're creating, I wouldn't be surprised to see a delegation of visitors that don't come in peace."

Ignoring the insult, Levi retorted, "See any dangerous outlaws on your scouting trip out there?"

Shiloh removed his hat and used it to fan the air, pretending to clear away the smoke. "No, not a one. I'm just waiting for your smoke signals to bring them directly into camp."

Levi sighed and stared at Shiloh. "You think George is still out there? Still looking for me?"

"Of course he is."

Absently studying a distant clump of scrubby trees, the only place an adversary might be hiding, Levi asked, "How do you know?"

"I know his type. Been dealing with 'em most of my life. With George it's a matter of pride. In his mind he has to get his revenge. You know the feeling."

"So why not just sit down right here and wait for 'im?"

Shiloh smiled at the obvious flaws in the plan. "Might work. Might not. I think we have—you have—a better chance in Amarillo. It's like in the military. If you have the opportunity, you choose the best place to make your stand."

For long moments Levi sat staring into his smoldering fire, considering Shiloh's reasoning. Finally, changing the subject, he said, "You know, my smoke signals just might bring in the killer of that farmer. That Ernest fellow."

"So you believe it was murder, not an accident?" Shiloh was on guard, cautious that Levi might be trying to manipulate him in some manner.

"That's what I think."

"And why do you think the killer would be out here?"

"Well, he—or they—can't be too far away. We're still pretty close to his farm."

"Yeah, Levi, whoever committed that murder is either miles from here or sitting tight, right close to where it happened. Assuming it was even a murder, of course."

"Right close? Who would stay right close?"

"Maybe those cowboys who discovered the body. Maybe he had something they wanted. Land. Money. Who knows what?"

"Maybe so," In the manner that Shiloh had come to expect, Levi sat in silence for several seconds, then looked directly at the gambler and continued, "Shiloh, I've thought about this a lot and I have a theory about that killing. It's just a theory, you understand. Nothing more. But then, nothing else makes sense.

At least not to me."

"Okay. Let's hear your theory."

"Well. Lots of Libby's story doesn't quite ring true. If some neighbor wanted her land so bad, why hasn't he taken it? Or at least tried? She couldn't stop 'im. That rusty old Winchester? It doesn't impress anybody. Another thing. If some big rancher wanted that land, the sheriff wouldn't be on her side. Not in my opinion."

"Go on."

"There wasn't any evidence that he was robbed, so it wasn't about money. At least, it doesn't appear to be. What else could it have been? Libby? Did some lonely cowboy want her? Nobody came looking for her, so she wasn't what they were after."

"Is there a conclusion to your detective work?"

"Yep. What if, just what if, she killed him for some reason?"

"Why? Why would she do that?"

"I've got no idea. Maybe she kind of went crazy out here alone. What if she found out he'd been seeing another woman somewhere? I don't know, just some dumb thinking of mine."

"Not so dumb, Levi."

"What?"

"Actually, I'm quite impressed. You're remarkably perceptive. I didn't think you'd pick up on that so quickly."

"What?"

"You have drawn some sound conclusions," Shiloh said. "She did kill her husband."

Levi sprang to his feet, spilling hot coffee on his shirt and pants as he did so. A look of surprise spread across his face. He was amazed that he'd been right, but he was even more surprised that Shiloh had trusted him enough to share the truth with him. "You know for sure?"

"She told me, but I already knew."

"Why did she do it?"

Shiloh briefly described what had happened at the Kaufman farm. As he concluded, Levi asked, "And that was why you chose not to stay with her?"

"Oh, no, that had nothing to do with it. You see, Levi, she only did what she had to do. She's no killer. I'd be more concerned about her feelings of guilt than about anything else."

"Guess I was wrong about that. I figured you left when you found out."

"Things are never that simple, Levi. I just realized that if I stayed, I'd be staying for the wrong reasons." Shiloh searched his surroundings with his eyes, as he remembered. "I could never adjust to her way of life, nor could she adapt to mine. Can you imagine me spending the rest of my life on that farm? I can't. Neither can I see her being happy in my world. It would be unfair to both of us. You have any more questions on that subject?"

"Just one. Actually, it's about that youngest boy of Libby's. Seth, wasn't it?"

"That's his name. What about him?"

"How old is he, anyway?"

"Libby said he's about four."

"And when were you there? Before this time, I mean."

Shiloh was quiet for long moments, staring steadily into the campfire. Levi grew restless, wishing he'd never brought this subject up. Clearly, Shiloh didn't wish to discuss the paternity of Libby's youngest son. Just as Levi was preparing to apologize, Shiloh fixed a steady gaze upon the younger man and said, "I visited the Kaufman farm less than a year before Seth's birth. Now I think it's best to leave that poor family in peace."

Levi fell silent again, obviously deep in thought. After a while, Shiloh chose to encourage Levi to speak his mind. "You certainly are pleasant company," he said sarcastically. "What seems to be eating on you today? Does the story about Libby trouble you?"

"No, Shiloh, it's something else. I've had something on my mind."

"Oh, hell. Not that again."

"Yeah, that." Levi hesitated and fidgeted in discomfort, desperately wanting to choose the right words. Unable to think of an adequate approach, he stumbled on. "Shiloh, you've been leading me around for several weeks now. Fact is, you haven't done much else, but look after me. You taught me to use my Colt. I thought I knew how, but you showed me that I didn't. You talk all the time about Texas and stuff. You can't stop talking about Indians, insisting it's information that'll be useful to me sometime in the future. You want me to learn things. I appreciate it, but I don't understand it. You could be making a fortune, the way you gamble. But you're playing nursemaid to me. Why?"

Shiloh's face took on an agitation that Levi had seen only a few times before, as he replied, "I thought we'd been through all that. Fact is, I'm not sure myself. Maybe I'm trying to repay society for some failure of mine. I've surely had my share. But let's try this again. I believe you have some promise, if I can just manage to keep you alive. You're still little more than a kid, but you'll grow up if you'll let yourself. You have to bury this guilt you feel about Jovita's death. Let her go. Sure, you can feel regret, sorrow.

"You should feel it, but you can't continue to live in the past. This state needs people like you, but it needs them alive, with clear heads that can find ways to solve problems. You've got a real chance. I'm afraid you'll waste it. I'll be a gambler and gunfighter until I die, but you have an opportunity to be something better. I wish somebody had done this for me. Look, Levi, maybe every man wants a son, so he can pass on his wisdom, or whatever he sees as wisdom. I'll never have a real son. At least not one that...maybe you're the closest I'll ever get. Just listen to me. Don't waste your opportunities."

Making no response to Shiloh's words, Levi said, "There's something else I'd like to know."

"There always is."

"No, really. This is important to me. Shiloh, you know things that other people don't know. In San Antonio I was around other gamblers, and they sure weren't like you. How do you know so much about the world?" Levi was having difficulty in putting his thoughts into words, and Shiloh recognized it.

"I've explained all that," Shiloh replied. "I've listened to the stories of people I played cards with. Ranchers, cowboys, soldiers, outlaws, even an Indian or two. I read newspapers sometimes. I may be nothing more than a gambler, but I care about what's happening, and I'm certainly not dumb. I learn pretty fast, and I remember most things I hear and read."

"That's still not quite it," Levi insisted. "Lots of people know things, but you don't just know. You *understand.* You can take something that happened in the past and use it to see what'll happen in the future. Gamblers don't do that. Gunslingers don't either. And, too, you care—about me and about this state. About the Indians, even. That's not much like a gambler either."

Now it was Shiloh's turn to fidget and squirm. Levi was invading his privacy, and it made him uncomfortable. Still, the two had become close. They were associates and companions, maybe even friends. Too, he had pried into Levi's life and planned to do even more of it in the future. "Yes," he said. "I guess I do owe you some explanations."

Shiloh explained that he had been born in Connecticut, the only child of a moderately successful small-town merchant. The family was religious. His father always had wanted to be a minister, but never had gotten the chance. It became an obsession for the father to see a son pursue the career that he had been denied. When Shiloh was born, both father and mother were ecstatic. Here was the future minister they had long awaited.

Having been molded from birth, Shiloh accepted his parents' goals for him. When he was sixteen, he was declared ready and was sent off to college to study theology, to become a Presbyterian minister. At first he did well. He was bright, and he always ranked near the head of his class; however, near the end of his second year at college, his problems began. One of the more affluent students, probably out of jealousy, began to ridicule him about the way he talked and dressed. This fellow student mocked him constantly and encouraged other students to do the same. His chief tormentor was clever and carefully avoided detection by the faculty. Finally getting enough, Shiloh caught this student away from campus and gave him a thorough beating. Shiloh's victim was humiliated but not really injured.

In an attempt to save themselves from possible punishment, the student and his friends reported the incident to the school administration. Confronted with a bruised and black-eyed accuser and several witnesses, Shiloh admitted that he indeed had whipped the boy. No amount of explaining would satisfy the school's headmaster and his faculty. Shiloh had broken the rules, and he had to be punished. Expulsion was the punishment. Shiloh was crushed. Although he hadn't really wanted to be a minister, he knew how important it was to his parents. The news of his expulsion was much more difficult for his parents than for Shiloh. Their dreams for Shiloh were shattered. They knew that now he never would achieve the success they wanted.

Shiloh wanted to save his parents further embarrassment and humiliation. Late one night he took a family horse and saddle, an old percussion pistol, an ancient double-barreled shotgun, and a few provisions. He quietly rode out of the small town and headed west. Along the way, he stole food, worked at odd jobs, and barely stayed alive. However, he was learning survival skills, which proved useful on numerous occasions. Two years later he was in Texas, a strong, resourceful, and cunning survivor of numerous hardships and confrontations along the way. In his travels he learned to use both a deck of cards and a Colt revolver. They had provided a good living ever since.

"And now," Shiloh concluded, "You know more about me than anybody else alive does."

Deciding that he had exposed enough of his soul, Shiloh fell silent. There were many questions racing through Levi's mind, but this time he respected his companion's privacy. Following Shiloh's example, Levi made no comment and asked no further questions. Silently, they huddled close to the small campfire as the chill of the night crept in. Then, after a respectable period, they allowed the fire to burn down and, securing their bedrolls, went quickly into the darkness.

Both men were up early the next morning. Shiloh had announced that they were near their destination, but he wasn't sure exactly when they would arrive. After a hasty breakfast Shiloh and Levi secured their belongings and broke camp. It was just about daylight as they headed northward, Shiloh leading the way as both riders silently remembered the conversation of the previous night. At some point about half way between daybreak and noon, Shiloh reined his horse off the road onto a narrow trail that led along the south bank of a dry creek. Slightly less than half an hour later, the trail descended into a cool, cottonwood-lined gorge, where a spring splashed out of solid rock and fell into a small pool at the bottom of the creek bed.

After drinking his fill, Levi lay out flat on his back in the soft grass beside the pool, closing his eyes and absorbing the warm sunshine like a young adventurous kid. He spent a few minutes in total relaxation, and then he opened one eye and looked over at Shiloh. "I want to talk about last night," he said.

"I don't. I've already said too much," Shiloh quickly replied.

"You don't have to say anything. But there's something I gotta say. Been bothering me for a while. Last night you were real honest with me. Made me realize that I haven't been that honest with you."

"Really? How so?"

"Well, I know you think I've been feeling guilty about Jovita's death. That's true, but it's only part of the story."

"And you want to get the rest off your chest."

"I guess I do. See, when I was shot and ended up at the Sandifer Ranch on the San Saba River, the people there saved my life."

"Yes, that's what you told me."

"One of the people that took care of me was a woman named Rachel Sandifer. It was her husband that owned the ranch until he was killed. I was trying to get over Jovita's death, but I started having feelings for Rachel. In a way I loved them both. I felt guilty. Sort of unfaithful, I guess. I didn't want to love Rachel because I was supposed to be mourning Jovita. At the same time, I have to admit that I had—that I still have—feelings for Rachel. I'm not ready to say it's genuine love, but it's sure feels like it. It's gotten all mixed up. I didn't want to tell you. You were helping me. Teaching me. I was ashamed. I didn't want to disappoint you. I didn't exactly lie to you. I just let you believe something that wasn't entirely true. Shiloh, I know this doesn't make any sense, but I just couldn't let you think I was a bad person, so I helped you believe something else. I'm sorry."

It was approaching noon, and the weather had been

unseasonably warm. As small beads of sweat formed on Levi's forehead, he wondered whether it was caused by the weather or the fear that Shiloh wouldn't understand his transgression. The momentary silence was broken by the raspy call of a scrub jay coming from somewhere down in the canyon. Back behind the two men, one of the horses snorted and stomped, fighting off either some parasitic fly, or maybe just impatience. The only other sound was the gentle, regular breathing of Shiloh and Levi.

"Look, you aren't mentally incompetent simply because you loved two women, Levi," Shiloh finally replied. "And it's certainly not necessary to apologize to me."

"Hell, Shiloh, you'd have to feel like I did—like I sometimes still do—to understand what I'm saying."

Shiloh turned to his companion. "Do you think you're the only man who's lost somebody he cared about?"

"You?" Levi asked.

"Me and about half the men that ever fell in love with a woman."

"I've seen the women in San Antone. I've seen them look at you when you were gambling. Even heard 'em talk. You could've had most any one of 'em you chose," Levi argued.

"Yes, except the one I really wanted."

"Was it Libby?"

"No! No! I'm fond of Libby, and I certainly could've done worse, but it wasn't Libby. It was long before her."

"What happened?"

Shiloh sighed and looked out across the small pool of water. "Oh, I think she loved me, but she didn't approve of my profession," he replied. "Mostly, I guess, her family didn't. Anyway, she married somebody else. It was a long time ago. It's over. This isn't a perfect world, Levi. You move on. You live with disappointment, and you try to get over it. Jovita's dead. Rachel's not. It's that simple. It doesn't require genius to figure it out."

"And you think I should just move on?"

"It really doesn't matter what I think. What do you think? That's what's important. That's whose opinion matters. If I don't teach you anything else, I want you to learn to trust your own decisions. Don't let other people decide for you."

Each man stood quietly, solemnly staring at the other. If a stranger had happened upon the two men at that instant, he would have been certain that they were sizing up each other in preparation for a fight. Nothing could have been further from the truth. In fact, they had just broken down any barriers that had remained between them. They had accepted each other as equals.

Shiloh and Levi rode on through the day, both men anxious to reach their destination. Late in the evening they peered into the darkness and saw the faint flickering lights of the relatively new town of Amarillo. Actually, it was scarcely a town; just a few clapboard shacks and some hastily constructed buildings formed the major part. Radiating out from the central portion lay a haphazard maze of campfires, supply wagons, and trash heaps. The cattle and farming industries in the area were in their infancies, and a commercial center was struggling to develop to meet their needs. However, at this stage its development was far from adequate.

Privately, each man breathed a sigh of relief at the sight of the encampment. The trip had been educational and inspirational for Levi, yet both men had experienced introspection that had caused discomfort. Now, with that behind them, perhaps they could get on to more important tasks. Levi was restless to see the Palo Duro Canyon and the rest of this strange, flat, open country. Shiloh was in a hurry to find some unsuspecting victims who were willing to risk their money in a poker game.

Chapter 17

They had been in Amarillo for only a short time, but already the two vagabonds had settled in and made themselves at home. It was fall, and the weather was turning cold, much colder than Levi had imagined it would be. Frequent north winds blew across the open prairie, chilling the young man from balmy San Antonio to the bone. He had managed to trade for a warm, fur-lined coat and additional heavy clothing, but still he had trouble avoiding the icy blasts of north wind.

Snow had fallen twice already, and it was still a week before Thanksgiving. During his second day in town, Shiloh had bought a heavy canvas tent—apparently one stolen from the Army—from a bearded, foul-smelling drifter. He had peeled off twenty dollars from a large roll of bills and handed the money to the man. Levi noticed with concern that the man eyed the roll and carefully sized-up Shiloh at the same time. In an instant Levi's hand dropped to the butt of his Colt revolver, openly challenging the man to make a move. Realizing his mistake, the man stepped backward and held up both hands about chest high, palms outward to indicate that he meant no harm. Whatever his initial intention, the man now knew that any aggressive move would be suicidal. The moment passed with neither man saying a word.

The next morning, Levi was sitting on the edge of his cot, stretching and rubbing his eyes when Shiloh entered the tent and remarked, "Boy! You've been working hard. The tent's in excellent condition, and our gear's clean and stored away. I suggest that we saddle up these two fine steeds that we ride, and we take a trip out to the Palo Duro Canyon, the most beautiful place in north Texas or maybe in all of Texas. We'll take a supply of food and spend a couple of nights. Have us a regular picnic."

"You're sure feeling your oats this morning. What got into you?" Levi replied, as he yawned and shivered in the brisk morning air.

"Must be the cool weather. Besides, I like the Panhandle. Amarillo I could do without, but still there are gamblers here. Not good ones, just gamblers."

"Yeah. Well, myself, I've seen some bad looking hombres."

"Not bad. Just cowboys and farmers with money they don't need. Itching to lose it to me."

"You'd better be careful," Levi said, like an overly protective parent. "Some fool will put a bullet in your back when you're not looking. I saw how the man that sold you the tent yesterday looked at your money."

"I was watching that clumsy old bastard. I certainly wasn't in any danger. I watch my back every second. Even when you don't realize it, I'm watching."

"Okay. We won't agree on that today. I guess I just see more danger in some of these people than you do. Anyway, let's go see your little old canyon."

The men rode side by side southward, out of Amarillo. Levi paid little attention to their exact route. He was much too fascinated by the almost perfect flatness of the prairie. "Some people call it the *llano estacado,* which a rancher once told me means 'staked plains,'" Shiloh observed.

"Staked Plains? Why that?"

"There are several theories. Really more like legends, I guess. One story says that the early Spanish explorers were afraid they'd get lost in the expanse of country, so they left a trail of stakes to help them find their way back. Actually those stakes probably weren't stakes like we think about them. Probably more like piles of rocks. Others say that early settlers couldn't find trees to tie their horses to, so they carried stakes to drive into the ground. Kind of a portable hitching post."

"Got any idea what story's right?"

"Probably none of 'em. Call it what you want, it was the home of the Comanche Indians for maybe two hundred years."

"What finally did 'em in, Shiloh?"

"Same old story. White man's diseases. White man's guns. White man's liquor. White man's treachery. White man's greed. We couldn't live with 'em in any kind of harmony, so we had to kill all their buffalo and take all their land. The last ones dragged themselves onto the reservation at Fort Sill in 1874 or '75. Least, that's what I was told."

"That wasn't long ago."

"No."

"You seem to know a lot about 'em."

"Yes. I've always been fascinated by 'em. They were an amazing civilization. Honest. Trusting. Sincere. All those good features I studied when I was trying to learn how to be a minister. Sometimes I'm not too happy about being a white man."

They rode on for a while in silence, then Shiloh saw fit to continue. "Most of all, I wish I could've seen them just once. Chasing a herd of wild buffalo. Their tough, little paint horses racing across the prairie right up beside one of those shaggy creatures. What a sight it must've been. Or maybe a band of those haughty, self-important braves all decked out and ready to go on a big raid someplace. Feathers and scalps tied in their horses' tails and manes. Paint all over themselves and their horses. All kinds of decorations and finery. I've heard men talk about it, but I missed it."

"Guess you were just born too late, Shiloh."

"Yes, for lots of things. Look how modern the world is today. Railroads everywhere. Newspapers. All kinds of new-fangled farming contraptions. Barbed wire going up around every little piece of prairie. Just look at this rifle of mine." Shiloh reached down and drew a Winchester Model 1873 from a saddle scabbard. He held it out at arm's length, openly admiring it. "This will kill a deer or a man from almost as far as you can see him. Things have gotten too easy. People too soft and lazy nowadays."

Levi was quite aware of changes taking place in his surroundings. As the two men had been busily engaged in conversation, they gradually had ridden out of the open prairie onto an equally flat expanse of land densely populated with scrubby mesquites. They appeared to be identical to the mesquites that grew in central Texas, but these were little more than bushes, most specimens growing no higher than the head of a mounted rider. An occasional juniper was scattered among the mesquites. Like the mesquites, the junipers were squat, bushy plants, maybe a bit larger than the mesquites, but nothing like the junipers Levi remembered. A little farther on, the vegetation changed again, and the junipers became dominant with a few mesquites scattered among them.

In another instant Levi would have made a comment to Shiloh about the changes in the vegetation, but the words never left his mouth. Shiloh was sitting motionless on his resting horse, staring off into the distance. Levi rode forward and joined his friend. There, stretching out before him almost as far as the eye could see, lay one of the most spectacular sights that Levi had ever seen, the Palo Duro Canyon. The men were located on the western rim of the main canyon. Levi would learn later that there were numerous side canyons, branching off in all directions, while the Palo Duro itself extended for miles along the course of the Red River. From his location Levi could look across and see the opposite rim, perhaps five miles across, maybe more. It was impossible to tell.

The slope below the western rim was a jumble of gigantic boulders, interspersed with clusters of trees, shrubs, and small plots of native grass. A purple-blue haze hung over the huge expanse of the gorge itself. Up high near the top of the distant rim stretched long bands of thin-layered white rock, apparently limestone, alternating with thicker, irregular bands of red clay. Long slivers of stone and clay projected away from the canyon wall like long, gnarled fingers reaching out into emptiness.

Far below on the floor of the canyon stood several tall columns of red clay, apparently sculpted by untold years of erosion. On the very top of one column rested a huge flat rock, perhaps almost as large as a wagon bed. Off to his left Levy spotted a huge block of solid stone, jutting out of the side of a small rocky hill and hanging off into space. The massive stone was marked with crevices and ridges and fissures, looking for all the world like a giant, wrinkled, horribly disfigured face.

Extending along the bottom of a small side canyon stretched a line of cottonwood trees in full autumn foliage. The leaves were yellow and gold and bronze, shimmering and turning in the early morning sun. Barely visible in the very bottom of the main canyon stretched a long, glistening silver thread, the Red River.

Both mesquites and junipers grew profusely along the walls and on the wide, nearly flat bottom of the canyon, and they were joined by a small bush that Levi hadn't noticed before. The plant grew in almost impenetrable clusters in many of the flat, open areas where, for some reason, mesquites and junipers were absent. Dismounting, Levi examined the plant closely, finding that while it grew only about two feet high, it had leaves and acorns somewhat similar to those on the huge live oaks of central Texas.

"It's some variety of oak. I've heard it called 'scrub oak,' but I'm unsure about the name. Tough little devil, isn't it?" Shiloh volunteered, as Levi examined the plant. Then, turning the subject back to the canyon, he continued, "Didn't I tell you this place was spectacular?"

"It's that," Levi agreed. "So much bigger than I imagined. And prettier."

"As I told you before, this was the last fortress of the Comanche Indians, along with some Kiowa and a few Cheyenne. A few miles up the canyon from here, they fought their last big battle. They lost. One of those Army colonels down in San Antonio told me about it. Claimed he was there, just a captain at the time. According to him, Colonel McKenzie caught the Comanche sleeping one morning and surprised 'em. Played a real trick on those clever devils, again according to my source. The night before, McKenzie had his troops mount up and march in the opposite direction Away from the canyon, that is. Of course the Indians watched this maneuver. Surprised as hell, I'd guess.

"Then in the middle of the night, he turned his entire command around and rode hell bent for the Indians' camp in the canyon. He got there about dawn. The Indian scouts spotted the cavalry riding down a narrow trail into the canyon. They probably could've defeated the soldiers at that point if they'd attacked, but they chose to turn back and protect their women and children. McKenzie's soldiers destroyed most of the Indians' food and supplies and camp, but didn't kill many Indians. Captured nearly all their horses and shot most of those." Shiloh paused and looked across at Levi. "You have to recall now, this entire story came from that colonel in San Antonio. I have to add that he'd had a few too many drinks at the time, and he was trying to impress a cute little bar girl who was hanging on his every word."

"Wait a minute," Levi said. "They killed the Comanche's horses?"

"Yes sir. Surely did. Over a thousand, best I remember."

"Why?"

"Probably afraid the Indians would steal them back. They would've, too. This way the Indians were mostly afoot. They lasted a while longer on the run, but they didn't have horses, and nearly all the buffalo were gone. They just couldn't make it. Most of 'em walked to the reservation at Fort Sill."

"Not a pretty sight."

"No, but it could've been a lot uglier. Only a few Indians were killed by McKenzie's men. I've always believed he spared those poor heathens on purpose. He could've killed nearly all of 'em. At least, that's my humble opinion."

"Your humble opinion?"

"Yes, mine and a few other people's."

"You admire those Indians, don't you? Now me...well, I guess I really don't. I've been told about some of the evil things they did. How they treated captives, especially women and children. How they raided and plundered and burned. But you admire 'em."

"Yes, I know about their violent side, but I admire 'em. You will, too, when you really understand 'em. No, I don't wish I'd been one. I like the way they ran free and answered to nobody. They weren't tied to some tiny farm, starving to death, like Libby and Ernest. They ran free and wild. Proud. If they were hungry, they went where the food was. I admire the way they lived. Maybe I do have something in common with 'em. I guess I could've been freer and wilder. I could've lived in the mountains out west, but I chose not to. I could've killed an elk or something and lived off the land. No, I don't wish I'd been a Comanche."

"Seems to me you live a lot like 'em, anyway. You go where you want to. In a way you live off the land. You don't answer to anybody. Sounds good to me. Lots like an Indian."

"Maybe so, but it has its disadvantages. Anyway, right now I need to make camp and get some supper started. We can talk about what might have been later. In the meantime, why don't you go on back out there and enjoy the view. It's even better just before dark."

It had been dark for well over an hour when Levi slipped into camp and wearily threw himself upon the ground. Neither man broke the silence for several minutes. Then Levi said, "Shiloh, remember a while back on the trail, when you were telling me how a Indian brave would have a dream and got his medicine?"

"Yes. I believe we talked about that. Why?"

"Well, exactly how did it happen, again?"

"Oh, it probably didn't happen the same way every time. Usually, the Indian lad went into a kind of trance, or spell, and might see most anything. Usually, it involved an animal of some kind. Some animals had stronger medicine than others. The eagle was quite desirable. So were the bear and the wolf. The animal that he saw in his vision was his medicine. It protected 'im, looked after 'im, and warned 'im about danger and such like."

"Can a white man get this medicine?"

Shiloh studied Levi for several seconds. Was this simple country boy testing him? Maybe playing some sort of game? "I suppose so, but that would be extremely unusual. Why? Did you have such a vision?"

It was immediately apparent to Shiloh that his companion had witnessed something unusual. "Don't know," Levi said, "but a strange event happened to me out there."

"Tell Papa about it, son," Shiloh replied, not yet ready to

treat the discussion seriously.

"Make fun of what happened to me if you want to, but it scared the hell out of me."

"I wasn't ridiculing the medicine," Shiloh said, carefully hiding his amusement. "I was joking with you. Anyway, what happened?"

"I sat down under a tree, a pretty big one. Cottonwood, I think. I felt kind of tired and sleepy, but kind of dizzy, too. Maybe a little like when you've been sick for a few days, and you're just getting well. I was partly asleep and partly awake, when I looked down the canyon and saw this huge animal slowly coming right at me. Big old white dog, except it wasn't just a dog. It was a wolf. Not a coyote. A wolf. He came closer, until he was just a few yards away. Close as that big flat rock over there." Levi motioned toward a rock, lying about twenty yards away. Shiloh listened closely, seriously, as he slowly rolled a cigarette.

Levi now studied Shiloh, seeking the reassurance of his mentor. The expression on Shiloh's face provided that reassurance. "It was like I was frozen, but not scared, just couldn't move anything," Levi said. "So close I could see the hair standing on the back of his neck. And, the big yellow eyes, serious and unblinking, staring right at me. Big old tongue rolled out, slobbers dripping on the ground. He was breathing real hard, panting like those dogs back in town. All of a sudden, he sat down on his haunches and started whining at me. I swear it was at me. Then he threw that big old head back and let out a long, loud howl. Did it two, maybe three times. Maybe you heard it."

Shiloh silently wagged his head from side to side. "No. I didn't hear it."

"Made the hair stand up on the back of my neck. Then he got up and just stood staring at me. The wind was blowing through his fur, moving it all over like his whole body was moving. All the time he never took his eyes off of me. Finally, he turned around and padded off. Was gone in an instant. Quick as he came. After he got down the canyon a ways, I snapped wide awake. Felt real funny. Kind of weak."

Shiloh continued to watch Levi carefully. He saw that Levi was serious. Finally, he said, "Maybe there's a logical explanation. Could it be a bitch with a litter somewhere close?"

"Don't think so. I thought of that. I looked. Nothing."

"Now, I don't want to annoy you, but I must ask you a question. Could you have been asleep and dreaming?"

"Nope."

"Okay. Sometimes we get really tired and we…oh, we imagine things."

"Not that, either."

"Well, my friend, there may not be a logical explanation. Sometimes strange things happen, and we don't know why. We just have to draw our own conclusions."

"You think it was a vision?"

"Honestly, I don't know. I wasn't there, and I probably wouldn't know if I'd been there. I do know one thing. Supper's getting cold."

"Yeah," Levi said. "But first there's something else."

"Okay. Go on."

"This isn't the first time I've seen that wolf."

"When before?" Shiloh asked.

"The night when we were looking at the Waggoner cattle herd, pretending they were buffalo. I couldn't sleep, so I got up and walked up that hill. While I was sitting there and watching the cattle, the wolf just appeared right in front of me. It wasn't any distance at all from me. After maybe a minute or two, it got up and trotted away. Didn't howl, just left. That time was different from the one tonight. It was sort of a…an introduction. This one was longer, more involved. Maybe it was meant to reassure me."

Shiloh slowly removed his hat and ran his hand through his hair. "And you didn't think it was important to tell me that you'd seen it before?"

"No. I thought the wolf just happened upon me that earlier time," Levi said. "Accidentally, I suppose. But now it's happened again. Must be more than a coincidence."

Shiloh smiled and nodded. "Yeah. I'd say so."

"So help me understand. What's going on?"

Sitting and staring into the campfire, Shiloh removed the cigarette butt from his mouth and tossed it into the coals. He rose and looked at Levi, slowly shaking his head. "I have no idea what this means," he replied. "None at all, but I'll bet you haven't seen the last of your wolf."

Shiloh and Levi finished supper in relative silence. As the darkness settled upon the ancient haunts of the Comanche Indians, the canyon and the surrounding area took on an eerie quietness that would have made the staunchest unbeliever consider the authenticity of Levi's medicine. The medicine gave Shiloh little trouble. Having witnessed many events that weren't easily explained, he could accept the Indians' spirit world. The greatest puzzle to him was the man sitting just across the campfire from him.

Shiloh noisily dropped his eating utensils into a tin pan beside the fire, and then he placed more wood on the campfire. The flames hungrily licked at the dry mesquite limbs, casting deep shadows and golden bronze bands of color upon the camp. Finally, Shiloh could wait no longer. "Levi," he said, "I've always been curious about your name."

"That's been bothering me, too. Do you think there's any

connection between my name and the animal I saw?"

"What?" Shiloh responded in surprise.

"My name. Wolfe. And the vision was a wolf."

"Yes. As a matter of fact, I did wonder about that, but I'm just as interested in your first name. Do you have any idea where it came from?"

"Just that my mom picked it out. Found it in the Bible, I think."

"Yes, I'm sure she did. It's Jewish."

"Is that so strange?"

"No. Not that it's Jewish. But there are things about you and your name that are a little unusual. Not that it means anything, you understand. It just causes me to wonder. Maybe I'm just naturally curious."

"What about my name?"

"Okay," Shiloh said. "Let's consider your whole name. Now, I've just mentioned that 'Levi' is Jewish. 'Wolfe' appears to be German. And there are several things I learned in Seminary. First, the Jews have been oppressed throughout history. The Bible tells us that, but it's also discussed in lots of historical documents. The Spanish, for example, gave 'em hell. Others did, too. The Jews moved about, looking for peace but seldom finding it."

"Why," Levi asked. "Why did everybody hate the Jews?"

"Not an easy question to answer," Shiloh answered. "Lots of reasons, I guess. They were different from most other people. Dressed differently. Talked with something of an accent. Most of 'em wore beards, even if other people didn't. They kinda stayed to themselves. As a group, they understood finance, and in lots of cases they controlled the money supply. They just had a hard time fitting into the community. So, yes, they were different, and sometimes that's enough to cause one group to hate another one."

"Okay. What does that have to do with me?"

"I'm wondering if maybe, somewhere in your family tree, your ancestors were German Jews who came to this country, looking to escape from harassment. Maybe they came to Texas in search of peace, even renouncing their religion and heritage. Maybe even learning to dress and behave like people around 'em. They might have done it out of necessity. In some countries, Jews were given a choice. They could convert to some form of Christianity, possibly Catholicism, or be killed. Some fled. Don't know about you, but I'd probably flee or become a Christian, given a choice."

"Sounds tough. Having to completely change."

"Not necessarily completely change," Shiloh said. "Sometimes families clung to certain parts of their Jewish faith. Certain rituals. Traditions. Methods of cooking. Dress. I don't know. Maybe other things. Ever see anything that seemed… well, different about your folks?"

Levi smiled knowingly and then replied, "Lots of things, but none of 'em religious. We didn't do a lot of religion."

Shiloh stroked his stubble of beard. "Yeah. I guessed that. Sometimes these displaced Jews gave up all outward signs of religion."

"Suppose my parents or my ancestors were Jews that fled to America. Why would I want to know that?"

"Right now you probably don't, but the time may come when you want to know about those family members that came generations before you. This might be a place to start."

A long silence passed between Shiloh and Levi. Finally, Levi said, "Aren't you gonna finish?"

"Finish?"

"Yeah. You were about to tell me about the Levi in the Bible, but then you went wandering off in another direction, kinda like those wandering Jews."

Shiloh slowly rolled and lit a cigarette, inhaled deeply, and then blew a fog of smoke into the air. "So I did," he said. "Okay. I'll tell you about your namesake. He was one of the sons of Jacob. Don't suppose your mother ever told you about 'im?"

"Nothing at all."

"I thought not. Well, Jacob wound up with two wives, even more if you count his concubines. To start out, though, he was working for this fellow who had a beautiful daughter named Rachel. Another oddity, don't you think? Anyway, Jacob loved Rachel, so he made a deal with his future father-in-law to work seven years in return for Rachel's hand in marriage. Well, after seven years, the man gave Jacob Rachel's sister, Leah, not Rachel, for his wife. Jacob took Leah, probably grumbled a lot, but took her anyway. Then Jacob agreed to work seven more years to get Rachel, also. That gave him two wives, Rachel and Leah."

"You're going somewhere with this? What's it got to do with this Levi person?" Levi interrupted.

"Damn! You're impatient. I'll get there."

"Sorry."

"Well, Levi was a son of Jacob and Leah. Number three, I believe. Really, it doesn't matter which one. Old Jacob lived a long time and got pretty wealthy. Kind of swindled his father-in-law out of his livestock, it appears to me. I suppose it got somewhat uncomfortable living right there in the same neighborhood, so to speak. So he moved his big family and herds of cows and sheep and such to another country where nobody knew 'im. While they were there, one of the natives abducted and raped Levi's sister. Then the man, a rather important person, wanted to keep her and make her his wife. So Levi and his brothers pretended to go along, but demanded certain things in return."

"Wait. Wait. Wait. He wanted certain things in return? What kind of things?"

"Well, all the men in town had to be circumcised."

"Circumcised? You mean...with a...knife?"

"I certainly do. Whacked right off. That was part of the plan."

"How so?"

"Well, a couple of days later every man in town was hurting quite a lot."

Levi shuddered and smiled across the fire at Shiloh. "I reckon so!" he said.

"Yes. So Levi and his brothers sneaked in and killed every man."

"Just because of the rape?"

"And they didn't stop there. They plundered the village. Took everything. Goods. Livestock. Even women and children. There was considerable hatred, I guess."

Levi considered this obvious understatement. "Considerable hatred? I think so!" Then he looked at Shiloh and considered again. "You told me this story to make me learn something, didn't you?" he asked.

Ignoring the question, Shiloh continued, "Now you'll notice some similarities between this story and yours, but the real point—to me at least—is obvious. Levi could've had his revenge by merely killing the one guilty man, but he didn't. He killed every man. Then he destroyed and burned and stole and kidnapped. On and on. He wouldn't let go. Couldn't find a stopping place."

"And you think I might turn out like that?"

"Not necessarily, but I think that possibility exists in every man," Shiloh said gently. "Some more than others, though. Some learn to enjoy killing and destroying. Levi, the thing I want you to see is that you can't afford to be like your namesake in the Bible. When you've had your revenge, let the hatred end. Don't let it devour you inside. Put it away and move on." Shiloh stopped for a moment. "Guess I just don't have a very high opinion of my fellow man. I can be a bit judgmental. Probably comes from my religious training."

Apparently the discussion was over. If Levi objected to Shiloh's admonition, he gave no sign of it. Shiloh decided that the events of the day had given Levi enough to think about, so he said nothing more on the subject. Instead, he said, "I would like to suggest that we go to bed. I'd like to rise early in the morning and explore this canyon some more. After another day or two, we'll wander back to Amarillo. I'd like to play a hand or two of poker."

Chapter 18

The afternoon sun hung just above the western horizon, as Shiloh reined in his horse. Then he slowly rode in a wide circle, searching the country in each direction. Levi watched with curiosity and some amusement, but he said nothing.

Finally, Shiloh nodded his approval and said, "Along that creek down there, Levi. That looks like a good place to camp. Fairly open. A few trees. Some wood for a campfire. There's even some pools of water in the creek. Yeah, it'll be good."

Still amused, Levi said, "Looks good to me."

Shiloh studied his companion. "Something got your funny bone all stirred up this evening?"

"Naw. Just watching you pick our camp. A man would think you were picking a place for General Custer to bed down that calvary outfit of his, whichever one it was."

"Damn, Levi, you should know that. Custer's outfit was the Seventh Cavalry, and, if you'll remember, it was a *cavalry* outfit, not a *calvary* outfit. Damn! Now, let me explain the difference. Calvary is a religious word, with Jesus on the cross and all."

Levi smiled sheepishly and replied, "Yeah. Yeah, I know what Calvary is."

"It appears that you think I'm being way more cautious than necessary. Well, let me tell you, son. I'm not. If I'd been guiding for the good General Custer—actually, he was a colonel at the time—he'd still be alive."

"How so?" Levi said, mostly to make sure Shiloh continued the conversation.

"Look around!" Shiloh ordered. "Looks peaceful doesn't it?

Well, Custer probably thought so the night before he died. This is dangerous country, Levi. Course there's that bastard that's after you, but he's just one. This country is full of bums and outlaws that would just love to sneak into camp and steal horses and kill anyone that stood in their way. There are lots of ways to die out here. Never take anything for granted."

"You're saying I'm not careful enough?" Levi said defensively.

"I'm saying we've both gotta be careful. That's all."

Levi looked off into the distance, imagining some villain that lay in wait. Then he turned his gaze to Shiloh, slowly smiling in the shadow of his hat brim. "You did this on purpose. Right. Led me right into it. This is another one of your endless string of lessons. You know what I'll say, so you led me into a trap. Oh, yes, you did, Shiloh. Right?"

"I never know what you'll say or do, so it wasn't a trap, if that even matters. But you can learn a lesson here, a real one."

"Is there any more to that lesson?" Levi asked, still curious.

"Just be careful who you trust. Who you believe. You're honest. You trust people. You mean well. You won't find those traits in everybody."

Levi and Shiloh unsaddled their horses. Levi gathered wood and started a small fire while Shiloh cared for the horses. Darkness slowly fell, and night sounds replaced the stillness. The two men sat on the ground, leaning against their saddles and bedrolls while they ate a quick meal and sipped strong coffee.

Shiloh's voice broke the silence. "About our discussion a while ago," he said.

"Yeah. More about trust?"

"Well, yes, but not exactly. I want to kind of talk on the subject of believing what other people say and do."

"So is this the same lesson or a second one?"

Shiloh ignored the sarcasm. "Oh, it's a little bit different, so maybe it's a second one."

"Well, at least it'll give us something to talk about."

"Now, if you'd rather go off to sleep, go ahead," Shiloh said.

Levi pretended to consider his choices. Both men knew what his decision would be. "No. No, it's early yet. You might as well go on," he said.

Shiloh rose and stepped over to the campfire. Reaching down with a dirty handkerchief, he grasped the handle of the coffee pot and carefully poured himself a fresh cup of coffee, and then he refilled Levi's cup. Both men sat and stared into the cups for some time. Shiloh rolled an ugly cigarette, lit it, and took a long draw. Slowly, he exhaled a thin cloud of smoke. "Let me start when I was in Divinity School," he said.

"That's where you were studying to be a preacher?" Levi replied.

Shiloh stared at the younger man across the campfire, smiling and shaking his head. "Yes. Sure. That's what Divinity School is. Can I continue now?"

"Sorry. Go on."

"There was an old professor there—he seemed old to me at the time—probably wasn't more than forty. Could've been forty-five."

"That's old," Levi remarked.

"Not to me. Not anymore," Shiloh said. "Anyway, all of us kids liked this professor. He was different. Not so stuffy. Kinda easy going. Not always serious. You know the kind. He enjoyed a good joke. Professor Lindeman, I think it was. Not sure what the title of his course was. Probably something like 'Philosophy.' Anyway, he had a habit of introducing us to important people in the world, mostly people we'd never heard of. Some of them were controversial. Needless to say, he wasn't the favorite of the

'Right Reverends' that ran the place—the administration."

"Bet he wasn't."

"Yeah. Well, one day he introduced the class to the writings of Charles Darwin."

"Charles Darwin?"

"Ever hear of him?"

"No. Can't say I have."

"Well, Darwin was a pretty religious man, but he had unusual ideas. Englishman, as I recall. Brilliant mind. He was a student of plants and animals, and how they intertwine in nature. He was part of that early awakening of science. Well, that's what I call it. A scientist might have a different way of saying it. Anyway, he started to study how different animals are similar, but still different, and he came up with some theories about how life changes over lots of time."

"Over how much time?" Levi asked.

"Depends. Could be millions of years, according to him," Shiloh replied.

"What! Millions?"

"Right. Millions, maybe more. Kinda upset some folks. But old Darwin had done his homework. He'd traveled around a lot. He'd found people that had skeletons of ancient fish and lizards and things that don't exist anymore. He challenged other scientists and religious leaders to explain them. They tried, but they couldn't, of course. Darwin said that the earth is always changing, and the living things that can best live with the changes have the best chances to survive. The ones that can't change will die off. This is 'natural selection,' which, I suppose, means that those plants or animals that are best suited for a certain place and time are the most likely to survive. In other words, nature selects those plants or animals." Shiloh stole a look at Levi across the campfire. "You have to understand that I'm not a scientist, but I'm trying to explain science to you. I'm at a disadvantage."

"So where is this idea about Darwin today?"

"Oh, it's still with us. Will be for longer than you'll be alive. Some people call it the theory of evolution. Others have a much more harsh term for it."

"And it sounds like you're saying that these scientists, like Charles Darwin, believe that living things probably have been around lots longer than most people believe, and that these things haven't always looked exactly like they do today? And maybe this could apply even to humans? Is that about right?"

"Yes. According to Darwin's theory, as I understand it, humans have been around for considerable time. I don't remember whether he said just how many, but several thousand years."

"What do you think about this evolution idea, Shiloh?"

"It's an interesting theory."

"Want to know what I think about it?" Levi asked.

"If you want to tell me."

"I think it's a big pile of horse manure."

"Now, see," Shiloh replied. "You've missed the whole point. Our discussion isn't really about religion and science. At the moment I really don't know which comes closest to being correct. I suspect there's not as much difference as you—as most people—see, but that's not important at the moment. Our discussion is about considering different choices. Different points of view. You jumped to a conclusion without enough evidence to fill a thimble. That's what I was afraid of. All you know about Darwin's theory of evolution is what I just told you, and already you've made up your mind."

"Well, it just doesn't sound right."

"Levi, if I can keep you alive long enough, you might amount to something some day. If you do, you've got to be one of the 'cool heads' in town. There'll be plenty of idiots that'll make snap decisions. There'll be a shortage of people able to weigh both sides of an issue, consider all possibilities before making a decision. You need to be one of those."

The two men stared at each other. "Look at me," Levi said, slightly annoyed. "Just look at me. Here I am. Dirty. Poor as a snake. Hell, I probably don't even have five dollars. I'm riding a horse that's probably stolen. At any rate, it isn't mine. I have a Colt revolver that isn't really mine. I have clothes on my back that once belonged to somebody else, and they're almost worn out. I haven't got anything, Shiloh. Besides that, I'm not educated, not like you. Hell, I never even heard of this Darwin person, and I don't know anything about Custer. I'm not all that free and easy around people. On top of all that, I'm trying to survive in this wild place, wanted by the law, and followed by a killer." Levi stopped and looked around, desperation in his voice. "And you think I might amount to something? How?"

"I don't know how, Levi. Believe it or don't, I don't have all the answers, but for some reason I'm spending time trying to save you, so maybe you could help me out and quit feeling sorry for yourself," Shiloh replied.

"And suppose some miracle happens and I survive my inevitable meeting with George Tompkins. What then?"

"Well, now you know about Darwin's theories on evolution," Shiloh said, attempting to take some of the seriousness off the subject. "That means you know more than most people. You won't always be right, but it'll be more likely."

"Seriously, Shiloh, how do I do this? How do I keep from making these snap decisions? I still have doubts about this Darwin person and his theories."

"That's okay, Levi. I'm pretty sure he sometimes had doubts. Just learn to give the other point of view a chance. It's like a judge that has to hear both sides in a trial." Shiloh stopped for a moment to consider his words. "Well, maybe that's not a real good example. I've seen some bad judges, but you get the idea."

"Yeah, I guess," Levi said. He tossed the remaining cold coffee from his cup into the fire, watching it sizzle and sputter. "I've got another question," he said.

"I figured you would," Shiloh said. "What is it?"

"What happened to the professor? Lindeman, wasn't it?"

"Oh, he was gone by the end of the school year. I suppose the school's administration dismissed 'im. It was their right to do so. After all, it was their job to teach religion. Having a man like him on staff was a pretty bold move. Didn't work out. Couldn't have a wild man like that upsetting their tidy little school."

Levi silently considered the professor's fate, and then he said, "That's rough, Shiloh."

"More than rough," Shiloh said. "The school kept the students from hearing a point of view that they'll have to face out in the real world. You see, Levi, that professor was trying to teach the students to think. He wasn't trying to destroy their religion."

The fire had burned to a small mound of glowing, copper-colored embers, and the night was mostly quiet. A bird that Levi couldn't identify called from somewhere in the distance. A coyote yapped in the hills.

"Is school over for now?" Levi asked.

"Yeah, I suppose. You can go home now."

"Think I'll just go to bed right here," Levi said. "I'm tired."

Both men unrolled their bedrolls, placed their Colt revolvers within easy reach and went to bed. Levi lay in the comfort of his bedroll, watching the millions of stars that spread across the expanse of the Palo Duro Canyon. He wasn't an especially religious man, but he knew that Darwin's theories about nature challenged those that he'd been taught.

Looking across at Shiloh, he saw the glowing ember of a

lighted cigarette. "Shiloh," he said. "Are you awake?"

"I am now," came the reply.

"Okay, so I've been thinking about Darwin."

"Good. That's what you're supposed to do," Shiloh replied.

"I have a lot of questions about just how this evolution thing works," Levi replied. "Maybe you can explain some of the details to me."

"Way over my head," Shiloh said, "but I have a small library of battered books that I carry in one of my saddlebags. I think I still have a copy of *The Origin of Species*, Darwin's first book. Professor Lindeman gave every person in his class a copy. You'll find Darwin's answers there. I left the aforementioned library in the tent back in Amarillo, but I'll give you my own personal copy. Now, go to sleep."

Chapter 19

Now that they felt safe from their pursuers, at least for a few days, Levi and Shiloh began to spend time with others. Shiloh spent most of his time among the rough, independent inhabitants of Amarillo. There was a colorful mixture of men who drifted like tumbleweeds through the area. Some were cowboys who worked on nearby ranches but spent as much time as possible in town, where they could enjoy cheap whiskey and cheaper women. Others were merchants, dealing in anything that could be bought, bartered, or sold. There were cold, silent, brooding characters that stayed to themselves and were respectfully avoided by everyone else. There were desperados, bounty hunters, mercenaries, and renegades.

Still others swaggered about, carrying heavy rifles, such as Sharps, Remingtons, or Winchester single shots, and few men dared to cross them. A few years earlier they had been buffalo hunters. Some probably arrived on the Southern Plains after the great buffalo slaughter was over. They were drifting, wandering, at loose ends, trying to find a new livelihood, now that there were no more buffalo to hunt or Indians to kill.

While this cross section of humanity attracted Shiloh, it was the one that Levi avoided. Shiloh went about the camps, rustling up card games anywhere he could. His fellow card players were not rich men. Many of them had little or no money, so he saw to it that he lost as many hands as he won. After all, he didn't want to scare off gamblers with lesser skills. In this situation the game itself was important, not the stakes.

Levi spent most of his time outside of town, riding the endless, open, treeless prairie and trying to imagine what it was like when buffalo had covered these plains and the Comanche and Kiowa Indians slaughtered, yet protected, them. Remembering the poverty of his own childhood, Levi visited some of the lonely, courageous homesteaders, who were trying to scratch out a living from a ruthless land.

Each time he looked into the faces of these hopeful but desperate pioneers, he remembered the tragic story of Libby and Ernest Kaufman. Occasionally he visited some of the ranchers who had transformed the plains from a lush sea of grass into a cattle-producing factory in short time. He rode through other areas once rich with native grasses, but now a denuded, barren wasteland that had been overgrazed and almost destroyed in only a few years.

Having spent his very early years in and around San Antonio, Levi was not prepared for the open quietness, the solitude, of the Panhandle. He was accustomed to huge oak trees covering the gentle hills and valleys of central Texas, to sparkling clear rivers lined with native pecan and cottonwood trees, and to dense thickets of junipers. He was familiarizing himself with a whole new world. It took some getting accustomed to, but he had to admit that he found a degree of raw beauty in this hostile country.

Both Levi and Shiloh maintained the vigilance they had adopted over the past few months. Each man went about his business casually and confidently, yet always aware that a mortal enemy could appear at any time. On his rides out onto the prairie, Levi practiced with the Colt revolver that constantly reminded him of Rachel Sandifer. Sometimes he picked out small targets on the landscape and practiced for accuracy. At other times he practiced drawing and shooting, striving not only for speed but also for smoothness and accuracy. He knew the day would come when he had to face George Tompkins, and he had a constant concern about Shiloh's tendency to flash his money about. He knew that he'd be well advised to stay in practice.

Although Levi and Shiloh had very different daily routines, they began each day with a discussion of plans for the day and then ended each day with a review of the day's major events. At the beginning of one day some time in November, Levi casually said to Shiloh, "Got a few minutes? There's something out here you've gotta see."

"What is it?"

"You'll just have to see it. I don't want to try to describe it."

Levi led the gambler down a row of rustic shacks to a point where they could observe the rear of one specific building, one that served as a restaurant for the settlement. Nestling down behind some boxes and other trash, Levi motioned for Shiloh to do the same. Already there was noisy clamoring inside the building, as men entered for an early morning meal. Occasionally, a dirty, shirtless cook came to the back door and scraped scraps of food into an open barrel.

They sat and waited for almost half an hour. They were getting cold and tired when a tiny shadow appeared, seemingly from nowhere, and approached the barrel. It was a small boy, not more than five years old. He was dressed in tattered pants and a dirty flannel shirt. It was a cold morning, but the child wore no coat or shoes.

"Who is that?" Shiloh asked in a hushed voice.

"An Indian kid. Comanche probably. An orphan, I think. For sure abandoned. I've asked around, and I've been told that his mother was Comanche. Nobody knows what happened to her. Probably dead. His dad was a white man, cowboy or buffalo hunter or something."

As they watched, the boy moved a box over to the barrel,

climbed up onto the box, and reached inside the barrel. He stood on the box and ate the waste food from the barrel. Hearing the back door open again, he jumped down and ran toward a mound of trash surrounded by a growth of weeds. As the cook came out the door, he spied the running child. Hurling a bucket of trash in the general direction of the child, he yelled, "Get outta here, you little bastard! Damned heathen!"

The child disappeared, and the cook went back inside. Levi and Shiloh slowly rose from their hiding places, went around to the front of the restaurant, and entered. They ordered coffee and breakfast and sat thinking about the discomforting sight of a hungry Indian child eating scraps of food from a trash barrel. It was apparent that Levi was greatly troubled by the plight of the young Indian. Shiloh let him brood for a while and then asked, "Well, what's bothering you today?" He knew very well what the answer would be.

"I've been watching that kid for several days now. It seems to me that we've done the same thing to him that we've done to his people. I guess he's kind of a symbol."

"Look, Levi, you can't rewrite history, and you can't solve all the problems in the world, or in this state, or even in this town."

"Maybe not, but shouldn't I try to help a kid out, if I see 'im in trouble? I'll tell you something, Shiloh. If that was a hungry dog or horse out there, people would feed it and care for it, most likely. But they'd just as soon see that kid die."

"Well, you have to understand how things are out here. Remember, these people grew up differently than you did. Just a few years ago, this was the frontier. I mean, the *real* frontier. Indians were scalping and raping and killing folks. Of course, white men were doing the same things to Indians, but we overlook that. A lot of these people had family members and friends that were captured and killed by Indians. They remember it, just like it was yesterday, which it almost was. They don't have much love for Indians, including Indian kids."

Levi was silent for a while, fully realizing the accuracy of Shiloh's remarks. After a while, Levi said, "Well, I'm gonna try to keep that kid from starving and freezing. Folks up here may not like it, but I can't just let 'im die. Already I've been putting food out for 'im. He knows it, too. Sometimes, he'll come and get the food, even if I'm standing out in the open, watching." After pausing for a few seconds, he continued, "Shiloh, maybe all this has something to do with that wolf in the canyon."

Shiloh scratched his head, considering Levi's strange remark. "Yeah. Maybe," he replied.

Over the next few days Levi managed to get a well-used coat and a pair of boots in a size that he thought might be right for the boy. He bought them from a farming family that had a son who had outgrown them. Levi carefully avoided telling the farmer what he planned to do with the clothing, fearing that the man and his wife might refuse to sell them if they knew.

Levi decided first to test the boy with the boots. He supposed that the kid never had worn boots or shoes in his life, but then he reasoned that maybe his mother had put moccasins on him at some time. At any rate, the boy seemed to be smart, and he had seen boots on white people's feet. In the early morning Levi walked out behind the restaurant and placed the boots near the trash barrel. Evidently, the boy was watching. By the time Levi got about thirty yards away, the boy darted out, grabbed the boots, and scampered away. As he departed, the boy looked directly at Levi. Levi was convinced that he smiled.

The next morning, Levi went to the same place, carrying the coat. This time Levi didn't lay the object down but stood near the barrel, holding the coat. The boy came out of the shadows and approached Levi, stopping about ten feet away. He studied Levi, black eyes shining and every sense alert. He was wearing the boots. Finally, mustering all the courage he could, the boy darted for the coat. At the last moment Levi pulled it back and grabbed the boy. The boy looked up at him, terror in his eyes. Levi smiled down at him and turned him loose, at the same time handing him the coat. The boy slowly backed away, never taking his eyes off Levi.

The boy was puzzled by the behavior of this strange white man. In his short life he had encountered many whites. Most of them had ignored him, pretending that he wasn't even there. Some treated him like a wild thing, something less than human, a scavenger like a coyote or a skunk. As long as he stayed out of sight and caused no trouble, he could live. Others, while not wanting to kill him outright, wouldn't have minded if he starved or froze to death. This man was different. He brought food and clothing. Maybe this white man would help. He would watch and see.

After a few days Levi began to notice that whenever he was walking around town, the boy followed him wherever he went. Levi would look back and see the tiny kid trailing along, perhaps thirty yards behind. Each day the kid grew braver and followed ever closer. After a few more days he was sleeping in a dirty old Army blanket, rolled up just outside the tent. Finally, the kid had adopted Levi.

"I believe you have yourself a new pet," Shiloh chuckled.

"Sure is amazing, isn't it? He really is kinda like a pet. People let 'im go wild, and now he has to be tamed. Just like a wild animal."

"What's his name?"

"Don't know."

"Well, he's Comanche, so you could call him 'Eats from Trash Barrel.'"

"Funny how we think alike," Levi replied, sarcastically, "I used the same reasoning but came up with another name." Levi squinted in the early morning glare and surveyed the Indian child's domain. "What did he look like up on that box, reaching over and eating out of that barrel?"

"I give up."

"Well, to me he looked like a bear cub, so I'm going to name 'im Little Bear. When he's older, he'll certainly want to change it, but it'll do for now."

"Fair enough. Little Bear it is."

Little Bear now had a name, approximately five years following his actual birth. The patronage of a white man somewhat legitimized the boy's existence for most people in town; however, not everyone felt that way. An incident that happened on a cold, blustery day in late November indicated the attitude some of the less forgiving citizens still held.

"Damn!" Levi shouted as he shivered between blasts of icy wind. "How cold does this place get?"

"Much colder than this," Shiloh replied.

Levi and Shiloh walked down the side of the busy road through town. Little Bear followed along some distance behind the two, playing with some imaginary toy, as children of all cultures do. Two cowboys who had spent far too much time in the saloon the evening before were riding past. Seeing the Indian boy, one cowboy grinned and leaned over and whispered something to the other. As the first cowboy pointed to Little Bear, the second one grinned back and nodded.

With an inhuman yell, one of the cowboys spurred his horse toward the boy, lariat wickedly cutting the air overhead. With a precision developed over many hours of practice, the cowboy dropped the loop around Little Bear and began to drag him down the street behind his galloping horse, with the other cowboy cheering him on. Both Levi and Shiloh whirled to see what was causing the commotion.

Instantly taking in what was happening, Levi drew and cocked his pistol, swung with the path of the galloping horse, and fired. His bullet struck the horse high in the neck, severing the spinal cord and killing him instantly. The horse went down in full stride, throwing the rider into the dirt several feet in front of the skidding horse. The sound of the shot attracted the attention of everyone in the vicinity. All activity stopped and all eyes were directed toward Levi and the cowboy.

The humiliated cowboy bounced quickly to his feet, ready to fight an entire army. Swaggering up to Levi, the man absurdly stormed out the obvious, "You killed my horse!"

"That's what I intended to do," Levi replied calmly.

"You fool. You could've killed me!"

"If I'd wanted to, but I didn't want to."

Dropping his hand toward the gun at his side, the man challenged, "Maybe I ought to just kill you."

With a voice as cold as the north winds, Levi replied, "I don't want any trouble with you, but if you'd like to be as dead as your worthless horse, just touch that gun."

The cowboy swallowed hard and looked around. Nobody was going to help. As Levi confronted the cowboy, Shiloh stood facing the growing crowd, his hand on the butt of his Colt, making sure some stranger didn't intervene. Finally, the man said meekly, "But I need that horse. He's all I've got."

Reaching into his pocket and drawing out a twenty-dollar gold piece, Shiloh politely walked over and handed it to the cowboy. "Here," he said, "I just bought your horse. Go buy yourself another one."

The cowboy glanced at Shiloh and then looked carefully at the gold coin. Through clenched teeth, he protested, "That was a good horse. He was worth more than that."

"Well," Shiloh replied, "look around. If you can find someone who'll pay more, I'll withdraw my offer."

Cursing a time or two, the cowboy pocketed the coin, turned around, and walked over to the dead horse. Without another word, he unbuckled the saddle, wrestled it away from the horse, removed the bridle, and walked away with them. The dead horse still lay in the middle of the street.

Little Bear brushed himself off and trotted cautiously over to the location where Levi and Shiloh were standing. With a rush he threw himself against Levi's leg, holding on tightly and sobbing. Levi gently stroked and comforted the frightened child, checking to see that no injuries had occurred.

Shiloh stood checking up and down the street. Turning slowly to Levi, he remarked, "Well, you didn't exactly do anything to avoid that quarrel, but I guess you were a little more careful that you would've been a couple of months ago."

Still angry, Levi looked at the gambler and snapped, "You saying I didn't handle that right?"

"Hell no! I'm not criticizing you. If I did, you'd probably shoot my horse!" The tension was relieved. Both men smiled and walked back toward their tent, closely followed by Little Bear.

Chapter 20

On the second day of December, Levi rose early and roused Little Bear from his sleep. The two grabbed some cold food and went to the makeshift stable to saddle Levi's horse. Levi had a strange, unsettled feeling that he didn't understand. It was a foreboding of some sort, as if some kind of hidden message surrounded him, and it was his job to unravel the mystery and to respond to it. He remembered the feeling he had when he saw the wolf in the canyon. This feeling was like that, yet somehow different—more urgent, more frightening, more threatening. Levi tried to put the feeling out of his mind. Today was supposed to be special, a reward for Little Bear. Today, they—just the two of them—would explore another part of the Palo Duro Canyon. They had invited Shiloh, but he had declined, joking that he had an urgent need to educate card players, not Comanche children.

The weather fit Levi's apprehensive mood. Dawn had broken clean and crisp and beautiful, like new money, he thought. Lifting Little Bear onto the horse behind the saddle, Levi had ridden a few miles from town, when the weather made a sudden change. A stiff, steady wind blew from the west, driving dust and weeds across the prairie. Clouds drifted in, quickly obscuring the warmth of the sun. Soon, drops of cold rain, intermingled with scattered snowflakes, began to fall.

Levi and Little Bear pulled their coats about themselves, thankful that they'd had the foresight to bring them along. For about an hour they battled the bitterness of the elements, but the storm showed no signs of abating. Knowing that the Indian child was at least as uncomfortable as he, Levi reined his horse into a small, obscure branch of the Palo Duro Canyon. While he built a fire beneath a sheltering ledge, his young ward scurried about gathering extra pieces of the dead wood that littered the bed of the canyon.

Comfort came slowly, but it came. The fire crackled and sputtered, and the accompanying smoke burned their eyes, as the damp wood resisted burning. However, at length the campfire caught up, generating enough heat for several men. Levi leaned back against the canyon wall, hoping to catch an afternoon nap but knowing that it was not likely to happen. Somehow he couldn't relax, unable to rid himself of the feeling of impending doom that he had felt since morning. He tossed another mesquite limb on the fire, sending a shower of ash and sparks skyward.

"Now, this is a white man's fire," he said to Little Bear. "Way too big for a Comanche." Levi expected a response. Receiving none, he went on, "What do you think, Little Bear? Your ancestors make fires like that?" Still there was no response. He turned about to locate the child, not frightened for his safety but curious about why there had been no reply.

Little Bear stood transfixed, staring at something to the left of Levi, behind a ledge and slightly out of the man's line of sight. Levi scooted a few feet forward, and then stretching his body far to the left, he peered around the ledge in the direction that the boy was looking. A huge gray-white wolf stood studying the child. Suddenly seeing Levi peer around the ledge, the wolf jumped backward in surprise, throwing a small shower of gravel in the general direction of the two people. Clearly, it was the same animal that had appeared to Levi earlier in the canyon, when he had stood beautiful and graceful like a marble sculpture in the Panhandle twilight.

But this time the animal didn't display his earlier majesty, standing with his head drooped and almost touching the ground. The tail also was different. Neither erect like a collie nor straight out like a fox, the wolf's tail curled down between his legs and back under his belly, like a cur that had lost his spirit. Whining pitifully, the wolf looked through lifeless eyes at Levi and Little Bear. His breath came in irregular, raspy bursts. He moved with pain, as if the pads of his feet were sore from a long journey over rocky, barren ground. "Something's happened!" Levi whispered, his fear and excitement growing. "Something's not right! This is a bad sign!"

Puzzled and frightened by Levi's behavior, Little Bear sobbed, "Is he hurt?"

"No son," Levi replied. "I think he's trying to tell us something. He wants us to go back to town, and we'd better hurry."

Levi's terror heightened as he approached the town. Since first seeing the wolf, he had been hoping, praying that his fears would be wrong, but he knew they wouldn't be. He knew he was about to experience something horrible. He just didn't know what. There was an unusual amount of movement in the streets, and a small crowd had gathered in front of the tent. The knot tightened in Levi's gut. In spite of the cold, he felt beads of sweat forming on his forehead and down his back.

As Levi neared the tent, an uneasy man approached him and said, "Better get down and come inside, Mr. Wolfe. Yore friend's been shot. Shot real bad."

"Who are you?"

"Folks just call me Red," the man replied.

"What...what happened?" Levi stammered.

"I wasn't here, but one of the men in town tol' me what happened. Seems like some stranger done it. Big man. We'd never saw him before. He come and asked where he could find you. Said he had a message from San Antone. Had an official-looking envelope in his hand. Somebody pointed to yore tent, and the big man thanked him. Real polite. Said he'd just wait 'til you come out. Didn't want to disturb you if you was sleeping late."

Red stopped and looked fearfully at Levi, wondering if the distraught man might hold him responsible. Instead, Levi maintained his composure and urged, "Please go on."

"Well, seems like yore friend—Shiloh's his name, right?" The man hesitated and studied Levi. Levi nodded and the man continued, "Well, Shiloh come out of the tent with a blanket draped over his shoulders. Had it up around his head and face. It was cold, you know. The stranger grinned real big and said something. Real slow, he pulled his gun. Took a long time, like he was taking as much time as possible. Shiloh didn't have no gun on 'im. Stranger shot him twice. It looked like two slugs in his chest. Then he done something real strange. Walked up and stood right over Shiloh. Just stood and stared. Almost like he couldn't believe what he'd done. Then he just stalked away, cussing."

"Where is he? Shiloh, I mean."

"Inside. We made 'im comfortable as possible," Red replied, nodding toward the tent.

Without another word, Levi went into the tent. Shiloh lay on his cot, covered with blankets. As Levi approached, Shiloh looked up and said, "Well, I think I found old...George Tompkins for you."

"George Tompkins?" Levi exclaimed. "Why in hell would George shoot you?"

"He was...standing there...grinning. I was all wrapped up in a blanket, so he couldn't see my face very well," Shiloh said, speaking with great pain. Each word and each breath was becoming more labored. "Looks like...he thought...I was you. Called me Levi...just started...shooting."

Levi turned to Red. "How bad is it?" he asked.

"Real bad," Red replied. "Real, real bad." He motioned Levi back outside the tent, out of hearing, and continued, "He won't make it." Shaking his head, Red turned away from Levi.

Levi went back inside and sat beside Shiloh's bed. Shiloh weakly opened his eyes. "You're going…after 'im?"

"Yeah."

"I thought so. Remember every…thing I…taught you," Shiloh said, struggling for the strength to speak.

"I won't forget a thing."

"I know…I won't last…long, but I'll live…until you…come back. Just be sure…you do. The boy needs you."

Levi stepped back outside the tent and motioned for Red. The man hurried up to Levi. "Where's the man that did this?" Levi asked.

"Bartender told me the man come in the saloon and said he'd know when you got back. Said he'd be waitin' over to the saloon."

Levi looked about and caught sight of Little Bear. The young Indian boy was staring up at Levi, speechless, tears streaming from his eyes. Levi placed his arm around the child's shoulders, trying to comfort him. Levi could imagine what was going through the child's mind. The boy understood enough English to know what was happening. For the first time in his life Little Bear had shelter and food. But just important, he had someone who would protect him. Now he might lose everything and be right back where he started. Mainly, however, he had grown to love Levi, who had become the father he'd never had.

Levi was apprehensive about the task ahead of him. Several months ago, when he first set out on George's trail, Levi had been driven by hate and vengeance. In Bandera he had extracted a measure of revenge. He didn't need any more. At first Levi had been alone in the world, responsible to nobody and responsible for nobody. Now he had Rachel and Matthew to be concerned about, and he had the Indian boy who was totally dependent upon him.

But Shiloh had trained him as well as anyone could be trained in the art of gun fighting. And what was it that Shiloh had taught him? "Use your senses. Take advantage of your opponent's mistakes. And most of all, a man who fights for a cause has a tremendous advantage over anyone else."

Well, Levi resolved, he would remember his training, and he would remember his cause. He would protect his friends, and he would avenge Jovita's death and the injuries inflicted upon Shiloh. Given a choice, he might flee to some place where he'd never have to face Tompkins, but he didn't have that choice. It wasn't possible. Tompkins wouldn't allow it. He had to kill the man or be killed by him.

Levi checked his Colt Peacemaker. "Strange name for such an instrument of death," he said to himself. "Oh well, maybe it actually will bring some peace to my world. I aim for it to give a lot of peace to Tompkins." The gun was fully loaded and functioning perfectly.

Walking briskly down the street toward the saloon, Levi was alert to everything around him. Heading toward the southeast, he knew the sun would be to his back. The wind still was blowing in brief gusts from the west, drifting light powdery snow and some dust before it.

As he approached the saloon, Levi caught a glimpse of a figure lurking in the shadows between the saloon and an adjacent building. "George Tompkins!" Levi whispered to himself, recognizing the hulking image. At first Levi thought Tompkins planned to try to kill him from ambush. Then he remembered that George had passed up opportunities to do that. What George really wanted was to perform the killing in a slow, methodical way, so that Levi would know what was happening, have time to think, experience genuine terror before dying. Hadn't he thought he was doing that when he mistakenly shot Shiloh?

The figure stepped quickly from the shadows into Levi's path. Levi was correct. It was Tompkins. "Well, look who's here!" George spoke sarcastically and smiled wickedly. "Seems like we keep running into each other, don't it?"

A sudden appearance didn't have the effect upon his intended victim that he had expected. Levi silently stared at Jovita's killer, unsmiling and unblinking. A tiny bit of self-doubt crept across the man's weathered face. A flutter of nervousness twisted and turned in his gut. The confident smile slowly faded. The man facing him was not the one he remembered. It was Levi, all right, but there was a change. In place of the tentative, uncertain youth there stood a calmly confident man, one who appeared to know what he wanted and how to get it.

There were other problems. Surveying his surroundings, he saw that he had been far too hasty, far too confident. He was looking directly into the blinding glare of the late afternoon sun, and the wind was causing flakes of snow and bits of dirt to fly in his direction, stinging his eyes and biting his skin. Could this upstart kid have out-maneuvered him, the experienced veteran of numerous such conflicts? Okay, so maybe he'd misjudged Levi. Maybe he had, but it wasn't over, not by a long shot. Maybe this kid—or man—could be conned out of the advantage he had, or maybe he could be coaxed into abandoning the field.

"Look, kid," George began, condescension heavy in his voice.

Before George could continue, Levi interrupted, "I think you'll find out I'm not a kid!"

"Okay. Okay. Let's talk about this. We've both lost friends. Ain't no need for any more killin'. Maybe we could call it even and go our separate ways."

"Don't think so," Levi said, flatly.

"You know I saved yore life. Shore, you remember. Down in Bandera. After I shot you, I followed you and put you back on that horses. Patched up yore wound. Did it more than once."

"Why did you do that, George?"

George was trapped. He knew why, and Levi knew why. Both men knew that George didn't want Levi to merely die. He wanted Levi to experience real terror, to beg for his life, to beg to be spared from a terrible death. He wanted Levi to stare into the smiling face of his killer, knowing what was about to happen. In anger George recognized the inadequacy of his carefully constructed plan. It was he who was experiencing terror, not Levi. He was caught in his own trap.

Levi repeated his question, "Why'd you save my life? So you could toy with me. So you could kill me in your own way. Right? Well, here's your chance."

In spite of his predicament, in spite of his terror, George wasn't ready to give up. There still might be a way out. Maybe he still could prevail over this kid. He moved a step to his left. Then another step. Maybe he could improve his position.

Levi's words cut like broken glass through the cold December air, "You make one more move, and I'll shoot you down just like you did Shiloh."

"That his name? Truthfully, I'm sorry about that. I didn't mean to kill 'im. It was a mistake." Tompkins quit moving. Levi knew what was happening. He was trying to engage Levi in casual conversation, hoping that he would lose his caution. "You know," George went on, "It's kinda like what you done to my friends. Just shot 'em down in cold blood."

A chill went through Levi. George was almost correct. Levi had given none of the three men much of a chance. But was that even important? What chance had they given Jovita? Levi felt perspiration forming on his brow. He drew a deep breath, saying to himself, "Don't let him get to you. This is too important to too many people." The crisis passed, and Levi was calm again. In spite of all his training, Levi knew he almost had let the man's talk unsettle him. Well, maybe he could do the same thing to George.

Forcing his voice into a flat monotone, filled with contempt, Levi said, "You've made a big mistake. You've bitten off way more than you can handle. You've gotten old and slow. Cowardly. Stupid even. Only people you can kill is defenseless women and unarmed men. Maybe you should crawl out of here on your belly, like a snake. Yep. A stinking, slimy snake, that's you. Go on, now, you worthless, cowardly bastard. Tuck your tail and run."

Enraged by Levi's rebuke, George clawed awkwardly for his pistol, knowing he had lost before he touched the Colt. The fiery glow of the sun was blinding, and the dirt and snow pelted his face, having more psychological than physical effect. George barely had lifted his weapon from its holster when Levi's first shot struck. The bullet entered his chest, knocking him backward, buckling his knees, and spinning him partly around. George felt the burning pain as the bullet ripped through flesh and shattered bone. He tried to scream as it tore through the aorta at the top of his heart, spilling blood into his chest cavity. Again he tried to cry out in pain, but no sound came from his mouth. Only a small trickle of frothy blood appeared in each corner.

As George's big body spun to the right, recoil raised Levi's gun well above the level of his head. He cocked the gun at the apex of its path upward and brought it back down to eye level in an instant. George desperately was trying to raise his pistol, but was failing. Levi's second shot struck just two inches to the left of the first one, forcing George to his knees. His small, pig-like eyes were dilated and unseeing, and his neck swelled out, as if it were about to explode. His shallow breath rattled in his chest. He tried to return to his feet, but he could not. Again he tried to lift his weapon but discharged it harmlessly a few feet in front of him. George toppled forward, falling heavily on the cold dirt street in Amarillo, stone dead.

Levi stood watching the motionless body of George Tompkins, making certain that he was in fact dead. Cautiously, Levi lowered the hammer on his Colt revolver. Satisfied, he turned and walked back toward the tent. Levi grew cold and dizzy. Both fear and relief swept over him. For months he had longed for the day when he would put an end to a pitiful life. Now he had done so, but it gave him no pleasure—just an empty, nauseated feeling in the pit of his stomach.

Chapter 21

Little Bear ran to meet Levi, laughing and crying with happiness. Levi scooped the child into his arms and held him close to his chest. Little Bear, still struggling to learn English, said nothing. Neither did Levi. The man named Red was kneeling beside Shiloh when Levi and Little Bear entered the tent. He respectfully rose and backed away so that Levi might approach. Upon hearing the movement in the tent, Shiloh opened his eyes and looked about. When he saw Levi, a faint smile crossed his face.

Lifting his head slightly off the pillow, Shiloh spoke haltingly, "I want to...to talk with Levi...alone." Red obediently moved toward the door, taking Little Bear's hand to lead him out. "Actually, the child...can stay," Shiloh continued.

When only Levi and Little Bear remained with Shiloh, the gambler addressed Levi, "I know I'm not...going to live. Wanted to make sure...that you...killed Tompkins. Knew...you would." Shiloh rested for a full minute and then continued, "Now, listen...I'm getting really tired. Give the kid...my horse and saddle. A Comanche and a horse...kinda go...together. Now, reach... under the bed."

Levi did so and pulled out Shiloh's rifle, the Model 1873 Winchester. Unlike so many of those in use at the time, this was a fancy grade rifle with a twenty-six inch octagonal barrel, not a short-barreled saddle carbine. "I wanted one that would reach out and do the job for me at long range," Shiloh had once told Levi, so he'd had the rifle custom made by the factory.

"That rifle...will do things your...old Henry only...dreams

about. I want you...to have it...but keep...the Henry. Someday your...grandchildren will...prize it. Also, take...my Colt revolver...in a few years...teach the kid...to use it...if you want to."

Shiloh rested again, breathing deeply, each breath making a harsh, raspy sound. He closed his eyes and lay still. A bit of panic overcame Levi, as he feared that his friend might have died. But then Shiloh went on, "Now, for the ...serious part. I have...a lot...of money. I want you...to have it. I have...no family. You're the only...real friend...I have. They...say I can't...take it with me." Levi started to protest, but Shiloh weakly raised his hand for quiet, and then he continued, "Use the money...anyway you...want, but you...take it. I want a...promise on that. If it... stays here...no telling...who'll end up...with it. Now promise."

Levi felt dazed and undeserving. It was almost as if he were being rewarded for killing a man. However, he had no other suggestions as to how to dispose of the money. Quietly, he responded, "I promise."

"Okay, see that...you do. Most is...in my money belt. Some's in the...hollow butt of...the Winchester. Rest is in my left boot. Now, for one last...thing. Bury me...out by the...Palo Duro Canyon. Don't let...anyone know...where it is. Then, you and... the great...Indian Chief there get back...to central Texas...where you belong."

"I'll stay here with you," Levi said.

"No!" Shiloh snapped. Then, more gently, he repeated, "No, Levi. I don't want...you to see me die. It's...it's not pleasant." Shiloh rested, again trying to gain strength. "Call Red...back in here."

Red entered quietly and stood respectfully in the background, well out of Shiloh's line of vision. "Red's here, Shiloh," Levi said.

"Thanks," Shiloh replied. "Red. Red, come on up here. Now

tell these...two about our little deal."

Red edged his way cautiously toward the others. He cleared his throat. "Well. It seems that Shiloh wants to...how do I put this politely?"

"You don't have...to be polite," Shiloh said. "Just tell 'em."

"Like Shiloh just said, he don't want his friends to watch 'im die. At least to him, it takes away his dignity." Red paused and studied Levi's reaction. Seeing none, he continued. "I'll hang around here. You and the boy stay in my tent. It ain't much, but it'll keep you outta the rain and cold." Red fell silent.

After a short period, Levi asked, "Is that all?"

"Not quite," Red replied. He shook his head slowly. "This kinda thing never gets easy," he whispered, glancing first at Shiloh and then at Levi. "We ain't got no real undertaker in this hell-hole-of-a-town. I kinda do the job. Nobody else wants to do it. I make the coffins and clean up the bodies and arrange for the burials. It ain't pleasant work. I shore don't like it, but it pays better than most work around here. Shore ain't no shortage of customers."

"And him?" Levi said, nodding toward Shiloh. "How did you get involved?"

"He was layin' there on the ground in front of his tent. Some vulture sent for me. He thought I'd pay him for the tip, I guess. I saw he was still alive, but hit real bad. We brought him in here, and that's when he tol' me what he wanted."

"And he wants us to stay while he dies?" Levi said.

"That's about it. After he's gone, I'm supposed to put 'im in the coffin and seal it up. Just to make sure we all understand his instructions, the sealing is permanent. Once sealed, it stays sealed. He doesn't want you to see him dead. Then my work's done. I turn the sealed casket over to you for burial. His instructions."

"And that's it?" Levi said.

"Purty much."

"Strange."

"Not so strange," Red replied. "I get all kinds of requests. This one's purty normal. He just wants you to remember him alive, not dead."

Levi now turned to Shiloh. "You hear all of that, Shiloh?"

"Sure. I'm not…deceased yet," Shiloh whispered.

"This is what you really want?"

"Yeah. It's best…this way, Levi. You may not think so…but it is."

Levi looked from Shiloh to Red to Little Bear. Then he looked again. "Then, I guess the decision is made." Looking again at the small Indian boy, he said. "Let's go find Red's tent, Little Bear."

Levi turned to go. "Wait, Levi." The weak voice came from Shiloh. "Levi, I know you and the boy think you need me." Shiloh laughed softly. "I sure…hate to go off…and leave you… without my…expert guidance. Looks like…I got…no choice."

"Shiloh, this isn't over," Levi said. "You can recover from this."

"No, Levi. No chance. Let me…talk. I'm feeling pretty weak." Shiloh fell silent. Red rushed to the bed and bent over. Not knowing exactly what to do, he held his head close and listened for breathing.

"He's alive, but unconscious," Red said. Turning to Levi, he continued. "Go get some rest. I'll call you if there's a change."

Just at daybreak, Red woke Levi. "Levi, he's gone. He died not long after you left. I just let you sleep. Nothing you could've did. I took care of 'im. Did my best work. Put 'im in my best coffin. Sealed it up real tight. Cain't nothin' get to the body. Anyway, I've done all I can do. Ever thing's ready for burial."

"Thanks, Red. You've been a real help. Let me pay you."

"No, thanks, Levi. Shiloh done paid me in advance. Real generous. I'm took care of."

On December the fourth, dawn broke clear and crisp over the Palo Duro Canyon, as the first sliver of light appeared just above the eastern rim of the canyon. Within a few minutes half the sun was visible, casting its rays into the purple darkness of the canyon and wiping away the shadows. Levi sat quietly, stoically, on the canyon's western rim, watching the sun rise and the canyon come to life. An old army blanket was draped about his shoulders, and his felt hat was pulled low over his brow. He sat cross-legged with a cup of coffee cradled between his hands. A small campfire crackled and hissed a few feet behind him.

Farther back stood a rickety old wagon that Levi had rented the previous day from the livery stable in Amarillo. At midnight he had loaded the casket into the wagon, and he had driven out of town. Just before his departure, he had lifted the sleeping Little Bear into the wagon bed, actually beside the coffin, and tied both saddle horses behind the wagon. He left the tent and some supplies behind, attempting to give the appearance that he would return. He had no intention of doing so.

Reaching the outskirts of Amarillo, Levi had headed south and eventually a bit east. His previous trips into the countryside around the town paid rich dividends on this occasion. The road was neither good nor well-marked, problems that were increased by the darkness. However, having studied the entire area on numerous earlier occasions, Levi had little trouble in finding his way. He got almost no sleep. Upon arriving at his destination, he hid the wagon and team of horses among some junipers and watched his back trail for a few hours. As he had hoped, no one was following, but there were individuals in Amarillo who knew that Shiloh had money. It was entirely possible that such a person might have been watching the tent when Levi left with the wagon.

As Levi sat enjoying the peace of the early morning, Little Bear came hurrying over and slid under the blanket beside him. Levi placed his arm around the boy and said, "Here, Son, let's warm you up a bit." He was startled by his own words. In his memory he had addressed the child as his son only once before. The responsibility of having a son actually frightened him, but, in effect, that was the relationship that had developed.

"Little Bear, there's some biscuits in the bag over by the wagon. Go get some if you're hungry," Levi told him. Little Bear got up and trotted over to the bag, reached in, and got two cold, hard biscuits. He began gnawing on one and solemnly handed the other one to Levi. Closely watching the child, Levi marveled at how quickly he was learning the English language, or what passed for it on the frontier. Little Bear snuggled back down under the blanket with Levi. They sat and waited for ten minutes, then twenty minutes, and then half an hour. The restless young boy began to fidget and squirm about, restless for activity after a long sleep. Finally, he looked up at Levi, puzzled by the long wait.

Levi returned the look and gave a slow smile. "Kinda wondering what we're waiting for?" Levi asked the child. Little Bear smiled back and nodded. "Well, I'm not sure. Guess I was about halfway expecting some help. There's lots of space up here. Don't know exactly where to bury ol' Shiloh. Thought my Indian medicine—or yours—might show me where." Little Bear nodded again. Levi wondered just how much of the conversation the boy actually understood. The two fell silent again, sitting and waiting. A quarter of an hour passed. Levi stretched and prepared to stand, when he noticed Little Bear staring intently into the distance.

At first Levi saw nothing, but then he saw it. It was little more than a dot on the horizon, but it was growing larger with each bound. "Dog?" Little Bear whispered.

"Pretty close," Levi replied. "Wild dog. Wolf."

By now the huge white animal was easily visible, padding along a game trail that paralleled the canyon. The wolf was now traveling more slowly, moving his large head from side to side, testing the air for strange scent and stopping frequently behind junipers or scrub oak to survey his surroundings.

Little Bear watched in amazement. He looked over at Levi, his round eyes sparkling with excitement, a huge smile spread across his face. Unable to contain his enthusiasm, he jumped up and ran toward the wolf, pointing and chanting, "Wolf! Wolf! Wolf!" Seeing the boy, perhaps for the first time, the wolf veered away from the trail and squatted beneath the largest tree in the area, a huge cottonwood growing in the head of a draw. The animal made a low growling-barking sound and then sprawled out beneath the tree.

"Well, that's our answer. That's where we'll plant Shiloh," Levi whispered. Little Bear gave Levi a sideways glance, to which Levi responded, "Sorry. Didn't mean any disrespect."

As Little Bear and Levi watched, the wolf got to his feet, barked a few more times and then turned back down the trail, walking in the direction from which he had come. After traveling only a few yards, he broke into a long, ground-eating trot and was gone within seconds. Levi and Little Bear walked over to the cottonwood tree. It took only moments for Levi to determine that the wolf had chosen wisely. This was a quiet and scenic spot on the rim of the canyon, restful and secluded, a marvelous spot to bury Shiloh.

It took Levi most of the day to dig the grave. Although it was a beautiful spot, the ground was hard and rocky. Levi was determined to place the body deep in the ground, having heard stories of coyotes digging up bodies that had been buried too shallow. While Levi worked with the shovel, Little Bear was scouring the area for stones to cover the grave, further discouragement for the coyotes and other scavengers. Several times while they labored, Levi and Little Bear spied the wolf standing silhouetted on the rim of the canyon, as if overseeing the proceedings. Occasionally, he would let out a long, mournful howl to the amazement of the two humans. Each time Little Bear playfully answered with his own imitation of the wolf's call.

With nightfall close at hand, Levi declared the hole deep enough. Standing in the bottom, he could look out only by standing on the tips of his toes. Levi half-carried, half-dragged the coffin to the gravesite and clumsily slid it into the deep hole. He had to climb down into the hole with the coffin in order to get it straight and flat on the bottom of the grave. Climbing back out, he stood looking down and, remembering the man who had taught him so much, saved his life on occasion, and been his constant companion. Most of all, he was a friend, the closest friend that Levi ever had

"I'm going to miss you, Shiloh," Levi said quietly, "and I don't even know how to bury you properly, but me and the kid will do the best we can."

With that, Levi went over to the wagon and soon returned with a battered, leather-bound Bible. He wasn't an accomplished reader, but he managed to do an adequate job of reading the Twenty-third Psalm. After that, he read a few additional passages, chosen at random, and then closed the Bible. "You won't be needing this," Levi said, referring to Shiloh's Bible. "Maybe I will. Anyway, I'll keep it." He placed the small book in his breast pocket. With a smile on his face, he looked down at the rough wooden box and said, "You didn't think I knew you had it, did you? Well, you're not so clever. I saw you reading it several times, when you thought I wouldn't notice." Looking upward, Levi said, "Take care of him, Boss. I know you will."

It took only a few minutes for Levi and Little Bear to scoop the dirt over the coffin and then to carefully scatter stones and dirt and limbs on top in what would appear to be a haphazard manner. Levi left no head stone, no marker of any kind, knowing that to do so might possibly attract grave robbers. He did, however, make a mental note of the grave's exact location, vowing that if he ever returned to the Panhandle, he would pay a respectful visit.

Levi left the gravesite reluctantly, feeling that he had done an inadequate job of performing the ceremony. As he had done so often in his short life, Levi silently wished that he were more articulate, more capable of expressing his feelings, and better equipped at choosing the best words to fit an occasion. Clinging to the thought, Levi said, "Well, there's no reason I can't do better. Shiloh did. I'm as smart as him." Then, with his first smile since burying his friend, he continued, "Besides, if I'm ever going to be as important as Shiloh said I would, I've got to learn to read better and write better. Even talk better. I do believe there's a school teacher down in central Texas who can help."

When Levi returned to camp, Little Bear was carefully tending the campfire, just as Levi had taught him to do. Beckoning the child, Levi said, "Come here, little man, let's talk. You know, if you're going to be my partner now that Shiloh's gone, we have to discuss things."

The child smiled at the adult and said, "Okay."

"Do you want to go back to town?" Levi asked.

The child's face darkened. He indeed had learned some

English. He knew what Levi was asking, and he didn't relish the idea of returning to a place where he had been treated like a wild animal. He looked squarely at Levi and replied, "No!"

"Want to go a long way off, where it's warmer and there's lots of big trees?"

"You bet!" the young Indian replied, using one of the local expression that he had adopted.

"Well, if we go, we've got to leave real early in the morning, a long time before daylight."

"Okay."

"Then let's go and eat some beans and get some sleep. We've got to leave about midnight. If there's any more bad guys out there, we don't want 'em to know what we're doing."

The campfire burned low, leaving little more than brightly glowing embers. Little Bear lay fast asleep in his blanket, apparently at peace with the world. Levi sat for a long while, staring into the golden glow of the fire, lost in memories of the past. He marveled at how profoundly his life had changed over the past few months, at how many people had left their marks on his life, and at how he had changed his way of measuring the importance of events and of people.

Just a few short months ago, his one obsession was to kill every member of a murderous gang of renegades. He thought George Tompkins' death would bring him peace. He had killed George and all his followers, but that had brought no satisfaction. True, he avenged Jovita's death, but that didn't bring the beautiful woman back to life. Her death was still just as real.

As he had done so often, his mind focused on Jovita. How many times had he lain awake at night, missing her gentleness, reliving their brief life together? But that was over now. Jovita always would be a part of him. He would never forget her, but he would learn to remember her without pain, without guilt, and without remorse. It would be difficult. Indeed, it already had been difficult, but he was coming to grips with it.

Then there was Rachel. At first he had denied his feelings for this headstrong young widow. It was not right, he had told himself. Jovita had just died. How could he allow himself to care for another woman? In spite of his self-doubts, he had done the right thing. "At least this once," he said aloud, "At least this time I made the right decision. I got away to sort things out and to find a solution, and I found it. I'm not an evil person for loving Rachel. It wasn't my choice to find her so soon after Jovita's death, but I had to deal with it, and I did."

Levi knew his mind was wandering, and that maybe many of his thoughts were senseless, incoherent ramblings of a thoroughly exhausted man. He had gotten almost no sleep the previous night, and this night was rapidly slipping away. He made one last trip around the perimeter of the campsite to ensure that everything was in order. He checked his and Little Bear's gear and then made sure the saddle horses were nearby. Finally, he lay down for a few hours of restful sleep.

Levi awoke suddenly, half expecting to find Shiloh holding a gun to his face, just as he had done so long ago in Waco. Instead, there was nothing except a clear, starlit night. The moon, almost full at this time of month, hung low, casting long eerie shadows along the slopes and cliffs that formed the walls and valleys of the canyon. Somewhere along the canyon rim, an owl hooted. Farther out on the prairie the yapping and howling of a pack of coyotes broke the stillness, as they hunted for a rabbit, a rat, or anything to ward off starvation for another day. Levi was glad that no one observed the shiver that passed down his spine as he gazed out over the spooky landscape. "No wonder the Comanches had such a respect for this place," he mused.

Little Bear was out of bed almost as soon as Levi was. Bouncing about and trying to help, the child was mostly in the way, but Levi was struck by the youngster's enthusiasm. "We go to place of big trees?" he asked, staring intently at Levi, fearful of disappointment.

Levi chuckled and replied, "Yeah, we go to place of big trees."

With Levi's reassurance Little Bear became even more animated, restless to begin the journey. "It's a long way," Levi reminded him, "We'll ride a long time. Bunch of days." In spite of himself, Levi used exaggerated hand and arm gestures, trying to be sure the child understood him. He knew it didn't help, but still he continued.

"Okay, bunch days," Little Bear replied, "We ride bunch days. You bet."

"Getting to be a real chatterbox, aren't you?" Levi laughed, knowing that the Indian child didn't know what it meant to ride a bunch of days.

"Okay, we go now?" the boy prodded.

"Yeah. Yeah, we go now. Just let me get a few more things taken care of."

While Little Bear rummaged about, looking for another cold biscuit, Levi caught and saddled their horses. His original plan was to leave the rented wagon and horses exactly where they stood, knowing they would be found and returned. It now occurred to him that to do that might reveal the location of Shiloh's grave. That was the one thing that he didn't want to do, so he harnessed the rented horses to the wagon and tied his own horse behind. Little Bear already had managed to mount his horse. This done, Levi drove the team and wagon a few miles away from the grave site, freed the rented horses, and abandoned the wagon. He smiled at the awkwardness of his maneuvers, but at the time he had no better plan.

Levi and Little Bear sat astride their saddle horses, each contemplating the long trip ahead. He made one more check to be sure he had packed all necessary gear and supplies. Looking at the impatient Indian child, Levi declared, "Let's go to the place of big trees."

Little Bear smiled and replied, "Okay. You bet."

Orienting himself on the Big Dipper constellation and the North Star, Levi headed south, away from the bustling cattle town of Amarillo. He estimated that it was two o'clock in the morning when they headed their mounts south. Although he was totally unfamiliar with the country they would be passing through on their trip, Levi anticipated no real difficulty. He wondered whether the trip would be hard for the five-year-old Indian boy. Although he had no way to even guess, Levi doubted that there would be undue hardship. After all, in his short life, Little Bear had endured intense suffering and hardship. This would be play.

"Tell you what we'll do, Chief," Levi said to Little Bear. We'll go slow. Take our time, just like me and Shiloh did coming up here. We'll enjoy this trip. No point in rushing things. Near as I can figure, we should get there a little before Christmas."

"Christmas?" Little Bear replied. "What Christmas?"

"A five-year-boy that doesn't know about Christmas?" Levi exclaimed. "Boy, you do have a lot to learn."

Chapter 22

Rachel Sandifer watched the day break cold and clear over the freezing waters of the San Saba River. A white blanket of frost lay on the dead buffalo grass, and a thin crust of ice lined the river's edge up against the shoreline. A narrow ribbon of water streamed from a crack in the limestone on the opposite bank, cascading some fifty feet into a clear pool of the river. Shrubs and weeds near the waterfall were crusted with a thick layer of ice, glistening and shimmering in the morning light like glass beads on a necklace. It had been unusually cold for the first half of the month of December, making the young woman wonder what January and February would be like.

As the first soft colors of dawn gave way to full daylight, Rachel stole a glance up the winding dirt road that led northward from her home toward the main road. The road then went south into town, and in the opposite direction northwest toward Brownwood and northeast toward Waco. She had looked hopefully in that direction thousands of times in the past months. It was the direction Levi had taken when he had gone away so long ago, and the one that he'd used when he first came into her life, more dead than alive all those month ago.

Rachel well remembered the day of Levi's departure. Her life as a rancher had seen its fair share of dark days. No, she had seen far more than her fair share. The day that she let Levi ride out of her life indeed had been one of the darkest. But deep down, she knew he had to leave, to find peace after the death of Jovita, and to come to terms with his feelings for her so soon after Jovita's death. Also, he thought he had to protect her and those close to her when George Tompkins came looking for him.

Oh yes, George Tompkins. At first she didn't take Levi's fears of Tompkins as seriously as she should, but then one day the man appeared at the ranch looking for Levi. Just as they had agreed, Rachel hid inside the house with a loaded, double-barreled shotgun while Oscar went out and talked with him. The man was friendly and polite, claiming he had information from Levi's friends in San Antonio about the charges against him. One look at him, however, and Rachel understood the dangers. She saw the seething hatred in his eyes, hatred that he tried to camouflage with charm. She watched, and she knew that Levi had made the correct choice.

As Levi had instructed, Oscar pretended to believe his story and told him that Levi had gone to Waco to visit a family member. She knew the torment that Oscar was suffering as he revealed Levi's whereabouts. She watched him bite his lip and fight back the tears as he wished Tompkins luck in his efforts to locate Levi in Waco. Then, as quickly as he'd appeared, he departed. However, his departure wasn't without incident. As he prepared to leave, he tried to engage Oscar in some good-natured small talk, perhaps hoping Oscar might carelessly relate additional information that he was holding back. Oscar would have none of it. He politely waited for Tompkins to mount and ride away.

As he swung easily into the saddle, he smiled broadly, looking directly at the window where Rachel stood, well hidden in the shadows, watching the two men talk. Then he said directly to Oscar, but loudly enough for Rachel to hear, "Tell the woman she can put the shotgun down. I'm leaving now." With a smile and a tip of his hat, he turned his big white horse and rode away, never looking back.

He had satisfied himself that Levi was no longer at the ranch.

Maybe he already knew where Levi was. Maybe he was just checking one more time to be sure. Maybe he was considering doing the same thing to her that he had done to Jovita, but decided it was too risky. At any rate he'd been gone for many months.

Glancing up the road again, Rachel saw two tiny objects on the horizon, barely visible in the morning haze that lay like a blanket over the rolling hills. For a moment her heart leaped, and she caught her breath. Then she forced herself to be calm, remembering past disappointments. How many times had it happened in the past? How often had she stood watching a rider approach, hoping against hope that it would be Levi returning, only to find that it was someone else? How many times had she been disappointed, bravely hiding her emotions from her loved ones, only to cry herself to sleep at night?

Maybe it was time to give up. Maybe she had lost again. Levi had promised to return within a year. Well, it hadn't been a year, but it was getting close. She looked again. The figures were much too far away for identification. It couldn't be Levi. Who would the second rider be? Levi had appeared at her ranch alone, and he had left alone. There wouldn't be anyone accompanying him. No, it couldn't be Levi. She was convinced that she would never see him again. She turned and walked back toward the ranch house.

From the distance Levi could see the ranch house. Wisps of white smoke drifted from the chimney, and reflections of the early morning sun played on the water of the San Saba River. The pungent odor of the juniper trees drifted across the ridges, reminding Levi that he was back in familiar country. Someone was moving about, barely visible, down by the corral. "Has to be old Oscar Carson," Levi said, more to himself than to Little

Bear. As they rested their horses on a small hill above the ranch house, Levi pointed out the prominent features of the ranch to the sleepy-eyed Indian boy that rode beside him. Little Bear tried without success to appear interested.

Levi waited on the ridge for an unusually long time. After all this time and anticipation, he was apprehensive about his return. What if Rachel had given up on him, sold out, and moved away? After all, she was under extreme pressure from outside sources to surrender her land. Maybe someone made her a reasonable offer, a legitimate offer, for the ranch, and she took it. It would be reasonable for her to consider such an offer. What if she had married one of the many eligible men in the community? Love or no love, she might marry for comfort and companionship, for protection even, perhaps hoping love would come later. What would he do? Could he handle another disappointment?

Again addressing the sleepy Indian boy, Levi said, "Well, Partner, are you ready?"

"You bet," came the unenthusiastic reply.

Touching spurs to his horse, Levi began the long ride down to the ranch, filled with hope and no small amount of fear. Little Bear followed. As he approached, he decided to circle below the house and go straight to the corrals. That way, Oscar could tell him everything that had happened since his departure. If things were really bad for him, if Rachel no longer wanted him there, then he and Little Bear could just move on, and maybe Rachel would never learn that he had returned. The two riders moved quietly through the mesquites and junipers, well hidden from the view of the house. However, when they passed a short distance beyond the house, they would be clearly visible to Oscar at the corral. The plan was working perfectly. Levi and Little Bear approached the corral, certain they had avoided detection from the house and hoping not to startle Oscar in his work.

As they came close, they could hear movement inside a small storage building at one end of the corral. As the door swung open, they waited for Oscar to step out into the sunlight. The figure appeared, but it wasn't Oscar. Instead, Rachel stepped out and looked up at Levi and Little Bear. She stood staring at them, unable to speak.

Finally, she managed to choke out his name, "Levi!"

Levi was as surprised and unprepared as she was. "I…I thought it was Oscar," he stammered.

"Oscar?"

"Yeah. From the hill I could see somebody down here. Couldn't tell who. Thought it must be Oscar," Levi said, still trying to quiet his nerves. "Truthfully, I was hoping it was Oscar."

Surprised at the reply, Rachel said, "Hoping it was Oscar? Why, Levi?"

"Well, I thought it might be best to talk first to Oscar. Talk to him before I saw you, just in case I wasn't welcome here anymore."

"Not welcome? For goodness sakes, why wouldn't you be welcome?"

Levi nervously pushed his hat back and brushed his fingers through his hair. "It's been a while. I thought maybe things had changed."

Rachel smiled for the first time, understanding his fears. "Levi," she said, "you'll never know how hard I've prayed for this day. I was so afraid I'd never see you again."

"He did come here, didn't he?"

Rachel nodded, remembering the day. "Yes. Oscar told him everything he wanted to know. Just as you told him to. I didn't want him to, but he did."

"Did you see 'im?"

She nodded again. "Yes, Levi, he was awful. He scared me.

I could see the cruelty in his eyes and in his face. For weeks I'd wake up at night trembling in terror. Is he dead?"

"Yes. He is. Someday I'll tell you the story."

Levi suddenly became aware that Rachel was staring intently at Little Bear. Levi had been so involved in his discussion with her that he had momentarily forgotten about the child. Intimidated by Rachel's gaze, the boy had ducked his head and was looking at the ground.

"Rachel, this is my young partner, Little Bear," Levi said.

"Little Bear?" she repeated, totally bewildered.

"That's right. Comanche Indian. Part anyway. Named him myself."

A thousand thoughts raced through Rachel's brain. "Does he have parents?"

"Doesn't seem to. He was abandoned and left to starve. He's another story for later."

"Does he speak English?"

"Quite a bit. He learns fast. In a few days he'll be talking your arm off."

Levi dismounted and motioned for Little Bear to do the same. Then he handed the reins of his horse to the child and asked, "Little Bear, would you take care of the horses?"

The child smiled at Levi, happy to have something to do that would take him out of the spotlight. "You bet!" he said, leading the horses toward the corral.

With the child busily engaged with the horses, Levi turned to Rachel and embraced her. Tears filled her eyes as she clung to him. "I was so afraid I'd never see you again," she said. "When I first saw George, I was sure I wouldn't. This is still a dangerous land, Levi, and these are dangerous times. When you were here before, I didn't have any idea just how dangerous. Lots of thing could've happened to you. One look into the eyes of George

Tompkins made me realize just how much danger you were in."

"Yeah, I guess there were times that I was in some danger, but you can forget about George. You'll never see him again. Course there're lots more just like him." Levi had known Rachel for only a short time, but he had learned to sense her moods and to read her behavior. In her last remarks he recognized a fear that hadn't been there before. "Never mind my problems, if that's what they are. How are things here in central Texas, especially here on your ranch?" he asked.

Rachel shrugged and looked away. "It's hard to say, Levi. It's sure hard to say. There are signs of trouble. Many signs. Sterling's death probably was an early sign. I hate to sound casual about his death, but it really was a sign. There have been other signs. We don't know how far it'll go. But at least you're back. God has answered my prayers."

Laughing softly, Levi said, "It wasn't just God that brought me back. You had something to do with it, but right now I want to know more about the problems here."

"Things haven't changed dramatically since you left. At least, the changes aren't visible. The Buzzard's Water Hole Gang—or the Mob, as some people call it—is still alive. There's a lot of lawlessness going on. Most honest people think the Gang's behind a lot of it, but we can't prove much. Probably couldn't get anything done, if we could prove something. Several families have been forced off their land. Mostly small ranches or farms, poor people mostly. One theory is that the Gang will work on the weaker settlers until it gets stronger, and then it'll go after larger ranches, like mine. I'm scared, Levi. I'm sure somebody wants this ranch, and I don't want to give it up." She spoke with a determination that told Levi she would be willing to die for her land, a genuine possibility in the lawless climate that seemed to be developing along the San Saba River.

Suddenly remembering that he hadn't seen Rachel's foreman, Levi asked, "You still have Oscar, don't you?"

She sighed and looked off across the rolling hills. "Oscar," she said, with dejection. "Oscar's a wonderful manager and rancher, and he's a fine man. He's part of this family. He tries to take care of me and Matthew, like we're his very own. Reminds me of one of those whitetail does carrying on over a new fawn. But he's not a match for some of the outlaws that have appeared in this county, Levi. He's older, and he's not as strong and as fast as he once was, and he doesn't accept his limitations. He's going to get himself killed trying to protect us. Still, he knows more about this land grab than I do. I suspect he's not telling me everything. Maybe you can get some information out of him."

"Where is he, Rachel?"

"Funny you should ask," she replied, as she pointed into the distance. "I can see him coming in now from the river. He's been down there checking some fence. They have a habit of getting cut. He'll be here in a few minutes. I'll go back to the house so you can talk."

Oscar was still a hundred yards from the corral when he recognized that the man standing with one foot on the bottom rail was Levi. He let out a yell that would have made an Apache proud, as he spurred his horse into a run. He was already dismounting when the horse slid to a halt. He ran a few yards to the spot where Levi waited. A huge smile crossed his face, as he grabbed Levi's hand and began to pump it.

"Lordy, I wasn't never so glad to see nobody as I am to see you," Oscar said. "I just knowed you was dead."

"My God, Oscar, did everybody think I was dead?"

"Just about. That was a mean lookin' hombre what come here. He scared me purty good, and he scared the hell outa Rachel."

"Well, he isn't gonna be back. He's dead."

"Dead? You mean *you* killed 'im?"

"Yeah."

"Damn, Levi, I knowed you right good. Seems to me that you wasn't 'specially good with a gun. Somebody musta showed you a thang or two 'bout usin' that Colt Rachel give you."

"Now, wait a minute, Oscar, I wasn't that bad." Levi paused and slid his hat to the back of his. Smiling easily at Oscar, he continued, "You're right, though. Somebody did teach me, somebody I want to tell you about sometime, but now I want to talk about something else. I want to talk about this ranch, this land, this part of the state. I want you to tell me what's going on here."

Oscar hesitated, not sure how to answer Levi. "Well, I'm not rightly sure."

Levi cut him off before he could continue. "That's what Rachel said. Don't hold out on me, Oscar. What's really happening here?" Levi's voice had an edge to it, as he struggled with growing annoyance and anger. He sensed that information was being withheld from him, perhaps in an attempt to protect him, and he wanted no part of it.

"That's what I'm tryin' to tell you, Levi. We don't have all the answers yet. We don't know much more than we did when you was here. Hell, I ain't tryin' to hide nothin' from you. I wouldn't do that."

Levi looked away, ashamed that he questioned Oscar's integrity. "Sorry. Didn't mean to accuse you. Tell me, is Rachel in danger of losing the ranch?"

"Well, there's considerable money borrowed agin it. Sterling done it. Didn't tell Rachel as fer as I can tell. Tryin' to pretect her, I suppose. She don't talk much 'bout it, but I thank she found out after he died. Probably right after you left, although she might of knowed an' jist didn't tell you. Owes 'bout five thousand dollars, I thank."

"But there's more than the money. Right?"

"Yep. Lots more. Let's see if I kin tell you what's happenin', near as I kin find out. You gotta understan', Levi, I ain't no big rancher or nothin'. They's lots goin' on that ain't told to me."

"I wish you'd tell me whatever you know."

Oscar looked away, gathering his thoughts. Well," he said, "I know one version of the story. May be accurate. May not be."

"Let's hear it."

"Okay. Several years ago, more than ten, probably more than twenty, some of them ranchers around here got tired of losin' their stock an' their crops and sometimes their lives. Outlaws wuz awful bad. Killers, rustlers, bandits of all kinds took a likin' to this place, this part of the state. It wuz a natural place fer 'em. Almost no law, country was just gittin' over the Civil War. Weren't enough Texas Rangers to go around. Sheriffs wuz either crooked as the outlaws or purty soon deader than George Warshington. They wuz lotsa cattle and horses that made easy pickins, and they wuz lotsa places to hide in these here hills and cedar breaks and such. The ranchers and farmers wuz at the mercy of the bandits, and the bandits ain't got no mercy.

"Well, seems like six of the biggest ranchers in the area at the time got tired of puttin' up with that damn nonsense, so they organized a vigilante committee fer they own protection. According to my understandin', they intentions wuz good. They just wanted to protect they selves from a crime wave that wuz sweepin' across the area. Hell, there weren't no law. Somethin' had to be done. Who could blame 'em? I suppose they wuz successful—at least at first. The original vigilantes should of disbanded and went back to legal ranchin', but they didn't. Them with the good intentions wuz purty soon replaced by men what wanted to use the committee fer they own benefit. The new vigilantes developed a purty sophisticated set of rules and ceremonies that wuz known only to gang members. They met at a kinda spooky place called the Buzzard's Water Hole for monthly meetins. They met with a prayer, accordin' to my spy.

"The members started workin' deals together. 'Brother-in-law deals' is what some people call 'em. Maybe legal at first, then purty shady. Finally, downright dishonest and sometimes even deadly. Some thank Sterling's murder wuz done by them coyotes. Some thank it maybe weren't even connected, just happened at 'bout the right time to make 'em look guilty. Maybe some killer wanted 'em to git the blame. Maybe one of the gang members wuz operatin' alone, without the knowledge and permission of the others. We probably won't never know the truth 'bout that.

"Honest folks don't know what to thank. Some hope it'll go away, an' it might. Don't thank so, though. Too much greed. It'll hafta be busted, and that's tough. Myself, I thank it'll rock along fer a while. Kinda drift in and out 'til finally somethin' hasta be done. It may take ten years of trouble 'fore we finally stomp this here thang out."

"I don't see why it's so hard to deal with," Levi argued.

"Lotsa reasons, Levi. First off, it's secret. Most law-abidin' folks don't got no idea who's involved. Might be a neighbor or a judge or a sheriff or all of those. Might be anybody. Might be most ever body. Oh, most folks got suspicions, but don't got no proof. These men is clever, and they're purty well organized. If they decide to kill somebody, they don't usually leave no witnesses."

Levi nodded slowly as he studied the distant hills. "Okay, Oscar. About this debt that Rachel owes. Who does she owe it to?"

"The bank. It's all legal. Course plenty of people hope she kaint pay it. They'd like to git her property from the bank. Why steal it if you kin buy it real cheap?"

"What if she had the money? She could pay the debt off, couldn't she?"

"Shore she could. She's already paid some. Course, if she paid up, she'd probably start havin' other problems. Right now, people're just sittin' back and waitin' fer her to go broke all legal like."

"And the bank? They wouldn't try to cheat her? You know how some businessmen think they can take advantage of a woman."

"Naw. Don't thank they'd cheat 'er. Actually, they're helpin' 'er. Give her extry time and all. They's some people here that ain't outlaws. Not yet, anyway."

"You're sure they're not involved in this Buzzard Water Hole nonsense?"

"Levi, yer askin' me lotsa questions. They's lots I don't know 'bout this thang. I thank Rachel's loan's separate. I don't thank the Gang has anything to do with it. Just remember, I could be wrong."

"Then, I'm gonna pay it off."

"It's a lotta money."

"I've got a lot of money."

"Better talk to her, anyway. She gits a mite touchy 'bout thangs. That red hair of hers should tell you somethin'. She's got that Irish temper. Besides, she's worked hard to save this here ranch. She may have a plan of 'er own. Don't do nothin' 'til you talk to 'er."

"Yes, you're sure right. I'll do that."

Chapter 23

He squatted on the edge of a small courtyard in front of the ranch house, watching while two children cavorted and played in the open area between the house and the San Saba River. One of the children was a rowdy, grinning, sandy-haired boy. The other was a quieter, more solemn, darker skinned and darker haired waif. He was somewhat smaller and somehow more out of place than his older counterpart. While the man watched, the younger child accidentally fell to the ground, apparently skinning his knees. The man straightened up from his resting position and started to go to the assistance of the child. However, before he could even begin to walk down to the child, the older boy picked him up, brushed the dirt from his skin and clothing and began to comfort him. Despite their obvious differences, the two boys were devoted to each other. This devotion pleased the adult greatly.

The man, Levi Wolfe, called out to the two boys, "Matthew. Little Bear. Is anybody hurt?" Both boys grinned at him and immediately went back to some game that only they understood. "Amazing," Levi said to himself, as the two kids continued to tumble and play in the cold afternoon sun. "Only thirty years ago, more or less, their parents would've been trying to kill each other. Now look at the two. Ripping and tearing like they've been friends forever. There's got to be a lesson there somewhere."

While the children tore about the yard like two young colts, Levi sat quietly watching and thinking. He'd been doing a lot of thinking lately. Like everyone else at the ranch, he had concerns, concerns about the future of the Sandifer Ranch. Concerns about his future there. Concerns about the spread of lawlessness in the area. Sometimes he wondered if he was up to the challenge. He smiled as he considered his prospects. In it all, he knew he'd confront those challenges and do his best.

Levi Wolfe had learned that there were many ways to confront difficulty. Once he had been inclined to sit back and let things take their course. But the events surrounding Jovita's death had persuaded him that the easy way was seldom productive, at least not for him. He had learned that he had to suppress his natural timidity and boldly confront troubling events, force them out into the open where they could be dealt with directly

Just face it head-on and solve it, he had decided. But would that approach work with Rachel? Could he assert himself and insist that she let him be a part of her life? Absolutely not. Not Rachel. Rachel would never respond positively to any kind of approach that appeared heavy-handed. A short time ago he was certain that Rachel was ready to marry him and turn over the operation of the ranch to him, to lean on him and free herself from a heavy burden. Now he wasn't sure. It seemed to him that she had been unnecessarily cool toward him lately.

Just where did he fit in with this woman whom he had traveled so far to be with? Certainly she was a different kind of woman than he had ever encountered before. She had learned to fend for herself since the death of Sterling, and she had learned to do it quite well. Her abilities to reestablish the ranch as a profitable business proved her worth as a businesswoman. Levi had only to ride through her herd of high quality cattle to see that she also had a quite thorough understanding of livestock. There were other indications of success and self-reliance.

Judging from the condition of the fields on her property, each clear of weeds and sewn with a good stand of oats, she had learned a bit about farming, too. The strangest thing, though, was a comment he had heard her make to Oscar a day or two ago. She had asked him to investigate the market for the native pecan nuts that littered the ground beneath the huge pecan trees that lined the course of the river. "From the looks of things, she'll turn 'em into gold," he said aloud.

"Turn what into gold?" The voice came from behind him.

In complete surprise, Levi whirled around, almost losing his footing in the soft dirt. "I didn't hear you come up," he stammered. Only a few feet behind him stood Rachel, the wind ruffling her clothing about her body, and the afternoon sun shining through her hair, casting highlights of brass and copper hues around her soft, gentle face. In Levi's mind she had never been more beautiful. With all his heart he want to take her into his arms and hold her close, but he didn't. Quickly regaining his composure, Levi continued, "I was just down here watching the kids, and thinking. Mostly, I was thinking, I guess."

"Thinking?" she asked. "What about?"

"Well, lots of things, really. Mostly about you. About me, too. Both of us."

"Thought so. Did you reach any conclusions?"

"Yeah. We need to talk." Then Levi remembered his own thoughts of a few minutes earlier. The present situation was one where abruptness might not be well advised. He had best proceed cautiously, with great diplomacy. "That is, Rachel—what I meant to say—there's some things that we might ought to discuss," Levi corrected himself.

Rachel smiled with satisfaction at Levi's sudden change in tone, his increased sensitivity. "Okay," she replied, "This is a lovely place. Let's sit here and talk for a while." Patiently, she waited for Levi to speak.

He looked out across the juniper-covered hills into the deep blue winter haze on the horizon. Choosing his words carefully, he said, "Rachel, I've always thought we'd have a good future here, and I thought you wanted it, too. Lately, the last few day, I haven't been so sure. You seem to be more interested in other things. I need to know where we stand. That's all."

Nodding her agreement, Rachel said, "Well, Levi, I do have a ranch to run whether you're here or not. Your return was quite a shock to all of us. A very pleasant shock. It took all of us a few days to adjust to it, and now we've adjusted and things have returned to normal. But you're right. Maybe I have had second thoughts, but not for the reasons you probably think. I don't want you to get into something you'll regret, and there are things here that many men would come to regret."

Rachel waited for a while, allowing Levi time to digest her words. "Rachel," he began, but she interrupted.

"No, I should continue," she said. "We really do need to get over this barrier, if we can. Levi, I love you very much, and I know you love me. You certainly seem to, but you have to decide whether a life with me is what you want. When you think it through, it may not be enough. It may not be worth the risk. Now, you already know all the reasons that you should marry me and stay here on this ranch. Let me remind you of some reasons why you might not want to. The first reason is because I'm me."

"What does that mean?" Levi asked lamely.

"It means that you need to realize who and what you're marrying. I won't change after the wedding. I'll still be the same. I look at some of the wives of the ranchers here, and it makes me sad. No. It makes me angry. They follow their men around, waiting on them, asking permission to speak. And I'm sure some of them get slapped around if the husband's not satisfied. That's not me, Levi, and it'll never be me. I rescued this place from near bankruptcy. I worked from sunup until dark many times, and with the help of Oscar—and God—I, or we, are doing better. I won't be content to bake cookies and have children for the rest of my life. Oh, I want to bake cookies, and I want to have your children, but that's not all I want. I want to be loved, but I damn sure want to be respected, too."

Levi looked at Rachel, completely surprised by the passion with which she expressed her wants and needs. In all the time that he had listened to her talk, he had never heard her say "damn" before. "And you think I can't provide what you need?" he asked.

Rachel shook her head vigorously. "No, Levi, that's not what I'm saying. It's not that I question your good intentions or your ability to provide. I just want to be sure that you really know me, and that you know I won't—I can't—change that part of me that wants success and involvement and respect. Remember, too, that you'll have to deal with other ranchers. They may not like the fact that your wife is involved in the details of running this ranch. It might make their wives restless, you know. You're an outsider, Levi. They can be pretty hard on an outsider."

"Rachel, I've learned to work with other people and to accept the ways they're different from me. Sure, we'll have disagreements, arguments. All married people do. Hell. All people do. But we can talk through our problems. I love you, Rachel. I want you to be happy. If helping to run this ranch makes you happy, that's okay with me. Better yet, you run the ranch and let me help. I don't worry what other ranchers think. I'll do my job the best I can. If that's not good enough, then they can say whatever they want."

She wondered how much more to tell him. "Okay, here's something else. I don't want to paint an impossible picture of my financial situation. Sterling was a good man. He knew cattle and horses and crops, but he was a poor manager. He didn't handle business problems very well. Probably, if he had lived, we'd have lost the ranch by now. With Oscar's help I've turned that around. We just might make it. I'd love to have your help, have you working side by side with me. But we might fail. A couple of hard, dry years might wipe us out. Are you ready for that?"

Thinking about the fortune that Shiloh had left him, Levi smiled at her and said, "Rachel, that's one area where I certainly can help. I promise you won't lose the ranch for money reasons. I'm not rich, but I have a little money put aside. If necessary, I'll use every bit of it to save your property."

Rachel studied him for several moments, not quite sure what he meant. Where would he have gotten money? When he left the ranch, he had little or nothing. He certainly hadn't been gone long enough to accumulate any significant amount. As Rachel puzzled over his remark, Levi said. "Now, what other worries do you have in that lovely head of yours?"

"Well," she replied. "There's always the Mob. Did you talk with Oscar about that fine organization?"

"Yeah. He filled me in. Didn't seem to know much, though."

"Nobody knows a lot, but if you stay here, you—and I—will have to deal with it."

"Rachel, I'm not afraid of those outlaws."

"You'd better be," she said, smiling at his lack of understanding. "You'd sure better be afraid of them, whoever they are. They haven't caused us much trouble, but they will, as soon as they realize I'm not going broke. As soon as they see you here, and they realize you're going to stay. As soon as they get stronger, they'll hit us, and nobody will be safe."

Levi paled and stared at Rachel. "So we'll face 'em. We'll organize. Isn't that a start?"

She nodded. "Yes, I believe it is."

"What can we do?" Levi asked. "I mean, immediately."

"Nothing, really. Not yet. Just be alert and take no chances. Don't let some worthless killer pick a fight with you, just so he and his friends can kill you and claim self-defense, knowing all the while that a friendly judge will let them off. Keep your ears and eyes open. Learn all you can. Try to identify honest ranchers and make friends with them. We'll need them. Identify members of the Mob, if you can." She paused for a moment and studied him. "There's something you should do immediately."

"Okay. What is it?"

"There's a strange man who lives in Norwood. His story about how he got here is stranger than yours. His name is Jake McIlroy. He's been here for only nine or ten years, but he's established a newspaper, the *Norwood Gazette*, and he owns a hotel and some ranching and farming land. He's married to a Lakota Indian woman, who's at least as smart and industrious as he is. You need to hear their story, but you need to hear it from them, not from me. If anybody knows what's going on in this little corner of the world, they do. I suggest that you drop in on Jake, introduce yourself, and become a part of his inner circle. The two of you should work together to confront the problem we're all facing.

"As soon as possible, I believe you need to become one of his best friends. I know the wife, Evangeline, but I don't know her very well. That's a failure on my part. I should be her closest friend by now. Now, you and Jake should work together, organizing this community to defend itself against the fight that's sure to come. That's where you start."

"Okay. I'll start immediately. Anything else?"

"Yes. One more thing. Watch out for those two young boys that are playing outside. To these killers, nobody's off limits. Not even two innocent boys."

Levi shook his head. "Strange, isn't it, Rachel? We may have to form a vigilante committee to get rid of a criminal gang that once was a vigilante committee."

"It could come to that, Levi. It certainly could." She was quiet for a while. Darkness had settled in, and the late winter evening was growing colder. Rachel pulled a warm jacket about her shoulders, then bravely turned to Levi, "I've loved you since you first came here, but you needed time to deal with your loss of Jovita. I respect that need, and I don't want you unless you can make a total commitment to me. I told you that before, and it hasn't changed. I can't compete with a person who's not here, who's a fond memory. I don't think you can love and still cling to the past, to your memories of Jovita."

Now it was Levi's turn to be reflective. He pondered her words at length. He had known that Rachel would be concerned about his feelings for Jovita, and he wanted to give her an answer. He wanted to be honest and forthright, and yet not create more doubts in her mind. He wanted to set her mind at ease. "Jovita will always be a part of me, just as Sterling will always be a part of you," he said. "We can't deny our memories, our past lives. I can never get her completely out of my memory, but I've dealt with the fact that she's dead. I've suffered a bad loss, but it's over. I'm ready to move on. I want us to be together."

"Do you love me? *Really* love me?"

"Yes, I do love you, Rachel. I know I haven't said it often enough. Sometimes, it's not easy for me to put my feelings into words. But I can learn. The fact that I once loved Jovita, and the fact that I still have warm memories of her doesn't mean I don't love you. I do. I want us to be married. The sooner the better. I want to be a part of your life and have you as part of mine."

"Well, Levi, I want to be sure you understand the size of the problems I face, the ones you're asking to be part of. I could lose this ranch to the bank, and I could cause you to be shot by some thief who wants to scare me away. You know all this?"

Levi's memories came flooding back. "Certainly, I do. I've seen hardships before. Lots of times. I've worked long, hard hours without rest or food. I've nearly frozen up in the Panhandle. I've been shot at. Hell, I've been shot. I'm not a coward. A man has to have something to live for, or he's nothing. I want to share everything with you. We can be partners in every way, share problems and pleasures. And we can share debts."

She nodded and smiled. "That's how it'll have to be. I want a partnership, an equal partnership."

"Fair enough. Since we like to discuss things so much, I guess it's a good time to talk about this. We're going to be a rather peculiar family, Rachel. You have Matthew, and I have Little Bear. Of course, he really isn't mine, but then again maybe he is. I know this for sure. We're all he has. Things may be a little awkward for a while, at least until we all get used to each other."

"Why? You've noticed how well the two boys get along. They're as different as daylight and dark, but they're inseparable. Neither one notices that their skin is different. We—you and I—can be just like them. We're pretty different, Levi, but we can follow their example. We can overcome our differences. We'll be as inseparable as those two kids."

"And what about Little Bear? Does it matter to you that he's an Indian?"

"Of course not. He already thinks I'm his mom, and I treat him exactly like I treat Matthew. On the other hand, some of the people around here might not accept him, especially the older ones. There still are some folks around who lost family members to Indians in the early days."

Levi studied the distance. "I had to be sure. He means a lot to me." He said. "I know he may have trouble fitting in. He has a lot of adjusting to do, but he responds to love and attention. God knows he hasn't had much of that. He needs you. He needs both of us."

It had been dark for some time, and both Levi and Rachel knew it was time for them to go inside. It was growing colder, and the boys probably needed attention. Still, they remained seated side by side in the stillness, now silently watching the full moon begin to work its way slowly across the winter sky. An owl hooted several times somewhere down on the river, soon to be answered by another one back up in the hills.

Then the silence returned, only to be shattered by a sound completely unfamiliar to Rachel. The sound began low and mournful, and then it grew louder and sharper, ending in a series of extended howls. It rolled across the hills and echoed in the canyons and river bottoms. The sound was repeated several times, and then all was silent again.

Rachel looked at Levi, clearly puzzled and somewhat disturbed. "A dog?" she asked.

"Wolf," Levi replied, smiling at her discomfort.

"A wolf? Levi, there aren't any wolves around here," she corrected.

"There's one now."

"Will it bother the livestock?"

"This one won't."

"Well, the other ranchers will kill it."

"I doubt they'll kill this one. They'll never find 'im."

"You seem to know a lot about this thing, Levi. Is there something you're not telling me?" Quietly, matter-of-factly, Levi told the story of his first encounter with the wolf, and its subsequent appearances at certain times.

When he had concluded his narrative, Rachel sat for over a minute, quietly considering what he had said. "Levi," she said, "that's the strangest story I've ever heard."

Levi gave her a quick look in the darkness. "You don't believe it?"

"I believe every word of it. I just don't know what to make of it."

"Shiloh said that there are things that happen that a white man just can't understand. Maybe an Indian can, but not a white man."

"Shiloh said that? Now, that's one man I wish I could've met."

"Believe me, you'll hear plenty about 'im from me," Levi replied. "Besides you and Jovita, he meant more to me than any person I ever knew. He taught me nearly everything I know. Things about this state and about how the world works. He taught me a lot about the Indians and why I should know about them. And he taught me how to use a gun. That may not sound important, but it's one reason I'm still alive. It may come in pretty handy here one day, too.

"He saved my life in more ways that even I know. Then he took the bullets that were meant for me. Rachel, he was just an unknown gambler, not much better than a common criminal to most people, but he was the smartest and best man I ever knew. If he'd lived at a different time, he might've been anything he wanted to be, but now he lies in an unmarked grave on the rim of the Palo Duro Canyon. Nobody will ever know just what kind of man he was."

"You'll know. So will Matthew and I. You'll tell us. Little Bear knew him. He'll remember. Don't think his life was wasted, Levi. I don't think it was."

"He ought to have had better."

"Levi, we really do need to go in. I know that Oscar's inside taking care of the boys, but I need to get them ready for bed."

Rachel was quiet for a moment, and then she began to laugh quietly.

"What's so funny?" Levi asked.

"Have you been paying attention to our conversation?" she asked. "It sounds more like we're discussing a business contract than talking about our future together. Besides that, it sounds like each of us is trying to talk the other out of the contract."

Smiling back at her, Levi also recognized the humor in the situation. "Well," he said, "I guess we're a little different from the usual...what word do I use? Lovers?"

"Sounds good to me."

"I'll ask you again," she replied. "Are you sure? Really sure? Are you ready to face the problems? No, the challenges here?"

"This is what I want, Rachel. This is why I came back. I came back for you. It's a decision I'll never regret, and I'll do everything in my power to make sure you don't regret it. I know there are problems here, but problems are everywhere. I want these problems, these challenges."

"Good," she responded. "Christmas is a happy time. How about a wedding on Christmas Eve? Christmas has always been a special time for me and Matthew. Somehow, that time seems appropriate."

"Good. That's perfect. Let's make the arrangements."

Their destiny determined and their doubts resolved, they slowly walked together through the darkness into the ranch house.

Chapter 24

Levi reined the horse to a halt. Dismounting, he led the animal over to a willow tree and tied him to a low limb. The horse snorted a couple of times, dropped his head, and shifted his weight to only one back leg, resting the other. Levi briskly scratched between the animal's ears, smiling as the horse shook his head and snorted again when Levi stopped scratching.

"You're a bit grumpy this morning, aren't you?" Levi joked. Patting the horse on the front shoulder, Levi remembered the night the two Mexican men gave him the horse. "Wonder where they got you?" he mumbled. "I'll bet somebody in San Antone was sure disappointed when you disappeared. Funny, I never even gave you a name. Doesn't seem quite fair, does it? Probably, you've called me several names in the past year. Well, I'll have to think of one for you."

He walked slowly along the cattle trail that paralleled the river for several hundred yards, then climbed up an embankment and passed among cottonwood, ash, and pecan trees. After a short distance the trail led away from the river up into the hills. It was early morning, just after sunup, one of Levi's favorite times of day, and this one of his favorite locations on the ranch. When his schedule allowed, he came here each morning. If that was not possible, he'd try to come in the late evening, another favorite time of day. Walking among the trees along the river, Levi breathed deeply, enjoying the fresh aroma of the new vegetation of early spring.

He noticed with satisfaction that the leaves of the huge pecan trees were just beginning to appear. "Ah, spring's here for sure," he observed. The different species of trees along the river and in the hills develop their leaves at different times, as late winter fades into early spring. Levi smiled as he remembered Oscar's botanical instruction on the subject, "Them mesquites is the last trees to leaf out in the spring. They're a shore sign that winter's over, and spring's here. Ain't never been no freeze in these parts after the mesquites set they leaves." Oscar had continued to explain other facts—as he saw them—about the various trees growing on the ranch. One of his observations was that pecans produce leaves later than most trees, but not as late as mesquites. Therefore, they are good indicators of the ending of winter, but not as good as mesquites. Moving quietly beneath the pecan trees, Levi could hear a pair of squirrels playing chase in the canopy overhead. "Reminds me of a couple of kids I know," he said to himself.

Following the trail out of the quiet river bottom, Levi walked through a savannah of junipers and live oaks. Clumps of grama grass stood in dry clusters, waiting for the warm sun and spring rains to flourish again. Along the slope of the hillsides stood patches of bluebonnets and Indian blankets in full bloom. In some places the two kinds of flowers were in separate bunches, while in others the two intermingled. The result was an irregular tapestry of unparalleled variety and beauty.

Finally, Levi stopped in a clearing on a small hill, really little more than a high mound of dirt rising perhaps fifty feet above the surrounding area. The point was surrounded by a small grove of oak trees with stunted native shrubs scattered among them. From this vantage point Levi could look to the right and see more than half a mile of the winding course of the San Saba River.

Off to his left lay a wide-open valley, an oak-and-juniper-covered savannah much like the one that he had just walked through. He sat down quietly and prepared to enjoy the world about him. Sitting at this location, he and Rachel frequently observed the large flocks of wild turkey that traveled up and down the river. Once, a curious turkey hen came within a few feet of Rachel, apparently trying to identify this human invader. Usually, he and Rachel saw the whitetail deer that are so plentiful throughout the region.

Somewhere far downriver he could hear the wild turkeys calling to each other, but this morning they weren't in view. As he waited, Levi became aware of other sounds that broke the stillness. Back out in the open meadow a woodpecker hammered out a message on a mesquite tree, seeking some hidden larva. A pair of large, black crows passed overhead, cawing loudly as they went. In an algerita bush nearer at hand, a brightly colored male cardinal fussed persistently as he foraged for food. As the sun rose higher in the eastern sky and the early morning grew warmer, the bushes and trees came alive with the chirping and calling and fluttering of dozens of different kinds of birds.

Levi had come alone this morning. Usually, Rachel accompanied him, but today was different. This morning he wanted to be alone, to reach deep inside himself and free any past memories that lingered there. Rachel knew he needed to be alone. She didn't know exactly why, but she recognized the need. In a way she surprised herself. She and Levi had been married for only a few months, but already they often communicated without speaking.

Although Rachel had no knowledge of the significance of today, Levi did. He had checked a calendar to be sure, and he had confirmed that today was the eighteenth of April. Exactly a year ago Jovita had been murdered. Looking toward the horizon to the south, he imagined where San Antonio must be located. Then he looked in the other direction and tried to visualize the location of Amarillo. Sitting here in the peace and tranquility of central Texas, enjoying the love of Rachel and the support of his new family, Levi found it difficult to believe that he had just passed through a year of such hate and violence.

It was difficult to believe that Jovita had loved him so passionately and then died so needlessly, that Shiloh had educated him in the ways of the frontier and then had died a death as needless and senseless as Jovita's. He had really experienced more in one year than most men could experience in five lifetimes. What forces had led him to this remote speck in the universe? How did he happen to find Rachel—and Shiloh for that matter? Was it simply chance, or was some other force at work?

He sat for a long time, drinking in the wonders of the beautiful land, enjoying the soft warmth of the sun, and the sweet fragrances of the spring flowers and new vegetation. As he sat, the sounds of the birds died away and all was silent. The hair bristled on Levi's neck and he felt a slight chill pass through his limbs. Then he heard it, a sound floating across the endless hills of central Texas, a haunting sound that at once commanded respect but also gave encouragement and promised better things to come. As in the past, the sounds began as a low mournful growl and then rose in crescendo to a long, sustained howl. It was repeated twice and then all was quiet. After a while the birds began their noisy chatter once more, and all was normal again.

Picking himself up off the ground and brushing loose dirt from his clothing, Levi slowly worked his way back down the hill toward the river where his horse was waiting.

Epilogue

Selena sighed and studied the ceiling. "Something like ten years ago," she said. "Seems like yesterday you walked out of my life, planning to marry a younger and prettier woman named Jovita."

Levi laughed. "I'm afraid I did."

"For two or three years I was convinced you were dead," she said. "Then I happened to open a newspaper from Norwood, Texas, a town I'd barely even heard of, and there you were—photograph and all. So, I enlisted some help, and I learned all about you. A young wife, Rachel, I think. A ranch on the San Saba River. And a long story about a mob. A pretty violent bunch."

"Violent? Yes. But they've been pretty well put out of commission, at least for the present. There are still some sympathizers hanging on, waiting for a chance to strike back."

"It's been a while, Levi. Let me ask you bluntly. Why are you here? Ten years is a long time."

"Yes. It's been a while, but conditions in and around Norwood are just now safe enough for me to leave for a few days." He paused for a moment, wondering if he should have come. "There are some people I once knew. Thought I might see if they're still here," he continued. "Hell, Selena, that's not why I'm really here. I've had questions for a long time. Only you can answer them." He looked away again. "Thought I'd simply ask."

"Levi!" she said. "Of course I'll answer any questions. Assuming I have the answers."

"Oh, you have the answers." Directing his gaze directly at her, he said, "It's always been so strange to me that a couple of Mexican men decided to rescue me from Sheriff Hammer's jail. They didn't seem to be all that sympathetic to my dilemma, so why did they do it? It was risky. They could've been killed. Or worse, they could've failed and been arrested. They'd have paid a high price for that attempt."

"I still haven't heard your question."

"Who did it? Who planned it? Jovita's mother certainly didn't. Father Pena didn't. A disgruntled deputy or city official that wanted to expose the sheriff for his incompetence? Not likely. So who?"

"You know, don't you?"

"It had to be you, Selena. Nothing else makes sense."

Now very serious, Selena broke eye contact and looked away. "At first I thought reason would prevail. After all, who really thought you killed Jovita? But it looked more and more like you might actually go to trial and be found guilty. So I visited Jovita's mother and told her what I planned. I was afraid she'd be cold and judgmental. Instead, she was kind and supportive of my plan. She thanked me! Me! And she knew…knew all about you and me. Still, she was the…the Christian she claimed to be."

Selena took a deep breath and continued, "So I did it, and it actually worked. We put you on a good horse, got your guns and saddle and a few other items from the boarding house, and sent you on your way. I thought you had maybe one chance in a hundred."

"That was optimistic."

"I went back to see Jovita's mother," she said. "She was elated and more optimistic than me. She said God would look after you. Maybe He did."

"I went to see Jovita's old home place," Levi said. "There was a new sign on the door."

"Yes. 'Jovita's Place.' It's a charity where poor women can come for help with housing, food, clothing, or protection. Most anything. Even for assistance with education, especially for college students. You still own the freight business that I sold you. We've used the revenue from that, and now we get donations from lots of businesses and private citizens. It's doing well. The idea came from Jovita's mother. She wanted to set up something in honor of her daughter. When she died, she willed her house to the charity, and it's now the headquarters." She smiled and winked at Levi. "Officially, the freight business still belongs to you. We'd like to continue to use that revenue for Jovita's Place."

"I can't think of a better use for it," Levi replied. "If I actually still own it, I'll gladly sign it over to the charity."

"Thank you."

Levi turned his attention to Selena. "And how about you? How are you doing?"

She frowned and looked across the room. "I'm now a rich woman," she replied. "And I'm young enough to enjoy my wealth. But I have this eerie feeling that things aren't right. Maybe it's a premonition. A warning. We have all kinds of people here in San Antonio. Sure, we have white people." She smiled. "Gringos. And we have a large population of Mexicans. Some are actual citizens of Mexico, but they live here in San Antonio. Then there are Mexicans that are actually U.S. citizens, but they may have relatives or close friends that live in Mexico. Almost everybody is aware of the political upheaval that's taking place just south of the Texas border."

"But wasn't it that way, back when I lived here?"

"No, Levi, it's more intense now. People are taking sides. Some support the dictator of Mexico. Others support one of several revolutionary leaders, such as Pancho Villa. There's a lot of strife all around. I'm afraid the various interests in this part of Texas will be drawn into it. It could have catastrophic results."

"Exactly what do you fear?"

"I hear conversations." She stopped and looked around, making sure nobody would overhear her. "Lots of people come into my businesses. Sometimes, they say more than they should. I think there might be an attempt by some officials—pretty important ones—to get the state of Texas involved, maybe in some crazy scheme to form a new nation out of south Texas and northern Mexico."

Levi leaned back and laughed. "Come on," he said. "Do you really believe that's possible?"

"No. But I think some people are dumb enough to try. It could result in a lot of bloodshed."

"If this happened, would you get involved?"

"I might not be able to avoid it," she replied. "If you have any thoughts on this, please share them."

"Yes, I do. This is playing with fire. Lots of laws concerning sovereignty are involved here, concerning both the U.S. and Mexico. If you have employees or friends that might be inclined to get involved, you should strongly discourage it. It would be good if you had ready access to good legal advice. Do you have it?"

"Yes. I have a law firm that advises me on matters concerning business."

"In my opinion, you need to learn as much about the law as possible. Is there a law firm that would let you come in maybe two or three days a week for a while? You could help them and they could help you."

"Interesting idea," she replied. "The firm I use will welcome my help, and it will give me that chance to learn."

"Good. I have another idea."

"Okay."

"There's a woman from Norwood who now lives in Austin. Over the past years she's written for newspapers in both towns. She knows more about the law than anybody I know. She's just waiting for the day when Texas allows women to be lawyers. I'd like to put you in contact with her. I suspect the two of you will have a lot in common."

"Who is she?"

"Her name is Willa."

"Oh, yes! I've read her material in the Austin paper. I'd love to meet her."

"Then I'll set it up. I suggest a first meeting in Austin's Driskill Hotel. It's large and elegant, and it attracts a lot of out-of-town visitors. Nobody would notice two beautiful women visiting in a nice hotel. After that, whatever the two of you decide."

They were silent for almost a minute, each remembering days that were lost forever. "Levi," she said. "You may as well know, I once loved you very much. It really hurt when I…I lost you."

"You did?" Levi said, shaking his head in surprise. "I never realized that. I thought I was the only one that had those feelings. You always insisted that you were way too old for me. I thought you really meant it."

"It was just a way to keep you at a distance, Levi. Actually, I was only about three years older." She smiled. "That is, if you were honest about your age."

"I was. Why did you…push me away?"

"I thought that if I didn't, I'd be holding you back from the future you're now living."

"Strange what one person can do to another, all in the interest of doing the right thing," Levi replied.

"Yes, it is," she said. "But it worked out for you? You're happy?"

"Yes. And you?"

"I'm good. I'm busy, and my life's rewarding. I'm good."

"I'm glad I came back to visit you," he said. "I had my doubts. Actually, my fears."

"Will I ever see you again?"

Levi laughed. "I'm pretty sure you will. Willa will keep me informed about your adventures."

There seemed to be nothing more to say. Both rose from their places at the table. Levi embraced her and gently kissed her. Then he turned and walked toward the door. She watched him leave. A small tear trickled down her cheek.

Author's Notes

The state of Texas is rich in history and folklore. Just take a look at one of the legends—maybe one with a grain of truth—that weave their way through history books and campfire stories. Make your own choice. There's no shortage of lost gold mines or sprawling cattle ranches or battles for justice.

These stories—these histories, these legends—are made even greater by the folk heroes that populated them. There are men like Colonel William B. Travis and James Bowie who, in the telling of their exploits in the Battle of the Alamo, take on a dimension that is larger than life. Or we might want to think about Sam Houston or Charles Goodnight or Captain Bill McDonald. Each one exemplifies greatness in his chosen profession.

However, if you take a closer look at details of their lives, different stories begin to emerge. These men were not infallible. They were not all-knowing, all-wise. They made mistakes, some of them huge mistakes. These men had problems in their personal lives, as well as in their careers. Some were sometimes indecisive, probably questioning earlier decisions. So, these were real Texans, complete with all the strengths and weaknesses that make them interesting, sympathetic, and admirable. These were *real* men with real successes and real failures.

That is how I've created Levi Wolfe. He is a man who makes mistakes, one who suffers humiliation and ridicule, and one who has trouble in making good decisions. Still, he never gives up. He enjoys some of the successes that real people get to experience. He never quits trying to find the right path. I have tried to make Levi a character with whom the reader can identify.

Levi is a truly imaginary character. He is not patterned after any real person, living or dead. He is the product of my imagination, nothing more. Other characters in my story—Rachel, Shiloh, Jovita, Oscar—also are imaginary. To me, these characters give Levi the strength to face struggles, both with himself and with others. It seems to me that George Tompkins is the one character that I created who has no redeeming qualities. He is truly evil. So is he believable? I think he is. I think there are real people out there who are the living, breathing equivalent of George. I'll let the reader decide.

My story begins in San Antonio, a city that was struggling to become a major metropolitan area following the disruptive influence of the Civil War. There were different factions in the city at that time. A large population of Mexicans—either actual citizens of Mexico or their descendants—made up one group, while Europeans—largely Germans—made up another. Then there were citizens of the United States that had found their way into the city. Yes, it was a cultural melting pot.

It was a place with quaint old shopping centers and majestic Roman Catholic cathedrals, as well as spectacular gambling halls and opulent houses of prostitution. It was a city of contrasts in almost every way.

Several books provide reading about the city as it existed at that time. Although most of them are currently out of print, copies exist in libraries and on the used book market. Here are some to consider.

San Antonio, City in the Sun, by Green Peyton, 1946.
San Antonio, a Historical and Pictorial Guide, by Charles Ramsdell, 1959.
The Alamo City, by Pearson Newcomb, 1926.
The Silver Cradle, by Julia Nott Waugh, 1955.

CPSIA information can be obtained
at www.ICGtesting.com
Printed in the USA
BVHW050438080722
641607BV00001B/8

9 781977 254191